THE VERY BEST OF THE BEST OF THE BEST OF SECRETS
VOLUME 1

THE VERY BEST OF BEST OF THE BEST OF SECRETS

VOLUME 1

From the Editors
Of *True Story* And
True Confessions

Published by True Renditions, LLC

True Renditions, LLC
105 E. 34th Street, Suite 141
New York, NY 10016

ISBN: 978-1-938877-56-8

Visit us on the web at www.truerenditionsllc.com.

Contents

HIJACKED!
We struggled to survive.

I was exhausted, *totally* exhausted. No one had told me it would be this way. I guess I had visions of nobly helping the devastated victims of the flood, without realizing what work would be involved.

When news of the terrible rains that had inundated the Midwest and had practically destroyed the tiny town of Middleton came over the radio and TV, we were all sympathetic. Our church group had discussed the situation and came up with the idea to help those people. "This is a chance for us to put our Christianity to work," one of the members said. "We can help."

The idea snowballed, and within forty-eight hours we had a crew of volunteers waiting at the airport. When one of the manufacturing plants in town heard of the disaster they donated their services of their company plane and pilots to fly us there.

Everything happened so fast. We were eager and excited. Quite an odd assortment, really. Reverend Costa was with us. Several teenagers took off from school to go with us. My best friend, Amber, went along and, of course, Keith, the guy I was planning to marry. A couple of housewives had decided at the last minute to join our gang.

We went to the town, dug in, and worked in the mud and destruction, helping as much as we could. It had been hard, backbreaking work, work that none of us were really prepared for. But what we lacked in knowledge and skills we made up for in our determination to assist these people who were so frightened, so devastated by the loss of their homes, and, in some cases the loss of a family member.

After a week, our job was done and we headed back home. I couldn't wait to take a nice hot bath, put on some clean clothes, and eat home-cooked food again.

As soon as I felt the plane move down the runway and lift into the sky, I leaned back against the seat, closed my eyes, and slept. Everyone seemed to be doing the same thing.

There had been so much laughing, teasing, and singing on our flight in. And Keith had sat beside me. Every few minutes he'd lean over and whisper, "Chloe, kitten, I love you." Or he'd say, "Just wait, kitten, the next time we go someplace on a plane it will be on our honeymoon." He'd squeezed my hand and the look in his eyes made me just melt inside.

Now that we were heading home we were silent, too worn-out

to sing or even indulge in conversation. About halfway there our pilot brought the plane down at a large airport to refuel. We all got off the plane and went into the airport. It felt good to stretch our legs. Most of us bought a snack to take back on the plane with us when we boarded it for the final leg of our journey.

We'd been flying about half an hour when I heard some noise coming from the back of the plane. At first, I thought that some of the guys back there had gotten into a discussion.

"Look back there," Amber, who was sitting beside me, whispered.

I stared toward the back of the plane watching as a man moved slowly up the aisle. I didn't know him. He wasn't part of our group. We were all dirty, disheveled, and weary. But none of us looked like him.

His clothes were muddy and hung from his tall, skinny frame like rags. An old baseball cap was perched at an odd angle on his head. Straggly hair hung down below the cap and brushed at the frayed collar of his ancient jacket.

He moved slowly up the aisle, heading for the cockpit and George Miller, our pilot.

"What's he doing?" I asked Amber. "What's wrong with him?"

"Chloe, he has a gun!" Amber said. "Look!"

He had just pulled the weapon from under his jacket and now he walked a little taller, with more of a swagger to his step, as if the gun gave him extra strength, extra courage.

One of the men in our group started walking up the aisle behind the man, but a second member caught his arm and pulled him down into a seat.

When the man reached the middle of the aisle he stopped. "I'm sorry to inconvenience you, folks," he announced in a loud voice. "But this plane is not going wherever you think it is. There's been a slight change of plans." He chuckled as if he thought what he had just said was amusing. "This plane is going to take me where I want to go. I don't want to hurt anyone—so don't force me to. Just do as I tell you and everything will be fine."

He continued his way up the aisle toward the front of the plane. When he reached the cockpit, he rapped sharply on the closed door. Without waiting for a response, he opened the door and stepped inside, closing the door behind him.

The minute he was out of sight everyone began talking, asking each other what this was all about.

"Who is he?" Amber asked in a whisper as though she was afraid he might hear her question. "He isn't part of our group."

"I don't know who he is," I told her as I huddled in my seat.

"Are you alright?" I turned to see Keith standing over me,

2

looking anxiously down into my face.

"Keith, who's that man? What does he want? What's happening?" I reached out to grab his hand. I couldn't keep the fear from my voice.

He hunched down beside me. "Honey, I don't know who he is. He wasn't on the trip. He must have gotten on when we stopped at that airport to refuel. I think he was hiding in the rest room."

"Is that gun real?" Amber leaned across the seat toward Keith. "Maybe it's just a toy," she said hopefully.

Keith shook his head. "It's a real gun," he said in a low voice.

"What's he doing now?" I wondered.

Keith glanced up the aisle toward the closed door to the cockpit. Just then we felt the plane veer to the right. "I think that answers your question. He's making George change our flight plan."

"That sounds like you're saying he's hijacking this plane." Amber sounded close to tears.

He reached across me and touched Amber's shoulder. "Amber, it's going to be alright. Just relax. George is a very capable pilot. He'll know how to handle this situation." Then Keith touched my face. "I have to go see if old Sam Grayson is okay." He stood up and walked down the aisle.

I turned slightly so I could watch him go. He seemed to fill the aisle. He was such a big guy—tall, muscular, but in spite of his height and strength, there was a gentleness to him, a tenderness. I waited till I saw him lean over to talk to Sam, placing his hand reassuringly on the old gentleman's thin shoulder. Then I turned back to sit straight in my seat. All around me people were talking among themselves in hushed voices. They couldn't understand what this was all about.

I leaned back against the seat and closed my eyes. I could still see Keith's face as he leaned over me, could still see the look of concern and caring and love that had made him hurry to me the moment the man was no longer walking up the aisle.

Keith—I'd never known anyone like him before. I'd dated a number of different guys. Most of them were pretty nice fellows and many of them remained my friends after we stopped dating. But none of them could hold a candle to Keith.

I'd been out of high school a couple of years now. Right after graduation I went to work in the office of my uncle's insurance company. I enjoyed the work and enjoyed the people I worked with. My life had settled down into a comfortable routine—I went to work, came home, had dinner with my mother and father and kid brother, Tom. Sometimes I'd have a date in the evening. Sometimes Amber and I would go to the shopping mall and walk around. Sometimes we'd go to a movie or to see a play at our local community theater.

Every Sunday I went to church. I enjoyed the services, found

Reverend Costa's sermons inspirational and uplifting. I joined a group of young adult singles and we had a lot of good times. We bowled together, went to football games together. Each Thursday evening we had a Bible class.

It was how I met Keith. One of the class members brought him as a guest and Keith started attending on a regular basis. Keith and I seemed to hit it off right from the beginning. We started dating, and after several months we knew we were in love. At Christmas Keith gave me an engagement ring. It wasn't large, but it was beautiful and I loved it because it represented our pledge to each other that we would soon be married.

Keith worked at one of the largest supermarkets in Crestville. In time he would work his way up to being the manager. He enjoyed his work and liked being around people. And people liked being around him.

Keith was a generous person, so giving of himself, of his time and his energies. Because of his connections we'd been able to get cases of food to take with us to Middleton. But that was just like Keith . . . always wanting to help others.

I think that was one of the things I loved most about him. I also loved his strength, his gentleness, and his sense of humor. He was fun to be with. He could find enjoyment in complex things like a debate on the plays of Shakespeare or in the simplest things. Some of our best times were spent just watching the sun set.

We often took walks. There's a national park near my parents' home and Keith and I often went there to walk along the winding paths, to watch the leaves as they changed from green to golden brown. They crunched under our feet as we meandered through the almost deserted area.

When winter set in, we hiked through the park bundled up in heavy coats and fluffy mittens. We'd take a thermos of hot chocolate, and after scooping the snow off a green wooden bench, we'd sit together and sip on the hot drink. Once, we built a snowman on a sloping hill and Keith wrapped his long woolen scarf around the snowman's fat neck. "I don't want him to get cold." Keith laughed as he tried to tie the scarf into a fancy bow.

When spring came, we walked through the park and watched the tiny flowers peeking up through the now warm soil. We touched the brand-new, not fully opened green leaves on the trees.

Keith was everything I ever wanted in a man. He made my heart sing when he spoke my name. I couldn't imagine ever wanting to spend the rest of my life with anyone else.

Our wedding plans were all made. I had my dress, a beautiful, very old white gown that my grandmother and my mother had worn.

4

Now it was my turn to wear it. Amber would be my maid of honor. It would be a small wedding, since Keith didn't care for fancy things. That was just fine with me. All I needed to make it totally perfect was my parents, Tom, Amber, Reverend Costa, and of course, Keith.

"Chloe, what's happening!" Amber's voice cut into my thoughts. "I think this plane's going down!"

I opened my eyes and looked around. She was right. The plane had begun to descend.

"Everyone, please fasten your seat belts," Keith announced from the back of the plane. "I think we're landing and it's imperative that you fasten your seat belts immediately."

My fingers shook as I tried to maneuver the seat belt. I looked around me. Everyone was sitting very still. They didn't seem unduly frightened, just sort of dazed by what was occurring.

"Where are we?" I asked Amber, who was sitting next to the window. "This can't be Crestville Airport. We haven't been flying long enough to be home. And besides, the pilot changed direction."

Amber looked out the window. "I don't know what this place is. It looks like an Army camp of some sort. There are barracks to our left, and I think those buildings over there are hangars. We're approaching a runway. I guess George is going to set the plane down here."

I tried to lean across Amber to take a look for myself but my seat belt restricted me.

"That's odd," Amber said, half to herself.

"What is?" I asked.

"There's nobody here."

"What do you mean, there's nobody here? Amber, you just said that this looks like a military base."

"But, Chloe, there's no one here—not one person. Not a car or vehicle anyplace. There's a landing strip, a runway . . . but no planes."

"But why?"

Before I could finish my question the door to the cockpit opened. The gunman stepped through it, still holding the gun in his hand. "We're landing here," he announced in a loud voice. "Now you folks just do like I say and no one will be hurt."

I could feel the plane settle onto the runway and glide along the surface. Then it stopped. No one said a word.

When the plane had made a complete stop the gunman turned to look back into the cockpit. "Get out here!" he ordered and he stepped aside slightly as George and Patrick, the copilot, stepped into the aisle.

"Tell 'em," the gunman ordered.

George glanced at the man, then turned to face us. "Everybody, we've had a change in plans. The gentleman has ordered me to land the plane at this abandoned military base. We're quite alone here. I don't want anyone to try to be a hero. If you do, it could mean the life of one, or of all of us."

"That's right," the man agreed as he pushed the gun against George's head. "Nobody acts smart and nobody gets hurt. Just do like I tell you. Now, I want all of you to unfasten your seat belts and leave the plane by the rear exit. Don't try anything either because I have the pilot right here. Just move out of this plane. Take anything with you that you will be wanting because once you get off this plane you will not be getting back on again."

He paused a moment. "I want to warn any of you who want to act brave and sneak back here later. I have planted a bomb on this plane. Once you get off, I will set it to go off if anyone sets foot inside. The detonator is here." He pointed to a bulge in his jacket pocket. "This little toy is lots of fun because if I see anyone even approaching the plane all I have to do is push a little button and—boom! No more airplane!" He laughed. "Now, get moving—all of you. Go over to that building straight across the way there."

I saw Keith start toward me. "Hey, you!" the man yelled. "The door is back that way. I said to head straight to the door. What's the matter? Can't you hear? You want to get someone hurt? Now get out that door!"

Keith hurried down the aisle toward the rear exit. He was carrying his jacket and a brown bag. That must be the snacks he'd bought at the airport, I reasoned. Following his example, I grabbed my navy blue jacket, my purse, and the sack of potato chips and candy bars I'd purchased when we had stopped to refuel. Everyone seemed to be doing the same.

Keith stood at the base of the fold-down steps and helped everyone as they stepped down onto the pavement of the runway. As I stepped down, he reached up his hand to assist me just as he had everyone before me. I stepped to one side, intending to wait beside him and then walk into the building with him.

"Go into the building, Chloe," he said.

"But, honey—" I started to protest.

He turned to look at me. "I said to go into the building. Now go." There was no affection in his voice. He spoke almost in a monotone. I stood looking at him a moment. He seemed different somehow. "Go on, Chloe." This time it was an order.

"Come on, Chloe." Amber took my arm and headed toward the building. I fell into step with the others and moved across the uneven pavement toward the one-story building. A faded sign hanging crookedly above the door said "office."

The first man to reach the door turned the doorknob and one by one, we stepped over the threshold. It took a moment for my eyes to adjust to the dimness of the place. We were in a large room about forty feet long and fifty feet wide. Close to the door was a large wooden desk covered with a deep layer of dust. The tile floor was dirty. The room was almost empty except for a battered old couch pushed under a half-boarded up window on the far wall. Several folding chairs were propped against the wall closest to the door.

"What's this place?" one of the men asked.

"Looks like it was once a recreation hall," someone observed. "There's a fireplace over there."

We moved around, examining the room. The windows that weren't boarded up let in very little light because they were so dirty.

"What are we supposed to do now?" one of the women wanted to know.

"I don't know," someone answered. "But don't do anything that will get him upset or we may never get out of here."

"Alright, everybody, just relax." We all turned to see George step into the room. "I'll tell you the rules of this game."

We all moved closer to him, eager to hear everything he had to say.

"Our plane has been hijacked by a guy named Marcus. In brief, he and his partner, a guy named Miles, were involved in a bank robbery. Right after the robbery they split up. Miles went one way and Marcus headed this direction in an effort to confuse the police. They're supposed to meet up here at this abandoned military base. Then they'll go on together to where the stolen money is hidden."

"Why did he bring us here?" someone asked.

"I don't understand the entire plan," George said. "Marcus wouldn't tell me much. Evidently hijacking our plane was the quickest and easiest way for him to get here."

"What happens now?" came another question.

"How long will we be here?" one of the women wanted to know.

George looked at the group of us crowded around him. "I can't answer those questions."

"Well, when is this partner supposed to meet Marcus?"

"From the way he talks, Miles will get here probably tomorrow morning. But I can't be sure."

"Why can't Marcus just let us get back on the plane and go home? He used our plane to get here so why can't he let us go now?"

"Look, everyone, I told you all I can." George sounded upset.

"Can't you let someone know where we are?" one of the teenagers asked.

George shook his head. "You heard what the man said. If anyone goes near that plane he'll blow it up. I wanted to send out a distress

7

signal but Marcus was watching me closely and there was no way I could. All I was able to do was contact Air Traffic Control and tell them we were deviating from our original flight plan."

"Well, then they'll know we're in trouble," a man said.

Again, George shook his head. "When the air traffic controller called me back to ask if I was declaring an emergency I had to tell him I was not."

"Why? You should have told him we were in danger!"

George stepped back slightly. "I had a gun placed against my skull," he said. "If I'd done anything to alert the authorities, Marcus might have pulled the trigger and then he would have turned the gun on Patrick. With no pilot and no copilot the plane would've crashed and you would all have been killed."

Everyone began talking at once and George raised his hand to get their attention. "Please, listen to me. I won't lie to you. This is a dangerous situation. But if you trust me, we can get through it. But you must do as I say, as Marcus says."

He stood looking around the room. "Let's get busy and get ourselves organized. It's getting colder out there and it's starting to rain. Some of you men and boys go out and see if you can find any wood . . . bits of lumber, tree limbs, anything. Bring them in here before it gets wet. Keith, you go over there and check out that fireplace and get a fire going."

Some of the men started out the door in search of wood. "Don't go very far," George warned. "Marcus is over by the plane and he's watching all movement outside this building. Get what wood you can find close to the building and do not go around behind the building."

George turned back to look at the rest of us. "Some of you women check and see what food we have. I think everyone bought stuff when we stopped at the airport for refueling. Bring all the food over here and put it on this desk. We'll figure out how much we have and how best to use it."

As soon as George saw us becoming active he went out the door. In a few minutes he and the men came back in, carrying some tree limbs and several large packing cases. They carried their finds to the fireplace and began to break up the wood. Keith pulled a book of matches from his trouser pocket and in a few minutes had a fire started.

"Alright, girls," Corinne Sloan called as she headed for the desk. "Let's see what we have to eat." Corinne was a large woman with a confident manner that quickly put everyone at ease.

She pulled several facial tissues from her purse. "Look at this filthy desk!" she scolded. "It looks worse than my desk at home." Quickly she dusted off the top of the desk. "Now, put the bags of food right here," she ordered.

I sat my bag with its potato chips, candy bars, and cheese crackers on the desk in front of Corinne. Then I started across the room to where Keith was helping the men stack the boards that just moments ago had been shipping cartons.

"Can I talk to you?" I asked, putting my hand on his arm.

He turned and looked at me. "Sure," he said.

We walked together a short distance away from the rest of the crowd. "What do you want?" he asked.

"What's really going on?" I asked him. "This is all so scary."

"What do you mean it's scary?" Keith looked at me. "We're just delayed a little from getting to where we're going. You'd better get back with the ladies." He motioned toward the desk.

"But, Keith, I—"

He turned and walked away from me, back to where the men were standing close to the fireplace. I started to follow him. He glanced at me. He didn't say a word. It sent such an odd feeling down my spine. What was wrong with him? Why wouldn't he talk to me?

Slowly I walked back to where the women were clustered around Corinne, examining the contents of the bags.

"Hey, you guys!" Corinne called across the large room to the group of men. "How about lugging this desk closer to the fire where it's warmer. We'll use it as a table."

I expected Keith to be the first guy to answer her call, but when the other men headed toward us, he just stood there beside the fireplace.

"Come on, Keith," one of the men called back to him. "You're big and strong. Help us move this desk for Corinne."

But Keith just stood there.

The men began to drag the heavy desk across the tile floor. "It sure is noisy," one of them commented.

"Wait a minute," Corinne instructed. "Let me check that thing out." She walked to the desk and pulled open the top drawer then pushed it shut. She opened the next one and closed it. Turning slightly, she opened the large drawer on the other side of the desk.

"Look at what we have here!" She held up a galvanized coffeepot. "That's what was making the noise. The guy who used this desk must have been a real coffee drinker."

"Good, we can have some coffee." Patrick grinned.

"Not without coffee to make it with," one of the women corrected him.

"What do you call this?" Corinne reached into the drawer and held up a tin of coffee. She pulled off the lid. "There's some in here, not much, but at least it will make us something to drink."

She carried the coffee tin and the coffeepot and the men began to drag the desk across the floor again. I looked at Keith, big strong Keith, standing there close to the fire. I couldn't believe he wasn't helping them move the heavy desk. Old Sam Grayson was there pushing, looking like he was about to have a heart attack, but Keith just stood there watching their efforts. What was the matter with him?

"Alright, we got your desk moved for you, Corinne," Patrick announced. "How soon do we eat?"

I knew these people were frightened, unsure about the situation they were in but they seemed to have a courage, a strength that let them tease a little in spite of the danger that surrounded us.

"You can't have coffee without water," a housewife reminded Corinne.

She started to laugh. "Look out that window . . . if that ain't water falling from the sky I don't know what it is."

"All you have to do is catch it," a teenage girl added with a giggle.

"Keith, you can take this coffeepot outside and set it where it can get filled with water. It might take a little while but time is one thing we have plenty of right now." Corinne held the battered old pot out toward Keith. He took it and handed it to Abe, a teenage boy standing next to him. "Here, take this out and get rainwater in it."

"But, Keith—" I started to say something to him but the look on his face made me stop. Abe, too, didn't seem to recognize the "new Keith" because he hesitated a moment before reaching for the coffeepot. "Sure, Keith," he said. "I'll go get the water."

"Don't go near the plane," Sam Grayson reminded the boy.

Abe pulled his denim jacket close about him and opened the door, letting in a blast of cold, rainy air. He was outside only a few minutes when he came back in. "Can somebody help me carry it?" he asked.

"Let me help," George said as he headed for the door. He returned a minute later with Abe. "This is like having our own running water," he said as he carried in the full coffeepot, careful not to spill the water.

"Bring it here," Corinne instructed. "Let's get something hot to drink."

We all gathered around the fireplace. Some of us used the folding chairs that had been leaning against the wall. The men had carried several small logs in and Patrick placed a board across them to form a bench. Several others pulled the battered old couch close to the fireplace. There wasn't room for all of us to sit down, but the rest of us stood close to the ones who were sitting.

I moved over to stand beside Keith. I tried at one point to put my arm through his but he sort of shrugged me aside. He didn't object to my standing beside him but he didn't seem to want me to touch him.

10

I was glad I was standing in the shadows. I didn't want the others to see the tears that threatened to spill from my eyes at any moment.

I couldn't really understand him. The man standing beside me seemed like a total stranger. He didn't seem at all like the man who laughed at the corny jokes I told him, who liked to tousle my hair, who loved to walk in the rain or in the snow with his arm around my shoulder, slowing his long stride to match my own.

Corinne fussed over the coffeepot, measured in some of the coffee from the tin, put the lid on the pot, and set it over the flames in the fireplace.

"I wish we had some marshmallows to toast in that fireplace," Abe teased. "Or some frankfurters. We could have us a real nice hot dog roast."

"That's just like you, Abe," someone laughed. "Always thinking of food."

Keith moved away from me, slowly circled around behind the group, and walked across the room away from the warmth of the fire, away from the comfort of our friends. He stood looking out the window that overlooked the runway.

I was about to follow him when Amber came over to me. "Chloe, I can't believe this is happening. How are we going to get out of this mess?"

"Everything'll work out fine, Amber. Just relax. Just think of this as an exciting adventure, something we'll have fun telling everyone about when we get back home." I tried to sound confident, but I certainly wasn't.

"If we ever do get back home." Amber sounded doubtful.

One of the women came up beside us. "Is there a ladies' room around here?" she wondered.

I glanced around. "What's that door?" I pointed to a door not far from where the desk had originally stood. When I opened it, I found it led into a short hallway. "There you go." I smiled at the woman. "Right at the end of this hall."

I turned to go back to Amber. As I moved across the room I glanced toward the window where Keith had been standing but he was no longer there. A quick glance around the room told me he was no longer with the group.

Where was he? What had happened to him? The group huddled around the fireplace seemed calm enough. They sat together, waiting for the coffee to finish brewing.

"Say, what are we supposed to drink out of?" Abe finally spoke up. "That coffee is starting to smell really heavenly but it won't do us much good if we don't have anything to drink it out of."

"Well, anyone who keeps coffee in his desk drawer and a

coffeepot to go with it surely must have cups around someplace," Corinne reasoned good-naturedly.

Corinne started opening the rest of the desk drawers. "And I'm right!" she said triumphantly as she held up four ceramic cups. "There are only four here so we can take turns."

"Who goes first?" someone quipped. "The ladies or the gents?"

"Maybe we should let the prettiest ones go first," someone suggested, teasing.

"Maybe the oldest should go first." Sam Grayson laughed.

The teasing continued with each one offering suggestions and each comment getting a laugh from the group. I looked around again. Still no Keith. Where was he? No one else seemed to notice Keith was not with us.

Finally, the coffee was ready. Reverend Costa stood before the group and led us in a brief prayer of thanks for the food and drink we did have, and for the shelter from the storm outside. He also prayed for divine protection during this crisis we were experiencing.

When the coffee was ready the members of our group began taking turns with the cups. Anyone who had a cup of coffee could choose one small item from the collection of food on the desk. Corinne said we had to ration out the food because we didn't know how long we would be here.

I was one of the last to be served and I had difficulty swallowing the coffee. It was bitter, but it was hot, and should have brought some warmth to me, but I drank it only because Amber kept urging me to. I nibbled at the half of a candy bar I had been allotted. The chocolate almost stuck in my throat.

I was afraid. Here we were miles from anyplace. No one knew where we were. No one knew what had happened to us. Rain was pouring down out of the sky and the wind pounded against the side of the building, making this God-forsaken place seem even more desolate.

Reverend Costa began to lead the group in some songs. Several others offered prayers for our protection. Someone recited some Bible verses. Hearing the familiar words of the hymns and the words of the Scriptures did help me feel more secure.

Finally, I moved away from the group. I went to stand by the window that looked out over the airport. As I gazed through the rain, I saw the door of the plane open and two figures emerge. Because of the near-darkness I couldn't make out who they were at first.

They were moving quickly toward our building, hunching their shoulders against the wind and rain. As they approached I could see that Keith was one of the two. The other one was Marcus.

That was where Keith had been. He'd gone back to the plane.

But Marcus had warned us not to even think of going near it. Why had Keith decided to take such a risk? And why hadn't Marcus destroyed the plane when he saw what Keith was doing? Approaching the plane was one matter—actually getting on that plane and spending some time inside with Marcus was an entirely different one.

I watched as the two men neared our building. I wondered what Keith would do if he knew I'd seen him come out of the plane? He would be angry, I was sure of that. As quickly as I could without drawing attention to myself, I walked back to the group that sat huddled near the fireplace.

I had just stepped beside Amber when the door opened and Keith and Marcus rushed into the room.

The singing stopped abruptly. Everyone turned to look at the two men standing near the door with water dripping from their coats.

"I told you there was hot coffee." Keith turned and grinned at Marcus. "Come on," he said casually. "Let's get some. And there's food here if you're hungry."

Marcus followed Keith across the room. Everyone seemed to melt back out of the way as they walked to the desk and picked up coffee mugs.

"Which of this stuff can we have, Corinne?" Keith asked as he pointed to the food on the table.

I could tell Corinne was apprehensive about being so close to Marcus. She stepped back a little. "Just help yourself," she managed to say.

"Here, Marcus, want a candy bar?" Keith offered. "Or how about some of these cookies. Take your pick."

Marcus unzipped his jacket. As the coat opened I could see the bulge of the gun he had pushed down into his belt. A chill went through me. Marcus reached for a couple of the cookies, then accepted the cup of coffee Keith handed him.

Keith glanced around at the group. "Go on with your singing, everyone," he encouraged. "It sounded good."

But no one made a sound. And no one moved any closer to the fire because Keith and Marcus were now seated directly in front of it, sipping on the coffee, munching hungrily on the cookies. Everyone seemed to crowd back into the shadows in an effort to keep a distance from the men.

Amber and I stood close together against the wall. I looked at Keith sitting there, saw him take a bite of the chocolate chip cookie, saw him grin at Marcus. "These aren't as good as my mom makes but they'll do," he commented. Marcus nodded and reached for another cookie.

The man sitting with Marcus was a total stranger to me. Here was a person who had sided with a criminal, a man who would sneak away from his friends and seek out the very person who was our enemy.

I looked down at my hand and saw the diamond engagement ring there. It was small, but it caught the flickering light from the fireplace and tried to sparkle even in the darkness. I'd been so proud of this ring, had felt so secure in the love it represented.

"What's wrong with Keith?" Amber asked softy. "He's acting strange."

I just shook my head and shrugged my shoulders. I didn't dare to speak. I knew if I said one word I would begin to cry. I didn't know what was wrong with Keith. All I knew was that he was not the man I thought he was. He'd ignored me from the very beginning of this whole nightmare. If he really, truly loved me he would've spent as much time as close to me as possible in an effort to protect me, to reassure me.

All he'd done was brush me aside, ignore me, make me feel like I was bothering him. And he wasn't much better with the rest of our group. He spoke to almost no one and refused to help out with the simplest of tasks.

I was afraid as I stood there in the shadows, afraid of the man sitting close by the fireplace who made no effort to conceal the gun he had in his belt. I had no idea what his next move would be, how long he would keep us here, what he intended to do with us.

Finally, Marcus and Keith finished their food. Marcus stood up, and when he did Keith was right beside him.

"Like I said before," Marcus said, "I'm sorry to have to put all of you through this ordeal. But it just couldn't be helped. I had no other way to get to this base."

He glanced around the group of people. "You're gonna be here all night. Don't try to get away," he warned. "I wouldn't like to harm anyone." He patted the gun that protruded from his belt. "If everyone cooperates and if things go according to plan you should be on your way home tomorrow."

Keith leaned over and whispered something in Marcus's ear. They both glanced toward the door. Keith said something else to Marcus, nodded, then took two of the folding chairs that were placed in a semicircle near the fireplace. Carrying the chairs he walked toward the door. I expected him to go back outside but he set the chairs directly in front of the door and sat down on one. Marcus sat on the other.

"You'd better try to get some rest," Keith said. He slouched down in his chair, leaning his head back against the door.

I couldn't believe what I was seeing! Marcus and Keith were blocking the door so nobody could possibly get out during the night.

The people who had been standing almost motionless during this entire scene now began to move a little. Corinne went to the desk, gathered up the food, and put it back into the bags.

"I guess we'll have to sleep in shifts, everyone," George spoke up. "We don't have enough chairs and seats to go around and it's too cold and damp to lie on the floor. Besides, there's nothing to cover up with." He pointed to several people and said, "You people can rest first."

Mr. Grayson put some more wood on the fire. One of the teenagers decided to sit on the floor and lean against the side of the desk. What movement there was seemed tentative and uncertain. It was one thing to be kept prisoner in this building during the day. It was an entirely different matter to be in the now-darkened building with Marcus and Keith just across the room.

I glanced over at the door. Keith and Marcus were sitting there, engrossed in a deep conversation. Marcus was pointing back toward the plane. Keith first nodded his head in agreement, then he shrugged and shook his head.

I looked over at him. I hated him, oh, how I hated him. And yet, somehow, in spite of all this, oh, how I loved him.

"Chloe, you have to do something, you just have to talk to Keith and find out what's going on!" Amber looked at me, her blue eyes bright with fear.

I glanced across the room to where Keith sat on the folding chair in front of the door. That door was our only escape from this prison we were in, from this horrible situation that seemed to get more terrible with each passing moment.

Marcus sat there beside him, his head slumped forward against his chest, his dirty old ball cap pushed to one side of his head.

But I didn't really see Marcus, didn't really see the man who had forced our plane to land at this deserted military base. All I could see was the gun that was pushed down into his belt, and the bulge in his jacket pocket which, he had warned us, contained a detonator that could totally destroy our plane.

"Chloe, you have to do something!" Amber looked close to tears. I knew how she felt; I wanted to cry, too. Not just because of the frightening situation we were caught in, but because all my dreams and plans for marrying Keith were gone. How could I ever marry a man who told me he loved me one moment and the next sided with the very person who was our enemy? I thought I knew Keith so well, I thought he was all I could ever want in a man. How could I have been so wrong? Maybe I should have been grateful that I'd found out about this side of him before the wedding.

I felt someone touch my shoulder and turned around to see

15

Corinne standing beside me. She had been so brave through all this. She had taken charge of seeing that we were fed from the meager supply of food we had. I knew I could not let her or the others down. Somehow I had to find a way to talk to Keith.

We'd slept fitfully during the night. The building we were in had once been a recreation hall for the military base. Now it was just a large, almost empty room that was very dirty and very cold and damp. No one moved about much. They were afraid that any movement might upset Marcus and cause him to do something that would harm one or all of us.

I glanced back toward the door. Marcus was awake now. He was talking to Keith and I saw him gesture toward where our plane sat on the empty runway. Keith grinned, touched Marcus's shoulder, and nodded. The two of them stood up and pushed their chairs to one side. Keith opened the door and went out with Marcus following closely behind.

The minute the door closed everyone descended on me at once.

"You've got to do something, Chloe!" a woman insisted.

"Talk to Keith, Chloe," one of the men demanded.

"Why is Keith acting like this?" Abe asked.

I looked at his face. He was just sixteen, such a nice boy, but he was afraid.

"Abe." I touched his shoulder. "I don't know any more about all this than you do. Keith has told me nothing. I don't know what made him turn to Marcus. I don't. . . ."

"Maybe Keith is really Marcus's partner," someone suggested. "Maybe there's no one named Miles. Maybe Keith has been in on this thing right from the very beginning."

A man objected. "Keith wouldn't do that! He can't be that man's partner!"

"Hey," someone spoke up, "you know, this whole trip was Keith's idea in the first place. He's the one who said, 'Let's help out.' Maybe he wanted us to be forced to land here."

Everyone was talking at once, some with the idea that Keith was in on the crime, and others denying such a thing was possible.

"Everyone, let's settle down!" The reverend spoke up. "We're upsetting Chloe. I think we all need a cup of coffee."

"It's ready now," Corinne answered. "Who wants the first cup?"

I hurried across the room to her. "Let me have one of those cups of coffee." I held out my hand. "I'll take it out to Keith."

"Chloe, you can't go outside. It's too dangerous," Amber insisted.

"That's right," George, our pilot, agreed. "Here, let me take it out to him."

I took the cup of coffee from Corinne and started for the door.

16

As I passed the large wooden desk I picked up two cookies. Reverend Costa stepped in front of me. "Chloe, you can't go out there," he said quietly. "It isn't safe."

Ignoring him, I continued walking toward the door. Abe opened the door for me and I stepped out into the cold morning air.

I heard the door close slowly behind me. I stood there alone, holding the cup of coffee and cookies.

The rain that had pounded against the building all night had finally stopped and the air felt clean and clear. I gazed around the empty military base trying to see where Keith and Marcus had gone. But I saw no one. I felt so alone, so unprotected. Now what should I do?

"Keith!" I called. The sound of my voice seemed to echo hauntingly in the distance and I shivered slightly as a gust of wind came around the side of the building.

I started walking, taking slow steps, moving away from the security of the building, from the protection of my friends.

Oh God, please help me, I prayed silently. Don't let Keith, or Marcus hurt us. Help me. . . .

"Chloe." At the sound of my name I turned to see Keith coming across the runway from the direction of the plane. "Chloe, what are you doing out here?" he asked as he neared me. For one brief second I thought I heard true concern in his voice. In that one instant I saw a look in his eyes, a tenderness. Or did I? Before I could be sure, a veil seemed to descend over Keith's face. "I asked you what you were doing out here," he said sternly. "You should be inside with the others."

I held the cup out toward him. "I brought you some coffee," I said. "I know how much you like a cup of coffee the first thing in the morning. And I brought you some cookies. I wish I could have brought more, but I had to leave some for the others."

He stood looking at me. He looked tired and tense.

"Here, take the coffee," I urged. "Can I get some for Marcus?"

"I'll take this to him," Keith said as he reached for the cup.

"Where is he?"

"He's in the plane."

"What's going to happen?" I asked. "Why are you with him? When—"

"Stop asking questions!" Keith snapped at me. "Just go and get another cup of coffee."

"But I—"

"I said to go and get another cup of coffee!" Keith ordered.

I turned and hurried back to the building. Someone inside opened the door when I reached it. I stepped inside.

17

The minute I was in the room a dozen questions were hurled at me.

"What's happening out there, Chloe?"

"What did Keith say?"

"Where is Marcus?"

"How soon will we get out of here?"

I ignored them and walked quickly to the fireplace. "Corinne, I need another cup of coffee," I told her.

She looked at me with such concern on her face. "Chloe, honey, are you alright?" she asked gently.

I nodded. "Yes, I'm okay. Please pour me a cup of coffee for Marcus."

She poured the drink into a yellow ceramic cup. I grabbed two more cookies and headed for the door. Abe opened it for me and once again I started walking toward Keith. He had not moved from the spot where I'd left him.

"I got some more cookies, too," I told him.

I handed him the second cup. But he couldn't take it because he held cookies in one hand and the first coffee cup in the other.

"Here, give me those cookies," I said, reaching for them. "I'll put them in your jacket pocket."

He started to give me the cookies, but both my hands were full, too.

I grinned. "Wait a minute, here," I told him. "Let's get organized a little."

I took the cookies I was holding and deposited them in his left jacket pocket. Then I reached for the cookies he was holding and tried to put them in his right jacket pocket, but they wouldn't go in. My hand brushed against something metal. I looked at his pocket. It resembled the bulge Marcus had pointed to yesterday in his own jacket pocket, when he announced that he had a detonator that could activate the bomb he told us he'd placed on the plane.

I felt a chill go down my spine.

"Put the cookies in this pocket," Keith instructed.

I pushed the two remaining cookies into his left jacket pocket.

"Now give me the cup."

I handed the cup to him. He took it quickly from me. "Now get back inside," he ordered. "And stay there!"

Then he was gone, walking quickly across the cracked pavement toward the plane. I watched as he hurried up the steps and then he was gone from my sight.

"Chloe, get back in here!" someone called from the doorway.

I turned and walked back into the building.

Again I had to face people demanding answers. I told them all

18

I could, which was really nothing. I began to shake a little. Someone handed me a cup of coffee and someone else led me to a chair close to the fireplace.

They all clustered around me. They wanted answers; they wanted reassurance. I said nothing, just sipped at the coffee. It wasn't very good, but it was hot and it sent warmth through me and I began to relax.

"Okay," I looked up at them. "I'll tell you what I know. Keith and Marcus are both on the plane. I have no idea what they're doing there. I tried to ask Keith some questions. He wouldn't talk to me, wouldn't tell me anything."

A collective groan went up from the group. They'd hoped to find out if or when we'd get out of here.

I turned sideways in my chair and looked at them. "Look, I'm sorry. I tried. I really did. But there was just no way to get Keith to tell me anything. I'm sorry."

Reverend Costa moved closer to me. "Chloe, you tried and we all do appreciate it. Now don't worry about it. You did the best you could."

Several others voiced the same thing and everyone seemed to relax a little.

We now had only two cups since Marcus and Keith had the other two. We began to take turns getting our share of the morning coffee. Everyone seemed restless, uncertain of what to do next.

Reverend Costa stood up in front of the group. "All right, folks," he announced. "We're going to have a contest. We're going to match the ladies against the men. I want all the fellows to sit or stand over here on this side of the fireplace and the pretty members of our group can stay on that side. You can sit, or stand, or whatever. Just get comfortable. And get your thinking caps on."

There was a shuffling of chairs as we hurried to do as Reverend Costa instructed. When we were all properly arranged he announced, "We're a church group so we are going to have a Bible spelldown."

"What's that?" Abe spoke up.

Reverend Costa grinned. "It's a chance for me to find out how well you've been paying attention to my sermons, that's what it is."

"But there are more women here than men," Patrick protested. "That's not fair."

"We have one extra woman," the minister agreed, "so we'll let Corinne serve as scorekeeper. I'll ask a question, and for each correct answer you give, your team gets one point."

After the contest ended, with the women coming out the winners, Reverend Costa announced that we would sing. We began singing church songs, but before long we were singing "Old MacDonald Had

A Farm" and other nonsense songs. I had difficulty joining in the entertainment. I couldn't keep my mind on the Bible questions and I couldn't remember half the words to the songs.

But you can only answer Bible questions and sing silly songs for so long. Eventually, we were once again a quiet, uncertain group. People drifted off in little groups of two or three and talked quietly amongst themselves. Some sat by themselves, deep in thought.

I walked to the window near the door and looked out. Several hours had passed since I'd given Keith the coffee and cookies. The cookies! That reminded me. . . .

I glanced around, trying to locate George. Seeing him standing near the desk with Patrick and Abe, I waited till he happened to glance my way, then I motioned for him to come over to me.

He stood beside me and looked out the dusty window at the emptiness that surrounded us. "Did you want something?" he asked.

"What I have to tell you is in the strictest confidence," I said very quietly. "Do you understand that?"

George looked at me. I knew he had no idea what I was getting at. "Sure, Chloe," he agreed. "What's wrong?"

I shrugged. "Maybe nothing. I'm not sure. But you're the pilot of our plane and that makes you sort of like the captain of the ship, doesn't it?"

He nodded. "Yes, it does. Does this have something to do with our plane?"

"It might. But I'm not sure. What is a. . . ." I hesitated. I wasn't sure how to ask this question. I wasn't even sure if I should be asking it.

"Go on," George urged. "What are you trying to ask me?"

I turned so that my back was to the window and I was facing him. "George, what is a detonator?"

His eyes got big and he just stood there looking at me. "What did you say?"

"I said what is a detonator? Marcus talked about one yesterday. Isn't that a thing that makes a bomb go off?"

George nodded. "Yes, it is. Why?"

"What does it look like? I mean, is it plastic or wood or metal?"

"It's metal."

"Is it very big? Marcus said he had one in his pocket, didn't he?" I asked.

"That's what he said," George agreed.

"Do you think he does have one in his pocket? Could one fit into a person's jacket pocket?"

George shrugged. "Yes, I suppose it could. It could be almost any size." He grabbed my shoulders. "Chloe, what are you trying to tell me? What do you know? What did Keith tell you when you were outside with him?" he demanded.

"Keith told me nothing. Honest, George, he said nothing. I asked him questions, but he wouldn't tell me anything . . . he just told me to get back inside and to stay inside."

"Then what is all this talk about a detonator, all these questions?"

I stood there, my mind in a whirl. I was torn between two conflicting emotions. On the one hand, I was deathly afraid of what would happen to all of us, of the possibility that Keith was in fact a part of this whole nightmare, that he was indeed Marcus's partner. If that were true then he was more of a danger to us than Marcus was because Keith had been a part of our group. He knew our strong points and our weak points. He knew the best ways to harm us. We were really more at Keith's mercy than we were at the mercy of Marcus.

I felt overwhelmed with apprehension, terrified that we could all be killed at any moment. But underneath my terror was a feeling, a subtle, almost buried feeling that I couldn't shake. I knew I still loved Keith no matter what he had done or was now doing. A part of my heart simply wouldn't let go of the beautiful love that Keith and I had for each other. A love that sweet and beautiful does not die easily and I knew I was clinging to it with all my heart. There had to be some mistake, some logical reason for Keith's behavior.

What should I do? If I told George what I suspected would I be betraying Keith? How would my telling George affect my love for Keith? Isn't trust the very foundation of love? How could I. . . .

"Chloe," George broke into my thoughts. "Chloe, what's wrong? What's all this talk about a detonator?"

I saw desperation in his eyes. He held the responsibility of everyone here in his hands. Their safety and well-being had been placed in his care when he accepted the position of pilot of this expedition. He felt it was imperative that we have any and all information that pertained to this situation that could in any way influence the safety of these good people.

"Why are you asking me about a detonator?" he asked softly so none of the others would hear.

I had no choice, I had to tell him what happened when I took the cookies and coffee out to Keith. I told him about accidentally touching something metal in Keith's right jacket pocket.

"Can you tell me how large it was?" George wondered.

"Not really. And maybe it wasn't even anything at all. Maybe I'm just letting my imagination get away with me."

"But you said it made a bulge just like the one in Marcus's pocket," George reminded me.

21

"Maybe that's just a coincidence," I told him. "It probably is nothing to be concerned about."

George frowned. "Maybe you're right. All guys carry stuff in their jacket pockets. Just because he had something metal in his pocket doesn't mean it was something dangerous, does it?" George didn't sound convinced of what he was saying.

Quickly, I turned away from him. It was the wrong move to make. George reached over and put his hands on my shoulders to turn me back to face him. "What's wrong, Chloe? There's something else, isn't there?"

Very softly, I said, "Keith never carries anything in his jacket pocket. He might carry keys or money in his trouser pockets but he doesn't like to have anything in his jacket pocket."

"What's the conference about?" Amber greeted us as she walked up to George and me. "You two seem to be in a pretty deep debate. Is something wrong?"

George shook his head. "No, Amber. We were just trying to figure out if it's going to rain anymore."

"I hope it isn't going to rain." Amber glanced out the window. "I've had enough rain to last me for quite a while. It looks like the sky is clearing. In fact, I think the sun is trying to shine through."

"We could all use some sunshine," I said, trying to sound casual.

Several others came over to the window so there was no more chance for George and me to talk. I really didn't have anything more to tell him anyway. In fact, I felt I had already said too much.

The next hour dragged slowly along. I moved about the room, chatted with old Sam Grayson, teased Abe a little, talked with Corinne about how to best use what little food remained.

"There really isn't much left here," she said with a frown. "I don't know how we're going to manage much longer."

"What about coffee?" I wondered. "Is it all gone?"

Corinne pulled open the desk drawer and lifted out the coffee can. Taking the lid off, she peered inside. "Not much. I might be able to get one more pot of weak coffee out of this. I already made two pots of coffee from the same grounds."

"Do you want me to help you make the coffee?" I offered. I figured keeping busy was better than standing around worrying about Keith, wondering why he was acting this way.

Corinne walked over to the fireplace and lifted the battered coffeepot from the hearth. "This needs to be emptied and rinsed out."

"I'll do that for you." I held out my hand for the pot.

"You shouldn't go outside," she cautioned me. "Let one of the men do it."

"No, I can do it."

"It might not be safe," she warned.

"It's probably safer for me to go outside than it is for anyone else."

"But what about Keith and Marcus?"

"Marcus seems to be staying in the plane and I'm not afraid of Keith. We're planning to be married soon, remember?"

Corinne gave me an odd look as though she was wondering how I could still consider marrying someone that everyone now considered a traitor. I couldn't bear to hear any comment from her so I headed quickly for the door, carrying the coffeepot in both hands.

Abe opened the door for me and I stepped outside. The air felt so good, so fresh, and there was even some warmth to it now that the sun was beginning to shine.

I stood a moment just outside the door trying to decide where to pour the old coffee grounds. Slowly, I began to walk along the length of the building. I kept looking over at the plane as I walked. There was no sign of anyone around. What was going on in there? What were Marcus and Keith doing? If Keith wasn't Marcus's partner, then when was Miles going to show up? Marcus had said that when his partner arrived we'd be released.

I reached the end of the building and glanced around the side. Water lay in puddles that had not yet had time to dry out. I tipped the pot over and dumped the twice-used coffee grounds close to the side of the building. I wished I had some water to rinse this ugly pot out with.

Water. What did Corinne intend to use for water to make more coffee? We had used rainwater to make our coffee yesterday and the first thing this morning. But now the rain had stopped and that had ended our water supply.

I stood a moment, wondering what to do. Where else could we find water? I moved along the side of the building till I reached the back. Maybe there was an empty barrel that had caught some of the rainwater. If we boiled the water, it would be all right to use.

I had just turned the corner of the building, when I heard a sound. Instantly, I stopped. What was that? It sounded like someone walking. I stood as close against the building as I could. Inside I could hear the voices of my friends.

There! I heard it again. Someone was coming! Maybe it was Marcus. He would be angry because I was out here behind the building. Maybe it was Miles. Miles didn't even know me. He might be even more dangerous than Marcus.

I stood perfectly still, but my heart was pounding so loudly I was certain everyone inside could hear it. Slowly, I began to inch along the building; the brick wall of the fireplace extended a small way beyond the wall I was creeping along. If I could reach the brick wall and get on the other side of it perhaps it would shield me from the sight of whoever was approaching.

The wall, however, was near a window and I ducked slightly because I didn't want anyone inside to catch a glimpse of me. Seeing someone outside might frighten him or her.

As I ducked I felt a sharp pain go through my ankle. I could still hear the approaching footsteps. I wanted to run, but the soreness in my ankle wouldn't permit that. I managed to get beyond the brick wall and tried to sink back into the shadows just as someone came around the side of the building.

I could hardly breathe, and between the pain in my ankle and the pounding of my heart, I felt as though I couldn't stand upright another moment.

"Who's there?" a voice demanded.

A charge of relief soared through me. "Oh, Keith, it's you," I gasped as I stepped out into the open. But as I took that step I started to fall. My ankle simply wouldn't hold me up. Before I could totally collapse Keith had crossed the distance between us. Almost instantly his arms were around me.

"Chloe, what are you doing here? I told you to stay inside."

"I came out to empty the coffeepot. Then I decided to try to find some more water so Corinne could make another pot of coffee."

"You shouldn't be out here," he insisted. "What's wrong with your foot?" He held his arms close about me and I leaned my whole weight against him. That helped relieve the pain in my ankle a little.

"I guess I twisted it," I explained.

"How bad is it?" He leaned down and touched my ankle gently. I winced a little.

I could feel him run his hands carefully across my foot. "Nothing is broken," he said, sounding relieved. "I think you're right. You just gave it a bad twist. But you have to get back inside and sit down and take the weight off your foot."

For a long moment I just stood there, savoring the nearness of him.

"Come on, I'm getting you back inside." He was practically carrying me. I let him lead me across the rough ground, let his strength take the pressure from my ankle. It felt so right to have his protection again, to feel the security I had always felt with him.

When we came to where I'd left the coffeepot he paused long enough to reach down and pick it up. His leaning forward caused him to brush close against me and I felt the rigid outline of something in his jacket pocket. As he concentrated on getting the coffeepot I turned just enough to get a good look at his coat. There was something in his pocket. Something solid with square edges that created sharp angles against the fabric of his pocket. I pulled away from him slightly, but as he stood back up he tightened his hold on me.

Carrying the coffeepot with one arm and supporting me with the other, Keith headed around the corner. I realized he was slowing his pace to make it easier for me to hobble along beside him.

Together, we approached the front door. "Now you get inside," he said firmly. "I'll go get some water from the plane and bring it to the door. Then Corinne can make her coffee."

He left me and headed across the runway. He paused a brief second and glanced back at me. "Get inside and stay inside. I mean it!" he yelled loudly. His tone was gruff, angry, almost threatening. I couldn't believe the sudden change in him. A moment before he'd been so concerned about my ankle. He'd held me close, had assisted me gently in making the trek from the back of this building to the front. Now he was striding quickly across the runway back to the plane without a second glance at me. What was wrong with him?

I opened the door and started to go inside, but had trouble stepping over the doorsill.

In an instant everyone was clustered around me. A dozen questions were hurled at me at once.

Then George came pushing through the people huddled around me. "Step aside, everyone," he ordered. "Let her get inside and get this door closed." He put his arm around my shoulder and I leaned against him as he led me to a wooden chair. I sat down and leaned forward to check my foot.

"I'm okay," I assured everyone. "I just twisted my ankle. It isn't bad. Keith helped me get back into the building. He took the coffeepot to the plane to get some water. He'll bring it here in a moment."

Corinne rushed forward and knelt in front of me. "Let me see that ankle," she said, carefully untying my shoe and pulling it off. Like Keith, she checked for any signs of a break.

"It's gonna be fine," she assured me. "It's just a bad twist. I know it hurts, but there's no real damage done. You just rest that foot a few minutes and it will be almost as good as new."

"Where's Marcus?" someone asked.

"I don't know." I shrugged. "I didn't see him. I just saw Keith."

Everyone moved off into little groups of two or three to discuss this latest event, to try to decide what was happening outside of this room, what was happening on the big plane out there.

When George saw that everyone had drifted away from me, he came over and hunched down beside me. "How's your foot?"

"It's lots better already," I told him. "After I rest it a little it will be fine."

"And how's Keith?"

"I'm not sure about that." I looked at George. Should I tell him about the object in Keith's pocket? But what could I tell him? I didn't even know what it was. Maybe it was nothing. If it was nothing and I said anything to suggest it was a detonator, then Keith would truly be labeled a traitor. How could I do that to the man I loved, the man who had been so gentle with me only a few minutes ago?

For a fleeting second I could hear Keith's concern as he asked me about my ankle. But that memory was instantly clouded by the thought of the harsh, angry way he had yelled at me and ordered me to get back inside the building.

Which one of these two men was Keith? Was he the gentle, loving, laughing guy I wanted to marry as soon as possible, or was he really a person to be wary of, someone who could be sweet one moment and harsh and demanding the next? And why had he deserted us? Was he really Marcus's partner?

"Keith's coming!" Abe announced loudly as he opened the door.

"Don't worry, Marcus. I'll get us some coffee." I could hear Keith yell as he approached the building. "And I'll see if there isn't something a little better to eat than those stale cookies."

Then he was striding into the room. He moved with a cocky arrogance as he came in the door. "Hey, Corinne! Here's your water. Now hurry up and get some coffee started." Why was he talking so loudly? He was almost yelling.

As soon as he was inside he stepped to the left of the door. He seemed so big, so overbearing, so demanding.

"Abe, get that door shut!" he ordered in a lower tone.

Abe hurried to close the door.

Keith instantly dropped the coffeepot to the floor, reached out and grabbed the first wooden chair he came to, and raced across the room.

As he moved with long strides he stated, "No one is to make a sound. I want no talking, no screaming. You are to do exactly as I tell you."

Everyone watched in disbelief as he lifted the chair and sent it crashing through the window. Several women let out muffled yelps, but because of Keith's just-spoken order, no one actually screamed, although the action and the sound of the breaking glass was startling.

Using the leg of the chair, Keith prodded at several jagged spears of glass around the window's rim.

He turned and faced us as we huddled all together. Everyone seemed to have gathered in a tight knot around the chair I still sat on.

"Now," he said in a tone of voice that held such authority and power that we all seemed to shrink before him. "You will do exactly as I say. There's no time for questions or explanations. Follow my

26

orders exactly or you could be killed in the next few minutes. Do you understand me?"

No one said a word, although several people nodded.

"Since you are the pilot of this plane you will help me," Keith said to George. "Come here."

George moved quickly to join Keith in front of the window.

"Everyone will go out through this window. George and I will assist you. It's only a very short drop from the window, just several feet. It won't hurt you. As soon as you get outside, move back into the woods a short way, but don't go very far. Do not under any circumstances go around to the front of this building. Do you understand me? If you go around to the front of the building you might get hurt. You are to stay together. No one is to separate from the rest of the group. Stay behind this building. Keep low to the ground."

No one moved. It was as though we were rooted to where we stood.

"Come on, Corinne," Keith said. "We'll start with you. Come here."

Corinne stepped up to him. In one quick motion Keith and George lifted her and eased her through the window. "Debby, you're next. Then Helen."

There was no particular order to our exit. One by one we were eased through the window. Gently, but quickly, old Sam Grayson was helped through and Reverend Costa.

I stood up. My ankle was still sore, but I could now walk on it. After everyone else was through, Keith lifted me up and carried me toward the open window. For one long, entirely too short moment he held me tight against him. I felt his heart pounding. His face brushed against mine and I could feel the roughness of his two-day-old beard. As he lifted me higher toward the window he whispered, "Kitten, I love you."

Then he was pushing me through, being careful that I did not get cut by the razor-sharp splinters of glass that still clung to the outer edges of the window frame.

I dropped to the ground and hurried the short distance away to where the rest of our group was crouching low in the tall weeds at the edge of the woods. Amber pulled me down close beside her.

"Are you alright, Chloe?" she wanted to know. "Did Keith hurt you? Is your foot okay?"

"I'm fine," I insisted. "No, Keith didn't hurt me and my foot is much better now."

I could hear the soft murmur of people whispering to each other, but I didn't really hear what they were saying. All I could hear was Keith's final words to me: "Kitten, I love you." I could still feel his arms as he held me as long as he dared.

I glanced toward the building. George climbed through the window and dropped to the ground, then scurried over to us.

"Where's Keith?" I asked him. "Isn't he coming out with us?"

"As I was coming out the window, Keith went out the front door," George told me.

"The front door?" That didn't make any sense at all. "Why did he go out the front door after he forced us all to climb out the window?"

"I can't answer that," George said. "But I know we have to do exactly as Keith ordered."

George raised himself up slightly on his shoulder so that everyone could see him. "Listen to me." He spoke just loudly enough so we could all hear him. "We must stay right where we are and we must stay together. Is everyone here?"

Quickly we checked the group. No one was missing.

I don't know how long we stayed huddled in a tight little knot trying to hide ourselves in the tall grass that bordered the stand of trees. Maybe it was ten minutes, maybe fifteen.

One of the women began to cry softly and Corinne moved over to put her arms around her and offer her well-padded shoulder as a comfort.

Softly Reverend Costa began to talk to us, reminding us of God's promise of protection, quoting comforting scriptures. He prayed for our salvation, and I could feel those around me beginning to relax a little.

I'd just shifted my position slightly in an effort to ease my still sore ankle, when the noise started. Shouting! More shouting! I recognized Keith's voice. Then I heard Marcus's voice, sounding angry and threatening. Keith was yelling again. There was a shot— then silence.

I began to tremble. I knew something had happened to Keith. He'd been shot. I just knew it! He was dead! He was gone from me. I began to cry. Not loudly, just very deep, silent sobs.

Corinne put her arms around me and I cried on her shoulder. Amber held tightly to my arm, trying somehow to comfort me. Neither of us said anything, but she knew that I believed that Keith was dead.

"Listen!" Patrick cautioned. "Do you hear that? Is that a plane?"

I strained hard to hear. Yes, I did hear it. There was a plane off in the distance. And another sound—what was that?

"It's a helicopter," George announced. "They're here! I knew they would be."

Then we were surrounded by confusion. Out of the blue, springtime sky they came—a military plane, a helicopter, police officers.

28

Keith came rushing around the side of the building. "It's okay, everyone," he informed as he hurried toward us. "You can get up now. The danger is over."

He headed right for me and then I was in his arms. I was laughing and crying at the same time.

Then I noticed it—the blood on his sleeve. "Keith! What happened to you? You've been shot!"

"It's nothing much." He grinned. "Marcus isn't such a good shot with that gun of his."

In answer to all the questions being aimed at him, Keith said, "Marcus trusted me. I made him trust me. But the only way I could do that was to make him think I had turned against all of you. He believed I had a message for him from his partner, Miles. So he let me come onto the airplane after he took us captive here. After I gained his confidence, I had to continue to keep him convinced I was on his side."

"That's why you sat there in front of the door with him all night, isn't it?" Abe asked.

Keith nodded. "I felt horrible treating you all like I did, but I had to stay with Marcus till I found a weakness in him that I could use against him. I had to make him really think I was on his side."

"What about the bomb?" Patrick asked. "Is there really a bomb?"

"There certainly is," Keith said. "Or there was one. It has now been defused by the police."

"Could Marcus really have set the bomb off?" Corinne wanted to know.

"Yes, he could have. That is until I managed to get his detonator from him." Keith reached into his jacket pocket and pulled out a rectangular metal object. I hadn't been mistaken. He had been carrying the detonator in his pocket. George glanced at me and grinned.

"How did you get it?" Reverend Costa asked.

"After I gained Marcus's confidence, he showed me the detonator, then stuck it back into his jacket pocket. It looked about the same size as the cigarette case George had left in the cockpit of the plane. When Marcus removed his jacket, because it was warm on the plane, I just substituted the cigarette case for the detonator. Marcus never realized the difference until a few minutes ago."

"What do you mean?" Amber asked.

"I used getting coffee as an excuse to get back into the room with all of you. Then I made you all climb out through the window because I wasn't sure what would happen next. I wasn't sure if the plane would explode or what would happen."

Keith turned and looked at me and held his arm tighter about my shoulder. "I didn't want any of you to get hurt. As soon as you were out here I went out front, called Marcus to the door of the plane, and challenged him by showing him that I had the detonator and was in control of the situation. If he defied me I could blow up the plane with him on it."

"That's what all the shouting was about?" someone asked.

"Yes." Keith nodded. "The next thing I knew Marcus pulled out his gun and aimed it at me. I charged at him, trying to bluff him, but he pulled the trigger. But I'm alright," he added quickly. "It's just a nick. Like I said, he isn't a very good shot."

"Where's Marcus now?" Amber questioned.

"There was only one bullet in the gun. After he used that on me he had nothing left to fight with. He started to run. I tackled him and held him while the plane and helicopter were landing. Then I turned him over to the authorities."

"How did they know to come here?" Corinne wondered.

George spoke up. "Because I managed to send out a distress signal before we got off the plane."

"George mentioned that to me as we were walking from the plane to the building," Keith explained.

"But I thought you said you didn't get to send one out," I said.

George turned toward me. "I didn't get to tell the air traffic controller that we were in an emergency situation. But I did manage to flip a switch that would send out a limited frequency distress signal. But I had no way of knowing if any local pilots would pick it up."

"Well, someone did." Keith grinned. "That's why that military plane and the helicopter are out front right now."

"Can we move away from here now?" Abe asked hopefully.

"Of course, you can." Still holding on to me, Keith started to lead the way around the building and everyone followed.

Everything happened so fast. In no time at all we were back on our own airplane flying home. We were met at Crestville Airport by worried, relieved families and friends. And of course the press was there with reporters and news cameras from national television networks to cover the story of our dramatic adventure.

For a week the newspapers and TV shows were filled with news items about us. It was exciting, of course, and it was fun, now that the danger was over.

It was kind of neat to read about myself in the newspaper. I cut out each clipping and put it in a scrapbook. But those newspaper items meant nothing to me compared to the one that ran on the society page five weeks later. There was a picture of me in my wedding gown that had belonged to my mother and to her mother before her.

Our wedding day was perfect with sunshine and flowers and lovely music. After a brief reception, Keith and I headed for the airport to fly to a quiet little country inn a thousand miles away for our honeymoon.

"I told you the next time we went someplace on a plane it would be to go on our honeymoon," Keith reminded me as we leaned back in our seats and felt the plane lift off the runway.

I looked down at my left hand and saw the beautiful wedding band that matched the beautiful engagement ring Keith had given me. These rings truly symbolized our unending love for each other. A love that could survive the fright and terror we had shared a month and a half ago. I sat beside Keith and felt perfectly happy, perfectly safe. I knew he would always keep me safe. I had married a hero.

THE END

I KNOW WHO ROBBED
THE BANK!

Over the entrance the clock showed five minutes before three, five minutes until closing time. It was a midweek midsummer afternoon and things were slower than usual in the bank. I yawned and began to straighten up my teller's booth. I stacked the bills and coins and sorted the withdrawal and deposit slips. I wasn't aware of what was going on until I heard a man say, "Hand over all your cash, and make it fast."

I looked up. A gun thrust over the counter pointed straight at my chest. My hands fell and foolishly clutched at the stacks of bills. "Shove 'em through, sister," he demanded. Too scared to do anything else, I pushed everything that was in front of me, about a thousand dollars, under the clear partition. As I did so, I saw a heavy-set man in front of me, wearing a light raincoat and a dark hat. A bright blue silk scarf came right up to his eyes, which were exactly the same shade as the scarf.

Scarcely believing what was happening, I looked beyond the man. At the other teller's booth next to mine, another man, dressed the same way, was holding up Mr. Kennedy. At the entrance there was a third man, similarly dressed, with a gun pointed at Max Winters, the guard. In the middle of the room there was still another man holding a gun on several people backed up against the wall.

The man in front of me had already scooped all my money into a canvas satchel and was walking backward toward the door. In a second he and the other three men were gone. Just as the door swung to, the burglar alarm screamed out—I don't know who set it off. Then the bank and the street outside were swarming with police and sirens were screeching, but the robbers got away. It was three o'clock.

Only then did I breathe. It had happened so quickly. Suddenly, the whole place was babbling. Mr. Kennedy leaned against the glass partition between our areas and wailed, "Oh, my God, this shouldn't happen to me—after twenty years! Fifteen thousand he took."

I had worked at the bank for three years, since I graduated from Rothberg Community College, but I had been in the teller's position only two months. I'd been so proud of myself for having gotten the promotion, but now I felt ashamed, as if somehow it were my fault that the bank had been held up.

"Everyone stays right where they are," a police officer ordered.

It was Captain Shadwick, head of our small town's police force. Captain Shadwick was also the father of my boyfriend, Vince. He strode over to my cubicle as if he didn't know me. "Tell me exactly what happened, Ms. Paulson," he said.

"I—I don't know," I stuttered. "All of a sudden that man was in front of me, pointing the gun at me, telling me to give him the money. I just gave it to him." I covered my face with my hands, sobbing. "I'm sorry, so sorry."

"Don't cry, Nicki," he said more kindly. "It isn't your fault. We're merely trying to get the facts." He asked me more questions, but all I could remember were those blue eyes. When he asked me how much money I'd given the man, I said, "I don't know for sure. Let me look at my note sheet." I looked around the counter, on the floor and in the wastebasket, but I couldn't find it. I must have given it to the robber along with the money.

Another policeman came into my cubicle and took me into a back office where they took our fingerprints. Long after the customers and the other employees left the bank, Mr. Kennedy, Max Winters, and I were finally allowed to leave. Mr. Kennedy was white as a sheet and shaking so much, he asked Max to drive him home. Captain Shadwick said he'd have one of his officers drive me.

"Oh, no," I said. "Please don't. It would scare Mom if she saw me drive up in a police car. I'd rather walk, as I always do."

"All right," he said, "but go straight home."

I got my purse and left. It was only a fifteen-minute walk from the bank to my house, but today it seemed everybody in town was out to stop me and ask about the holdup. Those who hadn't seen the police around the bank had heard the news on television or on the radio, and with the curiosity of small-town people they thought they were entitled to firsthand information. At least ten people asked me if I knew the man who held me up. "Of course I don't know him," I replied indignantly. "Had I, I would've told the police."

I was seething by the time I reached my own doorstep. Why did anyone think I had any connection with the gang who robbed the bank? I was just an innocent teller, and if I hadn't turned the money over fast, I might have been a dead one.

"Nicki, honey!" Mom cried, opening the door. "My poor heart just about stopped when I heard the news. Are you all right?"

"I'm okay, Mom," I assured her, closing the door behind me. "But how are you?"

She put her hand to her heart, gasping a little. "I'm all right now, Nicki, but I almost did have another attack. Come, sit down and tell me all about it."

"Later, Mom," I put her off. "Let me take a shower first."

33

She followed me to my room, prattling like an excited child. That was the way Mom was—like a child, a beautiful but spoiled child who demanded attention and needed to be looked after. That's the way it had always been, as if I were the Mom and she the daughter. When Daddy was killed in a car accident, Mom had clung to me, whimpering, "You're all I've got left, Nicki. You'll have to take Daddy's place."

So proudly, at the age of eleven, I shouldered the responsibility for my mom. She was small, only five feet tall and delicately pretty. I was as tall as she then, but before I stopped growing at about eighteen I was a lot taller, and I was just passing pretty.

We had no financial worries because Daddy had been a builder and owned two ten-unit apartment houses besides our house, which had been Mom's folks' home. The income from the apartments kept us well until Daddy's cousin, Ted Paulson, moved in on us. Daddy had come from a farming family in the southern part of the state. We had visited them once in a while but Mom and I had never met Ted because he was a merchant seaman and always away. It'd certainly been a surprise that summer day, two years after Daddy died, when Ted rang our bell.

Mom actually fainted when she saw him. At first glance he looked exactly like my father—tall, muscular, with the same color eyes and hair. But when you looked closer at Ted you saw the difference. He was bigger, harder. His eyes were a funny color that changed with his moods, and his hair was streaked with gray. He was five years older than my father would have been, but he had a lot of Daddy's charm, that is, as far as Mom was concerned.

As soon as Mom recovered from the shock and realized he wasn't her dead husband returned, she went all out to make Ted feel at home. To my thirteen-year-old eyes it was disgusting to see the way she flirted and fawned on him and fell for his phony compliments. It hurt me to think that she could be nice to this cheap copy of my wonderful daddy.

Six weeks after Ted Paulson rang our doorbell and moved in, he married my mom. I was supposed to like it! Oh, Ted went out of his way to try to please me at first, but I wasn't easily conned into liking him. After a while he just ignored me, and it wasn't long before he began ignoring Mom, too. He'd be flattering and loving toward her when he was home, but he was gone a lot. Even when he wasn't away at sea, he was always working on some big mysterious deal that kept him out nights and often away for weeks at a time. Now, at the time of the bank robbery, he'd been away nearly a year, heavens knows where, and Mom hadn't heard a word from him for ages.

As I came out of the shower, Mom was saying, "I'm just

34

frightened to death. Robbers! Right here in Rothberg, holding up innocent people. Suppose they come here? Maybe, like on television, they think you might talk and come here to get you."

"Oh, Mom!" I cried. "Don't be silly. Nothing's going to happen to me, or to you." I went to my closet and pulled out my jacket.

"You're not going out tonight, are you, Nicki?" Mom asked, her voice rising in panic.

"Why not? Don't I always go out with Vince on Wednesday nights?"

"Yes, but tonight—" Mom dabbed at her nose, sniffling back a tear. "Tonight I hate to be alone."

"You'll be all right," I said, leaning over to kiss her cheek. "Just lock the door and don't let any strange men in."

"Oh, I wish Ted were here," she wailed.

I snorted. "That's all we need—another robber!" Over the years Ted had reduced my mom's bank account to almost nothing, and he'd managed to get her to sign one of her apartment houses over to him.

Rather than listen to me sound off again on my stepfather, Mom left the room, saying, "I'll go put supper on, so you'll be through when Vince calls for you."

The thought of being with Vince calmed my jittery nerves. I may be a big girl, but inside I was scared. I wanted and needed a strong man to lean on and Vince Shadwick was my rock.

I loved Vince and wanted to marry him but not yet, even though he was always after me to name the day. There were two reasons why. The main reason was that Vince still had another year at law school. I didn't want to shackle him with responsibilities until he got his degree and started practicing, although he argued that he could support me on what he made working part-time in the county clerk's office. The other reason was Mom. Two years before, she'd had a heart attack and hadn't been really strong since. She depended on me so much that I hated to leave her—depended on me too much, Vince said.

Mom was unusually quiet during supper. We were just finishing our pie and coffee when Vince rang the bell. She looked up quickly, as though surprised. "That's Vince," I said, getting up.

"Oh, so soon?" She half rose, then sank back in her chair. I looked at her sharply. Her face was pale and her hand was at her throat. I started to go to her, but Vince rang again.

When I let him in, he put his arm lightly around me, saying, "Hi, beautiful." Then he pulled me closer and said, "Thank God, you're all right." For a few seconds I stood there, suddenly trembling in his arms. "Hey, you're not still scared, are you, Nicki?" he asked, kissing my forehead.

I smiled up at him. "Not any more—now that you're here."

"I wish I'd been with you this afternoon, or rather I wish I'd been there instead of you."

I laughed. "Mr. Kennedy was scared out of his wits, too."

"Oh, it's terrible," Mom said, coming into the living room. "My little girl exposed to holdup idiots! I'd like to almost die."

We turned to look at her. I felt my throat tighten. I knew the signs. Mom was working up to a high pitch, so that I'd stay home with her. I tried to ignore her. "I'll get my purse, Vince. The movie starts at eight. We don't want to miss the beginning."

I ran upstairs, powdered my nose again, and put on fresh lipstick. When I came back down, Mom was leaning back in a chair, and Vince was telling her that the bandits hadn't been caught, but that his father and the police were doing all they could to track them down. "But I'm so afraid for Nicki," Mom wailed. "The robbers might do something to her!"

"Don't worry, Mrs. Paulson," Vince said. "She'll be all right with me. Nothing will happen to her." He reached out to take my hand.

"I know she will be," Mom murmured, "but, oh, I wish you wouldn't go out tonight." She was panting now. "I've got this awful feeling that something terrible's going to happen."

Vince looked at me questioningly. "Oh, Mom," I cried shortly. "Nothing's going to happen. Just lock the door like I told you to. We'll be home early, I promise you. Come on, Vince, it's getting late."

I rushed him out the door, afraid to look back at Mom, afraid I'd weaken and give in to her panic, as I had so many times in the past. "You're sure you want to leave her, hon?" Vince asked.

I nodded and got into his car. We were late arriving at the movie, but it didn't matter. I couldn't enjoy it anyway. I kept thinking guiltily of Mom, the beseeching way she'd looked as we left, the real fear that was in her eyes. Before the movie was three-quarters over I whispered to Vince that I had to go home. He growled but got up.

When we were in the car, he said, "I can understand your mom being upset tonight, but every time we have a date she's pulled the same act. She's a clinging vine and eventually she'll sap all the life out of you, Nicki. That's why I want you to make the break now and marry me right away. She'll be okay once she gets used to being alone."

"Oh, Vince, please let's not talk about it now. Just hurry. I'm worried about Mom. I almost feel like she does, that something terrible is going to happen tonight."

Vince said no more, but switched on the radio. A news bulletin was on: "The holdup gang who robbed the Rothberg Bank has not been apprehended. It is believed they have gotten out of the state—" There was more but it meant nothing. It only served to heighten my nervousness.

36

He took me to my door. As we came in, I could see a light on in Mom's room upstairs. All was quiet. "Mom!" I called.

"Is that you, Nicki dear?" Mom called from the top of the stairs. "You're home early, aren't you?"

"Yes. I was worried about you."

"Silly!" I looked at Vince in dismay. Disgust was written on his face. This wasn't the first time I'd spoiled our date because I'd been overly anxious about Mom, only to come home and find her perfectly all right.

He touched my arm. "Now that you're satisfied about her, let's go somewhere for a drink or something."

I was about to agree when Mom called again. "Come on up, dear." Then she added in a sort of hushed voice, "I—I have something to tell you."

I didn't think much about it. Mom can make a great secret of what she's going to fix for breakfast or a new way she's decided to do her hair. Turning to Vince, I said, "I guess I'd better not go out again, darling." I put my arms around his neck and gave him a kiss.

Instead of pulling me close, he almost pushed me away, barely touching my lips. "Okay, Nicki. Go baby your mom, and if you ever decide to live your own life, let me know."

"Oh, Vince! Don't be like that," I cried, but he'd slammed the door behind him. His car started with an angry snort, and before the sound of the motor died down I was aware of Mom urgently calling me.

Wearily, I dragged myself up the steps. Mom took my arm and pushed me into my room, closing my door firmly behind us. Her hair was mussed and her face flushed. I noticed she was wearing a fancy new robe. She whispered, "He's here. He's come back."

I stared at her. "Who? The bank robber?"

She shook her head. "No, I mean your stepfather—Ted's back."

"Oh, no!" I cried. "Why did he have to come back now of all times?"

"You ought to be glad," Mom said. "We need a man around now to protect us."

I sighed. There was no use arguing. "Mom, the bank robbers are probably out of the country by now, but if they are still around, you can be sure the police will catch them. We're in no danger."

Mom sniffed. "Maybe not, but I feel a lot better with Ted home. He just got back from a trip to Europe. He brought me this negligee from Paris. Isn't it beautiful?"

I looked at the lacy, filmy thing. Ted always brought Mom presents like that—things more suitable for a mistress than a middle-aged wife, but Mom loved them. He always brought presents for me,

37

too, but I merely put them away on my closet shelf. I never let him have the satisfaction of knowing I liked anything he gave me.

I didn't have the heart to hurt her. "Yes, it's pretty, Mom," I answered her then asked, "Where's Ted now? Asleep?"

She nodded. "He was so tired. He and a friend drove down from New York. He was exhausted."

"Is his friend staying with us, too?" I asked.

"No, he didn't even come in. I was in the kitchen doing dishes when Ted walked in. I nearly died when he sneaked up behind me and put his arms around me. I thought he was one of the robbers."

"Ted shouldn't have done that," I said. "He knows how easily frightened you are. Did he know about the bank robbery, that I was held up?"

"Not until I told him," she said. "Well, good night, dear. I'd better get back to bed."

"Night, Mom," I said, kissing her.

I didn't realize how much the day had taken out of me until I lay down, but then I couldn't go to sleep. I kept seeing that gun, and the man with the scarf around his face. Then I'd see Vince, first smiling, then scowling as he'd been when he left. Then Mom—worried, frightened, excited, and then Ted's face, as I remembered it. Once he must've been a handsome man, but time and a rough life had hardened him. The last time he'd been home he'd had a broken nose. His hair had turned almost white and his skin was deeply sunburned. His eyes had had a peculiar yellow-green light.

His eyes had always bothered me—and frightened me. When he was in the house his eyes seemed to follow every move I made, but he had never actually made a pass at me, never put his hand on me, though sometimes I felt I'd rather have him beat me than stare at me. I remembered his broad, hulking shoulders and his square, brown hands. And I remembered his husky, rasping voice that grated on my nerves.

I was about to fall asleep when suddenly I sat up. That robber was about the same size as Ted. The hand on the gun had been square and brown. The hair—I didn't remember it, but the eyes had been almost the same shade. I shook my head. What was I thinking of? I had never liked Ted—still, that didn't make him a bank robber. It was just a coincidence that he'd returned from overseas the same day.

Finally, I fell asleep and awoke early to hear sounds of giggling and low laughter coming from Mom's room. It made me sick to think of my mom and that loser shut off together in a world of their own. And Vince had gone away in anger because I'd put my mom before him! Not anymore, I thought. I'll call him and tell him I'll marry him whenever he says, I decided.

I dressed and left home without seeing Mom or Ted, I didn't even turn on the television. I hadn't given the bank another thought, either, until I was out on the street and two or three people stopped me to ask about the holdup. From them I learned that the men had not yet been caught.

At the bank, Mr. Chris Rothberg, Jr., the vice president, said that they thought it would be better if I worked in the back office for a few days, at least until the holdup men were found. "Is Mr. Kennedy being demoted, too?" I asked bitterly.

"No, he's not," Mr. Rothberg answered. "And don't feel that it's a demotion, Nicki. We just want to protect you. The FBI has been called in because it's almost certain the criminals got out of the state. And there'll be a lot of curiosity seekers and newsmen around today. We just want to keep you out of the limelight as much as possible."

There was nothing I could do but go back, not to my old desk— another girl already had that—but to the empty desk where beginners usually sat. It was humiliating and I felt as if I were being punished for something I couldn't possibly have helped. And those cats in the bank really turned on me with claws bared. "Why did you give up the money so quickly?" someone asked. And another, "You saw the man. What did he look like?" Another asked, "Are you sure you don't know who he was?" But the worst jibe of all was, "What does it feel like to be fingerprinted?"

Of course I wasn't a criminal, but I sure felt like one before the day was over. I telephoned Vince at his office, but he was busy and it was nearly four before he called back. He was still mad at me, even after I told him I wanted to see him. I couldn't tell him about Ted because everybody in the office was listening, and I certainly couldn't explain to him then I wanted to get married right away All I could do was to ask him to drop by the house. Reluctantly, he said he'd come after his evening classes, about ten.

After closing time Mr. Rothberg asked me, Mr. Kennedy, and Max Winters to stay for more questioning. It seemed that they thought the robbery was an inside job, that one of us must be in with the gang. They asked us almost everything about our personal lives. I had to tell them that my stepfather was home from the sea, and that I was engaged to Vince Shadwick—things like that. Mr. Kennedy is a bachelor, about fifty, a churchgoer, a member of the country club, and generally above reproach in Rothberg. Max Winters has a large family and is always hard up for money. He has a teenaged boy in reform school, but he's never been in any kind of trouble himself. The grilling they gave us was awful, but finally they let us go home.

At home there was Ted, beaming and fatherly, handing out presents—costume jewelry, perfume, a beautiful hand-tooled bag from

Spain. And there was Mom, gushing and girlish, flitting around like a hummingbird over her man. The trouble at the bank wasn't mentioned until dinner was nearly over. "Have they gotten any leads on the holdup yet, Nicki?" Ted asked casually. I shook my head. I didn't want to talk about it. "Do they suspect anybody inside?" he asked, looking at me through new dark-rimmed glasses I'd never seen on him before. They made his eyes look black.

"I don't know," I said shortly, getting up from the table. "I'll do the dishes, Mom," I told her. "You and Ted go watch TV, go to a movie, or something."

She and Ted had been drinking wine with their dinner—the wine was another present from France—and she was a little tipsy. Ted said later, maybe. They went into the living room and before I was through with the dishes I heard them going upstairs, heard her giggling, "It's too early, darling!"

To keep from having to overhear any more, I stayed in the kitchen and cleaned out the cabinets and the refrigerator. Mom's a hit-and-miss housekeeper, and now that Ted was home, her housekeeping would be skimpier than ever. I worked with a vengeance, trying to work off my resentment toward Mom and my stepfather, and toward my helpless involvement in the holdup.

I was hot and sticky when I finished my cleaning, so I went up and took a shower and put on some clean clothes. When I came down, it was only quarter of ten. I straightened up the living room. Then I went to the window and stood watching for Vince's car.

The opening of a beer can made me spin around. Ted came into the room, carrying a drink. "Got anything to read around here?" he asked gruffly.

I motioned toward the magazines on the coffee table. He flopped down on the sofa and started riffling through them. "Where's Mom?" I asked.

"Asleep," he answered. "Couple of drinks and she's out like a light."

I turned back to the window. It was very quiet and still outside. Not even a leaf was stirring on the big elms that lined the sidewalk. I wondered if we'd get a sudden summer storm. It was terribly warm, but something more than the heat was bothering me. As if compelled, I slowly turned around. Ted had a magazine in front of his face but he was staring at me over the top of it. His big black-rimmed glasses were dangling from his right hand. As soon as he saw me turn, he put the glasses back on, but he wasn't fast enough. In that split second I saw his eyes reflecting the bright blue of the back of the magazine. And they were the same bright blue eyes that had confronted me in the bank! Ted's chameleon eyes had betrayed him! He stared at me now through the glasses as if daring me to say something, but I was speechless with terror. He might have a gun in his pocket. He might kill me, or worse, kill Mom!

Just then I heard Vince's car stop in front of the house. I gasped, "There's Vince," and ran from the room. Ted said nothing, but I felt if I said one word to Vince about my suspicions the worst would happen.

"Hey, what's the rush?" Vince asked, meeting me halfway on the walk and catching me in his arms.

"Oh, nothing," I panted. "I—I'm just glad to see you. I was afraid you were still mad, that you wouldn't come."

"Oh, honey, you knew I would," he assured me and started to kiss me but I broke away.

"Let's go for a ride. I—we can't talk here," I said.

He realized that I was upset about something, so he hurried me into the car and we drove off. "What's this all about?" he asked after we turned the corner and were on the highway.

"It's Ted—my stepfather—he's—" In spite of my fear I was about to spill everything about Ted, but a passing car honked at us and the driver called, "Hello, there." It was Vince's father, Captain Shadwick. We waved back.

I realized then that I couldn't tell Vince about my suspicions. He would have to tell his father and his father would have to arrest Ted. How would it look then to have his son engaged to a crook's stepdaughter? Or suppose I was wrong and that I was jumping to conclusions and Ted wasn't guilty? He would never forgive me, nor would Mom. Mom! With her bad heart, any sort of trouble or investigation might be the end of her.

Vince said, "Dad says they think someone who works inside the bank is in with the gang who robbed it."

"Why does he think that?" I asked.

"I guess because it all went off so smoothly."

I didn't say anything more. I couldn't. Now more than ever I couldn't tell Vince my suspicions about Ted—he'd think I was in on the robbery! I had to have more time. I had to give the police a chance to find the robbers themselves. Oh, God, how I hoped I was wrong about Ted. If I wasn't, I could never marry Captain Shadwick's son. Even if I'd had nothing to do with it, people would always think so. I shivered.

"What was it you wanted to see me about?" Vince asked. I moved closer to him. "It's nothing, really. My stepfather's back. And when he's there, Mom acts like an idiot over him."

Vince laughed. "If she's that much in love with him, he can't be all bad," he said. Vince had never met Ted. We weren't dating the last time Ted was home. "What did he ever do to you that makes you dislike him so?"

41

"Nothing really," I admitted slowly. "It's just the way he looks at me, the way he makes me feel. He's an awful character. He doesn't love Mom; he just uses her to get whatever he can out of her."

"Like what?" he asked. "What can you actually pin on him?"

"Oh, Vince, stop talking like a lawyer," I burst out. "There's nothing I can pin on him, as you say, but I just can't stand him."

He put his arms around me. "Well if you can't stand him, marry me now and get away from him." He kissed me.

I wanted to say, "Yes, let's get married tonight," but I knew I couldn't, not with Ted between us. "I wish I could, honey. Oh, how I wish I could," I said, sighing.

"There's no reason in the world why you can't," he said. "Your mom's got a husband to look after her now. And your arguments about my having to finish school first are nonsense. I can finish just as well being married as single. We won't be rich, but we won't starve."

"Vince, please, let's not talk about it now. I'm so upset about the bank and Ted and everything."

"All right, sweetheart," he said gently, slowing down to turn off the road. We parked at one of our favorite spots, on a little bluff overlooking the valley. He took me in his arms and for a long time there was nothing in the world but Vince and me and our love.

In the ten months I'd been dating Vince he'd never tried to make me go all the way, but that night we both got so keyed up we almost did. It was he who broke away. "My God, Nicki," he cried. "We can't keep this up. We've got to get married and soon or—"

A sharp crack of thunder and a blaze of lightning made us jump. "We'd better go," Vince said. "Looks like a storm."

We drove home with the lightning and thunder right behind us, but it didn't rain, and it grew hotter than ever. From the car we could see Ted was still in the living room watching TV, so I didn't ask Vince to come in. "But I'd like to meet your stepfather," he said stubbornly. "We'll have to meet someday if you're going to be my wife and I'll be a part of the family."

"Not tonight, please, Vince," I said nervously, starting to get out of the car. "You'll meet him soon enough."

"And when are you going to be my wife?" he asked, trying to pull me back into his arms.

"Oh, Vince, please!" I screamed almost hysterically. "Don't push me."

"If you really loved me, you wouldn't have to be pushed," he said, and then added, "Or is this thing between us just sex? You call me, you say you must see me, you fall into my arms. Is it just that you want me but you don't want to marry me?"

I couldn't take any more. Breaking away from him, I scrambled out of the car and ran into the house. I flew up the stairs to my room. There I threw myself on the bed, but tears didn't come. I felt like the summer night, charged with lightning and shaking with thunder, and there was no relief from the pressure.

Ted was still downstairs. I could hear him prowling around like a tomcat, heavy-footed and full of threat, as if he were waiting— waiting until just the right moment to do whatever he planned to do. But nothing happened that night.

And nothing happened the next day, except more questions at the bank, that is, for Mr. Kennedy and me. Mr. Winters was at home with a cold. Ted was out that night and Mom had no idea where. I hoped he'd gone for good but he came in about midnight. I was glad that the following day was Sunday and the bank was closed so I didn't have to go out. Mom was so wrapped up with Ted that she hardly noticed I was in the house, though in mid-afternoon, when she saw me taking about my seventh can of cola from the refrigerator, she said, "Nicki, it's so hot. Why aren't you out at the Y swimming?"

"Do you want to get rid of me, Mom?" I snapped.

Tears sprung to her eyes. "Of course not, dear," she said. "I just wondered. You're usually off somewhere with your friends."

"Well, I didn't feel like going anywhere today," I told her.

"Are you sick, baby?" she asked, reaching up to touch my forehead. I almost slapped her hand away, but managed to control myself.

"No, Mom, I'm not sick," I said patiently.

"Then you're going out with Vince tonight?"

"I don't know," I said, walking out of the kitchen. Vince hadn't called me since the other night and I had no intention of calling him again. But I wanted to see him. I ached to be in his arms again. We usually went to dinner or to the movies.

As I went out the back door to read under the shade of a huge oak tree in the backyard, I heard Ted come in and say, "Let's have another beer, honey." Mom giggled. I realized then that they were already on their way to a grand old time.

Later they went out in Mom's car and when they returned about eight o'clock Ted had to practically carry Mom in. I had dinner ready but he said they'd eaten, and he took her right up to bed. Poor Mom. With her bad heart, she shouldn't have been out drinking trying to keep up with a tough sailor like Ted.

While I was sitting eating dinner, Ted came into the kitchen to refill his highball glass. He'd switched from beer to whisky. He stopped and scowled at me. "What's a babe like you doing home alone on Saturday night? Where's that boyfriend of yours, that cop's kid I understand you're running around with?"

43

I started to say that I'd had a fight with Vince, but one look into his leering face and I knew I had to get out of the house. I couldn't stand being alone with him, with Mom sound asleep upstairs. There was no telling what he might do. So I said as civilly as I could, "I'm meeting him at a friend's house at nine. We're all going to the movies together." I'd dress up and go to a movie alone just to get out of the house, if Vince didn't call in the meantime.

Ted lost interest in me then, and went on to get his drink. He lumbered back to the living room to watch a boxing match on TV. I cleaned up my dishes and went up to dress. The door to Mom's room was open and I could hear her snoring softly. I tiptoed in to see if she was all right. Though her face was flushed and her makeup smeared, she looked like a tired-out teenager who'd flopped in bed.

I reached down to pick up her sandals, which she'd kicked under the bed. It was then that I saw the bag—Ted's big weather-beaten leather bag with labels from all over the world pasted on it. It was shoved well under the bed. I jumped as if the word, "Dynamite," had been written all over it. Something told me that bag held the evidence that would prove Ted was one of the bank robbers! My hands reached for it, but then I heard his heavy steps on the stairs. I jerked up and fled to my room.

I dressed quickly. I had no plan except to get out of the house fast, then come back after Ted was gone and search his bag. I was sure he would go out because of the restless way he was roaming around. Besides, his whisky bottle was almost empty. He would probably go to one of those taverns down by the river where the riffraff of town hung out. I'd never been in one of them, but I'd known ever since Ted married Mom that he kept pretty low company outside the house. He had never stayed in town long enough to make any decent friends.

Ted was sitting on the edge of Mom's bed, staring into space as I passed by to go downstairs.

I was halfway out the front door when the phone rang. I ran to answer it, hoping it would be Vince. A low, scratchy voice asked for Ted.

"It's for you, Ted," I yelled, putting the phone down. Then I hurried out and got into Mom's car, only to discover I didn't have the car keys. I didn't want to go back in to get them. I could walk to town, I decided. Although it was dark, I wasn't afraid. Our town was a quiet, peaceful place—that is, it had been until the bank was robbed.

As I walked, I made my plan. I would go to the drugstore, pick up a new lipstick and hang around for about half an hour, then I'd go home. Ted would be gone by then and I could sneak his bag out of Mom's room and search it. That was as far as my thinking got. I had no idea what I'd do if I actually found some evidence, but I knew I had to make the search.

44

The minutes dragged slowly by then I was on my way home again. As I skulked in the shadows, I felt like a criminal myself. In a way I was, wasn't I—hadn't I been withholding information from the police? I should have told Captain Shadwick about my suspicions Thursday night when I recognized Ted's eyes above the blue cover of the magazine.

When I reached the house I saw that the car was still in the driveway. Maybe Ted hadn't gone out, after all. Then I remembered the phone call. He'd probably been picked up by one of his pals. I hoped so. If he were still home, I would have to make up some story. But he wasn't in the living room. The TV set was off, but the lights were still on.

I went upstairs, clomping noisily so if Ted were home he'd show himself, but he didn't. The door to Mom's room was closed, but the nightlight threw a soft gleam from under the door into the hall.

Cautiously I explored the house to see if maybe Ted was hiding somewhere to trap me. When I was sure he was nowhere around, I went back to Mom's door. I couldn't just walk in. Ted might be there. I swallowed hard, forcing back panic. Lightly I tapped on the door, ready with the excuse, if Ted was there, of wondering whether I should put the car away.

There was no answer. All I heard were Mom's gentle snores. If Ted had been there asleep, he'd be shaking the roof with his snores. I put my hand on the cold metal doorknob, turned the knob slowly, and pushed the door open. Mom was sleeping just as I'd left her. There was no big, burly body on the other side of the bed. I sighed with relief.

I walked over to Mom. She didn't move. I didn't think she would. She was a heavy sleeper. I knelt beside the bed and reached one hand under to pull out the bag. My hand closed over its handle. Then I froze. I had no right to go through my stepfather's things. But it would be wrong not to. I listened tensely, but there was no sound in the house.

I pulled the bag out onto the rug. To my surprise, it wasn't locked. The fastener snapped open like a firecracker. I sat back startled. Then I got hold of myself and made my hands do my bidding. Out came the shirts and underwear from the top. Ties, a wool muffler, and a plaid silk scarf came next, but there was no bright blue scarf. Papers, matchbooks, cuff links, tie clips were in the side pockets. There were a couple of cardboard boxes, one containing some cartridges but there was no gun. Ted must have it on him. The other box contained some dice, cards, and miscellaneous junk. Then under some cardboard boxes, such as the laundry puts in men's shirts, there was a metal box. And it was locked!

I ran to Mom's dressing table and got her nail file. The box was made of cheap metal and had a flimsy lock. Even with my shaking fingers I didn't have much trouble opening it. The first thing that hit my eye was a comic book. I gasped. It was so ridiculous—a kid's comic book all locked up! I lifted the book. Underneath another comic book! I lifted it out but it was heavier, thicker. I started leafing through it and bills started spilling out. Between every page there were several bills—some old and used, others crisp and new, of all denominations from one dollar up to a hundred dollars! There were four more comic books, all bulging with money!

Stunned I sat back on my heels. What should I do now? Could I go to Captain Shadwick and say that I'd discovered money locked in my stepfather's bag? How stupid I'd look! I had to have more evidence. I leaned back over the bag and then I saw the gun at the bottom of the box. It was just like the gun the robber had held on me. Ted had to be the holdup man. I was scared to death of the thing, but my hand reached for the gleaming gun.

"What the hell do you think you're doing?" Ted's voice crackled through the room. My hand jerked around, but the rest of me froze. He was coming toward me weaving, his face contorted. Automatically my fingers curved around the cold steel gun. I'd never handled one in my life, but my finger closed around the trigger.

"Put that gun down!" Ted barked. "It's loaded!" But I couldn't put it down. I pivoted and then my hand was pointing the gun straight at Ted. I couldn't help what I was doing. Something inside me was making me do it.

Then I heard my voice squeak, "You were the holdup man. You took the money from me at the bank."

"Are you nuts?" he growled. "That's my own hard-earned money. Now give me that gun."

He reached out, but I yelled at him like a bad movie actress, "Stay where you are, Ted Paulson, or I'll kill you, you thief!"

My teeth began to chatter and I got icy cold all over. I must be crazy to talk of killing someone, even my stepfather. But if he got hold of the gun, he'd kill me. I knew he would. Now he stood at bay, half-crouched, his eyes gleaming yellow like a cat's. A piercing shriek stabbed my ears. My head flipped around. It was Mom, sitting up in bed, screaming, "Nicki, stop!"

That was all Ted needed. He pounced on me with the full weight of his big body. His hand grabbed the wrist of my hand, which held the gun. We were struggling fiercely to get it away from each other when it went off. The gun roared—then there was deadly silence. Even Mom wasn't screaming any more. She was lying in a heap on her bed; red blood was staining the white sheet clutched in her hands.

"Mom!" I shrieked. I had killed my mom!

Ted was on his feet, bending over her, yelling at me, "Get a doctor, an ambulance, quick!"

I couldn't move. Ted hit me hard with the back of his hand. "Move! You know her doctor. Call him and call the hospital for an ambulance. Do you want your mom to die while you sit there gawking?"

"She's not dead!" I mumbled unbelievingly.

"Not yet, but if we don't get help in a hurry, she will be."

I scrambled to my feet and raced downstairs to the phone. I dialed the first number that came to my head—Vince's. I was surprised when he answered, surprised that I had called him when I meant to call Dr. Kaye. "Vince—" I gasped. "It's Mom. I've shot her—get help." I didn't wait to hear his answer, for I realized I must call the doctor.

I reached the doctor and managed to tell him what happened. He said he'd get an ambulance and come as soon as possible. I hung up, for Ted was yelling for me to bring whiskey from the kitchen. I found the bottle and stumbled back upstairs.

Ted had Mom lying flat on the bed, a wet towel against her shoulder. He snatched the whiskey out of my hand and poured it into a glass, then held it to her lips. Most of it trickled down the side of her mouth, but she moaned a little. "She'll come around," Ted said. "She's out, but I think it's just a shoulder wound, thank God."

I sank on my knees beside the bed and took Mom's cold hand in mine. "Oh, God, Ted, suppose I had killed her, suppose she had died, suppose she does?"

"Who said you shot her?" he snapped. "It was my gun. It was my fault."

I grabbed at that. It was—everything was his fault. If he'd never come to our house after my father died, Mom and I would've had a nice, peaceful life alone, and she wouldn't be lying at death's door this minute. "Yes, yes, it was your fault," I stammered. "If you hadn't had that gun, if you hadn't stolen that money from the bank—"

"I didn't rob that bank, you stupid kid," he said. "If I had, do you think I'd be fool enough to hide here in this house, knowing you'd turn me over to the cops fast? You've always hated my guts."

"I don't believe you. You've lied and cheated and stolen from Mom for years. You've used her and spent her money—and I do hate you, Ted Paulson!" I'd never told him what I thought of him before. Now I felt a little shocked at what I'd said.

"That's no skin off my nose," he said. "Your mom loves me and I love her. Maybe I haven't been the best husband in the world, but from now on I intend to be. I've saved most of what I've made all these years at sea. Now I've got enough to retire and take care of your

47

mom, and the sooner you marry that cop's kid and get out of our hair, the better we'll like it."

"Ted—Nicki—" We'd been so involved in our argument that we'd almost forgotten Mom lying there beside us, nearly dead because of us. We both stared at her now. She was moaning, moving her head from side to side. "Don't fight, please," she gasped.

"Mom, Mom—" I cried, sobbing so loud that I didn't hear the front door open or the ambulance men coming up the stairs with a stretcher.

The doctor and Vince arrived at the same time, the ambulance and Captain Shadwick seconds later. Ted explained what had happened, but I was too unnerved to do anything but cry against Vince's shoulder as they took my mom away on the stretcher. "You come with us in the ambulance, Mr. Paulson," Dr. Kaye said. Turning to Vince, he added, "I guess you can look after your girl, huh?"

"Sure, doctor," Vince said. "I'll bring her to the hospital in my car."

Then his father asked me for my version of what had happened. I told them about my suspicions and what I'd found—the bag and the money were still lying there on the bedroom floor—and I ended my story with, "I still think Ted was one of the bank robbers, don't you, Captain?"

He shook his head. "I can see why you thought so, Nicki, but you were wrong. We've been working night and day on the case, and we've almost got it solved. Believe me, your stepfather had nothing to do with it."

"Then who—"

"I can't tell you now, but it isn't Paulson."

We put the money back in the bag and shoved it under the bed, but Captain Shadwick took the gun along. "There'll be an investigation," he told me, "but don't worry about it. Right now, just worry about your mom. Come on, I'll drive you to the hospital."

By the time we got there the bullet had already been removed from Mom's shoulder. She'd been given a transfusion because she'd lost so much blood and now she was under sedation. Dr. Kaye assured me that she would recover quickly. "But her heart?" I questioned.

He patted my shoulder. "Your mom's heart healed long ago, honey. She's a strong woman, even if she looks like a helpless little thing."

Mom did recover and was home again within a week. In that week my stepfather and I really got to know each other. "I can't blame you for what you thought of me, Nicki," Ted said. "I was an old sea dog when I met your mom, but I'm going to be a real husband and father now. I'll look after you both as I should have from the beginning."

He forgave me for my ugly suspicions and I forgave him for neglecting Mom, for I realize now that he does love her. He's still rough and tough at times, but Mom is happy with him and I'm happy for her.

Ted's coming home to stay made it easier for me to say, "yes" to Vince. We're going to be married before Christmas, and move into a small apartment. Vince still has a year and a half before he becomes a lawyer, but with my working, we'll get along fine.

I'm back in my teller's position now, but there's a new man in the cage next to me. Mr. Kennedy turned out to be the "inside man" on the bank holdup. He confessed everything and revealed the names and whereabouts of his accomplices. He'd lost a lot of money in some real-estate speculation and juggled some accounts to cover his "borrowing" from them. When he discovered the bank examiners were coming to audit the books, he staged the robbery to cover his tracks. The bandits were tracked down by the FBI and sent to a federal penitentiary. So was Mr. Kennedy. The gossip has died down now and things are pretty quiet in Rothberg. A new alarm system has been installed in the bank. It's supposed to be foolproof.

Ted and I had to go through an investigation, but neither of us were held responsible. It was ruled an accident. Ted had a permit for the gun so that was not held against him. He told the captain to keep the gun, though, for he has no more need of it. He says he's never going to sea again, except as a passenger. He and Mom are going to take a long second honeymoon trip just as soon as Vince and I are married. I wish them as much happiness as I know Vince and I will have.

THE END

THE CURSE OF
THE MOUNTAIN WITCH!

Inheriting the old one-room log cabin was a dream come true. Going back to it would be a return to the past, playing in the shallow creek behind Granny's old country store, making playhouses under the trees with soft, green moss for furniture, and eating fat, brown-crusted biscuits with red-eye gravy. It was a miracle. I had dreamed, somewhere in the back of my mind, of going home again, and now that dream had turned into a reality. The city could never offer the good feelings inside that the mountains gave, a kind of peace and security. The city was different; everything was fast and not very permanent.

I was born and raised in Carbondale on the edge of where the steep mountains began. When I was growing up, Mama and I lived in the back rooms of Granny's big country store. Daddy had died when I was a baby. My cousins and I used to crawl under the store and dig holes in the ground and have mud fights until Mama would tell us not to go under there anymore because of snakes. Then we would make tree houses and forts on the sides of the mountains.

Granny used to tell us kids about the cabin she had lived in years ago, up at Lily Valley when Grandpa was working up there. She also told us how the big flood came and washed all the railroad tracks and the little communities away and they were never rebuilt.

Sometimes in warm weather, Granny would load up all of us kids in her truck, take us to the cabin, and we would have a picnic in the yard.

When I was a teenager, Mama and I moved into our own house in town. By then, I had stopped playing in the creeks and climbing the mountains. Instead, every Saturday night my friends and I would ride around the monument in the middle of town, girls looking for boys and boys looking for girls. We would ride around the streets, go to the movies, and then go to the small barbecue and ice cream parlor afterward.

That's where I met Bruce, my husband. I was in the tenth grade and he was in the eleventh at the schools we attended out in the country. He was riding in a car full of boys and I was in a car full of girls. We started throwing ice at each other and then started talking, and that was it. He called me later that week, and the next Saturday night we went out on a date. He gave me his new class ring, and we had been in love ever since.

When Bruce graduated, he got a job as an electrician's helper with the local power company. He saved his money to buy us furniture, and when I graduated we had a big wedding. We laughed and said we should have served barbecue from the ice cream parlor at the reception instead of cake.

We both wanted to move to the big city seventy miles away. Most young people we knew wanted to do that. Bruce got a job with another electric company, and we moved into an apartment in the city. He took night courses and was soon promoted to foreman. I worked as a receptionist in a doctor's office. It was hard and we had to go without extra things, but eventually we were able to buy a modern brick house in a new development and Bruce was able to afford a new pickup truck.

Most important of all, I was pregnant now and the baby was due the end of September. We'd waited a long time for a child, so this baby would become the most important thing in our lives.

During the past years Mama and our older relatives had died, my cousins had scattered, and Bruce and I seldom went back to Carbondale. Still, there had been a longing to return to our roots. We often talked of a summer home in the mountains, and sometimes, we would ride up the dirt mountain roads through the hollows, and we'd look at cabins and wish we had one. We would go up the mountain road, where we'd parked as teenagers and had marshmallow roasts and were afraid of ghosts and flying fireballs in the woods. We'd been afraid, too, that there was a still hidden farther up the mountain, and that the moonshiners would blast us with their shotguns if we got too close to it.

Sometimes when we went to Carbondale, maybe once a year, we would try to return in our hearts to the past, but there was really nothing to hold us anymore—nothing—no land, no kin.

I really hadn't thought too much about the old cabin until that day in May when the phone call came. I'd stopped working by then, so I was home when the lawyer from Carbondale called. He told me that a distant relative had died and that I was now the owner of the cabin.

I nearly had a fit all day, waiting for Bruce to come home from work. I called his office to tell him the news, but he was out working at some site. I made his favorite supper. It was an old mountain supper, even though the greens came in a can instead of fresh from the garden. When I heard his truck pull into the driveway I ran to the front door and threw my arms around his neck.

"Mmm," he said, squeezing me back. "What did I do to deserve this?"

"You won't believe it," I said. "You just won't believe it!" I was so excited, I could hardly get the words out of my mouth.

"What?" he asked. "Tell me."

"You remember my granny's old cabin way back up in Lily Valley? It's ours now. How can we be so blessed? We have everything—this house, a baby on the way, and now our dream has come true . . . our own cabin."

Bruce kissed me gently on the lips. "We can go home again," he said.

That Saturday morning we drove up to Carbondale to sign the papers, and then we went to inspect our cabin. The air changed as we went into the mountains. It was cool and clean and different from the air in the city. We turned onto the road that curved like a snake up toward Lily Valley, and I giggled as we were jostled from side to side in the truck. It was like we were teenagers again.

Then we turned onto the gravel road that led into Lily Valley, with the mountains surrounding it like the sides of a bowl. We could look up in the distance and see the top of the mountain, which looked like the face of an old man.

There were a few older houses along the road and one back up in the dark trees, like in a cave. We saw cleared fields down in the bottom near the creek, with the tips of corn rising from the ground. On the top of a hill sat a white church with a steeple and a bell in it. White tombstones covered the side of the hill. Even from a distance, we could see flowers on the graves.

We reached the turnoff to our little road, which was by an old white house on the near side of the creek. An old lady was in the backyard hoeing, and she looked up and waved as we went by. We crossed the slanted bridge over the big creek, and I remembered that long ago bridges were made like this, slanted and with no railings, so that the water could run over it when the creek overflowed. Sometimes those creeks got mighty high.

"Remember those stories?" I asked Bruce. "The ones about the big flood years back? I remember Mama telling me that it rained so much, with all that water running off down the mountainsides, that water filled the creeks. There was a big flood and houses were washed down the mountain, with the babies still inside them crying."

"Yeah, and remember the story about the ghost in the attic?" Bruce asked. "It was just a shirt hanging there and everybody got scared."

We were home again, telling stories.

Bruce drove slowly up the road, which was now hardly more than a path with hemlock, rhododendron, and laurel branches hitting the sides of the truck. It was as though we were driving into a dark green cave, into a deserted world, yet the old lady's house was less than half a city block away.

Jumper, our dog, knew that this was a special trip, and he barked and jumped up and down in the back of the truck.

Suddenly, we were in the clearing—and there was our cabin. The front door hung off one of its hinges and the grass was above our knees. I had a feeling that the cabin was smiling at us, welcoming us to give it life again.

"I'm dreaming," I said. "This is too good to be true."

"Looks like we got lots of work to do," Bruce said as we climbed out of the truck. "Watch out for snakes."

We walked to the porch hand in hand. Bruce pushed the front door aside, picked me up in his strong arms, and carried me across the threshold.

Our eyes adjusted to the dark and I saw that furniture was still in the house. There was an old wooden bedstead, a table with two chairs, shelves on the walls, and there was the big stone fireplace, with a black pot and ashes still in it. It felt like we had stepped decades back into the past.

"Well, we better start cleaning if we're going to sleep here tonight," I said, brushing the spider webs out of my hair. Bruce carried the cleaning supplies and other necessities from the truck. I was glad that I had thought to bring buckets and a broom and soap.

"Let's go to the spring," I suggested, and we walked behind the cabin to where the steep mountain bank rose up.

The spring was more beautiful than ever. Cool, clear water dropped from between rocks to a tiny pool. Ferns circled the pool and a devil's helper, a long black flying bug, skimmed the top of the water.

We carried buckets of water into the cabin and I swept the floor, opened shutters, and washed the windows. I found an old enamel dishpan and washed the pottery dishes on the shelves. Bruce went to work cutting the grass.

When we were thirsty, we drank spring water from an old gourd dipper we found on the shelf.

"Best drink in the world," Bruce said as he wiped the sweat from his face. "You know, this doesn't really seem like work at all."

He carried the old feather mattress out in the yard and hung it across a tree limb in the sun. I was afraid it would be dusty after all these years, but it had been covered with an old sheet.

That evening I got our drinks from the spring where we had put them to keep them cool, and Bruce gathered fallen tree limbs from the edge of the woods and made a fire in the old fireplace. We roasted hot dogs on sticks and talked of how we would cook in the old black pot, though we did need electricity in the cabin.

Later, we held hands and walked down the path to the creek. Water, cold as ice though it was already spring, ran over smooth rocks, and we could see tiny fish in the still water around the rocks at the edge of the creek. We took off our shoes and waded in the water. We could hear a cow bawl on a distant hillside.

"We're home at last," I said, and we both had tears in our eyes.

As the sun was setting behind the top of the mountain, we walked barefooted back to the cabin. I lit the old lamp I had brought as we put the cover Granny had given me years ago on the bed. Then I blew out the lamp and we lay on the soft feather mattress. I rested my head on Bruce's chest, and we listened to the night bugs outside singing to their mates.

"I can't wait for the baby to grow up here in the summer," Bruce said. "We can fish in the deep part of the creek."

"And if it's a girl, she can make playhouses," I added.

With the flames in the fireplace flickering low, we made love in the old bed. It was a tender moment that we hadn't known in years.

The next morning we woke early enough to hear the roosters crowing in somebody's backyard. Bruce brought more water from the spring and as I was trying to scramble eggs in a frying pan over the fire, we heard Jumper barking. We went on the porch and Jumper was wagging his tail and looking down the road. The old lady we had seen the day before was walking into our yard. She looked like she was a hundred years old, her face was so wrinkled, but she walked as frisky as Jumper. A straw hat was on her head.

"Thought I'd come see my new neighbors," she said, offering her free hand. "Here's a chocolate cake. I'm Kristine Corbis, but everybody calls me Granny. I live right down the road, just a little piece, across the creek. You're Patty. I knew your granny and kinfolks well. Glad to see some life in this old cabin again. Glad to see there'll be a little one, too." She nodded toward my middle and smiled.

We sat on the porch and ate pieces of the cake for breakfast. Granny told us that she had lived in these parts nearly all her life and had plowed her land with her mule, who died twenty years ago.

Then she began to tell about the neighbors. "The Ferrys, they run the little store down the road a bit. And the Springers, they have grandchildren for your baby to play with one of these days. You remember Harley Collins? She's about your age, Patty. We all knew you'd be coming here. Harley says she went to school about the same time you did. She lives across the road and back up on the hill in the woods. Her husband and baby got killed in a car wreck, but she lived. It sure did do something to Harley. You remember her?"

My heart stopped. Bruce and I looked at each other.

"Yeah, we know her," Bruce answered.

"Sure," I said sarcastically. "She and Bruce were friends all right."

54

My mind began to wonder. Bruce and Granny were talking about gardens and I began to think of Harley. . . .

When Harley and Bruce were in the twelfth grade, they went to the same school. She was after him constantly. She would call him and write him love notes and put them in his locker. I could have lived with that without too much hurt, but what hurt me worse—made me mad, I guess—was the night she got drunk. Bruce's parents were off somewhere and Harley slipped into Bruce's bedroom. When he came home from the ball game—we were together at the game—she was in his bed. Bruce put her in the bathtub to sober her up, and then he rode her around until she got straightened out so her parents wouldn't know.

That was good of him, but the next day at school Harley told everybody she had slept with Bruce. By the day after that, it got to my school—you know how gossip travels. When I walked into history class during first period, everybody laughed right out loud. It was embarrassing. I didn't even know what was going on until somebody passed me a note. I read it with everybody looking at me, and then I started crying right there in class. I held my hand over my face so the teacher wouldn't see. I didn't believe that Bruce had done anything wrong, but I was mad that he hadn't told me before everybody else found out.

A couple of months after that Harley went down to South Carolina for a few weeks, and everybody thought she had an abortion. That was just gossip. Nobody thought it was Bruce's baby, but I was always afraid Harley would say that just out of meanness.

I guess I was still mad at her, and even after all these years I was still mad about something else that had happened back in our high school days.

One day I got home from school and found this pretty present wrapped up in pink paper with a pink bow and with my name on it by my front door. I took it inside and opened it up, thinking it was a late birthday present. It had white tissue paper crumbled up in it. I thought there was something really small in it and that somebody was teasing me by putting all that paper around it, but when I opened up the paper, there was a big black live spider in it.

I screamed and threw the paper down, but before I could step on the spider, it crawled away real fast under my bed. Mama sprayed the room with bug killer and I guess it died, but I had a hard time sleeping that night. I kept feeling something crawling on me, but it was probably my imagination. I never did find out who did that to me, but I always believed it was Harley.

When I graduated, Harley sent me a card. I sent her a card for her birthday after that. I thought that bygones were bygones and I sent her a wedding invitation. I guess I really did that for spite, I have to admit, but she didn't come to the wedding. She did give me a nice set of towels for a wedding present, though. I looked through them real closely, but there wasn't any spider hidden in them.

Hearing Granny mention her now, I knew I ought to feel sorry for her, what with her husband and baby getting killed. But I admit it wasn't easy for me to feel any warmth for Harley.

I looked back up and listened to the conversation.

"You have to plant by the moon," Granny was telling Bruce. "By the signs."

Then we told Granny that we planned to come back to the mountains every weekend so that we could plant and work on the cabin.

"I do need to put in electricity," Bruce told her, "so we can have a refrigerator. This fresh air will do Patty good. We've waited so long for this baby. It's our whole life. I want the baby to have some mountain roots."

"Well, good," Granny said. "If you feel poorly, Patty, I'll fix up a tonic for you. And Bruce, I have a little tonic for you, too." She laughed.

Granny invited us to church with her on Sundays, to the little white church up on the mountaintop that we had passed. We said we'd love to.

When she left, Jumper followed her out, wagging his tail. Bruce put his arms around me and said, "I saw that look on your face when Granny mentioned Harley. I don't know why you're still jealous of her. She was nothing to me. She won't bother us."

"Well, she was always after you," I said. Then I felt guilty. "I guess it's just hard for a woman to forget when somebody has been after her man. I'm sorry. I guess I should have charity in my heart for her, like the Bible says, especially after what she's been through."

"You're right," Bruce said. "You know you have been and always will be the only woman for me. She was kind of cute, though." He laughed.

"Oh, I remember a cute boy, too," I teased.

We laughed together and Bruce kissed me again. It was good to have the kind of marriage where we could tease each other.

We talked about Granny Corbis and our other new neighbors. They would be important to us, especially with our own kin dead. Granny, we thought, could be a real granny to our baby.

"Maybe we could have Christmas here," I said. "And a big fire in the fireplace, and the tree cut from our own land. But how could I roast a turkey over the fire? We do need electricity."

"You're right," Bruce said. "I don't want sandwiches for Christmas dinner."

"We can hang real fir or pine or hemlock around the front door, like in the old days," I mused out loud. "The real kind. Won't it smell good? I hate our plastic decorations."

"Do you remember where that idea comes from?" Bruce asked. "I remember my history teacher telling us. The early settlers thought that fir or pine trees would keep witches out because they would have to take time to count the needles. Then they couldn't come in and ruin Christmas for everybody."

"Maybe that would keep Harley out," I said sarcastically.

"You're being nasty," Bruce said. "But I love you."

"You're right. I'm sorry. I love you too." I kissed him.

We worked on the cabin all weekend and went back to the city on Sunday. All week we waited to return to the mountains. It's all we talked about. I went to the fabric store and bought red-checked gingham for curtains. We went back to the cabin Friday evening, and on Saturday morning Granny brought us some preserves.

"Take this, too," she said, handing me a brown paper bag. "It's leather britches."

"What's leather britches?" I asked.

Granny explained that leather britches were dried green beans. "It's a way to save them. You can dry some this summer. Thread them on a string."

That afternoon Bruce said he had to go down to Carbondale alone. I wanted to go, but he said no. I was worried that he was going to see Harley, he was acting so odd, but I knew that was foolish of me.

A couple of hours later I heard the truck coming up the road and ran to the front porch. "Close your eyes," Bruce hollered from the truck. I put my hands over my eyes and waited. I heard a thumping sound as Bruce got something out of the back of the truck.

"Open your eyes," he said. "Surprise!"

I dropped my hands from my eyes. Bruce had put two rocking chairs on the front porch.

"I got two of them so we can take turns rocking the baby," he said.

Our little cabin was beginning to look like a picture in a magazine.

We were sitting in the chairs when Jumper suddenly ran down the road, barking and growling. We thought it was Granny, but it was strange that Jumper was growling and acting afraid.

Around the little curve and up the road by the hemlock tree walked Harley Collins. She looked as though she hadn't aged a year since we'd seen her last. Her long hair hung down her back nearly to her waist.

"Well, Harley," Bruce said, getting up from the chair, "we heard you lived here. I'm glad to see you."

Harley ran up the steps and threw her arms around him, kissing him on the lips. He hugged her back.

Then she turned to me. "How are you doing, Patty? Heard you're pregnant." She looked me up and down.

Bruce sat back down in his chair and Harley sat on the steps. "Tell us what you've been doing with yourself," he said to her. Then he turned to me and said, "Get Harley a glass of tea, hon! She looks hot."

I went into the cabin to get the ice out of the cooler. I could hear her and Bruce laughing, and I was hurt that I was left out. I tried to tell myself that I was a jealous woman, but I just had a funny feeling about Harley. I knew Bruce was mine and he had never been hers, but it was hard to forget the pain of those high-school memories. I tried to tell myself that she'd had plenty of misery in her life, and I was lucky to have happiness.

I took two glasses of tea to the front porch, one for Bruce, too. Harley was sitting in my chair now. I handed them the glasses and sat down on the steps. Jumper sat next to me as though protecting me.

"When's the baby due?" Harley asked.

"In September," I replied.

"Hope nothing happens to you," she said. "Don't drink any snake eggs from the spring or they'll hatch in you."

Bruce laughed and reached out his hand to touch my shoulder.

Harley left soon after that, and I watched her swinging her hips as she walked down the road. She turned, waved, and blew a kiss.

"That was for you," I told Bruce.

"Don't pay any attention to her," he said. "She's pitiful."

I decided to stay at the cabin the first week in June and not go back to the city. I wanted to work on my flowerbed around the front porch, and I just didn't want to feel rushed. It was safe anyway, me staying alone. We had friends there, Granny and the others. My doctors in the city said that I was strong enough as long as I took it easy and didn't overexert myself.

I was very happy there. I could even see that I had more color in my face. Granny and I visited every day and she took me to the store in her old car. Every afternoon she and I watched the soap operas on her little TV. We laughed over who would steal whose husband.

On Friday evening Harley came to visit. "Where's Bruce?" she asked right off the bat, without even saying hello first.

"He'll be here soon," I explained. "He probably had to work late."

"You mean you could stay here all week and not worry about where he goes at night, down there in the city? He always was a skirt-chaser, you know." She laughed and rolled her eyes as if she knew something I didn't know.

I tried not to let my anger show. "Oh, he's been working on the baby cradle at night. He cut down an old oak tree back up the mountain, sawed it up, and is making a cradle for our baby."

I tried to change the subject and asked her about her job as a beautician. "What's the latest in hairstyles? Long or short?"

"Oh, everybody wants curly this year." She went on to tell me about permanents. "Bruce likes long hair, doesn't he?"

"He likes mine any way." I laughed.

"Seen any snakes up here?" she asked, changing the subject abruptly.

"No," I replied, but I felt a little uneasy and instinctively looked down off the porch to the ground. Then I was sorry, knowing she was just trying to aggravate me.

"Oh, well, maybe you're lucky. They're around," she said.

She talked a few minutes more and left. I noticed that she did not swing her hips this time—now that Bruce wasn't watching.

When I went inside, I closed the wooden door instead of just closing the screen door like I'd done all week. I thought of snakes. I hated to admit it, but Harley had gotten to me, after all. I knew I would have to get up to let Bruce in. When the knocking woke me up, I jerked, scared for a second.

"Why do you have the door closed?" he asked when I let him in.

I explained that Harley had warned me about snakes.

"Forget it," he said. "Snakes are scared of people. I got you a surprise again, a small refrigerator. I'll finish with the electricity tomorrow."

I was glad that Bruce was there. He made me forget Harley. All weekend we worked on the cabin. I decided to stay the coming week again.

"I'll miss you, babe, but I know this is good for you."

All that week Granny and I talked, and each day she gave me something new, like a jar of honey or a baby quilt she had used for her own children. There was a light that seemed to glow from her, a kind of goodness that I had forgotten about in the city. Sometimes she talked about her children, one dead and three others living in states far away. I felt like I was another child for her, someone in her life and she was a granny to me, something that I had missed having these last few years.

I talked about Harley to her. "Why is it," I asked, "that I always feel bad when she visits me? I just get a funny feeling inside, like she's out to get me. Am I crazy?"

"Don't pay any attention to her," Granny said. "She's not all there all the time, I think. She's probably jealous that you and Bruce are having a baby, what with hers dead. She just spreads darkness all over the place like a big black cloud. I remember her granny was mean as a snake, always thinking she could throw a spell on somebody. It's all in the mind, you know. But I do feel sorry for Harley. She's pitiful, really—always hurting and never having any happiness. But it's usually her own fault."

I was glad to hear that somebody else thought Harley was weird—and at the same time, like Granny said, I felt sorry for her.

Bruce arrived as usual on Friday, and on Sunday we went with Granny to the little white church. We had already been there with her, and I loved the church and the congregation. Granny said people got baptized down in the deep part of the creek, which I thought was very nice.

Afterward, there was a church dinner at the picnic tables under the big oak tree. All our new friends asked us how life was in the city. Granny had made a big pound cake, and there were three kinds of potato salad, ham, fried chicken, biscuits, and fresh blackberry pie.

We ate our dinner and laughed and it was wonderful—until I looked up and saw Harley standing beside me. I set my tea down on the table and walked to the next table to get some more fried chicken, actually to get away from her. She leaned up against the table, near my iced tea, and then walked away. I was glad she got the message.

I went back and picked up my tea, but the strangest thing happened. Now it tasted funny, but I drank it anyway. It didn't taste that bad. I laughed inside, thinking that Harley came around and poisoned everybody's happiness in some way. I thought: Harley stands next to my tea and makes it taste bad. Then I realized what a fool I was, having such an imagination. I was letting Harley get the best of me again.

Bruce had to leave early that afternoon to go back to the city. He had to go to work earlier on a job. I was lonely when he left and I felt a little sick, sort of woozy. I always felt alone in the featherbed where he had slept the night before, but now I was tired, very tired, as though my energy had been poured out of me. I went to bed early, pretending he was beside me.

I didn't know how long I had been asleep when suddenly I woke up with a start. I knew I had heard a strange noise, but I couldn't put my finger on what it was—maybe a bird or an animal in the woods. Then I realized that it was probably a bad dream from all I had eaten. I lay back down, uneasy but not afraid.

Then I heard a noise again, clearly this time. It was the cry of a baby. I sat up again, pulling the covers up around me. I listened, but I didn't hear it again. I was sort of dizzy and everything was blurry. I thought that surely it must have been an owl or something, not a baby. How could a baby be crying outside? I was nervous but not scared out of my mind.

The next thing I knew it was morning, and when I went down to Granny's I asked her what the sound could have been.

"A baby crying?" she asked. "Must have been your imagination." She stared back up toward the woods with a grim look on her face and then smiled. "It's nothing. Nothing. Just sounds in the woods. You know pregnant women get jumpy."

Granny taught me to crochet that day, and the next afternoon Harley came to visit. She told me about her hard day in the beauty shop, standing on her feet all day. She seemed concerned, too, about how I felt, and I felt guilty thinking bad things about her.

"I need my hair cut," I said, just making conversation. "It hangs on my neck and bothers me."

"Tell you what," Harley said. "Let's go down to Carbondale. We'll go to the beauty shop and I'll cut your hair, give you a new style. Then we can grab a hamburger somewhere."

I was glad to get my hair cut and agreed to go. I was glad to go somewhere new.

We went to the beauty shop and Harley cut my hair, but I still had a funny feeling when she was messing around my head with something sharp. I could feel her fingers on my head and I felt strange inside. When she was through, I started to pick up my hair from the floor but Harley pushed me aside, saying I didn't need to stoop over. Then she picked the hair up and put it in a paper bag. I wondered why she didn't sweep it up and put it in the trashcan, but I thought that Harley was just a very neat person.

We ate in a restaurant and then stopped off at the small supermarket. All in all, it was pleasant, surprisingly, and Harley didn't mention Bruce once.

When we got back to the cabin, she carried one bag of groceries into the house for me. I was amazed at the energy she had. She nearly ran into the cabin with the bag before I could get halfway out of her car. Maybe she's not so bad after all, I thought. Then I noticed that she had carried her pocketbook with her into the cabin, and I wondered if she thought I might steal something out of it if she left it in the car. Then I thought: It's just my stupid imagination again.

After Harley left I put the groceries away and went to bed. I was trying to go to sleep, but Jumper was sniffing around the bed and that aggravated me. "Get up here, you silly dog," I ordered, and he jumped on the bed and curled up by my feet. For once, I slept soundly, probably because I'd had such a pleasant day.

The next morning I slowly opened my eyes and stretched out in the bed, wishing that Bruce was beside me. I sat up and put my feet onto the floor. My right foot felt something round and smooth and cool, something that had not been by my bed before. I jerked my foot back up and looked at the floor.

My heart instantly pounded and my hands shook. It was a snake! I screamed and Jumper woke up and looked over the edge of the bed, too. He froze for second and then jumped like lightning on the snake. Dogs have an instinct about where to bite, I guess, and he grabbed the snake behind its head and shook it. I could see his teeth biting into the snake, and when it was dead he dropped it to the floor.

I was sure it was dead, but I wanted to be doubly sure. I crawled across the foot of the bed and slowly crept across the room to the fireplace to get the poker. Then I leaned over the edge of the bed, raised the poker, and hit the snake as hard as I could. Jumper looked down at the snake and whined.

I eased off the bed again and shoved the poker under the snake and carried it out to the front yard. I threw it on the ground and Jumper ran round and round the snake, watching it, ready to pounce again if he had to.

I was still standing there, when I heard a voice.

"What is it, child? What is it?" Granny called as she came panting across the yard. "I was outside hanging up clothes on the line when I heard you screaming. Are you all right? What is it?"

I couldn't speak, but Jumper was still barking and dancing around the snake. Granny looked down.

"Oh, child, it's a blacksnake. Why did you kill it?" She saw the poker still in my hand. "A blacksnake is a good snake. Eats rats. Well, I'll hang it up on the tree." She picked it up by the tail with her bare hand and slung it across a low limb.

"Why did you hang it up?" I asked.

"To make it rain," she answered. "Didn't you know that? Hang a dead snake in a tree to make it rain. We need some rain real bad. That snake wouldn't have hurt you. Just scared you to death, I guess. Come on down to the house and sit for a while."

"No, I can't be afraid in my own home. I'll stay here."

"You're right," Granny said. "Don't worry. Things like this happen. There's no need to be afraid."

All day I worked, and then I went down to Granny's in the evening. She didn't mention the snake, trying to keep my mind off it, I guess.

I finally went home before dark and looked at the ground before every step I took. I glanced into the woods and thought I saw eyes staring at me, but I reminded myself I was being foolish again.

I tried to stay up as long as I could at home, but when I couldn't keep my eyes open any longer I went to bed. I knew the Lord would protect me.

I didn't wake up the whole night, and when I opened my eyes in the morning and saw the sun shining across the cradle that Bruce had finished, I knew how silly I had been. After all, I thought, didn't I come from these tough mountain women, too? I wondered if living in the city had made me soft.

I was sitting at the table, drinking my morning coffee, when I happened to glance over at the fireplace and saw something brown and wrinkly on the hearth. I got up to pick it up, thinking it was trash, and then dropped it and screamed. I felt as though my hand had touched fire. It was the skin of a snake and it was brown, like that of a copperhead.

I ran out of the house and down the road to Granny's, hardly able to breathe. Jumper ran at my heels. One of my sandals fell off and the rocks hurt my foot, but I didn't stop to get it.

"Granny! Granny!" I yelled as I ran into her house. "I found a copperhead skin on the fireplace."

"Child," she said, patting me on the arm, "it's not time for snakes to shed their skins now."

But I insisted that she go with me to the house and see for herself.

"It was probably here for years," she explained after she'd taken a look. "It's so dry, it had to have been here for years. Maybe the wind blew it down the chimney. You know that snakes often live in little nooks in the roof."

I stayed down at Granny's the rest of the week to get my nerves calmed down.

When Bruce came for me on Friday night, I could hear Granny whispering to him. "It's just her being pregnant," she confided. "Women get that way. That snakeskin could have fallen out of the rafters. It looked old, and that blacksnake—well, you might not see another one for ten years."

Bruce and I went up to the cabin. I wasn't afraid with him with me. He put his arms around me and said, "Babe, I love you and I want you not to worry so much. You know what this baby means to us. You have Granny and Harley to take care of you."

I pulled away from him. "Harley? I don't want her around me now. I just have this feeling that I can't put my finger on."

"I know you're jealous of Harley, but you don't need to be," Bruce said. "There was never anything between us. She's just lonely. I'm her old friend and so are you. We were never more than friends— and not good friends at that. I have a feeling that she wants to be close to you."

Speak of the devil and there she appears! At the moment we were

63

talking about Harley, she came walking up the road.

"How are you doing, Patty? You look peaked," she said. This time she didn't speak to Bruce first. "How are things going up here? Seen any ghosts?" She laughed. I remembered that she always did like spooky things.

"How did you know?" I asked. I was mad that she was minding my business. I forgot that she had been nice to me that other day.

"Know what?" she asked.

"That I got scared," I replied.

"I read it in the clouds," she joked. "No, I don't know what you mean. This is kind of a scary place, though."

I looked up at the clouds, and they were dark and heavy and were moving across the tops of the green mountains.

Bruce and Harley looked up, too.

"Sure looks like a bad one coming," Bruce said.

We could hear thunder in the distance and saw bolts of lightning flash across the mountain.

"Guess I'd better go home," she said, "before I drown."

The wind began blowing and the trees bent from the force. We sat on the porch watching the clouds cross the mountains until a loud crack of thunder seemed to jump off the top of the cabin and pop in our ears. Bruce put his arm around my waist and we went into the cabin. It was dark now and we were tired, so we went to bed and listened to the rain pounce and dance on the tin roof. It was better than a tranquilizer or a shot of Granny's tonic.

The next morning the sun was out and drops of water glistened on the trees like diamonds. I walked barefooted to the spring and stooped over to dip my bucket into the cool water, but something suddenly caught my eye.

I focused my eyes on what I had halfway seen. There were little round eggs, about the size of marbles, lying in the bottom on the sand. I dropped my bucket and stared at the eggs. They were snake eggs!

I felt as though a hand had grabbed my throat, and at first I couldn't scream. Then I screamed as though the sounds were coming out from deep within me.

Bruce came running from the cabin.

"What is it, honey? You look like you've seen a ghost."

"Look," I gasped, pointing to the water. "Look!"

"What?" He took my hand tenderly. "I don't see anything." He looked at me real funny.

"It's snake eggs, there in the water. Just like Harley said."

He dropped my hand, bent down, looked into the water, and dipped his hand in and scooped up the eggs. He held his hand out to me. I stepped backward, away from him.

"Oh, honey," he said and laughed, "it's just little white pebbles. Probably washed down the mountain in the rain. Don't be so nervous. Maybe you need to come back to the city with me for a while."

I felt embarrassed, even in front of my own husband. I had always been so strong and now I was acting like a baby. I did go back to the city because I was worried about getting so upset. The doctor said nothing was physically wrong with me. It was pleasant, I have to admit having modern appliances again. I turned the water on and off in the kitchen sink just for fun.

I was glad to have a real bathroom instead of having to go to the outhouse. I decided that when we went back to the cabin, I would decorate the outhouse with the leftover wallpaper from my city bathroom. I made Bruce his favorite meals every night. I saw my city friends, and they teased me and said that one of my legs was shorter than the other from standing on the side of a mountain. I invited them to come and stay for a weekend soon at the cabin.

Though I was happy to be with Bruce, there was a feeling that pulled me back to the mountains, as if a spell had been cast on me and I could not resist it. I wanted to go back and finish working on the cabin because the next summer I would be busy taking care of the baby.

"Let's go back to our real home this weekend," I told Bruce. "I just feel that I need to be there. I believe I'll stay next week, if you think you can do without me. I need to see about my tomato plants."

When Friday rolled around, we got in the truck and went back to the mountains. I was glad to be home. I hadn't been sleeping well in the city air, and I knew I would sleep fine in the fresh mountain air. It was just different.

"Missed you," Granny said when we got there. She was helping me clean up and sweep out the week's dust. "You've got a little color in your face now."

When it was time for Bruce to leave on Sunday, he asked, "Are you really sure you want to stay here?"

"Yes," I said. "I need to. I really need to. Only two more weeks and then I'll come home."

"I understand," Bruce said. "But I'll worry about you. You do have Granny Corbis and all of our other friends." He didn't mention Harley.

When Bruce left, I went down to Granny's and ate supper with her. It was like eating in heaven—mountain people can really cook. She had chicken and dumplings, green beans cooked with bacon grease, hot biscuits, and her own apple butter that was made from apples froth her own trees.

Afterward, Granny walked me back up the narrow road to the

cabin. We could see the glowing pink sun going down behind the mountains.

Monday went by as usual. On Tuesday, Granny and I went down to the shopping center in Carbondale. She said she wanted to buy something to send to her great-grandchildren on their birthdays.

"Bless my soul," Granny said as we got back into the car. "I can't believe all the things I see, like a door opening when you step on the floor. Used to be, it would take two or three hours to come down here in a buggy. Now it's hardly an hour." I laughed to myself because Granny drove as slow as if she was driving a horse and buggy.

"You haven't seen anything yet," I said. "Have you ever seen moving stairs?" I told her I wanted her to come to the city and visit with me for a while.

When we got back home, it was getting dark and I was tired as could be and thirsty, too. I now had the small refrigerator that Bruce had brought when he finished putting in electricity, and I went to it to get a glass of tea. I thought I had put the pitcher on the top shelf, but now it was on the second one. I worried that my nerves were getting bad again.

I undressed and put on my nightgown and got into bed. I was beginning to feel a little dizzy. It was strange. I was tired, and my head was fuzzy, but I was still awake. I wanted to go to sleep. My eyes stayed open, though, as though rocks were holding my eyelids up.

Sometime later, I heard a noise. My eyes were shut and I tried to open them and I tried to sit up and look around the room, but I could hardly hold my head up. Then I heard the sound again, like a baby's cry. I could feel my heart pounding, but I could hardly move. It was as though a landslide had fallen on me. I could still hear the baby crying. I wondered if it was my baby inside me crying. I wondered if it was a baby on the mountain. If it was, I knew I had to save it.

I wanted to get up, but I couldn't. I tried to move my head. The crying grew louder. I could feel Jumper standing stiff on the end of the bed. I tried to make myself wake all the way up. I was half asleep and half awake, but I could hear what was going on. I wanted to jump up and find out where the cry was coming from. I heard it again and it seemed to be floating around the cabin. Then I heard it again at one side of the cabin and then at the other side. It seemed to last a whole hour. I could barely turn my head to look at the clock. It was three in the morning.

Jumper jumped off the bed and ran around the room. I tried to get up again but felt paralyzed. Then the sound disappeared. There was absolute silence.

The night bugs that usually made noises made no sounds at all. I made no sounds at all. And then they began again in a few minutes as if the intruder had left. I tried to stay awake to listen, but I finally fell asleep.

It was nine in the morning when I woke again and I turned my head toward the clock. I was surprised at myself for sleeping so late, and then I remembered hearing the baby crying and my feelings of helplessness. I could get out of bed now, but I still felt tired. I tried to think about the night and wondered if it had been a nightmare.

I went down to Granny's and told her what happened.

"It's your nerves again," she said. "Getting time for the birthing."

She walked me up the road home later. She stood by the porch and looked off into the thick woods and then said, "I'm going to get some spring water."

I stood on the corner of the porch and watched her. She went to the spring and then walked around the cabin, looking at the ground.

"What are you looking for, Granny? I thought you said there was nothing to be scared of," I said.

"There's not," she answered. "I was looking for some pretty white rocks to put around my dahlia bed."

Granny knelt down by the steps, stooped over, and looked under them. She put her hand under the step and pulled out a lock of hair, long, dark hair just like mine.

"Did you throw your hair under here?" she asked.

"Where in the world did you get such an idea?" I demanded. "Harley cut my hair and picked it up and put it in a bag."

"Oh," Granny said. "I see."

"See what?" I asked, still puzzled.

"Oh, nothing."

Granny went home and I stayed in the cabin, but I had an uneasy feeling in my stomach. I was still not nervous enough to go back to the city, though. That evening I walked down to Granny's so that we could go to prayer meeting together.

We went to the church up on the mountainside. It was pleasant to talk with the other neighbors in the valley. Some were bragging about their gardens, the squash and the corn and the cucumbers. I talked about my garden, which amounted to five little tomato plants and two peppers.

When prayer meeting began, I sat in the row opposite Harley. I looked at the songbook, and then I happened to glance up and out of the corner of my eye saw that she was looking straight at me. I looked right at her, and she stared at me.

Then she smiled as if she had a secret that I didn't know. Suddenly, I realized what the lock of hair meant. It was a hex, and I laughed to myself at Granny and Harley believing it.

After the preacher finished his Wednesday-night sermon, we

sang the closing hymn. I glanced over at Harley when we were on the last verse. As soon as the preacher prayed and gave his last "amen," Harley walked quickly out of the church without even shaking the preacher's hand.

Granny and I went back to her house for cake, and then she walked me home as she usually did. Everything seemed quiet, too quiet, and then I noticed that Jumper wasn't at the road to meet us.

"I wonder where Jumper is," I said.

"Out in the woods probably, or down in the field chasing a rabbit," Granny said.

We started up the steps. "Want to sit for a while?" I asked. Then I looked down and saw Jumper lying on the ground in the shadow of the steps. He was trying to raise his head. Then it hit me that something was wrong with him. I looked closely at him and saw that his nose had been gashed open. It was a red, raw cut, and deep. I had to lean against the porch post to keep from fainting.

"Oh, no!" Granny exclaimed as she leaned down to pick up Jumper. "Must have run into another critter," she said. "You stay here and I'll go and patch him up. He'll be okay."

I watched Granny carry Jumper down the road. I could see her talking to him like he was a baby. Granny had a way with animals, the same as Harley did, or so Granny had told me.

I sat in the rocking chair until it was completely dark, waiting for Granny to come back. Then I went into the cabin and reached for the string to turn the light on. I jerked it, but the bare light bulb did not come on. I got a funny feeling in my stomach for a moment and stepped backward out the door. At that moment Granny was coming back up the road.

"Why are you here in the dark?" she asked. "It's dangerous. You might trip over something."

"I was sitting here worrying about Jumper and just went inside right before you came, but the light wouldn't come on. Burned out, I guess," I said.

"Let me see," Granny said. She stepped inside the door, walked to the middle of the room, and pulled the light cord.

"What's that smell in here?" she asked. She pulled a chair under the light and climbed up on it.

"I noticed it, too," I said. "Sort of moldy or earthy smelling. What do you think it is?"

Granny turned the light bulb and it flashed on. "Why, it was unscrewed. You better not be climbing up here anymore. You might fall."

"I didn't unscrew it," I said.

There was a silence between us then that you could have cut with a knife. I wanted to scream, but I was afraid to make a sound. Granny sucked in her breath. We stared at the bed.

Two copperheads, big around as my wrists, lay coiled on my bed. They raised their heads, stretched out, and then plopped off the bed onto the floor.

"Stand still," Granny whispered. "Where's the ax?"

I motioned toward the front porch.

"Keep your eyes on them," Granny whispered again. "Don't let them out of your sight."

Granny slowly stepped down from the chair and crept toward the front porch. I looked at the snakes. I could see the pits in their heads. They looked dangerous.

Granny was now easing up toward the snakes. I wondered how she could kill two at once or whether one would get away. She eased even closer. The snakes' heads turned toward her. Their tongues flicked in and out. I eased back out toward the door. I felt as though my feet weighed fifty pounds each.

When Granny got within three feet of the snakes, she slowly raised the ax high enough to put some force behind it. One snake darted toward Granny's leg. Granny did not move. Then wham, quick as a bolt of lightning, she chopped one snake in two. The other one jabbed its fangs into Granny's thick leather shoes. She raised the ax again quickly and hit that one. Its body hung together by a narrow strip of skin.

I breathed out as though my breath had been trapped inside of me.

"Go outside, child," Granny said.

I went out to the porch and stood there, still shaking. Granny came out carrying the snakes on the ax. She threw them on the ground and then picked them up, one at a time, and hung them in the tree. I could see what she was doing, even in the dark.

"Well, we'll get rain anyway. I knew I smelled something in there, that earthy smell. Snakes smell in mating season. Did you know that?" Granny asked.

"I don't want to know," I replied.

"Come on home with me," Granny said. "I think you've had enough upsets. I do think it's awfully strange, all these things happening to you. I wonder. . . ."

I was glad to go home with Granny. I slipped under her clean sheets and went to sleep in only a few minutes. I felt that I had been run over by a big truck. I couldn't go back to the cabin until Bruce came on Friday. I sat on Granny's porch, waiting for him to pass by.

When he got there, Granny told him the story, and my hands started shaking as though I were living through it again. Jumper's nose was better and he knew that something was wrong. He sat pressed up against my ankles.

"I guess Patty better go back to the city now," Bruce told Granny. "That baby is important to me, and Patty is, too."

As much as I loved my cabin home, I was ready to leave after all that had happened. Bruce and I talked about closing up the cabin for the fall. It would take a few days to do, so he called his boss to ask for the time off.

I did want to spend the last few days in the cabin cleaning it up, though I couldn't sleep in that bed. On Saturday morning the three of us walked up to the cabin. The dead snakes still hung in the trees. I didn't want to admit it was because of the snakes, but it had rained some every day since they had been in the tree.

I sat on the front porch while Bruce and Granny went into the cabin. Granny carried the ax. They searched the room from one end to the other and there was no hole anywhere that they could find where snakes could crawl through. Bruce used Granny's ladder to climb on the roof and look for holes, but there weren't any there, either.

That afternoon Granny, Bruce, and I went downtown to the hardware store to buy a gallon of cedar oil to pour around the cabin. Maybe that would keep the snakes away, Granny said.

We went back and Granny gathered up all the bedclothes. She took them down to her house and boiled them in the big black washtub out back when the rain stopped for a while.

I needed to pack up the things in the cabin, but I would walk to the middle of the room and stand there, afraid to move. So I sat on the front porch while Bruce closed and fastened the wooden shutters. I could see over the mountain that huge black rain clouds were coming. The tops of the trees bent in the strong breeze. We hurried back down to Granny's before the rain hit.

It rained steadily all night, and when we got up in the morning, and looked out, the creek had risen. Granny was afraid that the water would wash her garden away and drown her vegetables.

"I haven't seen rain like this in many a year," she said. "Reminds me of the old days. Doesn't rain so much anymore."

The next day the rain stopped, but dark angry clouds still covered the sky. They were below the tops of the mountains, which were blocked completely from view.

We headed up to the cabin and saw that the water was nearly up to the bridge. I had a feeling that the rain would wash some of the evil away. I was able to walk into the cabin without my heart pounding, but I still could not go near the bed.

I washed out the tiny refrigerator so that it would be clean when we came back later, maybe at Thanksgiving with the baby. Maybe by then I could forget what had happened. Bruce took the ax, chopped up an old tree that had fallen from the wind, and stacked the logs between two trees so that the wood would be dry and ready to burn when we came back.

At least, I thought, the snakes will be gone in winter.

In a way, I would be glad to return to the city because I was feeling bad.

I was sweeping the hearth when a clap of thunder shook the house as though something had dropped on the roof.

The devil's beating his wife, I thought, remembering that old saying about thunder.

Bruce came into the house sopping wet. The rain was so heavy that it sounded like someone was throwing rocks on the tin roof.

"It'll probably pass," Bruce said, but another clap of thunder roared and the light went out. We looked out the front door and the rain was coming down so fast that it looked like jiggling rods of steel.

Suddenly, a pain went through my back and stomach. It was dull but felt as though somebody had punched me with his fist.

"Oh!" I moaned and bent over.

"What is it, honey?" he asked, looking anxious. "Are you okay?"

Another dull pain crossed my stomach. I squinted my eyes and clenched my teeth. "It can't be!" I said. "It's a month too early. The pain is coming too fast."

"Lie down," Bruce said. He took my elbow and tried to help me to the bed. "Maybe you're just tired out."

I pulled away from him. I couldn't touch that bed even though it had fresh covers on it. I sat down in the chair by the table and rested my head on my arms. There was a continuous dull ache now in the bottom of my back.

"Go get Granny," I said, trying to breath. "She'll know what it is."

Bruce put his coat over his head and went out the door.

I sat there and listened to the rain on the roof. I wondered how women long ago could have had babies without going to the hospital. A sharp pain went through my stomach and I had to lie down. I just had to.

I slid out of the chair onto the floor and hit my head on the table leg. I felt as though every drop of energy was pouring out of me. The pain went back and forth like the flashes of lightning I saw on the tops of the mountains. I felt like thunder was booming inside me, and that a tree had been struck by lightning and had fallen across my stomach.

I wanted to close my eyes, but I looked at the floor in front of me and saw dust that I had not swept up. I could see under the bed and wondered if a snake was under there watching me. Jumper licked my

71

face. All of a sudden I was lying in warm water and I wondered if the roof was leaking.

Another sharp pain cut through me. I sucked in my breath, trying to stop the pain. I wanted to scream for Bruce, but the words came out only as a moan. I wondered why he had deserted me. I thought I saw the snakes crawling toward me and I tried to get up but the pain was too great.

In the distance I could hear footsteps, and I wanted to scream out for whomever it was to save me from the snakes.

"It's covering the bridge," I heard Granny say.

"Where is she?" Bruce gasped, not seeing me at first.

"Oh, mercy," Granny said. "Put her on the bed."

I could feel Bruce picking me up.

"No, no," I begged. "Not on the bed!"

"We're here," Granny said. "Don't worry. We'll take care of you." I could feel her hands brushing my hair off my forehead.

Another pain hit and I screamed.

"We have to get her to the hospital," she told Bruce. "Cover her with this blanket."

I could feel him carrying me toward the front door. Another pain tore inside of me and I squeezed my fingernails into his arms without meaning to. The rain fell on the blanket and dripped off into my face as he carried me through the yard. Granny opened the truck door and Bruce lifted me inside. Granny got in beside me and I leaned on her. I could feel the truck beginning to move. I could hear the windshield wipers go slosh-slosh.

"Oh, no," Bruce said as he slammed on the brakes. I jerked against Granny and another pain slashed through me. "The bridge is gone."

"Lord help us," Granny said softly. "It's like the great flood all over again!"

Bruce backed the truck up the road and he and Granny carried me back into the cabin. I could feel them putting me on the bed, but I couldn't speak because of the pain.

"Get those sheets out of that box," I heard Granny say.

After Bruce got the sheets, he held my hand and wiped the sweat from my face. I felt like a hundred-pound rock was on my stomach smashing me. Then the rock exploded into a thousand pieces. I felt the snakes crawling on me, and I screamed because I thought I was in a pit of vipers.

Then suddenly, somewhere in my dazed mind, I heard someone else come into the room.

I heard Granny say, "How did you get here?"

In the foggy distance I could hear Harley answer, "I was walking

72

in the woods looking for herbs before it started raining."

"Get out," Granny said. "This is all your fault with your jealousy and thinking you can work spells and your way with animals. Get out!"

Harley laughed and I heard the door slam.

With that, the worst pain of all ripped through my body and I bit into my lip and tasted blood. Then there was emptiness and I could hear the rain pattering on the roof. For a moment there was silence and then I heard a baby cry.

Oh, no, I thought, I can't go through this again.

Then I went into blackness. . . .

It was morning when I woke up and the rain had stopped. I could see sunshine through the cracks in the shuttered windows. Granny was sitting next to the bed holding something wrapped in a blanket in her arms. Bruce leaned down and kissed me gently on the lips.

"I would like for you to meet your new son," Granny said, getting up and placing the baby in my arms.

In a little while there were footsteps on the porch and the preacher and a man from the church came into the room.

"We've got the bridge fixed up again," the preacher said. "The flooding was strong enough to tear it loose. That was some storm. Thank the Lord you all were taken care of."

Bruce took me in his arms and carried me to the truck. Granny carried our little son.

When we got to the hospital, the doctor said, "You mountain women are the toughest women I have ever seen."

I didn't go back to the cabin when I got out of the hospital. Bruce, the baby, Jumper, and I left from the hospital for the city. Granny was there to tell me good-bye for the next couple of months.

We drove to the city and I was glad to be in a house without the fear of snakes. Bruce had put the cradle in the truck and brought it to the city. The baby lay peacefully in it, his little eyes closed, sleeping. We'd named him Brian. Someday I would tell him of his mountain background and what his mother went through bringing him into the world.

A week later we got a letter from Granny. It looked like chicken scratch and read:

They found Harley's body down the creek. It was stuck in the limbs of a tree when the water went down. I guess she drowned the night of the storm. She was pitiful and I think you need to forgive her for trying to hex you because she was jealous. She only hurt herself. Hope to see you soon.

Love, Granny

By summer, little Brian was so chubby and healthy and beautiful that it took my breath away to look at him. I'd been thinking, too, how good it would be to spend some time in the mountain air again, and when I mentioned it to Bruce he said he'd been thinking the same thing.

So with one big breath I put that terrible time with Harley in the past. She was dead now, and couldn't do any harm to my family. We packed our things and left for the cabin on a hot Friday evening. Bruce took two weeks off from work.

Everything was just like we'd remembered—all the good parts, anyway. I'd written Granny that we were coming, and she'd gotten the place aired out. She and I talked about Harley once, and then we never mentioned her again. Granny said she figured Harley had put something in my tea that time I'd been so dizzy and sleepy, and she'd made that crying-baby noise I'd heard. She also hurt Jumper so she could put the snakes in the cabin. She was trying to hex me. In her sick mind, she thought she could do something to get rid of me so she'd have Bruce all to herself. But, like Granny reminded me, Harley was gone, and I had my family safe and sound.

By the end of our two weeks there, I'd really been able to forget all that had happened. The sweet mountain air, the simple life, and Granny's loving presence all served to heal my bruised spirit. I told Bruce I wanted to stay at the cabin for the rest of the summer with Brian, and he hugged me so tight I thought my ribs would crack.

It's a Friday night and summer is nearing its end. I'm sitting on the porch with Brian, waiting for his daddy to come for the weekend. Jumper is right beside me, as usual, and Granny is in the cabin pouring herself a second glass of tea. It sure feels like home here, and I know when Bruce and I close up the cabin this fall, it won't be for good. We'll be back again in the spring, just like the birds, the grass, and Granny's garden.

THE END

IN LOVE WITH
A FIREFIGHTER!
He's my hero

"**M**ommy, it's on fire—it's on fire!" Jack was screaming for me. I ran back into the kitchen as quickly as I could. My seven-year-old was standing with his back against the kitchen table, too scared to move. On the countertop, the popcorn popper I'd picked up at our church flea market that afternoon was spitting sparks while giving off great clouds of smoke.

"Jack!" I shouted at him, grabbing his arm and spinning him out of the kitchen. "Run! Run outside and pull the fire alarm!" He stared at me without moving, his eyes fixed on the smoking popper. Then, suddenly, he took off like a shot. I thanked God I'd had the sense to teach him where the fire alarm box was, and how to use it.

The popper wasn't on fire yet, but it soon would be. It had to be unplugged, and fast. I reached for the plug, but I was too late. The hot oil had exploded into flames. I screamed and yanked out the plug. The plastic lid had come off, and it was spitting flaming oil and popcorn everywhere. I pulled on my kitchen gloves and shoved the popper into the sink basin, turning on the water full blast.

The moment I did that, I knew it was the wrong thing to do. Smoke and steam flew up into my face. Flaming oil flew everywhere. My kitchen curtains caught fire. A drop of hot oil hit my arm and I screamed in pain. The curtains burned like tissue paper, as the roll of paper towels next to the sink caught fire, too.

It was beyond my control. Choking, blinded by the smoke, I ran from the apartment. Outside, I found Jack standing by the fire alarm box. At least we're safe, I thought breathlessly. Jack had pulled the fire alarm, now he just stared as I stumbled down the front steps. I took him in my arms, holding him just as tightly as I could, and prayed the fire department would get here before everything we owned was destroyed.

It seemed the fire engines took forever to come. The street was totally still, seemingly deserted. Then we heard the distant faint whine of sirens.

"They're coming, Mom!" Jack shouted. "They're coming!"

I couldn't speak. I kept imagining flames spreading throughout the apartment. All I could think was: Hurry! Hurry! Hurry!

Then the huge red bulk of a fire engine came flying down the street. Even before it came to a screeching halt, a fireman had leaped off and was running toward us. He was a big man with clean, even features.

"What happened?" he demanded.

"The popcorn popper," I sputtered, already feeling an enormous sense of relief. "It got too hot. There was smoke everywhere. I tried to douse it with water, but the oil flew everywhere. The curtains—"

He cut me off with a look of utter disgust. "Is there anyone else in the building?"

"No," I answered. "Just Jack and me. The second floor apartment is vacant."

"That's one good break," he growled angrily, then raced back to the fire engine. He shouted to the other fireman to keep ready, then grabbed a big portable fire extinguisher from the truck, and charged up the steps two at a time.

On the sidewalk, Jack and I waited anxiously. I glanced over at the other firemen, but they didn't seem to think the situation was too serious. I wished I had their calm, but then, it wasn't their apartment that was burning.

Finally, the big fireman came out again, the empty extinguisher dangling from his hand.

"How bad is it?" I asked anxiously. "Is the fire out?"

"Yes, the fire is out," he said through clenched teeth. His face was dark from the smoke, and he was breathing heavily. His eyes were glaring at me angrily as if I'd done something terribly wrong.

I was grateful he'd come, but his unfriendly attitude rubbed me the wrong way.

I was about to tell him so, when he said, "Your kitchen will need a lot of cleaning up. The curtains are ruined, and the place is still full of smoke. I opened the windows to air it out. Where'd you get that crummy popper from anyway?"

I told him I'd bought it at a flea market, real cheap. "Can it be fixed?" I asked innocently.

His strong face darkened with anger. "Lady," he said bluntly, "throw the damn thing out! The wiring's shot. You're lucky the whole building didn't burn to the ground. The only thing you did right was pull the plug. Throwing water on a grease fire is the stupidest thing you could have done. You should thank your stars you and the kid aren't on your way to the hospital right now."

I was flabbergasted. How dare he talk to me like that? Without another word, he walked off, swung onto the fire truck, and the engine pulled away.

I was so angry I couldn't speak! I was going to call the fire chief and the mayor's office, and report that nasty fireman. Then Jack, tugging at my sleeve, brought me back to reality.

"Mom, I'm getting cold. Could we go back inside now, please?"

"All right, honey," I said softly, pushing back my anger. We went in slowly, dreading the mess I knew we'd find.

My kitchen was in ruins. The shock of actually seeing the damage stopped me cold. A chemical fire extinguisher had been sprayed all over my stove and sink. The popcorn popper was a charred mass of plastic and twisted metal. There was a deep burn in the counter top. My curtains were charred rags.

It was too much to deal with then and there. I turned my attention to Jack. He'd been very brave through it all, but he was only seven years old, and now the reaction to all the excitement was setting in.

The clean-up will have to wait, I told myself. I'd have to get Jack to bed soon, or he'd never be able to get up for school in the morning.

It took two long bedtime stories and half a dozen lullabies before Jack was ready to sleep. As I tucked the covers around him and kissed him good night, I thought again of how lucky we'd been that evening. There was quite a mess to clean up, but the damage had not been serious. It could have been much worse. If only that fireman hadn't been so rude to me. . . .

Cleaning the stove, I fixed myself a strong cup of coffee and set about clearing away the damage so Jack and I could at least have breakfast in the morning. It was nearly midnight when I finally finished. I was physically exhausted.

Suddenly, there was a knock at the apartment door.

That's all I need, I said to myself. I made it a practice not to answer the door after dark. A woman alone learns to be cautious. I waited, hoping whoever it was would go away.

But the knocking came again, a little louder this time. I was afraid Jack would wake up, so I went to the door. I slipped on the safety chain before I asked, "Who is it? What do you want?"

A man answered, "It's Fireman Buck, ma'am. I'd like to talk to you for a few minutes."

I unlocked the door and opened it a few inches, keeping the safety chain on. "What is it?" I repeated coldly. "I was just getting ready for bed."

"I understand," he answered, his tone different, almost apologetic. "This will only take a few minutes."

It took a few moments for me to make my decision to open the door. "All right," I said. "But, please, my little boy is sleeping and it's very late."

He came in slowly, a big man looking sheepish and very tired. It didn't take more than common sense for me to guess he'd had a hard day.

"You look beat," I said.

"I am," he admitted, giving me a half-hearted smile.

"Would a cup of coffee help?"

"A cup of coffee would be just what the doctor ordered."

I invited him into the kitchen. He sat down with a sigh that made my heart go out to him. But I fought back my feelings and busied myself with the coffee, vaguely wishing I had done a more complete job of cleaning up. I had no idea why he'd come back, but it certainly wasn't for a cup of coffee.

"You said there was something you wanted to talk about?" I asked as I set the coffee in front of him. "What is it about, Mr. Buck?"

"Ryan," he said, picking up the cup. "Ryan Buck. I'm off duty now. And—I'm sorry. I don't know your name."

"Denise," I told him, taking a seat, "Denise Dobbs." I felt a bit uneasy about being on a first name basis, but there wasn't any real harm in that. I'd asked him in—I could always ask him to leave. From the eager way he drank the coffee, I could tell that whatever was on his mind there was no hanky-panky involved. He really looked dead on his feet.

For the second time, I had to put a tight rein on my thoughts and feelings.

"Denise," he said, "this is fine coffee." I acknowledged the compliment with a nod, but said nothing. He drank again then continued. "But what I really came here for is to apologize."

That caught me off-balance. "It's okay," I said, thinking of the mess he'd made of my kitchen. "You did what you had to do to get the fire out."

"Well," he said with a smile. "I apologize for that, too, but I'm mostly sorry for the way I barked at you this evening. Grease fires are nasty business. I guess I've seen one too many people make them worse by doing the wrong thing."

"Like throwing water on them?" Now I could even laugh a little at my own stupidity.

"Exactly," he said. "I've seen it happen lots of times. Still, I shouldn't have taken it out on you."

"Apology accepted," I told him. "And next time I buy a secondhand appliance, I'll test it out before using it, too."

"Good thinking," Ryan complimented me. He had a soft, easy smile that made me think he was a very nice man when he wasn't under the pressure of his job.

There was an awkward silence. Neither of us knew what to say next. The weariness crept back into his face.

"Bad day?" I asked, breaking the silence.

"They're all bad days," he said in a tone that shocked me. "When we got your call, we were coming back from another fire. A rooming house, one of those old buildings that go up like a tinderbox. A family was trapped on the third floor—a man, his wife, and two children."

I could sense his anger and pain. I wanted to comfort him, somehow, but I couldn't find the words. Then Ryan took a deep breath and finished his coffee. "I'm sorry—I'm keeping you up. Listen, what I wanted to tell you is, tomorrow night I'm giving a lecture on fire safety at the Y. I'd like you to come."

The invitation took me by surprise. "I just might," I replied. I really didn't know what else to say. Fortunately, he ended the conversation by getting up and stretching.

"I hope so," he said, as I walked him to the door. There, he turned and looked at me. His eyes seemed so clear, so intent, I had to look away. I was tired, and a lot of things I didn't want to think about were rushing into my mind.

"Good night," I said, closing the door quickly.

I was afraid of him reading my mind from the expression on my face. I was glad when I heard him start up his car and drive away.

Getting up the next morning was rough. I woke Jack at the regular time, but he got dressed slowly and I didn't have the heart to rush him. My mind seemed to be elsewhere. And then, at breakfast, he asked me a question that threw me for a loop.

"Mom, what was that fireman doing back here last night?"

I tried to make light of it. "You little devil, I thought you were asleep!"

"I was," he answered, wolfing down his French toast. "But I heard voices, and I snuck a peek to see who it was. Did we have another fire?"

"No." I laughed aloud. "We certainly did not! One was enough, thank you. That fireman came back to make sure we were all right, and to say he was sorry for messing up our kitchen."

"But he had to do that, didn't he, Mom?" Jack asked. "If he hadn't, the whole building might have burned down."

"Yes," I replied. "It's his job."

"Like Daddy's job was to be a policeman?"

That hit me hard. Jack's father had died when he was only a year old. We rarely talked about him now. I was sure Thomas would be proud of his son, but to hear him mentioned like that threw me into an emotional whirlwind.

"Yes," I answered, trying to stop my voice from quivering. "He was doing his job, just like Daddy. Now finish your breakfast and no more questions. If we keep this up, we'll both be late today."

That quieted him. Soon Jack was out the door, hurrying to school. I usually had time for a second cup of coffee before leaving for work, but this morning was different. Knowing I was doing the wrong thing, I went back into my bedroom. Unable to stop myself, I pulled open the top drawer of my dresser and took from it the few precious mementos I had of my dead husband.

Spread across the dresser top, it was a pitifully small collection for three years of perfect love and happiness. There were our wedding pictures, another one of Thomas and me at the seashore when I was pregnant with Jack, one of him in his policeman's uniform. There was a news clipping that outlined, in five short paragraphs, how Officer Thomas Dobbs had answered a robbery call and been shot in the back by a kid high on drugs and scared out of his wits.

That was it. Everything else I'd burned in those terrible days when I was trying to make a new life for myself and Jack—a life without my husband. Tears came to my eyes as I remembered selling our little dream house, all our furniture, the nice things I could no longer afford. Jack's whole world came apart. It was a long time before he began to get over his father's death.

In the end, I'd sworn to myself that I'd never let myself love another man who had such a dangerous job. Thomas had been an honest, hardworking policeman, and it had killed him. I'd built a wall around my heart and I intended to keep it there. For Jack's sake. For my sake, too.

With tears in my eyes, I carefully picked up my little treasures and put them away. I took one last look at the photo of Thomas in his uniform, and for an instant, I seemed to see Ryan Buck's face, too. But I forced the thought from my mind, put the photo back with the others, and went to get ready for work. Brooding never helps, I told myself sternly. What's done is done.

Years ago, after I'd lost Thomas, I'd learned how to keep busy and not let my emotions take control of me. But that morning, it didn't work. My mind kept drifting back to the excitement of last night. I kept thinking of what it would be like to have a husband and lover again. That thought made my heart beat faster in a way I'd nearly forgotten—so quickly and passionately, it frightened me.

The invitation to the lecture kept gnawing at me. Around eleven, I finally called Elaine O'Malley. I guess you could say Elaine was my best friend. I'd met her at Thomas's funeral. She was also a policeman's widow, though she had remarried and now had two beautiful children. Elaine was also a member of a group of policemen's widows who met to give each other advice and support.

She was the one person I knew I could talk to.

It didn't take long to explain my situation.

"I know exactly what you're going through, Denise," she said. "I went through the same thing. After Robert's death, I swore I'd never let myself get close to anyone again. But then I met John, and, well—you know the rest. I guess that proves the old saying that time heals all wounds."

I knew what she was hinting at, and it scared me. She thought I might be falling in love with Ryan Buck, and she was telling me it was all right. That was exactly what I didn't want to hear. I wanted Elaine to help me be strong. I didn't want to be hurt again.

"But what about Jack?" I pleaded. "It's different with you and John. He's an insurance salesman. This man is a fireman. What if Jack should take a liking to him, too, and then something should happen to him? I'd like to hear his lecture, but I'm afraid of him getting the wrong idea!"

Elaine's light, good-hearted laugh came over the line. "Denise, you're putting the cart before the horse! Jack probably does need a father now that he's growing up, but all this man has done is ask you to a public lecture. For all you know, he's already married. Go to the lecture, learn what you can, and let whatever else happens, happen. You've got to learn to live one day at a time. You can't be afraid forever."

With a sinking heart, I thanked Elaine for her advice. She hadn't given me the answer I'd wanted, but she was right. Ryan really hadn't asked me for a date or anything. But my worry was, what if he did? Would I have the strength to say no?

I wasn't afraid. I couldn't even think about missing his lecture. I had seen Ryan weary and angry. Now I wanted to see him in a fresh uniform, smiling, talking about something he knew and cared about. I thought of Thomas's first days on the police force, how proud he'd been, and felt tears coming to my eyes.

All right, Denise, I told myself. You're going. But only for the lecture.

I phoned Mrs. Terwilliger, the lady who watched Jack after school, and asked her if it was all right if he stayed until eight or nine. There was no problem. She had two little ones of her own, and they both loved when Jack stayed for supper. My son liked it, too. I promised her I wouldn't be too late. For the rest of the day, it was easier for me to keep my mind on my work.

I got to there just as the lecture was starting. Close to a hundred people were there, and the place was packed. I took a seat at the back, glad it was so crowded and waited for things to begin.

A representative of some citizens' group was chairing the meeting. She made a few introductory remarks, then introduced Ryan Buck and another fireman. Ryan was to give the presentation while his partner demonstrated various kinds of home extinguishers and safety techniques.

I settled back to listen and learn, but it was only later that I thought about fire safety. For the moment, I was too busy watching Ryan to think about anything else. I heard his voice, but not his words. While his partner demonstrated how to use a fire extinguisher, my eyes were on Ryan, who stood off to one side, scanning the crowd.

His eye caught mine. He smiled faintly, and a chill ran through me! Elaine was right—it wasn't Ryan Buck I was afraid of, but my own feelings. For the rest of the meeting, I was torn between staying and running out. As soon as the chairperson began thanking people for coming, I bolted for the door.

I rushed for the lobby and hurried into my sweater, my fingers nervously fumbling with the buttons. Ryan Buck struck some deep chord in me, and I was terrified. I didn't want to fall in love again! I wanted to go home, back to my safe, secure world.

"I'm glad you could make it," said a deep, already-familiar voice behind me. "Did you enjoy the lecture?"

I turned slowly, trembling, trying to compose myself. All the details of his lecture rushed back to me at once. Like not throwing water on a grease fire. Making sure all appliance cords are well insulated. Never throwing open a window because air feeds a fire.

"Yes," I stammered, "it was very good." I didn't dare say more.

"Listen," he said in a low voice, "I'm sorry about last night. I was beat. I've been thinking about it, and I'd like a chance to make it up to you—"

"How do you know I'm not married?" I cut him off, my voice shrill with panic. "You know I have a son. What about my husband?"

"Do you really want me to answer that?"

"Yes!" I boldly challenged him. I was praying for some avenue of escape, anything that would keep me from saying yes.

"I was all through your apartment last night, checking to see if anything else was burning. Two bedrooms, two single beds. I guessed you were divorced."

I knew then there'd be no escape. "I'm not divorced. My husband is dead. He was a policeman. He—he was killed on duty."

Ryan's face softened. He stepped back, his eyes regarding me in a new light. "I'm sorry," he said, but it was too late now. All my tension and fear and loneliness were finding release in tears. I was trembling slightly now, feeling a tremendous sense of relief as my grief finally came out. It felt so good to see such concern in a man's face again. I'd been so lonely, for so long—but had never admitted it even to myself. And now, to find someone who cared, someone who understood what I'd endured. . . .

He reached out to comfort me. But the moment he touched me, I automatically jumped back, away from him.

"I'm sorry, too!" I blubbered through my tears. I wiped my eyes with the back of my hand. "I have to be going. Jack—my boy—I have to be going!"

Without looking back to see if Ryan was following, I charged out into the night. I ran all the way to the bus stop.

For the next two weeks, I tried hard to forget Ryan Buck. During the week, I buried myself in work and living. On weekends, I made sure Jack and I always had someplace to go, and something to do. One Saturday, we spent the entire day at the zoo. The next weekend, we went to an amusement park. By the end of each day I was always dead tired. But when I tucked Jack in, and tried to sleep myself, I was always nervously restless, unable to sleep.

My desires, my needs, so long repressed, now refused to leave me alone. When I did manage to sleep, I'd dream constantly—wild, passionate dreams of a strong man holding me, loving me . . . I always woke up trembling, still exhausted. I knew that if Ryan Buck came knocking on my door then, I'd have been unable to resist him.

The third week after the lecture brought me some peace of mind. There was a whole morning at work when I didn't think of Ryan at all. Soon, I'd be back in the safe, secure cocoon I had woven myself and my son. Then, one Saturday afternoon, the phone rang—and my fragile house of cards collapsed.

"Hello," said a deep, husky voice. "This is Ryan Buck. Remember me?"

Remember him? My knees turned to water. My heart pounded. I was on the brink of telling Ryan to come right over—we'd spend the day together—when I went numb with anxious fear. Have him come over? Have my heart broken again? I couldn't do it! I just couldn't say the words!

"Of course, I remember you," I choked out, keeping my voice as cool and level as I could. "What can I do for you, Mr. Buck? Is it about the fire?"

"No, it's not about the fire," he answered cheerfully, brushing aside all my defenses. "You were pretty upset the last time we spoke. I didn't know if it was something I said, but if it was, I'm sorry."

"No," I managed to interrupt. "It wasn't you."

"Well, I'm glad to hear that." Ryan laughed. "Look, I think I have a handle on how you feel. I was married a few years back. My wife died of cancer. I thought I'd never get over it, and maybe that feeling of loss will never be completely gone. But life must go on. When I met you, I said to myself, 'There's a gal I'd like to know better.' But you were so upset I thought I'd wait a few weeks before calling you. You know what I'm trying to say?"

He was saying everything I didn't want to hear. I wasn't ready for this. Maybe I never would be! I had to stop it.

83

"No, no, no!" I muttered into the phone, shaking my head. "I'm sorry, I can't—"

"You never know until you try," Ryan said firmly, but kindly. "Listen, I'm through in half an hour. Suppose I just come over? Maybe we could go out for a hamburger or something with Jack. Just get to know each other better. What harm could there be in that?"

It was as though he were standing there before me, his handsome face smiling, his strong arms reaching out for me. For an instant, I wanted to scream: Yes! Come over right away! But then my fear possessed me. How could I possibly risk another heartbreak?

I panicked and slammed down the phone. I grabbed my sweater, and Jack, and ran from the apartment. I had to get out fast!

"Mom, where are we going? Why are we running?" Poor Jack— I'd taken him completely by surprise. But this was too complicated for me to explain. I thought quickly and made up a likely story.

"I forgot to tell you," I explained breathlessly as we rushed to the bus stop. "There's a new kid's movie downtown, and tonight's the last night. I just remembered. If we catch the next bus, we can just make it in time."

"Oh, wow!" Jack was delighted.

We were breathless when we got to the bus stop. In my hurry, I hadn't checked a bus schedule. We must have just missed one, because we had to wait nearly twenty minutes for the next. Each passing minute ate at my nerves until I was ready to scream. Ryan could come driving up the street any minute.

At last, the bus came. We were both thankful, but for different reasons. Jack climbed into a seat next to the window, and I sat beside him, glad that no one driving past would be able to see me.

But I'd sat down when Jack yelled, "Mom, it's him! It's the fireman—the fireman!"

My eyes shot wide open. "What do you mean? Where is he? Where?" I sat up immediately and looked out the window but I saw no sign of Ryan Buck anywhere.

"He was on a fire engine, Mom. It came past us on the other street when we stopped at that red light. That fireman was on the back of the truck."

"Jack, it couldn't have been," I said, trying to deny what I knew in my heart was true.

"It was, Mom!" Jack repeated earnestly. "I've been watching all the trucks since our fire. This is the first time I've seen him. Wow! Wait'll I tell the kids at school!"

Suddenly, all my doubts and fears were resolved. I knew what I had to do. Grabbing his little hand, I hurried with Jack toward the front of the bus.

"Where are we going?" he asked. "Are we going to the fire?"

"Yes," I said, "but you'll miss the movie."

"That's okay," Jack answered with glee as we got off the bus. "I'd rather see a fire!"

It seemed to be a big fire. In the next block, great clouds of black smoke were rising. I could hear the high-pitched sirens everywhere. They made my head ring. It didn't take much to be able to guess where the fire was.

"Come on!" I told Jack, offering him my hand. "Let's run!"

What did I think of as we ran? I thought of Thomas. He'd have wanted me to be happy, too. He wouldn't have wanted me to lock myself and his son in a world that refused to let love in for fear of being hurt.

I thought about Ryan Buck. I thought about the way I'd felt every time he spoke to me. I thought about his eyes, now weary and exhausted, now trying to smile. Ryan was lonely, too. He needed someone—perhaps the someone that he needed was me. . . .

I thought about how foolish I'd been, how I almost let my chance for another love slip by. I ran all the faster to reach the fire.

An old tenement was burning. Three fire trucks were already there, huge hoses gushing waterfalls into the raging flames. As we ran to the crowd of spectators, a fourth truck, its ladder extended, pulled into position against the blazing building.

I realized there were people trapped on the top floor. And that Ryan Buck was climbing that ladder. . . .

Holding Jack close, I pushed through the crowd. It was a real struggle, but we did get through. Beyond the crowd were television reporters with their cameras and microphones. We ran past them, too, our eyes glued to the top floor, and to the fireman nearly at the top of the long white ladder.

A fire chief blocked our way. "Lady, you can't go any closer. Get back."

"Please!" I begged him. "You have to let us by!"

"Lady, you're crazy!" he told me. "Whatever's in there is lost. You've got a kid—you're both alive. Be thankful. Now get back! We're doing the best we can to put it out!"

"But you don't understand!" I cried. The roar of the flames blocked out my voice, but I kept on screaming. "I don't live there! I have to find somebody! I have to know! Is Ryan Buck up there?"

Understanding lit up his face. "Buck? From Station Three?" He looked up then, and so did I. There was no need for him to answer. I knew who was up there. I knew it as surely as I knew I loved him. The danger he was facing made me shiver.

Everyone in the crowd was watching as Ryan Buck reached the

top of the ladder. He stepped off, onto the steeply sloping roof of the third floor, and then walked toward a closed window, where flames leaped and danced behind the glass. With his ax, he smashed the window. And then he stepped into that blazing inferno.

The whole crowd gasped at once. Then suddenly, the roof caved in! It collapsed all at once, with a hideous roar. A huge geyser of flames gushed up into the sky.

The crowd gave out a low moan, like some wounded beast, and I screamed aloud, "Oh, God!" I had run here to watch Ryan die. . . .

I staggered forward a few steps. My senses spun the same way they had when I'd heard about Thomas. I closed my eyes, trying to shut out this new tragedy, but the roar of the crowd cheering made me open them again.

I tried to look away from the burning building, but Jack's voice, sounding like he was at the other end of a long, dark tunnel, pulled me back. "Mom, it's him! It's him!"

I looked up. Miraculously, Ryan was back on the ladder. And he had a small child slung over one shoulder as he started down.

This time no one stopped me when I rushed forward. I stopped right next to the fire engine, murmuring, "Thank God! Oh, thank God!" as Ryan slowly came down with his precious burden.

When his feet finally touched ground he handed the unconscious child to the paramedics. Wearily, he pulled off his big gloves. The other firemen were congratulating him. Cameras swung around in his direction. The child's grateful parents were thanking him and he was doing his best to smile, but I could tell the heat and smoke had nearly been too much for him. Then he looked up. Our eyes met, and for a moment, the entire world held still.

In that moment, without a spoken word, we told each other our deepest truest feelings. Then I ran to his arms, all my fears forgotten. And his first kiss told me all I wanted to know. We clung together completely oblivious of the tumult all around us.

Then Jack was with us. He was grinning. Ryan motioned for him to come closer, and we both hugged him. Suddenly, we were a family. . . .

Later, we talked. I told Ryan everything about Thomas, my pain, my fears. At the end, I admitted I loved him with all my heart. No matter what kind of work he did, I'd still love him.

Ryan talked, too. Before his wife had become ill, he'd considered quitting his job because it was so dangerous and it worried her. But then she died. There was an emptiness in his life, and he knew it could be filled by helping people the only way he knew. He had to stay with it because firefighting was a very important job, sometimes a matter of life and death.

I had to admit he was right. If not for him, that little child would have died. Or Jack and I might have been badly hurt when our popcorn popper caught fire. His job, like Thomas's, had to be done.

I can accept that now. Ryan and I have been married for three years. He's a wonderful husband, a fine, exciting lover, and a good father to Jack. I still get cold shivers whenever he's working, whenever I hear a fire siren. I've learned to live with that. Our days and nights together are wonderful, filled with laughter and love, and I take them one at a time. For me, it's the only way to live.

THE END

I WOULDN'T CHANGE PLACES
WITH ANYONE

"Don't you ever come around this place again, if you know what's good for you! Get over in your own trashy part of town and leave us decent folks alone!" Mrs. Richards shouted. My sister and I crept out of the yard while the other children laughed cruelly at us.

"Don't worry, Cathy," I said, fighting to hold back the tears in front of my younger sister. "We're as good as they are any day!" Cathy was crying as though her little heart would break and I tried to cheer her up. How could I have known that Mary Richards's party was just an invitation for us to come and be humiliated? We'd even brought a present. They were probably laughing about it now, as we trudged down the dirt road to our trailer park outside of town.

"They called us trash!" Cathy sobbed. "Why is it so bad that Daddy works on the oil wells, Jenna? I don't understand." She began to cry again. I tried to explain that Daddy did hard, honest work, while Mary's father worked at a desk in the bank. Often, Daddy was out on the drilling platform in thirty below zero weather. The bad part was that we traveled all the time to new homes and to new schools. Daddy went where the work was—and we went with him.

"What's wrong with Cathy?" Mom asked. "She was crying when you came in." Mom looked worried. She always tried to protect us and yet make us ready for the world. I explained what had happened. "Now, Jenna, I know you have enough sense not to let that girl's remarks hurt you. Try to help your sister to understand." Mom put her arm around me. "You always know what to do, Jenna—I can count on you. Now set the table, honey—Daddy will be home soon."

Mom bustled around the small kitchen, taking biscuits out of the oven, stirring some pan gravy, setting a hot pie close to the window to cool. A lot of people made fun of our home, but I wouldn't change that place, with all the love in it, for anything in the world. Mom and Dad made our trailer a palace. Cathy and I knew we were loved and wanted.

"Hello, any of my beautiful girls home?" Dad called as he came in. Mom went to him, hugging him tight, even though he still wore his greasy overalls. Cathy and I also ran to kiss him.

"Hey, take it easy!" Daddy teased. "I just wanted a welcome home, not all the love you have." We laughed and sat down to eat.

After supper, Cathy and I went to our bedroom to do our homework. I could hear Mom telling Dad about our party humiliation.

"By God, Lena, I just don't understand why those people are so cruel to kids. This 'oil field trash' gets to me. Those snobs heat their homes and fuel their cars with what I help bring out of the ground—I wish they'd think about it sometime." They talked some more. Soon, I got ready for bed and went to sleep.

The incident was never mentioned again. We stayed in Castroville long enough for me to finish high school. I wasn't the smartest kid in the class, but I got all I could out of school because Mom and Dad said it would help me in the future. I got a job in an oil field supply company in town after graduation. I really liked the job—I was the only girl in the office, and I did all the office work and telephone orders. Many of the men who came to the office were Daddy's friends. I enjoyed their good-natured jokes.

About a month after I started working there, Mr. Jenkins, the office manager, called me into his office. "Jenna, I want to tell you we're very happy with you. We're giving you a raise."

I blushed because he went on to say how much he appreciated someone my age that had a sense of responsibility about work. "I'll be leaving here, soon, Jenna. The company transferred me. Would you be interested in handling the office work up there for me? It would be a step up for you because it's a larger office and you can learn more. There's also more money. What about it?"

"Oh, Mr. Jenkins—I don't know what to say! When would I have to leave?" He filled me in on the details and I ran home to tell my folks. They were real proud of me, I could tell. The next few weeks were a whirlwind of excited activity. I said good-bye to my folks and had a short talk with Cathy.

"I don't care what you do or where you go, Jenna," Cathy said, "you'll still be oil field trash to decent people. I'll never forget that party, and I'm never going to. I'll never be trash again to anybody when I get out of here."

I tried to calm her, saying she'd surely forget some day, and be happy. I worried about her, but I had too many other things to do, and in the rush, I forgot all about our talk.

My new job was exciting. I began to meet a lot of people in the office and was invited to many social gatherings. I was also dressing a lot better. I wore classic suits and dresses, and really cared for my appearance. Soon, I was dating some of the young engineers who worked out of our central office. I loved to hear about their work and their ambitions.

One day, I had to take a geology report out to one of the rigs a few miles away from the office. It started to rain when I left and I got lost a few times. And then I ran off the dirt road and got my tires stuck in the mud that oozed over the hubcaps. My clothes were a mess. All

I could do was to sit in the car and hope someone would come along.

An hour or so later, a field service truck rattled down the road. "Got some trouble?" a voice called from the cab. It was still raining, but I rolled down the window and told the man my troubles.

"I can't help the car, but I can help you." He grinned. "Wait a sec—I'll carry you over to the truck." His hard hat was pulled low so I couldn't see who he was. I opened the door and he picked me up and carried me to the truck. Then he went around to the driver's door and climbed in.

"Here, let me turn on the cab light so you can move that stuff around on the floor. I'm sorry it's such a mess in here." The light went on and I almost gasped.

This was the most incredibly handsome man I'd ever seen! He looked rough and tough, like most oil workers do, but there was gentleness to his laugh and he was terribly concerned about my comfort.

He started the truck on the slippery sliding journey back to town. "My name's Bobby Knight, and my rig here is called Sandy, after my kid sister. What's your name?"

"Jenna Rowan," I said. "I work in our central office."

Bobby said he was familiar with the office there, but he was working in the fields right now. He'd been moved down from Canada to South Dakota. He looked like a hardworking man. His hands were calloused and dirty, and the hard hat tilted back on his head had oil smears and scratches on it. He reminded me of Daddy a little. He dropped me off at the office and drove away before I could introduce him to anyone. It was near quitting time, so I went home.

I heard from my folks regularly. They even came to visit my first summer away, staying in my apartment. Mom liked the way I'd decorated the place. I was getting to be more of an office manager, but I was still interested in the fieldwork. Also, I still worried about Cathy, so I called home one day to speak to Mom about her.

"I worry about her, too," Mom said. "She seems to be happy away at college. She was always ashamed of what she was, I guess. Of course, we're happy she wants to better herself. I really think all her feelings stem back to that awful party." Mom talked on about Cathy, saying she never brought young men home, even though she'd had a good job before she went off to college. Cathy never mentioned her folks to her new friends—they just stopped outside the trailer and picked her up.

A year later, startling news came—Cathy was marrying a young man she'd met in college. He was a law student, and he came from a wealthy family. They'd be by to see me when they went on their honeymoon. There was no mention of the actual wedding. When I phoned Mom, I was shocked to learn that Cathy hadn't invited Mom or Dad! Then I remembered she hadn't invited me, either. . . .

I continued to work in the office of the oil company. Now I had several girls under me. My routine was shattered one day when an oil-splattered man strode up to my desk and tossed a stained report sheet on my desk.

"I wish you'd—" I started to show some irritation at the dirty paper when I heard the man laugh.

"Now don't you get stuck-up on me! A man rescues a lady in distress—and this is what he gets!" It was Bobby Knight! "Look, Jenna—I remembered your name—I've got about four days in town before I go back into the field again. Want to go to a party tonight?"

I was overwhelmed. He looked so handsome and devil-may-care. "I'd rather not. But thanks anyway."

He chuckled. "This is such a nice bunch of people. It's all engineers and office personnel. We're having it down at the Legion Hall. Hey—come on!" I hesitated, and then smiled my approval. "Great! I'll pick you up around seven, okay?" I smiled again. I started to give him my address, but he waved me off. "Got it already. In fact, I got it the night I brought you in."

Bobby picked me up at seven and we went to a nice place for a few drinks before the party. We also had supper there—steaks and a fine salad. When we arrived, the party was in full swing. Bobby took me around and introduced me to everyone he knew. There were a lot of jokes and good fun between Bobby and the others. He was well-liked, and I could tell the other girls were green with envy because he was my date. It wasn't very nice, but I enjoyed their envy!

"You're a terrific dancer, Jenna," Bobby murmured in my ear. "I'd really like to see more of you—a lot more. I guess this kind of gypsy life I lead isn't too interesting to a girl like you, but I'll be settling in an office in about a year or so, I hope." He went on to tell me how he'd started on the rigs right after high school and had worked his way up until he ran his own drilling crew. It paid well, but he was ambitious and wanted to get into management. I was interested, and told him all about my dad. "I'm oil field trash from way back. Dad worked on rigs all his life. He's worked them from Texas to Canada to Saudi Arabia. I guess I understand your life."

Bobby grinned in pleasure. "Of all the luck! I end up here and pick a rose out of an oil patch. How lucky can a man get?" Bobby held me tight, and then kissed me softly on the neck. I turned my head slightly and we kissed full on the lips. Shivers of excitement surged through me. My heart pounded and I leaned on him for a moment. "I will see more of you, Jenna, don't worry about that." Once we found the common ground of oil, we spent the rest of the evening talking about famous "characters" my father and Bobby both knew.

"So you really knew Otis Billings in Wyoming? My God, that guy is a living legend!" I smiled at Bobby's boyish excitement.

"Bobby, I really did enjoy this evening." I leaned against the door before entering my apartment. Bobby kissed me several times, and then held me against the rough wool of his heavy coat. Hardly trusting myself to resist him, I pulled away. I smiled a good night to him and closed the door.

We were inseparable after that night. Whenever Bobby was in town, we spent all his free time together. It was getting serious and we both knew it. We needed a little time, and, fortunately, Bobby was called back to Canada for a week. I was disappointed because I wanted him to meet my sister when she showed up. Bobby expressed his regrets, but he did have to leave.

I was excited, terribly eager to see my little sister. I hadn't seen her for several years. Now, Cathy was a married woman! It didn't seem possible. I scurried around the apartment, dusting and straightening, making some snacks and goodies. The kitchen smelled heavenly. I always remembered how nice the kitchen smelled when Mom baked. Suddenly, there was a knock on the door. I flew to it and flung it open. I grabbed my sister.

"Cathy!" I cried, "Oh, Cathy—I'm so glad to see you!"

She was happy, but a little embarrassed by the emotion I displayed. "Heavens, Jenna, you'd think I'd returned from the dead." She seemed cold, a little distant. She wore a stunning two piece suit that set off her slim figure.

Cathy looked the apartment over carefully before she entered. "I guess this is the best you could do here, but you've done wonders with it. Oh, Jenna, this is my husband, Martin Wentworth."

Her husband stood tall behind her. Martin was immaculately dressed in a fine business suit. He had on a silk shirt and very expensive shoes. But he seemed very friendly. I liked him.

"I'll just shake hands for now. You can kiss me later when you get to know me better." Martin laughed, and so did I.

"Please, Martin, save your common jokes for other people," Cathy said coldly. "Oh, dear, would you please run down to the car and get the things I brought for Jenna?" Martin was disappointed—he wanted to stay and talk, I could tell that.

"Have a chair, Cathy," I said. "I'll bring out something to eat." I ran in the kitchen and brought out the little snacks I'd made.

Cathy looked over the tray and took a small piece of cake. "Still cooking like Mother. Well, you'll get over it." She nibbled on the cake as she looked around the apartment. I was bursting with a hundred questions, but Cathy began talking first.

"I suppose Mother and Dad told you about my not inviting them to the wedding?"

I said they had. "I'd assumed they couldn't make it, with Dad working all the time."

"That's hardly the reason, Jenna. They could have made it. That's why I didn't invite them."

I was shocked. "Why, Cathy! You know they're so proud of you, finishing college and marrying a lawyer. Being at your wedding would have been the greatest thing in their lives. Mom always worried about you so much. She—"

Cathy turned her head away in exasperation. "Jenna, really! Martin's friends and family would have been—well—disturbed, if I'd asked them to the wedding. I mean, they really don't know how to dress, or anything. I just couldn't." She looked back at me, daring me to criticize her decision.

"Is that why you didn't invite me, either, Cathy?" I asked.

"Oh, no, Jenna, I did want you there! It's just that there wasn't time and I didn't know if you could get off work." Cathy seemed angry, but a little nervous.

"You could have written to me or phoned me, Cathy. You know you're my only sister, and I always thought the world of you. Are you afraid I wasn't good enough for you?" I was getting angry, but just then Martin came in and we both put on a good front for him.

We talked for about an hour. They'd brought me a gift of a clock and a silver tray. I was overwhelmed—these things must have cost a lot of money. Martin was genuinely friendly and interested in the work I did, but Cathy always steered the conversation away from any mention of the family. Martin seemed puzzled by that, but he was gracious enough not to mention it.

Just as they were getting ready to leave, there was a knock on the door. I couldn't imagine who it might be. I went to open the door.

"Hello, pretty lady! The man of the year is here." It was Bobby.

"I thought you were going to be away all week, Bobby!"

"I was, but the company changed its mind again, so here I am. Ready to go out tonight?" He stopped talking. "Oh, I'm sorry—I didn't know you had company. I'll come back later. I just got in from the field, as you can see." His khaki shirt and pants were splattered with mud and oil and a streak of black ran across his cheek. It made him look like a naughty little boy.

I invited Bobby in and introduced him to my sister and her husband. Martin shook Bobby's hand and made a few light jokes about his appearance. Bobby laughed heartily at them. There was no joking with Cathy, though. She barely acknowledged his presence.

Bobby felt the coolness and apologized for intruding. I went with him into the hall.

"Look, Jenna, I'll call you tomorrow, okay? You must have a lot to talk about with your sister and I'll just be in the way." I protested and said we could all go out that night for supper. Bobby said he'd call before he came over, and I returned to the apartment.

"You go out with him?" Cathy asked shocked. "I thought you had enough of grubby men! Jenna, you can get someone better than him." Her remarks were cruel—they were intended to be.

"Now just a minute, Cathy," Martin said. "I like Bobby. He seems like a nice guy."

I interrupted them both. "Look, Bobby will be over later and we can go out for supper, okay?"

Cathy answered, "We can't stay that long, Jenna. We really have to get on the road. We promised some people we'd be at their place tomorrow. I'd really like to stay. Maybe some other time."

Martin began to protest that they'd planned to stay with me for a few days. Cathy glared at him. "We must be going, Martin. If you don't have a sense of responsibility towards our friends, I do."

"Oh, please stay, Cathy!" I begged. "I haven't seen you in so long."

She turned and said, "I'm sorry, Jenna, but maybe some other time. We have to go now, Martin." He shrugged his shoulders and followed her out the door. When the door closed, I threw myself on the couch and sobbed.

"What's wrong, Jenna?" Bobby asked over the phone. I blurted out the whole story—how Cathy didn't want to stay with me, and that she apparently didn't like him. He said he'd be right over. When he arrived, we talked for a long time. I was still crying, but he bucked me up a little. "Look, she's a little upset now, just married and all. Give her another chance, Jenna, please?" I started sobbing again. Bobby was so kind—kinder than my sister could ever be. I threw myself into his arms.

"Oh, Bobby, you're so good! Please, don't ever leave me— please, don't!" His strong arms circled me and drew me closer. He kissed the tears from my cheeks.

"I don't know about that sister of yours, but you're good enough for me. Will you marry me, Jenna?" I said yes in a rush of joy. Suddenly, my world was a happy place again. I was giggling like a schoolgirl when we phoned Mom and Dad. They wished us the best and promised to come to the wedding.

We didn't waste any time. We rounded up Bobby's friends, and Mom and Dad drove up for the wedding. I wore a white gown Mom had made for me, and Bobby looked marvelous in his wedding suit.

Our reception was noisy and fun. My parents really liked Bobby and told me so. That made me even happier.

Right from the start my life with Bobby was glorious. I always waited eagerly for the time he came home, and I felt like a real woman, cooking and keeping house for the man I loved. Bobby was a wild lover but a tender and caring person when it came to quiet moments around the house. We lived that first year in a kind of bliss I thought existed only in dreams. . . .

One night, our phone rang. "Jenna, this is Martin Wentworth. Could I talk to you for a minute?" I was dumbfounded. I hadn't heard from Cathy or Martin since their visit a year ago. "Look, Jenna, I just wanted to say I'm really sorry about the way Cathy treated you. I guess I wasn't man enough to do anything about it. But I want to apologize now. We're getting a divorce and I just wanted to square things with everyone before I took off. I'm going to Europe on business for a few months. Cathy's living with another man. She has been for several months now. I guess he has more money than I do."

Martin's voice choked for a minute. "I think you're one of the better people in the world, Jenna. I only wish I'd met you instead of your sister. Look, this is getting a little too sentimental. Please tell Bobby I wish him all the luck in the world, and I know you two are happy. I just wish I was." The phone clicked and the line was dead.

I was astonished at this turn of events. My first thought was of Cathy, how unhappy she might be—but then I knew she'd always be unhappy, no matter where she was. Cathy would never be satisfied with anyone or anything.

When I hung up, I heard Bobby putting something in the refrigerator. "Who was it, Jenna?" he called from the kitchen. Tears rolled down my cheeks. They were tears of happiness. I had found my life and the right man to share it. Few women could say that.

"It's just someone asking how we were getting along. I'll tell you about it later." I wiped the tears from my eyes and walked into the kitchen.

"You oil field trash are all right!" I cried as I threw myself in Bobby's arms. I told Bobby I loved him at least a dozen times before he could recover.

"It takes one to know one." He grinned. Then he gathered me in his arms and kissed me until I was out of breath. "The only trash around here is in the garbage can under the sink," he growled in a fake gruff voice. "I'm holding all the treasures in the world right now." I smiled at him through tears of joy. I was oil field trash and proud of it.

THE END

I GAVE BIRTH IN
A FLOOD!

Standing beside the kitchen window that morning, I watched the bare trees bending in the wind. When we had moved in, it had been Indian summer, and the trees in our backyard had been bursting with green leaves. Now, the wind rushing through the bare branches made a lonely sound.

Behind me, the kitchen radio was blaring. A radio announcer was giving the day's weather forecast: "There's no change from our earlier forecast. Snow is expected to develop around one o'clock this afternoon, accompanied by strong easterly winds. We expect an accumulation of eight to sixteen inches. More snow tonight, often heavy, with gusting winds. Partial clearing by tomorrow afternoon."

Len snapped the radio off. Sitting down, he picked up the newspaper I'd placed beside his juice, and flipped to the sports section without looking at me.

Even so, I made myself smile at him. "Hi, honey. What'll you have for breakfast?" I asked. "Eggs? Toast?"

"No, thanks, Desiree." He still didn't look at me. "I'm not hungry, and I'm late, anyway. I'll grab something in town."

Did he hate the sight of me? Why wouldn't he look at me? Was it because I was eight months pregnant and looked bloated all over? Quickly, I pushed the hurtful thought away. "Len, the weatherman says we're getting snow—lots of it. And bad winds, too."

He shook his head. "I have a business to run, remember? Anyway, these weather guys don't know beans. Last time they said there'd be snow, we had three inches of rain. The storm will probably drift off to sea." He put on his jacket and headed for the door, then spoke over his shoulder. "I may be a bit late, Desiree. I have to see a man after work. He wants me to come down to his store and give him an estimate on some siding."

"Again?" I cried. I'd promised myself I wouldn't get angry and argue with him, but the anger was beginning to spurt through me. "Sure, you have a business! I know all about your precious business! What I want to know is whether you realize you have a wife—and a baby that's going to be born in a few weeks! What's the matter with you, anyway?"

His mouth was set tight, and he had that angry, trapped look in his eyes that I hated. Without a word, he banged out of the house, his footsteps pounding down the porch steps to his pickup in the driveway. In a second, I heard the engine start up, and then the squeal of tires as Len backed out into Barnet Street. He couldn't even wait to let the engine warm up, he was so anxious to get away from me!

He seemed to hate me and this baby I was carrying. It hadn't been that way when I was pregnant with Chelsea. As always, when I thought of our first baby, my eyes blurred with tears. Len had been so happy when I'd told him I was pregnant that time. He'd put his arms around me and swirled me around the room, telling me he loved me.

We had waited two years for me to get pregnant, so I shared Len's joy. I'd come from a large, happy family, now living out of state, and though I missed them, I'd hoped to start another large family of my own. He was just as anxious for kids, even though he was an only child. His mother had had complications following his birth, which stopped her from having more children. In fact, Mother Darrell was the one shadow in my otherwise happy life. She'd keep looking at me, and often she'd shake her head.

"I hope you have an easy time, Desiree," she'd say. "You're built so slim! I'm that way myself. You know, I almost died. . . ."

I didn't tell her that my obstetrician had explained to me that I had a rather narrow pelvis. That would have got her going! I wasn't worried at all, because Dr. Hanover had explained that though he'd rather have me deliver in a normal way, he could perform an immediate Cesarean section if the baby were too large, or if I had any difficulty with the birth.

For seven months, everything went well. Then, for no reason, something happened. I awoke one night with a deep, clutching pain that tore through my body. When the pain came again, Len insisted I go to the hospital.

I don't remember much about that night, except that there was pain and blood. I lost a lot of blood, so much so that the doctor was afraid I might die. "Get that transfusion into her, stat!" I heard him say. "We might lose her, too!"

Too? I remember puzzling over that small word as I slipped into unconsciousness. I didn't realize that Chelsea, our beautiful daughter, had died after just a few moments in this world. I found out when I woke up that evening and found Len kneeling beside my hospital bed, his face pushed against my pillow, his wide shoulders shaking with sobs. "Oh, Desiree!" was all he said, but I knew. I knew.

I recovered quickly. At least, my body went back to being what it used to be. Inside, I felt empty, and never so much as when Len drove me back to our quiet city apartment. I'd steeled myself to see Chelsea's things in the "baby room" which was to have been hers—but when I went into that room, it was bare. There was no crib, no bassinet—nothing.

"What happened to Chelsea's things?" I gasped.

"Ma took them," Len said. "She felt you could cope better if you weren't reminded. . . ." He put his arms around me. "She's right, honey. I don't want you remembering."

I knew he was trying to make things easier for me, but that empty room made me feel worse, not better.

"Chelsea was our baby," I cried, "not just a bad memory!" I pulled out of his arms. "Len, we can't just act as if she never existed!"

In the days that followed, I tried to talk to him about Chelsea. He always changed the subject. Mother Darrell didn't help, either. She wouldn't so much as let the word "baby" cross her lips.

A wall of silence seemed to be building between Len and me—a silence in which "baby" and "Chelsea" were never mentioned. Slowly, that silence seeped into the rest of our marriage. We weren't as close as we'd been, and when we made love, it was never the complete sharing of body and soul that we'd had before. Len began spending more and more time at his job with a roofing and sheet-metal company. He went to work early and came home late, just to eat and sleep. We got to the point where we hardly talked at all.

Then one day, Len came home earlier than usual, his face awake and alive with enthusiasm. "Desiree," he began, "how'd you like to move to a place called Bay Point? It's on the coast, right on the ocean."

The thought of leaving the city and all its bad memories certainly appealed to me. "Tell me about it," I said.

"Well, there's a business for sale in Bay Point—a roofing business. It's established, and I could make it grow even more. I heard about the business from one of the guys at work." He paused. "It'd be a good investment, Desiree. We'd have to put down a lot of money to start with, but we'd get it back in a couple of years."

He explained that Bay Point was a wealthy town with lovely, old homes owned by rich people who lived there during the summer, as well as by wealthy retirees. There were also sections of town where young people like us lived.

"There'll be a hundred new homes in that area in a few years," he enthused. "Desiree, it'll be something for our future."

We sat and talked about it, longer and more freely than we'd done since Chelsea's death. We didn't stop talking, either, when we realized how late it was getting. For once, our bedroom didn't look like a cold and lonely place, when Len put his arms around me and pulled me close to him.

"I love you, Desiree," he whispered. I clung close to him, knowing that the wall of silence between us had dissolved.

That night, we made love, joyously wrapped in the silver moonlight that filtered through half-drawn drapes. Our bodies shared something so beautiful, I wanted to cry. Later, in Len's arms, I knew we'd find our old closeness and happiness in our new home.

It wasn't until he was well into negotiations to buy the Bay Point Roofing Company that I realized I was pregnant. At first, I was shocked, because I'd been practicing birth control ever since Chelsea's death—something Len had insisted I do. When I thought back, however, I realized that the baby had been conceived that beautiful night when we made love in the moonlight.

Our lovemaking had been so wonderful and spontaneous, I'd forgotten to take my usual precautions. I was delighted that we were going to have a baby, but Len wasn't.

"How could you have been so careless?" he fumed. "Now I'll have to call the Bay Point thing off!"

"Why?" I asked. I'd already talked to Dr. Hanover, who'd recommended an obstetrician near Bay Point. "There's this Dr. Manfredi there, and he's wonderful. There's also a hospital, just fifteen minutes away in Verselles, north of Bay Point."

Len still looked mad, so I added, "Listen, don't worry, honey. This time, we'll have a healthy baby!"

"Who said I was worrying?" he snapped. We were quiet for a moment. Then he sighed. "It's just that it's so soon after—after the last time."

I hugged him, forcing his arms around me. "Len, let's be happy," I whispered. "A new business, a new home, a new baby—it's all going to be wonderful!"

Bay Point was wonderful. I loved its sandy, curvy coastline and the stately homes that were built near the seawall. One of the nicest areas was a place called Braddock Park, where wealthy, retired people had built up a community. These people could fish, paint, or just enjoy their lovely homes and gardens. I told Len that when we started making money with the business, that was how I wanted to live.

The home we rented wasn't as nice as the ones in Braddock Park, but it was everything I wanted: a big, old-fashioned home. The neighborhood was quiet because most of my neighbors were summer people who wintered in the city. I might have missed the city's noise and excitement, but I had my hands full, helping Len at our new store.

I loved working with him. While he attended to the technical end of the business, I met a lot of the people who lived in Bay Point. As our baby slowly grew within me, more and more women came over and traded pregnancy and delivery stories with me. I didn't mind; talking about babies just seemed to bring the day when I'd hold our baby in my arms closer—but Len didn't like it.

"Desiree," he said, "this isn't some baby clinic. We're running a business here."

"I know, but there isn't any harm in swapping experiences," I said lightly.

He didn't say any more—until a few weeks later, when an elderly couple came in to buy a screen door. While the man talked to Len, the woman came over to me.

"How far along are you, or are you sick and tired of that question?" she asked. Her smile was warm and friendly, and I liked her immediately. We began to chat, and I told her I was going to Dr. Manfredi. She nodded. "Dr. Manfredi, yes. He's a good man. Henry knew him when they both worked at St. John's Hospital."

After the couple left, Len read me the riot act.

"Desiree, what's the matter with you? You tell perfect strangers everything!"

He was beside himself, and one thing led to another, with us both yelling at each other and me ending up in tears.

We made up after that, but it wasn't a complete peace between us. Len got furious every time the word "baby" was mentioned in the store, to the point of being downright rude to customers. Eventually, to stop the unpleasantness, I stopped going to work there. He seemed relieved that I did.

I tried to keep busy. I walked a lot—up to the beach, to the Episcopal church on Sundays. It was at church that I met Ginnie and Henry Penn, the elderly couple who had come to our store some time ago.

"How lovely to see you again," Ginnie said, her eyes so full of welcome that I felt warmed through and through.

The Penns insisted on driving me home after services, and they made arrangements to pick me up every Sunday. I grew to like them very much. Henry was rather quiet; he didn't speak much, and I noticed his hands shook a lot, especially his left one. Ginnie, when I got to know her better, explained that her husband had been a surgeon, but now had Parkinson's disease, which causes tremors. "But it's controlled," she explained. "Rest and medication have done wonders for Henry."

Ginnie's friendship meant a lot to me, but the Penns' serene happiness was hurtful contrast to the problems that Len and I were having. We'd seldom argued before, but now we were at odds constantly. We hassled about the incredibly long hours Len was putting in at the store—and about other things. And yet all of it was a cover-up for Len's strange reaction to my pregnancy. . . .

I sighed, watching the gray clouds fill the sky. Another long, dreary day ahead of me. I wished there was something to do. Housecleaning? I'd already done that. Phone someone? It was too expensive to call my family long distance, and I'd quit talking to

Mother Darrell because her gloomy prediction about "another hard labor" depressed me. Ginnie? Perhaps I could call Ginnie, just to chat.

She seemed glad to hear from me. "Why not come over this afternoon?" she suggested. "I'm going to bake bread. Or if the walk is too much for you, I can pick you up in the car."

I told her I'd walk, that I needed the exercise. Her cheerful voice had done me good, and I began to do some chores around the house. It drained me, though. The baby seemed unusually heavy pressing down against my spine. Finally, around noon, I lay down for a short nap, hoping it would refresh me for my walk to Ginnie's.

I must have fallen more deeply asleep than I'd meant to. The phone's ringing woke me out of a deep sleep. "Desiree," Ginnie's voice said when I groggily picked up the receiver, "I'm so relieved to hear from you! I thought you'd started over to Braddock Park already."

I glanced at the bedside clock. It was nearly one-thirty! "I guess I fell asleep," I apologized. Then I realized what she'd said. "Is something wrong?"

"Look outside."

I glanced out the bedroom window and gasped. Huge flakes of snow were falling thick against the windowpane. As I watched, a gust of wind smashed snow against the side of the house.

"It started about an hour ago," Ginnie said. "Is Len home?"

"No, but the store isn't far from home." Now that I was wide awake, I could hear the sound the wind was making, the heavy gusts making the house shake and rattle.

"Do you need anything?" Ginnie asked. I said I was fine. "Sit tight, then, dear. Take care of yourself, and I hope Len comes home soon."

When I'd hung up, I dialed Len's business number. The phone just rang and rang. He had to be on his way home. I got out of bed and went to the kitchen to heat up some coffee. As I did so, I looked out the window. The world had changed! Everything was white—streets, trees, sidewalks. It was as if I was staring out at a new world. I clicked the radio on, and immediately an announcer's voice came over the air: "Easterly winds gusting up to eighty miles an hour are expected. It hasn't begun to snow in the city yet, but the prediction is that it will begin soon. . . ."

The minutes clicked by. I began to worry about Len. Two o'clock came and went. Three, and still, he didn't come. Where was he? Had he left the store and gone to see someone? Was that why he was taking such a long time to come home?

By four o'clock, the weather forecast was much more ominous: "Snow drifts have turned major highways into miles of wilderness.

101

Traffic is at a complete standstill, and several highways have been closed. Secondary roads have also been closed. Travelers who can do so are advised to seek shelter. The storm has not yet reached its peak. . . ."

I panicked.

Had Len had an accident? As if in answer to my fears, the wind, wailing like a banshee, tore at the roof. I heard the clatter of shingles. "Len!" I whispered. "Oh, Len, where are you?"

The baby inside me moved, and I pressed my arms against my middle. The weight of the baby pressed against my spine, and my back ached. I began to walk around the house to ease the discomfort.

At four-fifteen, the phone rang. Len! I raced to answer it, but it was only Mother Darrell, worried about us. "Len isn't home yet?" she asked. "Oh, dear God, where is he?"

"Everything's fine, Mother Darrell," I assured her. But my hands were shaking when I replaced the receiver.

I no longer wanted Len home with me; I just wanted him to be safe. I watched the kitchen clock as if it were an enemy. Four-twenty . . . four-thirty . . . Suddenly, I heard something above the scream of the wind. I ran to the door and tried to push it open, but it wouldn't give.

I strained and pushed until finally it cracked open a few inches. Snow was piled on the top step that led out of our house! I grabbed a broom and started sweeping the snow away from the step so I could open the door wider. Then I went out into the blizzard. The wind screamed at me, hurling snow against my face, practically tearing the door out of my grasp.

Now I could see Len's pickup truck moving along the street! I was so relieved and happy, I didn't stop to think. I lunged forward, forgetting that the steps were under several inches of snow. I lost my balance and rolled down the stairs. Though the snow cushioned my fall somewhat, pain lanced through me.

The breath was knocked out of me momentarily, but then I struggled to sit up. Suddenly Len was bending over me, pulling me to my feet. "Desiree, are you all right?" Panic showed in his eyes as he tried to brush the snow off me. "Honey, are you okay?"

"I lost my balance," I said. I wanted to tell him how happy I was that he was home, but then he began to yell at me.

"Are you crazy, Desiree, coming out in this weather? Why didn't you stay in the house? If you'd done that, you wouldn't have fallen!"

Still lecturing me, he hauled me to my feet and propelled me into the house. He was turning around in the hallway to scold me some more when suddenly, I gasped. A knifelike pain sliced through me, then changed to a gripping, spreading agony. It was a remembered agony; I'd felt this pain before the night Chelsea was born.

"Oh, God!" I whispered.

His expression changed, his anger turning to fear. "Desiree? It hasn't—started?" he whispered.

"It was just one pain. It's probably nothing. I'm not due for another few weeks."

Ignoring me, he strode over to the phone. "I'm calling Dr. Manfredi," he said. "I don't want to take any chances. I think you should go to the hospital!" He waited, and then I heard him say, "Dr. Manfredi's answering service? Tell him that I'm taking Desiree Darrell to the hospital. Tell him to meet us there." He listened. "Yes, I know about the roads."

I began to tell Len that there was no need to panic, but the pain came again. I gasped, clinging to the back of a chair. Then he supported me. "We're going now," he said.

Quickly, he got me into my coat and then half carried me outside, through the deep snow to the truck. In the few moments we'd been in the house, snow had built up on the pickup's windshield and more snow was falling, blasted along by the wind. As I climbed into the truck, I wondered how we'd get to the hospital in this weather.

"We'll make it," Len assured me, as if he'd read my thoughts. He climbed in next to me and threw the truck into reverse. "We'll go down Barnet Street and pick up Route Twelve. From there, it'll be a quick trip to the hospital."

I couldn't see any road on which to turn. I couldn't see anything! Len rolled down the window to stick his head out.

"This has to be Route Twelve," he muttered. Then: "Damn it, it's the wrong street! I know it is! I'll go back to Barnet and start over." His voice was strange, high pitched. I realized he was close to panicking.

I wanted to reassure him, but I was scared myself. In a few moments, we'd be completely lost.

Then I screamed. Something had been hurled against our rear window with such terrific force that it smashed through the glass. I turned, horrified, and saw an enormous chunk of ice wedged in the broken window.

"The wind threw it!" My voice rose into a scream. "It picked that block of ice up and threw it! Honey, what's going to happen if—"

"Don't think like that!" Len said savagely. "I'm going to get you to the hospital!"

"But what if we can't get through?" I wailed.

"We have to get there." His voice broke off in a rough sob. Wonderingly, I touched his cheek. He was crying—the way he'd cried when Chelsea died.

"I've been so scared, Desiree," he confessed softly. "I was afraid something like this would happen if we tried for another baby. Ma

103

said it might kill you to have this second child. It was so bad for you last time that I never wanted to put your life on the line again. I tried to make you see that, but. . . ."

"Len?" I forgot everything then, the pain, the storm. "If you were so worried, why did you keep avoiding me? You acted like you hated me."

He put his arm around me, pulling me against him. "I knew we'd been drifting apart after Chelsea. I knew you wanted another baby, but I was too scared of losing you to take that chance. I thought that if we started out fresh at Bay Point, things would be better. But then you got pregnant." He shuddered. "I tried to think everything would be okay. But as you got bigger with the baby, I got more and more afraid. I didn't want you to see how afraid I was, so I pretended to have to work . . . to be mad . . . anything rather than let you see how frightened I was. I didn't want you to be frightened, too." He paused. "Hate you? Desiree, you're my life!"

At that moment, I felt something give way inside me; something wet, trickling down my legs. My water had broken! I tried to speak evenly. "Len, how far are we from the hospital?"

"I don't know. This isn't the highway. Can't you hear the sound of the waves?"

In the distance, I could hear a pounding, crashing noise. "We're near the sea, Len. Where are we?"

"It's got to be someplace near Braddock Park," Len said. "I'll head back. I'll try for the highway again."

But I knew there wouldn't be time. Pain was beginning again, bunching, tearing pain. My baby was fighting to be born.

"Braddock Park is where Ginnie and Henry Penn live," I whispered. "And he's a doctor. Maybe—" My words were cut off by the pain, and I could taste my own tears and blood.

"Desiree," he said, "Desiree! Oh, God, what am I going to do?"
Ginnie Penn's story:

The snow started falling around noon. By one o'clock, the wind was howling, flinging the snow against the house. During lulls in the storm, I could hear the surf pounding a few blocks away. I called to Henry to ask if he'd heard the latest weather forecasts, but he wasn't even interested in the storm.

"What time is it, Ginnie?" he demanded. "Is it time for my program yet?"

I looked at him sitting in the living room, and my heart turned inside me like a heavy, hurt thing. It had been a joke in the beginning, his watching the soaps. Dr. Henry Penn, once too busy to even sit down and eat his dinner, now had time to watch soap operas in the afternoon! Instead of laughing, I wanted to cry.

"Ginnie?" His voice wasn't quarrelsome, just tired. "Ginnie, are you there?"

Physically, Henry was better than he'd been for some time. Medication and rest were helping control the Parkinson's tremors that had made him quit surgery several years ago. Mentally? Again, I felt the heaviness in me.

"I'm here, honey." I went up behind him and rested my hands on his stooping shoulders. Once, those shoulders had been broad and strong.

The stooped shoulders were just one symptom of the Parkinson's disease that had been diagnosed several years ago. At the time, Henry had been one of the most respected surgeons in Massachusetts.

I think Henry suspected what was going on before I did, because about the time I became seriously worried, he'd already decided to go into the hospital as a patient for tests. The tests confirmed what he feared—he had Parkinson's Disease.

He took his sentence quietly. "I'll have to leave surgery," he said. "They'd tell me I can go into some other branch of medicine. Pathology, perhaps, or research." His lips twitched into a smile. "We might even be able to take a vacation together, dear."

I wanted so much to cry, but I didn't dare, or Henry's courage, too, would crumble. "That would be nice," I'd said.

We spent a month by the seashore—a beautiful, bittersweet month. We both loved the sea, the stretches of beach, the cries of the gulls. Henry got some work done on a medical book he'd been writing. I puttered around, collecting shells and reading.

When we returned to St. John's Hospital, he appeared much better. Don Nicholas, the chief of pathology, was understanding and tactful. He helped Henry settle into his new work. Everything went well for a year. And then his health began deteriorating, ending in a complete physical breakdown. For a long while, he was very sick.

When he at last recovered, there was no choice for him but to give up medicine completely. "At least for a while," Don had advised. "You're always talking about that month you spent by the ocean. Get a nice home by the sea for Ginnie and yourself. You've spent your life helping people, and now you should live for yourselves."

Henry didn't argue with Don. As for me, I was so grateful he was going to be all right that I didn't think twice about his being forced to retire. Financially, we were well off. Our children were married and living out of state with their own families. These could be the golden years we'd dreamed of when we were young.

It worked, in the beginning. We bought a home in Bay Point, where we had summered so happily. Henry and I began redecorating our large house, and I was delighted when some of our neighbors pitched in to help. Elliot and Wilma Farrington helped us paint and wallpaper, while Kevin McCartney, who lived a couple of blocks down from us, brought over his tools.

Kevin was a retired carpenter, and he'd laugh heartily at the efforts Henry had made to fix things around the house. "Hey, we should stick to what we know how to do, Doc," he'd tease him. "You take out tonsils, and I'll put up shingles, okay?"

Henry just laughed, at first. He seemed to enjoy Elliot's and Kevin's company in the early days. Elliot even convinced him to invest in his big hobby—CB radios. Elliot had a whole CB base in the attic of his home, and he and Henry would talk over their radios like a couple of mischievous kids. Kevin McCartney and his wife, Anne, would come over to play cards, or just talk.

And then, suddenly, Henry's mood changed. He didn't want to talk to anyone, or see anyone—not even me.

"What's the use?" he'd snap at me if I suggested inviting someone over. "We'd just talk about the same old things. Damn it, Ginnie, we're all over the hill out here!"

From then on, it was all downhill. When our neighbors came over, Henry would sit in a chair quietly, not saying a word to them, and they soon stopped coming over. He even stopped talking to people we knew when we met them on the street or in church. We'd always been churchgoers, but now he had to be dragged there every Sunday. "I don't want to go. Why do I have to do things I don't want to do?" he'd demand.

All he wanted to do was sit in front of the television, watching soap operas and letting his life drift away. Not even a blizzard could distract him from that.

Suddenly I remembered that Desiree Darrell planned to come over that day. I frowned at the snow whipping across the yard. Surely she wouldn't have started to walk to in this weather! To reassure myself, I hurried to the kitchen and phoned her, waking her from a nap. She hadn't even known about the storm!

To do something to distract myself, I began baking banana nut bread. As I did so, tears slowly slid down my cheeks. I'd often baked when Henry was a young chief resident at St. John's. He loved the smell of the bread then, and when he came into the small apartment we lived in, he'd put his arms around me and rest his cheek against my hair. "The best perfume in the world," he'd murmur. "Love is the smell of homemade baking."

The phone rang. It was Anne McCartney. "Everything all right at your place, Ginnie?" she asked. "It's awful out here." I told her it looked pretty grim where we were, too. "At least you're not so close to the water," she said, sighing. "The weather forecast says that they're afraid of flooding at high tide. That's around ten tonight, isn't it? I want to leave, but Kevin says I'm crazy." She paused, and when she spoke again, her voice trembled. "I'm scared, Ginnie."

A new blast of wind and snow slammed against our house like a giant fist. "Look," I told her, "we've had all kinds of storms here, and we've weathered each one. Don't worry!"

Yet when I hung up, I knew I was scared, myself. Not just of the storm, but for Henry. The thought I'd been suppressing all day long finally burst into my mind: Henry has changed. He doesn't want to do anything. He doesn't even seem to want to live.

The afternoon had changed to evening by now, and the bread in the oven was giving out a good aroma. Henry didn't notice. He slept in his chair, while a commercial came over the television screen. I can't stand this, I thought.

At that instant, the doorbell rang and then someone pounded on the door. At the same moment, the phone began to ring. Henry woke up and rose shakily from his chair, looking at the door, then at the phone, and finally at me. "What?" he began feebly.

"You get the phone, okay? I'll go to the door," I told him.

I hurried to the door and looked out the peephole. I could see nothing, and the loud knocks came again. Henry was talking into the phone.

"It's Elliot," he said haltingly. "Some guy has been knocking on his door, asking for me. He wanted to know if something was wrong. . . ."

Just then, I heard this voice shouting outside: "Dr. Penn! Dr. Penn! Let us in! It's Len Darrell! My wife's having a baby and she needs help badly!"

Desiree! I yanked the door open and tried to budge the stuck storm door. Then I realized that foot-high accumulations of snow were blocking the door. Len Darrell, his hair plastered down with snow, was staring at me. He grabbed my arm. "Mrs. Penn, Desiree—"

Henry joined me at the door. "What's going on?" he demanded querulously. "What's happening?"

Len turned to him. "Dr. Penn, please! I was taking my wife to the hospital . . . her water broke . . . we got lost! Can I bring her here? Can you help her?"

"Bring her in quickly!" I cried.

Len ran back toward the truck that was parked where our driveway was supposed to be. He sank thigh-deep into the snow, but struggled on. As he pulled open the truck door, a dark shape sank into his arms. A blast of wind sent snow against my face. The snowflakes seemed like bits of stinging glass. Henry plucked at my sleeve.

"Why is he bringing her here, Ginnie?"

I explained, "You remember the girl we drive to church—Desiree Darrell? She's having a baby. They couldn't make it to the hospital."

"But he can't bring her here! I remember she told you she had a bad time with her first pregnancy." He turned and headed for the telephone. "I'm calling the hospital in Verselles," he mumbled.

But there was no help there. The hospital told Henry that all available ambulances were out. Several of them were stuck in drifts. As he was hanging up the phone, we both heard a long, suppressed moan of pain. Desiree Darrell, her face the color of ashes, leaned in Len's arms. "Upstairs!" I ordered. "On our bed! The doctor will examine her and see what he can do."

Henry didn't move. He stared as Desiree was helped up the stairs. "Henry!" I whispered.

He shook his head slowly. "I can examine her, but that's all," he told me.

Slowly, he went up the stairs after Len and Desiree. I hurried to the kitchen and made some coffee to relax Len. As I was at the stove, the lights flickered and went out.

Desiree's moan, coming at that moment of blackness, made goosepimples crawl over my skin. I heard footsteps. "Mrs. Penn?" Len Darrell was shouting. "The doctor needs a flashlight and candles!"

"All right. I have some candles in the kitchen, and a flashlight, too." I found the flashlight first, then a candle, which I lit and stuck onto a saucer. As I hurried up the stairs with them, I nearly collided with Len. "What does the doctor say?" I asked him.

"He hasn't said anything." There was another groan of pain, and Len's face was ghastly in the candlelight. "Oh, dear God," he moaned, "I knew this was going to happen. I'm going to lose her!"

"You stop that!" I tried to calm him down. "It sounds worse than it is. Now you take the flashlight and go downstairs. There are more candles in the living room—go find them."

He nodded and hurried downstairs. I went on up toward our bedroom and met Henry, who was waiting by the door.

"How is she?" I whispered.

"Not good. The baby's breech."

Oh, no! I thought. A narrow pelvis, and a breech delivery!

"You have to help her!" I whispered.

"How? I can't do a Cesarean here, and you know it! Ginnie, she's got to go someplace else. I can't help her!"

I felt cold all over. "Henry, she can't go anywhere else! You're a doctor. Okay, you can't operate. But can't you do something to help?"

He took the candle, turned away from me, and went back into our bedroom.

Len came hurrying up the stairs with the flashlight and two more candles. "Has something happened to Desiree?" he asked.

"The doctor's with her." I spoke much more confidently than I felt. Then I thought of something. "Mr. Farrington next door has a CB base. Maybe he can get some help for Desiree."

Giving me a panicked look, he rushed down the stairs. I heard the wind roar as he opened the door and slammed it shut. Then I went to the bedroom and went inside.

Desiree was lying on our bed, her face ghost-pale. Her hands were clenched by her sides. "Stay with her, Ginnie," Henry ordered. "I have to get my instruments." He gave Desiree what he thought was a smile, but which was really a ghastly twitching of his lips. She grabbed my hand.

"Is it so bad?" she gasped.

I smoothed her hand gently. "Oh, now, doctors always use that deep, serious voice. It makes them feel important."

That made her smile, but she was convulsed with pain immediately afterward. She clung to my hand so hard that it was almost black and blue later, but at the time, I was too caught up in worry over her to feel anything. Downstairs, I could hear Henry talking to someone on the phone.

"Where's Len?" Desiree asked. "Couldn't he stand watching me?" I explained where Len was, and she closed her eyes. "Am I going to die, Ginnie?"

"Of course not!" Before I could say another word, a series of strong gusts rattled the house. Desiree screamed weakly as something smashed against the bedroom window. Splinters of glass flew over the bed, and a huge, heavy object bounced across the floor.

"Desiree!" Len shouted as he came hurtling through the bedroom door. "I heard you scream!" He stopped, staring at the shattered glass.

"It's nothing," I said. "The wind just blew this chunk of ice through the window." The ice was at least two feet wide and a foot high. Gusts of wind screamed into the room through the broken window, so I tried stuffing bath towels into the opening.

"Do you have an old shutter?" Len said. "Plywood? I can fix that."

"In the basement. I'll show you!"

But Desiree reached for my hand. "Please, Ginnie, don't go!"

Len hurried down the stairs.

In a few moments, Henry came into the room. "I've just spoken with Dr. Manfredi," he told Desiree. "He and I discussed your case, so I can help you." His voice seemed stronger, but he looked pale. "He doesn't think you'll have any problems. At last measuring, your baby was small, so it should be born easily."

Desiree smiled and closed her eyes. Henry drew me aside.

"It's not good," he whispered. "Manfredi only confirmed my fears. It's going to be hell for her. When the time comes, I'll have to get that baby out quickly, before its oxygen supply is cut off. Ginnie, I'll need all my instruments sterilized."

I nodded. "I've started a fire downstairs in the fireplace and get the cast-iron pot in it."

He turned back to Desiree. It seemed that his stooped shoulders straightened a little as he went over in his mind the once-familiar procedure of delivering a baby. Downstairs, I heard the door slam open, then Wilma Farrington's voice. Len answered, "I'll go—as soon as I fix this window," he said.

"Go where?" I asked as he passed me on the stairs, lugging a sheet of plywood.

Wilma replied, "Elliot's been listening to the CB base all evening. When we heard about Desiree, he started trying to raise some help. They're going to try and send someone. They're rescuing people along the coast in trucks and boats."

"In what?"

Wilma tried to smile, but her eyes were frightened. "The Coast Guard is afraid we're going to get flooded in this area. Waves are breaking over the seawall and the tide's coming in."

I glanced at the clock in the living room. It was nine-thirty, half an hour to high tide. "We're three blocks from the ocean!" I protested.

"Maybe so. But have you listened to the ocean, Ginnie?"

I shook my head. I'd been too involved with Desiree. I placed the pot of hot water on the fire, positioning it, and as I bent down, the wind dropped for a second. I heard a bursting, angry, bellowing sound. I looked at Wilma.

"Now you've heard it," she whispered.

"My God—the McCartneys!" I gasped. "They're right on the ocean! What else did Elliot learn on the CB?"

"They're calling for volunteers to help evacuate people who live near the water. Elliot wanted to go. Thank God, he's too old! I came to ask Len if he wants to go. He's doing no good here, and people like Anne and Kevin McCartney need him."

Len came down the stairs. "The window's boarded up," he told me. "I'm going next door. If the coast guard needs me, I'll go." He drew a shuddering breath. "Dr. Penn said it was better for me to get out and do something."

"Go ahead," I said. "We'll take care of Desiree."

Wilma said she'd stay with me. "The walk over here was bad— snow and wind and that God-awful sound of the waves," she said. "I'll stay here and watch the water if you want to help Henry."

So I went upstairs and sat beside Desiree, washing her face as the contractions came and went. Henry said that she was dilating well, and encouraged her to push. He told her she needed all her strength and will to push.

Time seemed to freeze. Wrapped in a cocoon of arrested pain, Desiree's body tried and tried to force the baby out. Her hoarse groans of pain drove out the sounds of the storm. However, maybe because I was now listening for it, I could hear the booming of the waves smashing against the seawall. Henry didn't pay any attention to the storm. His attention was all on Desiree, and he kept encouraging her.

"It's looking good . . . you're really dilating beautifully . . . you'll soon be ready to have this baby. . . ."

But in spite of his words, I knew it wasn't going well. Desiree was tired from pushing and from the pain. She'd been in hard labor for hours! "I'm beginning to see the baby now," Henry said, but his eyes didn't match his encouraging voice.

"Ginnie?" Wilma called from the doorway. "I was listening to the radio—I got a local station. The waves are coming over the seawall!"

"But is the wall holding?"

"You don't understand. The waves are coming right over the wall! Huge waves. Rescue teams are trying to get everyone out."

Desiree had overheard. "You've got to get out of here, Ginnie," she whispered. "You and the doctor. Nobody can help me. . . ." I hurried to her, encouraging her, lifting her so she could push with the contraction. She was too tired to do more than push weakly.

"Desiree, you've got to keep pushing!" Henry commanded.

I turned back to Wilma, and our eyes met. The McCartneys! we were both thinking. What had happened to them? Wilma came on the other side of Desiree and steadied her.

Smash! The whole house rocked violently with the impact. Wilma screamed, and even Henry was startled. "What in God's name?" he began.

I ran into the hall and looked out of the window. A car had been hurled against our garage, but it wasn't the wind that had thrown it there. Water was running down the street, lapping at the steps of our house. It was flowing rapidly, powerfully! As I stared, the water tossed another car end-over-end into a house farther on down the street. Then it retreated, and as it did so, I saw a dark figure splash into the water and struggle across to us.

"My God!" Wilma screamed. "Elliot!"

Elliot made it to our door, wading waist-deep in water. "Tide's coming in," he gasped as Ginnie and I pulled off his wet clothes and bundled him in blankets. "I heard it on the CB. Whole houses are floating in Verselles. It's not as bad here yet."

"Not bad!" Wilma cried, but he stopped her.

"Honey, it's going to get worse. It's not high tide yet, and the waves are boiling over the top of the seawall." He looked at us, trying to grin. "Didn't want to be alone if—something happened," he said to Wilma.

She put her arms around him and began to cry. Upstairs, Desiree was crying, too—hysterical sobs. I hurried wearily up the stairs, listening for the crashing sound of the next wave. I stopped by the window in the hall to look out—and wished I hadn't.

The sea was like a wild animal. Water didn't run past—it surged, it crushed! I saw a roof float past, and then an enormous wave carried away part of the Farringtons' front porch.

"Ginnie!" Henry shouted. As I hurried into the bedroom, our house shuddered from the sea's battering.

"The Farringtons are downstairs," I whispered to Henry. "The waves are coming over the seawall!"

"When the Coast Guard gets here, you go, Ginnie," Henry ordered. "This house may stand—and then again, it may not. I don't want to take a chance of you being hurt."

"What about you?"

Instead of answering, he took my hand. "She's giving up, Ginnie. She's got it into her head that she's going to die. She's calling for Len. Where is he?" I explained, and he nodded. "It's just as well. He'd go to pieces seeing her like this, and that would finish her."

Desiree's eyes were closed and sunken. Her cheeks were gray. Henry shook her shoulder. "Desiree, do you feel a contraction coming? The baby can't be born without your help!"

She mumbled something, but her body tried desperately to push. At the same time, I heard a sound I hope to God I'll never hear again. A cracking, smashing sound, and then a roar that seemed to fill the whole world. Footsteps hurried up the stairs as the Farringtons ran up ahead of the flood that filled our living room. When I ran into the hall and looked down, I saw a swirl of rolling, icy, black water.

Wilma was crying and clinging to Elliot. "We're going to die," she whispered.

Henry called me back to Desiree's side. "We've got to help her push," he said urgently. "You do this, Ginnie. . . ."

I did as he told me, and she began to moan and push, and I helped her. Henry bent over her. "I see more of the baby, Desiree!" he said. "I'm going to give you something to deaden the pain, and then I'm going to cut a little, so that the baby will have an easy time coming out. All right?" He looked at me with eyes that said: Help me!

I would have given my soul to help him, but I had an awful fear that nothing anyone could do would help Desiree—that she was beyond human help. She just lay there, eyes closed. Then she said,

"Len . . . Len is dead, too? He's out in the storm and he's dead. He never came home from work. I'm dying, and I'll go with him. . . ."

She was delirious with pain. In the hospital, they could have helped her. Here. . . .

My eyes met Henry's. He looked frustrated and helpless.

Smash! The sea hit us again. From the hall, Wilma called, "Houses are floating by like—like a kid's bathtub toys!" The waves receded, smashing against us again.

Henry shook his head. I was afraid—so afraid. As if reading my mind, he said, "Ginnie, I'm scared, too. None of us might survive this. But I have to believe I can help Desiree have her baby. And you have to believe that, too."

Somehow, across all the years we'd shared, I'd never loved him as much, or been so proud of him. Without a weapon in his hand, he was going to fight for Desiree's life. "I do believe it," I said—and, as I spoke, some of the fear went away from me.

Then Elliot shouted, "Here they come!" Above the roaring of the storm, I could hear another sound—the sound of human voices. "They're coming to get us!" Elliot shrieked, beside himself with relief.

Wilma ran to the bedroom and looked in. "How is she? Did she have the baby?" I shook my head. "Well, you can't wait for her to have her baby! We have to leave right now! Can't we just—take her with us?"

Henry shook his head.

"You may be trapped here!" Wilma cried.

"You go," I said. "Desiree can't be moved, and so Henry will have to stay. He's a doctor."

Out in the hall, Elliot yelled, "They're sending a boat out to get us to the amphibious duck. We'll have to wade through all that water downstairs to get to them, so we'd better hurry."

"Go with them, Ginnie," Henry urged.

I just smiled at him. Henry, I thought, I just found you. Do you think I'm going to leave without you? Do you really think that life without you would mean anything to me?

I turned back to Desiree, helping her push, willing her to fight harder for her baby and for herself. "Okay," Henry said sharply. "I see the baby's behind now." He reached and withdrew a small gray leg. Then another. . . .

"Desiree!" It was Len's voice. I hadn't heard him coming up the stairs in all the noise. "Desiree—what's wrong with her?"

Henry didn't look at him. "Push—push with everything you've got!" he ordered. But Desiree just lay there. She'd given up. She'd had enough fear and pain, and she was beaten.

113

Len got down on his knees beside the bed, pushing me out of the way. He didn't touch her, but he put his lips close to her ear. "Desiree," he said, "Sweetheart, push for me!" She didn't stir. "Honey, you're doing fine. You're having our baby. . . ."

Her body contracted weakly, and she pushed—but it wasn't hard enough. I saw the perspiration on Henry's forehead as he picked up the forceps.

"Push!" he shouted at Desiree.

She paid no attention. "Len," she whispered, "you were right. I'm going to die."

"No!" Len cried. "Desiree, you're going to live. Our baby's going to live. Work with the doctor. Please help him bring our baby."

I closed my eyes, and heard Henry's labored breathing.

"Desiree, I've been out there helping to rescue people who were stranded," Len went on. "Down by the seawall, we saved two people who were literally up to their necks in water. They were clinging to their roof. The wife was exhausted, but the husband kept hanging on to her, keeping her from going under." He drew a deep breath. "What I'm trying to say is, that I'm here to hold on to you now, honey! I'm here to lend you my strength and my—my heart and life and everything else."

"That's it!" Henry said. "Now push again. Push! Hard!"

"I copped out on you, Desiree," Len was saying. "I was so afraid of losing you. Now I know that was stupid. How could I lose you? You're my soul. A man can't lose his soul." He was practically shouting in her ear.

And then Henry pulled back and held Desiree's baby in his hand. Deftly, he cut the cord, and a hoarse, little cry filled the room.

"Desiree and Len, you have a son," Henry said. "A fine, healthy son!"

"Doctor! Anyone up there? We can't wait!" a voice yelled from below. "You got to come now!"

I wrapped the baby in one of the blankets Wilma had brought and put him in Desiree's arms. "Wrap them both up warm," Henry ordered. "They have to be warm on our way out of here."

I don't remember much of how we left the house. It was a nightmare—all of it. The blizzard, with its wind and snow and churning, icy water, was a nightmare. Our journey in a small boat that ferried us over to a larger amphibious rescue craft was a nightmare. How we made it, I don't know. But I wasn't afraid. We'd gone through too much that night to be afraid.

During the rescue operation, Desiree snuggled her baby, her face white but peaceful, and so happy. Her husband stayed with her and the baby, whispering to her as if they were the only two people in the world.

Henry supervised getting Desiree onto the rescue craft, making sure that the dressings he'd quickly used on her were holding. Then he left with Len and came over to sit beside me. "We did it, Ginnie," he said. "Son of a gun."

"You mean you did it!" I put my head on his shoulder, and the tears ran down my cheeks and chin. "I love you," I whispered.

"I love you, too." His voice had a wide-awake wonder to it.

"Say, Doctor." One of our rescuers was bending close. "We'll take you folks to the Episcopal church in town. We're using it as an emergency hospital. There are medical supplies there, and we've rounded up one intern and one nurse. They'll sure be glad to have you!"

Len's voice cut in, fervent with gratitude. "They'll be getting the best doctor in the world! The way you took care of Desiree in the middle of all this hell—it was a miracle, Doc. A miracle."

Birth is a miracle, I thought.

Carry it one step further, and say that the rebirth of love and trust, such as I'd seen in Len's and Desiree's eyes, is a miracle, too.

But these had been a third miracle this night, for which I would spend the rest of my life thanking God. Looking into Henry's strong, confident face, I knew that the third miracle had been the greatest one of all. . . .

THE END

HER EYES BEGGED
FOR HELP

I first saw the old woman when I walked by the park on my way home from work. She was sitting on a bench, trying to pull a threadbare sweater around her shoulders. It was too small to reach around her. Wisps of gray hair straggled out from under a dirty old hat; a pair of army boots were on her feet. She was desperately clutching an old bag, the very weight of which seemed to pull her toward the edge of the bench.

A group of teenagers came by. "Hey, look at the old wino!" one boy jeered.

"Aw, she's just an ordinary hag," another said.

Squish! One of them threw an overripe tomato at her. It just missed her face and squashed on the bench, red rivulets of juice running down her leg. Without thinking, I ran toward the old lady to help her. When the boys saw me coming to her aid, they ran away, cursing and throwing insults at both of us as they left.

I turned to help the old lady, only to find her glaring at me.

"Here," I soothed, thinking she was upset. "Let me help you." I put my hand out to take her heavy bag.

She pushed me away so roughly that I staggered and almost fell.

"Why did you push me?" I asked, surprised.

The old lady muttered several guttural words, but I couldn't make out what they were. The nasty tone of her voice, however, made it plain that she was rejecting my help.

"Okay." I walked stiffly away, angry. Curiously, I was also dissatisfied with myself for walking away so easily. What had she been trying to say?

I watched her out of the corner of my eyes as she slowly dragged herself to the alley in back of a small restaurant. She was going through the garbage can! Horrified, I watched as she selected various items from the can, wrapped them in an old napkin, then carefully stuffed the napkin in her bag.

Oh, no! It looked as if she was going to take that garbage with her to eat! Just then she looked up and saw me staring at her. She shook a fist at me.

I turned away. The nerve of her! I went home and put her out of my mind.

Several weeks went by before I saw her again. It was a cold, rainy day and the chill seemed to seep into my very bones. As I turned the corner, I saw a stooped figure huddled in the doorway of a florist's shop. As I got closer, I saw it was the same old woman that had been in the park. She half-sat, half-lay on the doorstep as if she were too tired to go any farther. She carried the same dilapidated bag, clutching it in a death-grip. I walked slowly by, thinking she was either asleep or unconscious. She wasn't. One beady eye was open and gave me a hateful glare. I hurried on by.

So much for thinking of being a Good Samaritan! Forget her, I told myself.

The next day when I went by, I noticed that the florist's shop was closed but that the old lady was still lying in the doorway. I walked quickly by and averted my eyes so I wouldn't catch another hateful look. Well, at least it wasn't raining. She should be more comfortable than yesterday.

When I left work that evening, I caught a ride with one of my coworkers and didn't pass the little shop or see the old lady.

Why did she come into my mind, then, during the night? Several times, I caught myself thinking about how pale and sick she had looked, lying in the doorway. In spite of the hateful glare she had given me, I somehow sensed a plea for help behind her crusty exterior.

But maybe not. Maybe she was a genuine bum who drank all the time and lived on the streets.

Thoughts of the old lady lying in the cold doorway disturbed my sleep. It must have been very cold for her during the night, and she seemed to have had nothing but that threadbare sweater to cover herself with.

I awoke with a headache in the morning and called myself a fool. Why was I losing sleep over an old lady I didn't even know and certainly didn't care to know? I turned on the TV for the morning news and half-listened while I ate breakfast. Suddenly some words caught my attention:

" . . . and anyone who knows the identity of this woman should call Memorial Hospital. She was found unconscious last night in front of Rick's Flower Shop. Police who found her say she may have been lying there for several days. They are looking for any relatives she might have. Her condition is poor."

My attention was riveted to the screen as the news showed a police ambulance attendant picking up an old woman from the street.

Yes! It was the same old lady I had seen in the park and in the doorway. How sad! Oh, well. I guess now the police will track down her relatives and see that she is taken care of.

I had too much to do without worrying abound an old woman I didn't even know.

My weekend errands included the bank, the dry cleaner,

Autumn's Boutique, and the grocery store. And, if I had time, a stop at St. Michael's rectory to arrange for a Mass.

I staggered home around four o'clock—exhausted—my arms loaded with groceries. I sank into a chair and eased my shoes off of my aching feet. I decided to relax for half an hour while I watched the five o'clock news.

I almost dozed during the news. My eyes flew open when I heard the newscaster mention a "bag lady" that the police had found in a doorway the night before. The reporter pleaded for any relatives or friends who might know who she was to call police headquarters. She was unable to tell the police anything herself.

I leaned forward to catch every word but then the TV camera switched to a fire.

I turned the set off. What was it to me if that old lady had any relatives? Someone was sure to turn up eventually and claim her.

I put a chicken potpie in the oven. That and a salad would be my dinner. While the pie was baking, I put all the groceries away.

I lived alone, and while it was lonely occasionally, it did have a few advantages. Fast cooking was one of them. My meals-for-one were usually tasty and nutritious, but definitely not fancy.

I guess that being single at the age of thirty-one did qualify me as a spinster. I still had hopes of marriage someday, but I knew that my chances were getting slim.

My job certainly didn't help my marriage prospects at all. I worked in an all-female environment as an assistant librarian. The work was interesting and the pay was good, and so I stayed. On the few occasions when I felt boredom creeping in, I firmly repeated the job's advantages over and over to myself.

I put my potpie and salad on a tray and watched a favorite mystery program while I ate. But I couldn't seem to get interested in the show. I just couldn't get that old lady out of my mind!

Why should I get involved? I kept asking myself. But I knew I wouldn't rest until I either called the hospital to inquire about her, or went there in person.

I decided to go to the hospital. As I dressed, I told myself I sure was a fool to get involved. I'll probably get another rejection for my trouble, I thought.

The elderly woman at the hospital admissions office was very courteous. I explained why I was there, and she looked at her records.

"Oh, I believe you mean the 'bag lady' we admitted yesterday. Her condition is fair."

"Why is she called a 'bag lady?'" I asked, puzzled.

"Unfortunately, she is one of many elderly women who have no home. They wander the streets carrying everything they own in a bag.

We get lots of them here, and often when it's too late to do anything for them."

"It's hard to believe that this can happen in a civilized society," I gasped.

"Yes, but it is difficult to help them. Some of the women really have no choice. Others actually like living on the streets and don't want to be helped."

"Do you think I could visit the woman who was brought in yesterday?"

"You'll have to have permission. If you'll wait over there, I'll call the supervisor."

I walked over to the waiting area and picked up a magazine, but I couldn't concentrate on the words. My thoughts were filled with questions concerning the plight of these elderly women. Why wasn't something done to help them?

A trim, attractive woman approached me.

"Hello, I'm Miss Givner, Floor Supervisor. Your name?"

"Miss Meadows."

"I understand you want to visit the woman who was brought in yesterday?"

"Yes."

"Are you a relative?"

"No . . . I'm not even a neighbor. I saw her on the street several times, and I worried what would happen to her."

"You have good reason to worry."

Miss Givner took a deep breath. "She seems to be extremely hostile—perhaps because we can't understand her. She seems to be speaking Slovak—maybe Russian." She looked at me eagerly. "Do you speak Russian, by any chance?"

"No, I don't." She was so sympathetic that I was sorry to disappoint her.

"Say, wait a minute!" I said. "I just remembered. My sister-in-law has an aunt who is fluent in Russian. I could call her and ask her to come over here. Maybe she could understand the woman."

"That's a wonderful idea. Would you call her?"

"Sure." The clerk offered me the phone at her desk and I quickly looked up the number. I dialed and waited impatiently for Aunt Ruby to answer.

"Aunt Ruby?"

"Yes. Who is this?"

"This is Joyce Meadows. Do yet remember me? Your niece is married to my brother?"

"Of course I remember you, child."

"Aunt Ruby, you do speak Russian, don't you?"

"Yes. I was born and raised in Russia until my family emigrated. Of course, that was more than forty years ago. Now I speak only English. Why?" Her voice became terribly agitated. "I'm not in trouble with the government, am I?" Aunt Ruby was getting very upset.

"No, no, Aunt Ruby. This has nothing to do with the government. There's an elderly woman who is a patient in the hospital here. She speaks only Russian. I mean, we think she speaks only Russian. Could you come over to the hospital and listen to her? Perhaps you can find out what she's trying to say."

"In the hospital, you say? Poor soul. Of course, I'll come. Tell me which hospital it is and how I can get there."

I gave detailed instructions to Aunt Ruby on how to get to the hospital.

"Did she say she would come?" Miss Givner asked hopefully as I hung up the phone.

"She should be here in about forty-five minutes. It will take her that long to dress and get the bus."

"Let's hope this will be a lucky break for our patient." Miss Givner smiled at me. "I have to go back to the third floor now. As soon as your friend arrives, have the clerk call me. We'll go to see the patient together."

True to her word, Aunt Ruby arrived in less than an hour. I greeted her with an affectionate hug.

"It was nice of you to drop everything and come over here," I told her.

"Well, someday I'll be old, too, and maybe need the help."

"Never. You'll never be old."

"You're soft-soaping me!" But Aunt Ruby smiled—she was pleased.

I asked the desk clerk to call Miss Givner, and within minutes, she appeared. After introductions were completed, the three of us went to the third floor and into Room 327.

The old lady had her eyes closed and she looked very sick. Aunt Ruby walked close to the bed and spoke softly to her.

A change of facial expression told us that the old lady understood the words. Her eyes were still tightly closed, but she stirred and mumbled something. Aunt Ruby took her hands and held them between her own.

Suddenly the old lady's eyes flew open and she gave Aunt Ruby a soulful look. A torrent of words burst from her mouth and she gripped Aunt Ruby's hands so hard that Aunt Ruby winced.

"What's she saying?" Miss Givner asked eagerly.

Aunt Ruby ignored the question for a moment as she spoke

gently to the old lady, then listened closely as the woman spoke. The old lady burst into tears.

"What's wrong?" I asked as I hurried close to the bed.

"There's nothing wrong," Aunt Ruby answered. "They are happy tears."

"Did you find out who she is?" Miss Givner questioned rather anxiously.

"Her name is Irena Valon. She understands most of what I say. She's crying because she finally has someone who can understand her."

"Can you ask her if she has any relatives we can notify?" Miss Givner was determined to get her information.

"She says she was living all alone and the landlord evicted her," Aunt Ruby relayed. "She keeps calling for 'Terry.' I'll ask her who that is."

Aunt Ruby held the old lady's hand and talked to her for a long time. She didn't get much conversation back, but Mrs. Valon shook her head several times.

Finally Miss Givner suggested that we were tiring Mrs. Valon, and had better leave.

Mrs. Valon held Aunt Ruby's hand tightly. It was obvious she didn't want her to leave. Aunt Ruby spoke a few quick words and leaned over to kiss her gently on her cheek. My own eyes felt moist as I saw the tears pour down Mrs. Valon's face.

The three of us left the room and went down the hall. Aunt Ruby wiped a tear from her eye.

"It's sad," she said finally. "The landlord evicted her and she has been living on the streets since then. No one would rent to her because she had a dog. She refused to get rid of him. But the dog ran away from her and she hasn't been able to find him. That's why she walks up and down the streets. She's looking for her Terry."

"Then Terry is her dog!" I exclaimed.

"Yes."

"How long has it been since the dog ran away?" I asked.

"I don't know yet. She's heartbroken. Seems the dog is the only family she has. She came here to live with her son, and he was killed in an accident. She couldn't speak English and no one understood her so she lived like a hermit. Irena was afraid to approach anyone. Because she lived behind the iron curtain, she was deathly afraid of the police or any authority. The dog means everything to her."

"If she lost her dog in the last few weeks," I suggested, "maybe it will be at the pound."

"Yes, I think you may have a good idea," Aunt Ruby agreed.

"It's worth a try, isn't it?" I put my question to Miss Givner.

"Perhaps." She seemed a little reluctant.

I turned to Aunt Ruby. "It's the only lead we have right now. Ask her to describe the dog right down to the tiniest detail. And, more important, ask her why the dog ran away."

"Good. I will."

We all went back to Mrs. Valon's room while Aunt Ruby asked her the questions. The old lady talked very excitedly, words pouring out of her mouth in a torrent. Finally, she sank back against her pillow, exhausted.

"What happened to her dog, Aunt Ruby?" I asked, bursting with curiosity.

Aunt Ruby eagerly translated, relishing the spotlight.

"She was in the park, her dog on his leash, when suddenly another dog came running down the path toward them. Terry gave one strong lunge at the other dog, a female, and his leash gave way. Both dogs streaked out of the park in a flash. Unfortunately, there was a concert going on at the other end of the park that day, and there were police all around. Mrs. Valon was paralyzed with fear. She thought that if she asked for help, the police would put her in jail.

"She ran from the park and hid in an alley until the next morning. Then she started her search for Terry. She has been walking up and down the streets all day every day since then. It's been about three weeks. She's completely exhausted."

Mrs. Valon looked bad. Her breathing became heavy and erratic.

"We must let her rest now," Miss Givner said decisively. She patted Mrs. Valon's hand. "Now, don't worry. These two ladies will find Terry for you."

The old woman's tears overflowed again.

We left. Miss Givner went back to her nursing duties, and Aunt Ruby and I caught the bus to the pound.

They didn't have her dog. We described him: a black Labrador retriever type, gentle, one white spot on his left front paw, and one white spot on his neck. He was wearing a red collar. The attendant was very patient while we explained all the circumstances, but he didn't have any dog that even came close to fitting our description.

"Sorry I can't help you, ladies," he said. "Only thing I can think of is to suggest you put an ad in the paper."

"Why didn't we think of that ourselves? We'll do it," Aunt Ruby said.

"Sorry if we caused you any trouble," I apologized. We had taken a great deal of his time.

"No trouble at all," he replied.

"Here are our names and phone numbers," I offered. "Please call us if a dog that looks like Terry is brought in. If you call my number and there's no answer, please call this other lady's. I work till five."

The man wrote the information down in his book and we left. We were terribly disappointed.

"It was only a long shot, Aunt Ruby," I said. "We couldn't expect to just walk in and find her dog."

"I suppose. Just the same, though, it's discouraging. What will we tell her tomorrow?"

"We'll tell her that we hope to find Terry soon."

I paused. "Gee, I just happened to think . . . if we do find her dog, what will we do with him? We can't take him to the hospital, and she doesn't have a home."

"We'll cross that bridge when we come to it. The first thing is to find the dog. We'll go down to the newspaper now and put the ad in, okay? We might get a call tomorrow."

"Okay." Then I clapped my hand against my forehead. "Oh, no. Tomorrow is Sunday, Aunt Ruby. We can't get any answer until Monday night at the earliest."

We placed the ad, and Aunt Ruby and I parted at the bus stop. I promised to call her if I had any news about either the dog or Mrs. Valon.

I felt a surge of real affection for Aunt Ruby. Even though she wasn't a blood relative, she kindly included me in her large number of nieces and nephews out of the goodness of her big heart. Impulsively, I leaned over and kissed her cheek before she left on the bus. She shrugged, but I knew she was pleased.

I ate dinner in front of the TV again and went to bed early. It had been a long, tiring day. I got up early for Mass and went right to the hospital from church to visit the old lady.

Mrs. Valon looked old and feeble, but she managed a weak smile for me and eagerly grasped my hand. The smile wasn't really for me. I knew she wanted to know if I had any news to give her about her dog.

I spoke a few words to her very slowly and pantomimed our search for her dog. I didn't know if she understood me or not and I couldn't understand what she said.

She grabbed my hand and kissed it. I was embarrassed, but afraid to hurt her feelings by jerking my hand away. I left. She still didn't have her strength back and she needed lots of rest.

I called Aunt Ruby to tell her how Mrs. Valon had kissed my hand.

"I just can't believe she's the same nasty woman who glared at me in the park," I said. "Why did she hate me then?"

"Oh, child," Aunt Ruby explained, "she didn't hate you at all." She paused. "Fear! That's what it was. She was afraid of you."

"Afraid of me? Why, that's ridiculous. I only wanted to help her."

"Ridiculous to you, but not to her. She thought you wanted to have her locked up. She's afraid of any authority." Then Aunt Ruby asked me if I'd had any response to our ad for Terry.

"Aunt Ruby, we can't possibly get an answer until tomorrow night," I reminded her. "The paper isn't printed until afternoon."

"I keep forgetting. Well, call me tomorrow and we'll go to the hospital together."

"No, Aunt Ruby. You'll have to go alone. Mrs. Valon understands you and would enjoy seeing you more than me. I'll stay home in case anyone calls."

"Okay. I'll call you after my visit."

"Thanks, Aunt Ruby. Good night."

The next day I hurried home after work and waited impatiently. No one called. A week went by, and still, no call. Aunt Ruby visited Irena every night. Time was going by, and soon she would be well enough to leave the hospital.

On Friday, Aunt Ruby stopped at my apartment.

"Lord, child, I don't know what we're going to do," she said. "The doctor says Mrs. Valon can leave the hospital next Tuesday if she has someone who will take care of her."

"Maybe we can find a nursing home near here," I suggested.

"But she'd be alone with no one who understands her," Aunt Ruby said sadly.

"Why don't you take her to your house?" I asked this jokingly, but stared when I saw the serious look on Aunt Ruby's face.

"That's just what I intend to do," she stated firmly.

"Oh, no," I breathed, shocked. "I know it would be wonderful for Mrs. Valon, but what about you? You'd have to take care of her, cook for her, be responsible for her. That's too much for you to take on."

"At my age, you mean," Aunt Ruby snapped, ready for an argument.

"No, I didn't mean it had anything to do with your age," I mumbled.

"Yes, you did, and rightly so. But since my Irving died, I've rattled around in that big, old house all alone and lonely. So, we'll be company for each other. She told me she gets a small Social Security check. We both think she will get the most for her money by paying room and board to me instead of giving it all to an old folk's home." Aunt Ruby spoke almost belligerently, preparing for an argument from me.

"You've been planning this behind my back all along, haven't you?" I said.

"Yes." She laughed, delighted. "I feel I'm getting the best of the bargain. The money Mrs. Valon pays me will help to pay for a few extra bingo nights."

I hugged her. "You're a doll, Aunt Ruby—just a doll."

Aunt Ruby became serious. "There's only one problem," she said.

I looked at her questioningly.

"Terry. We still haven't found Terry for her."

"Do you want to call the newspaper and renew the ad?"

"I don't think we will get an answer now."

"It won't hurt to keep the ad going one more week," I suggested, wanting to cheer her up. "I'll pay for it."

"You're a good girl, Joyce," Aunt Ruby said, patting my shoulder.

"And there's something else we can try," I said. "I'll call the radio station and see if I can maybe persuade them to tell about Terry on their local news program."

Aunt Ruby hugged me again. "You are a good girl."

The radio station cooperated, but we didn't get any response from that appeal, either. The newspaper ad continued with no results. I began to feel that we'd never find the dog. He's probably been hit by a car, I thought.

Monday came and it was time to make final plans to take Mrs. Valon home to Aunt Ruby's.

"Wait for me at the hospital tomorrow, Aunt Ruby," I said. "I'll hurry over right from work and we'll share a cab to your house. After you and Mrs. Valon are settled, I can take a bus home."

"After you have dinner with us," Aunt Ruby insisted.

"All right." I gave in easily, knowing what a good cook she was. "I'll have dinner with you, then I'll go home."

Our plans went like clockwork. The next day Aunt Ruby and Mrs. Valon were ready to leave as soon as I got to the hospital. Mrs. Valon looked very pale sitting in the wheelchair, a nurse ready to take her downstairs. She bade a tearful farewell to all her nurses and to Miss Givner at the downstairs door.

Our cab pulled up and we made it to Aunt Ruby's house in less than twenty minutes.

"I hope you like your new home, Irena," Aunt Ruby said.

Mrs. Valon's face spoke volumes. She gave Aunt Ruby a trembling, lopsided smile. Obviously, she was afraid to believe that someone cared.

We both helped her to an easy chair. I unpacked her pitifully small wardrobe from a bag—two nightgowns, three dresses, and some frayed underwear. Her only shoes were the old boots that were on her feet. I made a mental note to buy several pair of soft bedroom slippers right away.

Aunt Ruby's delicious dinner included stuffed cabbage, mashed potatoes, dumplings, and lots of strong coffee.

But Mrs. Valon was too excited to eat. She couldn't seem to

believe that she would actually live in a real house. She kept touching the table and her chair, as though afraid they would disappear.

Then she started to cry softly. "Terry. . . ."

I shrugged my shoulders in defeat and looked at Aunt Ruby. Neither our newspaper ad nor the radio announcement had brought in a single call. Now too much time had gone by. Terry would never be found.

The telephone rang, interrupting our thoughts. Aunt Ruby looked at me in surprise.

"Who would be calling this late?" she asked, puzzled.

"Sit still, Aunt Ruby. I'll get it," I ordered.

"Hello?" I said.

"Hello. This is Paul Reed."

The name meant nothing to me.

"Paul Reed from the SPCA."

"Yes?" I felt my heart begin to pound.

"Are you one of the ladies who was looking for a dog here a few weeks ago?"

Oh, my gosh! He was calling about Terry!

"Yes, yes," I cried eagerly. "Have you found him?"

"I'm not sure. A dog was brought in an hour ago. He's part Labrador, all right, and he's black. But he doesn't have a collar—"

"But you think he might be the right dog?"

"It's possible—that's about all I can say. Can someone come down to look at him?"

"Of course. We'll be right down."

"The dog isn't in good condition," he warned.

"What's wrong?" I asked sharply.

But the line was dead. He had hung up.

I turned to see two pairs of eyes staring at me.

"For heaven's sake," Aunt Ruby begged, "tell us. Did they find Terry?"

"Now don't get your hopes up too high," I answered cautiously. "They did find a dog. It may be her dog and it may not be. Mr. Reed said the dog didn't have a collar and—" I stopped. I had better not tell them what he had said about the dog's condition.

Amid a great deal of incoherent talking, crying, and confusing suggestions, all three of us finally got into a cab and were on our way to the animal shelter. Mrs. Valon's face was flushed and she was obviously so excited that I worried about her blood pressure.

"Perhaps she should take one of the pills the doctor prescribed for her," I suggested to Aunt Ruby.

She waved her hand in a negative motion. "Later; Later." She raised her eyes up to the heavens. "It's a miracle," she said reverently.

"The Blessed Virgin answered my prayers."

"Now just remember it might not be Terry," I cautioned.

"It will be," she said complacently. "I also prayed to Saint Jude."

We pulled up to the animal shelter and I paid the driver while Aunt Ruby helped Mrs. Valon out of the cab. Slowly they walked up the steps to the door.

I hurried after them, and we entered the building together.

"Is Mr. Reed here?" I asked the man behind the counter.

"He's out back. I'll call him," he replied.

In a few minutes a tall, heavy-set man walked in. I remembered his face now, but I hadn't remembered his name when he called.

"We're here to look at the black Labrador," I explained. Quickly I introduced Mrs. Valon and told him she was the dog's owner.

"Nice to meet you," he said, smiling. "Now, remember it might not be your dog."

Mrs. Valon's smile wobbled, almost as if she understood what he had said.

"Would you ladies come this way, please?" He led the way to the back of the building where the animals were quartered in cages. He stopped in front of the very last one.

"Oh, no!" I cried out involuntarily. Mrs. Valon began to sob loudly.

On the floor of the cage, a large black dog lay as if he were dead. He was emaciated and one leg was in a splint. Both ears were chewed and torn. But all our attention was riveted on his paws.

All four paws were raw with sores that had been treated with some kind of salve.

Mrs. Valon sobbed hysterically. "Terry!" she wailed. There was no doubt in her mind that that was her dog.

Mr. Reed looked at her sympathetically.

"What's wrong with the dog?" I asked.

"Starvation, mostly. Apparently, he hasn't eaten for weeks. The police told us that they received complaints about a large dog roaming the park, but they couldn't get close to him. He's been running day and night—possibly looking for his owner. That's how he injured his paws."

He paused for a long moment. "It's just plain luck that we got him. Someone called, and this time the police were able to get him because he was too weak to run. They brought him here and our veterinarian did what he could for him."

"What does the doctor say?" I asked.

"He's in bad shape. He'll need lots of care just to pull through."

Aunt Ruby interrupted. "And that's what he'll get when we take him home. Lots of good care." She put her arms around Mrs. Valon and spoke to her rapidly in Slovak.

"What did you tell her, Aunt Ruby?" I asked.

"I told her that we two old ladies are going to give him the best care in the world."

Mrs. Valon tugged at Aunt Ruby's arm, imploring.

"What does she want?" I asked.

"She wants to touch Terry." She looked hopefully at Mr. Reed.

Without a word he opened the cage door and swung it wide. Irena reached a trembling hand to the dog.

"Terry," she crooned. "Terry." She stroked every inch of his fur, tears springing to her eyes when she gently touched one of his paws— paws worn sore trying to find her.

The dog lay so still I really thought he was dead. I looked at Mr. Reed questioningly. His eyes mirrored my question. "I'd better get the vet," he said hurriedly, leaving.

How sad, I thought. We found him too late!

"Terry," Mrs. Valon pleaded.

I thought I saw a small movement. It was so slight I wasn't even sure I had actually seen anything.

And then it happened: Terry wagged his tail! True, it barely moved, but it did move. It was the most welcome sight there could be to three pairs of watching eyes.

"He wagged his tail!" I shouted happily, hugging Aunt Ruby.

Mrs. Valon's whole face broke into one big smile.

"Yes," Aunt Ruby agreed rather smugly. "I told you Saint Jude listens to every prayer."

That was the beginning of Terry's recovery. Aunt Ruby moved him to her house where the two old ladies fussed over him endlessly. They spooned liver soup, chicken broth, and other homemade goodies lovingly into his eager mouth. Each day he was a little better.

I stopped to visit one night, about a month after Terry had first come home. He ran to greet me at the door, and I petted him and scratched him behind his ears.

"Why, Terry looks just great Aunt Ruby," I said. "How many saints did you pray to for him?" I kidded.

"I prayed to all the saints," Aunt Ruby replied seriously. "And it wouldn't hurt you maybe to pray a bit more yourself and soon you would have a man. No nice young girl like you should be living alone."

"Oh, no," I groaned. "Not again."

"It wouldn't hurt you to keep trying," Aunt Ruby insisted. "Tomorrow, first thing, I'm going to church and light a candle for you and—"

"—and pray to all the saints," we said in unison.

And even though I laughed, I thought to myself: Maybe that's not such a bad idea!

THE END

FOREVER LOVERS
We keep crossing paths

Certainly I don't hold my parents responsible for what happened—Lord knows I've made enough mistakes of my own. But I do know I never would have married Peter if things had been different at home.

I also know now that marrying to escape a miserable home situation is like jumping from the frying pan into the fire. And I had a miserable home all during my childhood and adolescence, that's for sure!

Fight! Fight! Fight! Day and night, that's all my parents did. I think I was conceived in an extremely rare period of truce.

For years, I felt guilty, as if the bickering were my fault. After all, weren't they staying together to give me a home? I know now that I shouldn't have felt responsible! I was their excuse for staying together, but the real reason was that neither one of them would admit defeat by being the one to start divorce proceedings!

Growing up, I vowed to myself that if I ever had a child, I'd never allow such things to go on in my home. And I tried to keep that vow—God, how I tried—but how little we know when we're children.

I never brought any of my friends home with me. And that, of course, was a reason to wage war!

"No wonder Beth is ashamed to have her friends over," my father would roar. "Look at this messy house!"

"The house looks messy because I'm too busy making nice clothes for Beth. If you earned enough money to buy her decent things, I'd have time to clean the house!" Mother would scream back.

Neither of my parents stopped to think that the never-ending hostility between them was why I didn't want my friends around. I spent as much time away from home as I possibly could, and that wasn't all bad. In fact, some really nice things came from my desire to escape my unhappy home.

I did most of my studying at the library. It was the librarian who, because I was there so much, gave me my first job. I dusted and straightened books and saved the money I earned for college expenses.

I desperately wanted to go to college, but there was no way my parents could swing the tuition. So I took a job in a drugstore, figuring I'd work and save more money, and apply for a scholarship. I was sure

I wouldn't be able to attend college and work at the same time—the reason I'd done so well in high school was because I'd had so much time to study! So I was spending all the time I could at the drugstore. The owner thought I was the best worker he'd ever hired and was constantly bragging about me.

"You don't find many girls like Beth anymore," I heard him say over and over. "Nowadays, kids do as little work as they can, yet they still expect to get good wages! Not Beth! She's here early, she stays late if we're busy, and she never complains about overtime!"

"That old man makes you sound like a saint," my best friend, Jillian, said more than once. "I wonder what he'd say if he knew the real reason you're in his drugstore so much is to get away from your folks."

Jillian was the only one who knew about my home life. I'd even dared to have her over, after she confided in me that the peaceful atmosphere in her home was false. "My parents fight quietly. They smile and pretend to be friendly, while all the time, they get in little sharp digs! And at least your father doesn't sleep around!"

Of course, I didn't tell my boss any of this. I just let him think I was very special. And that's exactly the words he used when he introduced me to his son, Peter.

"Son, meet Beth, a very special girl. Now that you've finished college, you'll be head pharmacist around here, so you'll see a lot of her. I think Beth puts in more hours here than I do!"

Peter was extremely handsome, with dark hair and eyes and white, white teeth. I soon learned that a number of girls liked him, but he was, despite his good looks, a quiet, shy, serious person.

For some reason, Peter took to me right away. He asked me for a date the day after he came! He was a really nice person, so much so that Jillian was quite impressed, to say nothing of my parents.

I couldn't believe it! For the first time in my life, my folks agreed on something: They both liked Peter. In fact, when Peter insisted on picking me up at home for a date, they invited him over for Sunday dinner. And that Sunday turned out to be one of the happiest days of my life. We had a lovely dinner. Later Mother and I did the dishes while Peter and Dad watched television.

We were like a family—a real family, at last. Dad joked and Mother laughed, and Peter seemed to think they were great. I thought a miracle had occurred. I was so happy!

But the minute Peter left, things returned to normal. Not quite as loud, or as angrily—but my folks started arguing again.

I cried myself to sleep that night.

A month later, when Peter asked me to marry him, the idea really appealed to me. I couldn't take much more at home—certainly

I couldn't stick it out for as long as it would take me to save money for college. Besides, I really did care for Peter. He was sweet, and his kisses were gentle and loving. I was sure life with him would be serene—nothing like I had at home. But was that enough for marriage?

When I asked Peter that, he smiled. "It's enough for me, Beth. I love you and I want you to be the mother of my children. We'll have a good life together."

My parents were all for the idea. Jillian was sure it was the most wonderful thing that could have happened. "He's as handsome as a movie star, and he's going to inherit a good business someday. You don't have to knock yourself out going to college."

Looking back, I can't believe how mixed-up my thinking was! But I guess that's why divorce courts are so busy. People get married for a million reasons other than the right ones.

Peter and I were married on a beautiful day in June. Our honeymoon was at his parents' cottage on a beautiful lake far from civilization. Peter loved to fish, and he was excited about having a whole week at the lake. I'd never done any fishing. Soon I found that sitting in a boat for hours wasn't my idea of a good time. I was used to keeping busy every second.

"Wow, you certainly are a squirmer!" Peter teased as I kept shifting around in the tiny boat.

"I'm used to—well, a bit more activity," I said.

"Relax—you'll learn to love it out here."

In the evenings, Peter wanted to watch the news. I'd rather have listened to romantic music while we danced on the patio in the moonlight. Peter said he'd rather stay indoors, away from the mosquitoes. So I sat and pouted, looking through the screen at the moonlight on the lake, resting my chin on my hand, waiting for the news to be over.

Peter was a sweet, thoughtful husband, that was for sure—our lovemaking was absolutely magic. So why was I so jumpy?

On the spur of the moment, I turned on the stereo—loud—switched off the radio and stood in front of my husband. "I want attention!"

A big smile spread across his face. He reached up and gathered me on his lap. "My little girl," he whispered. "My sweet little girl."

"I'm a pest, that's what I am," I said with a sigh. "I'm not sweet at all!"

"And I'm not a storybook lover, Beth. But I do love you, and I'll take good care of you all our lives."

"And I'll learn to please you, Peter!"

"Darling, you do please me! But just try to relax. You don't have to be working every second." He hugged me close. "When you have your own home to care for, you'll calm down and maybe even enjoy it."

We'd already picked out an adorable apartment. I was anxious to start fixing it just the way I wanted. I soon found that that didn't take long! I whisked through the decorating and furnishing in no time. I wasn't home from our honeymoon two months when I found myself with time dragging. I suggested going back to work at the drugstore, but Peter wouldn't hear of it.

"There's no reason for you to work anymore. Besides, you've always driven yourself too hard. Dad said you outworked any other girl he ever hired!"

I didn't want to make waves, so after Peter left for work in the morning, I'd dive into my housework to keep from climbing the walls. By ten o'clock, I was twiddling my thumbs and watching children's shows on television.

I don't think there's ever been a woman any happier than I was the day I found out I was pregnant! I wanted that baby desperately.

Our first was a little girl. So was our second. Our third was supposed to be a boy for Peter, but that baby was a girl, too. My life was busy every minute, crowded with little-girl needs and little-girl love. I tried to get pregnant again, hoping for a son for Peter. But something had gone wrong—I couldn't have another child.

Though Peter was disappointed, he took me in his arms and said, "I've four little girls, and that's enough children for any man." He still called me his "very own little girl."

The next few years were happy, filled with activity. Then, one by one, the girls were off to school. I found myself with time on my hands again. This time, I all but insisted on going back to work, but Peter was even more determined that I stay home.

"One of the kids might need you during the day," he argued.

"I wouldn't work full-time, honey."

"We really don't need the money, Beth! And the kids and I need you at home."

"Well, damn it, maybe I need to get out once in a while!" I retorted.

The girls all cringed, and Peter's eyes filled with surprise.

Our oldest daughter whimpered, "Gosh, Mom, you sound just like Grandma!"

I whirled and rushed from the room and to my bedroom, where I buried my face in a pillow and cried. All the years of my marriage, I'd bent over backward to keep a peaceful house. To have my child say I sounded like my mother was a real blow! I knew my parents upset the children with their fights. Only now, their battles were toned down considerably. I think they tried to put on a good front for Peter and the girls. I wonder what my own family would have to say if they ever heard a real knockdown fight like my folks used to have!

That night when Peter came to bed, I turned my face to the wall and pretended to be asleep. The next day, I complained to Jillian that I didn't have enough to keep me busy. She suggested I take some courses at night school.

"You planned on studying art when you went to college. Why don't you see if any of the schools are offering something in that line?" She shrugged. "Who knows, you may be another Grandma Moses!"

The more I thought about studying art, the more enthusiastic I became. Peter thought it was a good idea, too. So I found a class that started soon, and I enrolled.

That's how I met Marc.

A small group of us were sitting in a corner, talking, waiting for the instructor. I felt his presence before I saw him. The others kept right on talking, but for some reason I was silent.

I felt as though someone had opened a door and warm, sweet air was flowing in and all around me. I turned slowly and looked straight into Marc's eyes. For a moment, I thought I recognized him from somewhere. The same look of recognition flashed across his face, disappeared, and was replaced by a puzzled frown.

Just then, someone called out that finally our instructor had arrived. "Hey, Marc, what do the students do when the teacher's late?"

He smiled and walked to the front of the room, where he introduced himself and asked that we introduce ourselves. "We'll be going on a first-name basis in class. It's easier for me—I'm no good at remembering names." He stopped, hesitated, then added, "But I do remember faces!" He looked straight at me when he said that.

For the next hour, I listened. I set up my easel and worked some, but I really can't remember anything that was said or what went on around me. Strange emotions were flooding through me—emotions I couldn't identify—emotions that were making me feel suddenly, achingly alive.

Then, suddenly, the room and the people all fell into sharp focus. I was aware that the lesson was over. The others were just leaving. Flustered, I began to collect my things.

He was there beside me, very close. "I'm sure that what I'm about to say came over on the Mayflower—but don't I know you from somewhere?"

I stopped what I was doing and studied him. He wasn't really handsome—in fact, he had rather rugged features that looked like they'd been just casually thrown together.

"No! I'd remember your face if I'd ever seen you before—but I also have the feeling I should know you!"

Just then, one of my brushes fell to the floor. We both bent to pick it up. Our fingers met, and—

It was impossible—but it happened—it was happening. . . .

It was as though an electric shock was passing between us. Not a high-voltage shock, but a very distinct tingle. Then Marc said sharply, "Darling, you shouldn't have kept me waiting so long!"

I answered without thinking, "But I couldn't find you!"

We both jumped back, stood staring at each other. "My God!" he exclaimed. "What was that all about?"

I started to shake. I felt tears stinging my eyes. I reached out to support myself and touched his arm. Again I experienced the tingle, only this time it was nowhere near as strong. And then his arms were around me, comforting me, and I felt like nothing I'd ever felt before—as though I'd finally come home after a long, long journey.

"I'm sorry, but I—I—" He stopped talking as he hugged me close. "It doesn't make sense, but I was about to say that—"

"That what?" I asked, my face close against his chest.

"Well—" He pulled away from me. "It was on the tip of my tongue to say, that because you took so long—we've messed it all up again!"

"Messed what up?"

"Dear God, I don't know! I said it wouldn't make any sense!"

Suddenly we both realized we were standing with our bodies pressed together. Neither of us pulled away. And then he was kissing me and I was kissing him back, hungrily, passionately—as though I'd longed all my life for his lips on mine and now nothing was going to break us apart.

I should have felt shame—guilt—something other than complete joy. But there was only abandoned ecstasy. . . .

We lay in each other's arms, shaken by what had taken place, unable to understand, trying to sort it all out. We were surrounded by a golden glow—it was more than the afterglow of satisfying lovemaking. It was like nothing I'd ever experienced or heard about.

"I don't want to ever let you go," Marc whispered. "I have the feeling that if I do, I may lose you—" he hesitated. "I almost said again just then! That I'd lose you again! What does it mean? Oh, God, what's happening to us?"

"I don't know! And right now, I don't care! Whatever it is, it's the most beautiful thing I've ever known—and the most frightening."

"Don't be afraid. Oh, darling, don't be afraid!"

"But I don't understand any of this! I want to stay here with you, and I know I can't. I—I wish I knew what will happen next!"

He pulled away and shook himself. "Yes!" he exclaimed. "We've got to get ourselves together and think!"

He pulled me back into his arms. "Slowly now—one thing at a time!"

Looking up into his face, I said what I was thinking. "I love you, Marc! I don't know how that can possibly be, since it defies any sensible explanation. I only know I love you."

"And I love you," he whispered. Through us both there coursed that beautiful, electric thrill. We clung together, our lips warm and sweet.

Finally he drew away. "Beth! We do have to talk—to think this out! Yesterday I didn't dream you existed—wait now! Maybe that's not right." He frowned, thinking, shaking his head. "It almost seems that perhaps I—I—" His voice trailed off.

"What?" I asked.

"Well, it's like I've a faint memory, the way it is sometimes when you wake up and know you've been dreaming, but you can't recall any details of your dream. And then again, maybe it really isn't a memory, perhaps it was a dream I had once. I see you standing by the water—the ocean, maybe—and you're wearing a long, old-fashioned dress. Sounds silly, doesn't it?"

"It makes about as much sense as everything that's happened to us this evening."

Suddenly Marc's face clouded over. "I'm married, Beth—if you can call it that. My wife is a hopeless invalid! She ran her car off an embankment two years ago, injured her back, and she refuses to try any new therapy that might heal her."

"How long have you been married?" I asked.

"Only three years! I swore for years I'd stay single, but then I met Cheryl. Our first year was really nice. Then Cheryl had a miscarriage. She started to drink. She was drunk when she wrecked the car and nearly killed herself. She's drunk half the time now! Cheryl stays in bed all the time—yet she gets roaring drunk. I can't figure it!"

"I'm married, too. Does it sound strange when I say happily married? We have three daughters, all in grade school. I love my family dearly."

A look of anguish shot across Marc's face, followed by a look of concern. "Your husband will wonder why you're late!"

"Yes, he will! He worries about me a lot—calls me his little girl, in fact—" Then I cried, "But I don't want to leave you! I have this terrible fear—"

"I know, darling. I feel it, too—that we'll never meet again! I feel it, too. But we will meet again—believe that! My love, I don't intend to lose you again!"

135

He pulled me to my feet, stood holding me close. "Would it be safe for me to have your phone number, or would you rather I didn't?"

"You can call me anytime during the day. And, please—call me!"

"I will," he promised.

We said good-bye in the parking lot. I was halfway home when it hit me! I was an unfaithful wife! But then a warm sweetness flooded through me, as I realized I could no more have stopped those magic moments with Marc than I could have stopped breathing.

When I got home, the girls were all in bed. Peter was asleep in front of the television. Seeing him there, obviously waiting for me, almost made me cry. He was such a good man—such a good father. Gentle, kind Peter—it would kill him if he ever learned what I'd done during the few hours since I'd seen him last!

I shook him gently. He woke, smiling. "Well, how's my little artist?"

I turned from him so he wouldn't see my face. "It's late, Peter. Let's go to bed."

In bed, Peter reached out for me. I pretended to be asleep. He put his arms around me and stroked my forehead. Minutes later I could hear him breathing deeply and knew he was asleep again. I wept silently.

Early the next morning, after the kids and Peter had gone, Jillian stuck her head in the door. "Hey, Grandma Moses, how'd the art lesson go?"

She stopped short, walked in, and sat down, studying me, "Okay! Want to tell me about it? It's written all over your face that something's bothering you."

I whirled around. "Does it show? Oh, God, I wonder if Peter noticed anything."

I told her about Marc—oh, not how we'd lain in each other's arms—I couldn't tell her that! But the part about thinking we'd met before—somewhere, sometime. . . .

"I've heard of that before," she said. "It's called déjà vu. What did he look like?"

"Well, he stops just short of being homely. His features are rather rugged."

Jillian breathed a deep sigh of relief. "Well, I'm glad he's nothing special! It might wreck your marriage if he was."

"But it all seems so strange," I said, wondering how I managed to keep my voice so steady.

"A lot of people believe we're born over and over—and that sometimes we meet the same people in this life we've known before in another life." She was thoughtful for a long time. When she spoke again, she chose her words carefully. "Beth, I've been going to church all my life. I sincerely believe what I've learned there. Mainly that if a person truly repents for his sins, God will forgive him. I also believe that once forgiven, a person should not repeat his sins. Maybe some souls, even though they're forgiven, try to make up for bad things they did in a former life. Maybe they come back and—"

I gasped at that, remembering the strange words Marc and I had spoken when we'd first touched.

"Darling, you shouldn't have kept me waiting so long," he'd said. And I'd answered, "But I couldn't find you!" Then he'd said, "Because you took so long, we've messed it up again."

"Beth!" Jillian cried. "You look terrible. Are you sick?"

I sat down, staring at my friend. "No, I'm not sick. It's just that— well—some of what you said hit home! Maybe my instructor and I did, well, know each other before."

Just then, the phone rang. Instinctively, I knew it was Marc. As I started to answer it, Jillian grabbed her purse and dashed out. "I just remembered—I've got an appointment at the dentist's. I'll call you later."

I hurried to the phone. It was Marc. After I said hello, the line was quiet for a long time. Finally, he said, "Beth, it really happened, didn't it?"

"Yes," I whispered. Then I said, "Marc, my best friend just told me some things that sounded strange, but made sense—about living many lives. . . ."

He listened, and when I'd finished, he said, "You think we may have known each other in another life, and that we sinned, and now we have another chance to undo our wrongs?"

"Something like that! It sounds weird, doesn't it?"

"According to the way we've been taught to think—yes. But since last night, I've been doing some reading. At least half the people in the world believe in reincarnation."

"Marc, we must be very careful not to hurt anyone. We took an awful chance last night." My throat tightened so I could hardly continue. "What if someone had seen us?"

"Last night we were carried away by sudden emotions that we couldn't handle. We'll have to be sensible, but—" He paused. "I don't think I can wait until next week's class. Could you possibly get out sometime this week? We've got to talk, Beth!"

"Oh, Marc, I don't know! We'd be seen!" I exclaimed.

"You could stop by my home. I have people coming and going all the time. I give private lessons, too, besides the classes I teach. No one would think anything of it, if you stopped by and stayed."

"What about your wife?" I wondered.

"She never leaves her own room. It's at the other end of our house."

"I do want to see you!"

137

His voice was eager. "Come this afternoon."

After lunch, I drove to his home. He was waiting for me. I walked through the door, looked at him, and then walked straight into his arms. Our lips met—it was the same as before. We were hungry—starved—for each other. "You know what?" I whispered. "It's going to be like this every time we're alone. We'll think we're just meeting to talk, but—"

"I won't lose you again! Beth, I won't!"

"But sooner or later, someone will find out. Then where will we be? We'll either have to stop seeing each other entirely, or we'll have to sneak around."

His voice was desperate. "What can we do?"

"For now, just hold me! Hold me—"

Too soon, it was time for me to leave. Again, when we parted I felt that lost, empty feeling. "Call me tomorrow?" I asked. He nodded, his eyes mirroring the same torment I felt.

Halfway home, I knew I couldn't hack it. I simply couldn't face my husband and children, as mixed up as I felt. I stopped and called Jillian.

"Where've you been all afternoon?" she wanted to know.

"Do me a favor, Jillian? Cover for me. I'm going to tell Peter I've been with you and that I'm going to be with you a while longer. And please don't ask questions."

There was a pause. Then, "Sure, honey. Okay."

Then I called the drugstore. I asked Peter to take care of the girls until I got home. After I hung up, I got back into my car and started to drive. I don't know exactly how long I drove, or exactly where—but I found myself turning in a dead-end street when I suddenly realized I was in the parking lot of a small church.

The church door was open. I walked in, trembling. I knelt and started to talk.

"God, I don't understand what's happening to me. I'm so afraid—oh, God, tell me what to do. . . ."

Suddenly my mind became clear, really clear, for the first time since I'd met Marc. And I knew exactly what had to be done. Maybe we had known each other before, loved before, lost each other before. Or maybe there was just tremendously strong chemistry between us and we'd actually met for the first time yesterday. Whatever it was, I knew we shared a rare and beautiful relationship. And the only way to keep it that way was never to let it hurt anyone else. I cried then, but my heart was at peace.

When I got home, Peter had fed the girls and put them to bed. He was watching the news. He didn't ask questions—he'd accepted my lie. I prayed I'd never have to lie to him again.

Marc phoned the next afternoon. I was calm as I told him, "I'm not coming to class again—and I won't see you."

"No!" he interrupted. "No!"

"We proved yesterday that we can't just talk when we're alone. So if we talk at all, it'll have to be by phone!" I suddenly found it almost impossible to speak. "Please, Marc, help me—"

"Oh, Beth, Beth—I don't think I can!"

We talked then for a long time. I promised not to give up the idea of painting.

"You have real talent, Beth, and there are other classes. Finish the painting you started in my class."

So I enrolled in a new art class. My instructor was an older woman. I continued to work on my painting. Actually I couldn't really remember doing the preliminary work. I'd done it while I was still in that strange state of mind I'd experienced while in Marc's class.

Every day, Marc and I talked by phone. He agreed it was best that we didn't see each other. "I can take it, as long as I can still talk to you, know you're near, and you're all right."

Those first few days away from him were the worst. I found myself snapping at everything the girls did. And nothing Peter did pleased me. They were all hurt and confused by my nasty temper. Then one day, Peter snapped back at me. Before I knew it, we were having a real yelling fight. Suddenly, right in the middle of saying something, he turned and left the room!

"Don't you dare turn your back on me!" I screamed after him.

My three girls were staring at me with huge, miserable eyes. That only added to my own misery. "Go out and play!" I ordered.

Later that evening, when the girls were in bed, Peter said, "Beth, something has been bothering you lately. I've waited for you to tell me what it is, but for some reason you've preferred not to. But it's spilling out—making the girls and me unhappy, too. Don't you think it's time to talk it over—before our home starts to sound like your parents'?"

"Peter, that's the first time you've ever come right out and said what it's like in my parents' home."

"Honey, it was always an embarrassment to you, the way they carried on. And I've always known how it hurt you. It burns me up the way they put on such an act for the girls—the same way they did the first time I met them. Why couldn't they have tried that hard to make life pleasant for you during your childhood?"

"You knew all that right from the beginning?" I exclaimed.

"Small-town gossip." He smiled. "The neighbors weren't deaf."

"Peter, I swore years ago that my own home would never be like that!"

"Until now, it hasn't been, but, honey, sometimes you really try too hard. I wish you'd relax! You're always on the run. I used to watch you at work in the drugstore and I'd think: 'If I ever have anything to say about it, that girl will have the best of everything! She'll have time to stop and smell the roses!'"

"Peter! That's really romantic! You really do love me, don't you?"

He looked surprised. "Of course, silly little girl! Have you ever doubted it?" Then he drew me close. "Oh, I know—I'm not the kind of guy you read about in love stories."

"You're the most gorgeous man I know!"

He grinned sheepishly. "The other girls I dated always expected me to behave like a movie star. I could never live up to their expectations. After a few dates, they found me dull."

"You're not dull! You're a dear, sweet man who gets up in the middle of the night—even when it's freezing—to go down to the drugstore and fill a prescription."

He beamed. "Well, I never knew how to say romantic things, but I tried in other ways to show you how much I care for you." He dropped his eyes and searched for words. Then finally he said, "Beth, would you teach me to dance?"

"But—but you never wanted to!"

"Oh, yes! I always wanted to. But I'm the original two-left-feet character. I didn't want to turn you off with my clumsiness."

And he was awkward, though not terribly so. We laughed and had a good time, and the girls peeked at us through the staircase rails, giggling and whispering. Later, we all had cookies and milk.

That night Peter didn't try to make love to me. I was glad he didn't. He didn't ask again what had been bothering me lately. I began to think my husband was a very wise man, in many ways.

The next day when Marc phoned, I told him about my pleasant hours with Peter. We two could discuss anything and everything.

Marc said, "I'm happy you and Peter are on such good terms— but I'm jealous, too, because he has you and I don't. And I've something to tell you, darling. Last night I was so lonesome for you, I drove by your house, parked, then walked slowly by, listening and watching."

"Oh, Marc! You did?"

"Yes. I saw you through the windows dancing with Peter. I wanted to rush in, grab you, and run away with you!"

"Oh, Marc! You were miserable while I was enjoying myself!" I cried.

"This has got to be the strangest relationship I've ever heard of." He laughed. "Would you believe that as miserable as I was because I wasn't the man holding you—I was actually happy because you were happy! Do you know what I did?"

"Tell me!"

"I went home, took my oils into Cheryl's room, and told her I'd decided to paint her portrait. She was so surprised, she just sat there gaping at me. So I told her, 'Cheryl, we used to have great times together, but since you lost the baby and had the accident, you've shut me out. At least this is one way we can spend time together'."

"What did she do?"

"She burst out crying! And when I asked her why, she said it was because she didn't want me to paint her looking so terrible. So I answered right back that she couldn't expect to look like her old, beautiful self the way she'd been drinking—the way she'd refused to do anything but stay in bed, without even trying therapy."

"How did she react to that?"

"She asked, 'Marc, was I really beautiful?' I said she was one of the most beautiful women I'd ever seen—and about the most fun to be with!"

"That sounds better!"

"She thought so, too. She perked up and asked me to just sketch her first. She'd make herself beautiful again for the portrait."

"You mean she wants you to paint her portrait?"

"Yes, she really does! It's the first positive thing she's done since the baby."

"I wonder why she's finally reacting positively?"

"Beats me! Unless it's the way I approached her—right out—no holds barred—nothing held back. I told her off, instead of feeling sorry for her and treating her like the invalid she's made herself."

"Children are like that sometimes. They demand to have their own way, but if you lay down the law, give them a good talking to, they seem relieved."

There was a long pause before Marc spoke again, softly, "Beth, have I told you lately that I love you?"

"Not since yesterday!"

"I do love you—more than I can ever put into words," he whispered. "And I'm aching to see you."

"I don't think we should see each other."

"Do you think we'll ever be able to see each other without acting like a couple of teenage kids discovering sex for the first time?"

"Sometimes I wish that was all it was with us. If it was—"

"I know," he interrupted, "but it's much more and we can't handle it! Well, I've got a student due any minute. I'll call tomorrow."

But he didn't call the next day, or the next. By the third day, I was as jumpy as that cat on the hot tin roof. Finally, when Marc did call, I was so glad to hear his voice I almost cried.

"Marc! Are you all right? I've been out of my mind with worry!"

"I'm fine. And forgive me for not calling. I've been busy every second during the daytime and I didn't dare call at night. I can't talk but a few minutes now. Beth, you'll never guess what's happening! I can hardly believe it myself!

"The other night, when I took my canvas and paints into Cheryl's room, she was not only cold sober—she was all fixed up and anxious to see me. While I worked, we talked. She asked if I'd take her to therapy. I was so excited I couldn't work after that, so we just talked. All this time, Cheryl thought I blamed her for losing the baby, and she's been deathly afraid of—"

"Of losing you," I finished. "She clung to her bed, knowing you'd never abandon an invalid."

"Right! But she's really trying now. She still has her beautiful sense of humor."

"Marc, I'm so happy for you!"

"But I hear something in your voice," he said softly.

"I know now what you were feeling. I'm jealous—yet, believe me, I'm happy for you and Cheryl."

"Oh, Beth! God, how I love you, but we—neither of us—can be living in two places at once."

I laughed. "I know! And not too long ago, I'd have said it was impossible to love two men at the same time. But I do!"

"I know! Hey, I've gotta run! I'll call when I can. Oh! By the way, how's your painting coming?"

"I'm making real progress. My teacher is impressed."

In fact, my new art teacher was very interested in my painting. Just the evening before, she'd studied it and exclaimed, "You've told me you're not working from another picture or a photo—and that makes your work even more astounding! Why, it's almost as though I were actually standing in the room you're painting! It's obviously an old inn—early American period—or maybe eighteenth-century England. Your shading is perfect, the way light from the fireplace dances on the walls, the beams in the ceiling. . . ."

I glowed at her praise. I assured her again that maybe, long ago, I'd seen a similar picture and was working from a vague, hazy memory, but that I couldn't remember ever having seen such a room.

Peter and the girls were impressed with my painting, too. Peter remarked that Great-aunt Marie would certainly be interested in it when she came for her yearly visit.

Great-aunt Marie was a spinster, almost ninety years old. Every year, she made the rounds of her relatives, and strangely almost everyone looked forward to her visits. She wasn't like a lot of old people, cross and full of complaints. Instead she was a constant source of interesting tales. If anyone in the family wanted to check on something regarding the family, they called Great-aunt Marie. She always arrived on an early-morning plane, and she usually kissed half a dozen people good-bye when she departed. She made friends fast!

When Great-aunt Marie arrived, I met her at the airport. My heart sank when I saw her being helped along by the stewardess. That had never happened before. She had aged a lot since we'd seen her last. My heart ached with the realization that she wouldn't be with us much longer.

But she kissed the pretty girl assisting her, took my arm after kissing me, and said, "I've brought a small trunk with me. I hope you've driven the station wagon, so we can have it loaded right on. I'd hate to have it sitting around here."

Later that evening, as we all sat in the living room, she said, "I know the girls have been dying to see what's in my trunk. Now's the time I want to show you! First, the things are very precious to me and I've brought them here for you to keep, just in case. . . ."

Her voice trailed off. She reached over and unlocked the trunk. "I've chosen Peter to keep these mementos of our family's past because he's always been so responsible. He'd never let anything happen to them. And you, Beth, I'm going to ask you to write down everything I'll be telling you—things I remember that should be recorded." She rested for a moment, then continued. "I know you won't mind, Beth—you've never been able to sit still for a minute— always working like the devil was on your tail!"

She opened the trunk. There were loud ooh's and aah's from the girls. There were pictures, old diaries and letters, a powder horn, buttons from Army uniforms, fragile lace and embroidery—the treasures of a family carefully preserved by a loving old aunt.

During the next week, Marie and I worked. She talked—I took notes, using a tape recorder. There were stories of hard work, adventure, tragedy, and hilarious incidents. We went over birth certificates, slowly constructing a family tree.

When she became tired, I'd type what we'd discussed. It was all very interesting—but there was one box that drew my attention and affected me strangely. At first I thought it was because the story Marie told concerning the box was such a sad one. Later, though, I began to wonder.

The story was told to Great-aunt Marie by her great-grandmother. It concerned her oldest brother, Samuel. He had been a hardworking man who owned a large and profitable inn in a New England town. Samuel married late in his forties—and then he chose a young girl he'd hired to work in the inn.

143

She and Samuel—her name was Anne—had two daughters and a son. Almost as soon as they could walk, the children worked in the inn, washing tankards, sweeping floors, running errands. Apparently Samuel was a man who believed in hard work for his family.

Anne was a lovely person with a sunny disposition. She worked cheerfully, often practically dancing from customer to customer. And then one evening, a seaman stopped by. . . .

Anne and the seaman fell in love. Apparently they met secretly for some time before Samuel found out. He beat Anne and locked her in a bedroom. But she escaped and disappeared. At the same time, the seaman left town.

Four months passed. One day Samuel left and was gone for a week. When he returned, Anne was with him, weak, pregnant, and close to death. There was much gossip, but nobody ever heard the real story. Had the seaman deserted Anne? Was he dead—by the hands of the raging husband? To this day, that part of the story remains a mystery.

But the rest of the story the entire family knew. Samuel was constantly after Anne, making her work night and day, never letting her forget her "sin." Only now Anne didn't accept things quietly. She screamed back at her husband, fighting him every inch of the way. The inn became famous for the brawls that went on daily between Samuel and Anne—in fact, people called it the Brawlin' Inn!

One dark night, there was a particularly bad fight. Samuel struck Anne as she was standing near some stairs. She fell. Two days later, she lost her baby. That same night, Samuel died of a heart attack.

For weeks Anne lay close to death. When she finally was able to be up and around, she'd completely changed. She was now quiet and very serious. From then on, she worked hard, silently, and was never known to turn down anyone who asked for help. She'd stay up all night to nurse a sick person, walk miles to help out when an extra hand was needed.

The inn soon became more of a hospital, and Anne never charged for her labor. Her children loved her dearly, but she never could forget the one she'd lost in a fight with Samuel. She blamed herself for that child's death. After her children were raised, she gave the inn to them. She went into a convent where she lived out her life.

The box that fascinated me so much had belonged to Anne. Inside were curly locks of hair tied with ribbon, a wooden cross that must have belonged to Anne while she was in the convent, some pretty seashells, and one other thing.

Very carefully folded, tied with faded ribbon, was a strip of exquisite material. Even back then, material such as that must have cost a small fortune. It looked as though rainbows were woven into the material, and the colors were still lovely, except for the frayed edges.

Tears came to my eyes as I wondered about the person who had folded that fabric so carefully and tucked it away. Then I returned the material to the box, and the box to the trunk, deciding I'd had quite enough of the past for a while. It was depressing me. I was glad Marie and I were nearly finished with our work.

Marie stayed with us nearly a month. When we kissed her good-bye at the airport, we were all pretty sure it was our last good-bye—but for some reason, it wasn't really a sad time. She waved happily, walked to the plane alone, and went cheerfully off to whatever the future held for her.

During the time of her stay, I'd talked to Marc only briefly, so the day after she left we talked for hours. I'd known it was coming, but it was still hard to accept when Marc told me that he and Cheryl were moving south, where the climate would be easier for her.

"What do you think, Beth? The thought of moving—losing you—tears at me!"

"You know what must be done, Marc. And, honey, we won't really lose each other. Love—true love—never dies. I think it lives on in people's hearts—in their souls—it becomes what they are."

"Then I want to get it over with as quickly as possible!"

Marc sold his house, and then he and Cheryl had a huge lawn sale to get rid of everything they didn't want to move to their new home. And I saw Marc one last time. . . .

We were all out for a drive that Saturday. The girls wanted ice cream. After we bought them cones, we were just riding around. Suddenly Peter said, "Hey look! There's a lawn sale." Well, of course it was Marc's sale.

I didn't want to get out of the car, but Peter and the girls pulled at me.

The yard was filled with all the assorted things people collect. They'd cleaned out the attic, and there were antiques sitting all over, and a sign that said More Inside.

The girls ran around squealing. Peter was talking to a pretty girl who leaned on a cane, about an old musket. I wandered into the house, hoping to see Marc, yet afraid I would.

He came down the stairs carrying an armload of old magazines. When he saw me, he stopped, carefully set the magazines on the floor, and walked toward me. The house was pretty empty except for us. Outside, I could hear people talking, moving around.

He touched me carefully, and between us there flowed that strange current. He took me in his arms and kissed me hungrily. When we broke apart, he whispered, "We can't live in the same town, can we? We'd meet and it would always be like this between us." I could hear his voice thicken with emotion. Tears streamed down my face, for in truth there was a bond between us that neither time nor distance would ever change.

"I'm glad now that I'm here," I said. "That we have this chance to say good-bye."

He grabbed me closer and hugged me tightly. Then he whispered, "But not really good-bye, my darling, for I promise you this: We'll meet again."

Just then I heard a door slam. My oldest girl called, "Mother, just wait'll you see what Daddy bought me!"

"What is it, Kaitlyn?" I called, pulling away fast.

"And Daddy bought Dawn an old doll and Alicia a music box," Kaitlyn chatted happily on as the chest of drawers was loaded in our station wagon, as the children and Peter and I got in and drove away.

But just before I got in the car, Marc's fingers touched mine and our eyes spoke our silent, final farewell. I turned as we drove away— he raised his hand and waved. . . .

I've never spoken to, or seen Marc since that day.

Time passed. . . .

In fact, as time went on, I found I was strangely at peace within myself and happy, too. And Peter has been so happy lately. He's especially pleased when I go fishing with him. I've caught some pretty big ones! I can even clean them. In fact, that's where we're all heading this weekend. The girls love to fish, too. We're a very happy bunch.

There's just one more thing I want to tell you: One Saturday, I was cleaning Kaitlyn's closet. I came across a box filled with old clothing. "Where did you get this horrible stuff?" I asked her.

"Oh." She giggled. "It was in one of the drawers of that old chest Daddy bought me at the lawn sale."

I was about to throw the box out. But something made me hesitate. I examined the clothes more carefully. They were really old! Then something caught my eye. It was an old blue sweater, full of holes and falling apart—navy blue it had been, the kind a sailor might have worn. There was one pocket. I reached inside and pulled out something carefully wrapped in a piece of parchment.

My heart stopped at the sight of it! It was a piece of material exactly matching the piece that was in Anne's box.

Was it coincidence? All of it? Was my painting of the old inn— the strong feeling that both Marc and I had of having known each other before—the fact that the material in Anne's box matched the material in that tattered sweater in Marc's attic, all just happenstance?

Was my growing up in such a tumultuous household for some

reason? Is it ordained by fate that Peter and I are learning to live together in peace and understanding? Are Marc and Cheryl doing the same thing for the same reason?

Were Marc and I the lovers of long ago? Are we destined to meet and love again . . . and again . . . and again, through all eternity?

THE END

Criminal Confession:
MY DIRTY SECRET!
I can't tell my husband

The valuable gold earrings were missing! There was no mistake. After my frantic search I knew they were gone, and for one horrifying moment I was hurled back in time to the past I had tried so desperately to forget.

I had a new life now, a new love, and a new happiness that could all be destroyed by the discovery of my terrible secret. As I stood paralyzed with dread, the memory of how it had all begun flashed before me.

I'd been in my senior year of high school then. One day, after the final bell rang, there was the usual mad scramble for books and belongings. I was hurrying down the staircase when I heard someone call my name.

"Darla! Darla Seaver! Wait up."

I spun around to see Dave Anderson taking two steps at a time to catch up with me.

Dave had recently transferred to Hauppauge High. Although we'd only exchanged a dozen words on the way to or from classes or in the cafeteria, he seemed like a nice guy. Ever since I'd first seen him, I'd thought Dave was attractive. He was tall and lean, had a friendly grin and an easy, confident manner. A lot of the other girls agreed with me. That's why I couldn't have been more surprised that day when he ran up to me and said, "I just wondered if you've already got a date for the dance after the basketball game Friday. If you don't, I'd like you to go with me."

About five different things ran through my mind at the same time—all reasons not to accept—so I hesitated. I was flattered that Dave had asked me, but there were a number of things I'd have to work out if I said yes.

But as I looked up into Dave's smiling face and imagined how I'd feel walking into the gym after the game as his date, I impulsively said, "No, I don't have a date and yes, I'll go with you."

His grin broadened. "Great. Where do you live so I can pick you up?"

That was the first problem—my folks. Quickly, I hurdled that obstacle by saying, "I work at Witherspoon's Department Store, so you could pick me up there at six."

Dave agreed, and we decided that we'd go somewhere for a burger before the game.

It was only when I was on the bus heading home that I realized what a lot of figuring out I'd have to do about Friday night. To begin with, mine wasn't the ordinary, everyday kind of family that most high-school kids have. In fact, my home life was anything but normal.

A few years ago, Mama had joined a very strict religious sect that had extremely rigid rules. It wasn't even a church, really, just a group of believers who had broken away from a fundamentalist church because they didn't think it was strict enough. They believe that wearing makeup, high heels, fashionable clothes, or even cutting your hair was sinful. To them, drinking, smoking, or dancing was from the Devil himself. So, I knew if I even mentioned going to a school dance, Mama would forbid it. Dad, who didn't go along will her religious beliefs, was just as strict in his own way. He didn't want any boy "hanging around" and since he liked to go out to a tavern and drink beer after work on Fridays, he wanted me staying home with Mama.

So telling the truth about my date was out. I'd already tried arguing and persuading my parents to let me participate in some school activities and knew it was no use. I didn't like lying, but I'd found it was the only way I could do anything.

I had to sneak lipstick and mascara into my handbag and apply them at the bus stop before school. If I wanted to do something like go to a movie or to a school play, I had to make up something about going to the library.

Studying was all Mama understood because she knew I was trying to keep my grades up; I was working for a scholarship to a teacher's college. For me, the dream of college was my only hope for an escape from my rigid, unhappy home. But in the meantime, I had to have some relief from my mother's constant sermonizing and quarrels with Dad about his "sinful habits."

My whole life at that point had become a struggle to be free, I guess. I just tuned out a lot of what went on in my home and lived in my own dream world most of the time I was there.

Even working at Witherspoon's was part of my fantasy existence. Being around all those beautiful clothes, jewelry and accessories, luxurious furs, leathers, and delicate lingerie was a welcome change from the barren life at home. To Mama, life was supposed to be hard, and sacrifice and doing without was what it was all about. But I longed for warmth, beauty, and lightness. I was determined to be and live exactly opposite from my parents—someday.

When I got home, Mama was packing Dad's lunch while he sat at the kitchen table watching the portable TV. Mama was singing hymns under her breath, I knew, because she felt the TV was as bad as movies and never turned it on when she was alone in the house. She smiled her faded smile at me as I paused at the kitchen door.

149

"I'm going to my room. I've got some studying to do," I said.

For the first time Dad acknowledged my presence, and as I started down the hall to my bedroom, his harsh voice followed with a list of chores he wanted done.

"Okay!" I called back.

Reaching my room, I shut the door behind me, shutting out the sound of his voice, the TV, and Mama's monotonous humming. It was such a relief to be in the one room in the house where I could express my longing for pretty things.

I'd used as much imagination and as little money as I could to transform the small, plain room into a haven. I had painted the walls pale yellow, made bright, flowered curtains and cut out pictures I liked from magazines and pasted them on colored construction paper for frames. I'd made throw pillows for my bed and dyed my chenille bedspread a bright yellow.

I did have studying to do, but all that was on my mind was how I was going to work things out for my date with Dave on Friday night. Of course, going to work from school was easy—Mama expected me to do that. But how could I explain coming home as late as I would after the dance? It would be near midnight at least—about the same time that Dad would be getting off the swing shift at the plywood mill. I flopped on the bed and closed my eyes. I had to think of something! Whatever it took, I was going out Friday night!

I'd missed out on most of the fun of high school so far. Dave's asking me was important, and I wasn't going to let my entire senior year slip by without ever having attended a single dance. Then I realized I could tell Mama there was a meeting on Friday of the students who were eligible for scholarships—which was true.

Of course, it was immediately after the last class, not in the evening. But Mama wouldn't have to know that. She knew the honor society's faculty advisor, Miss Jacoby, often met with those of us who were applying to colleges. I'd just say I would be going to the school after I finished at Witherspoon's, which was also true. I'd be going to the gym, actually, but that didn't have to be explained.

With that all worked out, I could now concentrate on what to wear. I wanted to look really great. Dave was such a good-looking guy, and I wanted him to feel proud of me.

I got up and looked in my closet. Most of my clothes were basics I'd bought with my store discount at Witherspoon's; I couldn't afford most of their merchandise on my wages. I thought of all the lovely things they had, rack after rack of beautiful clothes I'd love to wear: luxurious sweaters in luscious colors; blouses of silk, lace, cotton; smartly tailored jackets, skirts, and pants. Most of the people who shopped at Witherspoon's had lots of money.

150

I felt a hot surge of anger rise up inside me. It just wasn't fair that some people had everything they wanted and others, like me, hardly anything.

I took out a pleated skirt and a tailored blouse from the closet and held them up to myself in front of the mirror. The outfit needed something to spark it up, I decided.

I turned and opened my dresser drawer and carefully shifted the piles of underwear. Underneath was the lining paper and I slipped my hand under that and brought out a bright scarf. It felt cool and silky as I tied it around my throat. The colors—rust, gold, and bronze—were a perfect complement to my oatmeal-colored blouse and beige-tweed skirt.

I'd taken the scarf from Witherspoon's a few weeks ago, but had never worn it. I'd been too scared to. I was still stunned that I'd done it. Oh, I'd taken a couple of things before. Not anything big or terribly expensive, just a couple of packages of pantyhose, a bra and some bikini panties, hair clips, and a cute little lapel pin I couldn't resist. There'd been dozens of them and no one ever missed anything. At first, I was amazed that I'd taken anything at all, and more amazed when I found I could get away with it. I couldn't believe how easy it was, and I always rationalized that taking things like that wasn't really stealing. Some of the stuff was just piled on the tables for sales; I didn't think it was even inventoried.

Besides, I worked hard at Witherspoon's. I often stayed after closing, helping someone else close out her register, or worked extra when things were rushed, and I didn't always put it on my time card. The amount of merchandise in the store was staggering. How could they ever miss the few small things I'd taken?

This scarf was different, though. It was a designer one, and pure silk. I knew how much they cost and I could never have afforded to buy one. Maybe that's why I'd never dared to wear it yet. The pattern was so unique, and anyone would recognize the designer signature.

I took it off, folded it carefully, and put it back in the drawer. I refused to feel guilty about it. They had so much of everything, I reminded myself, and I had so little. Evening out the scales a little wouldn't hurt anyone.

We were busy on Friday afternoon at Witherspoon's, but around four o'clock I took my break. In the employees' lounge I washed my face and carefully applied my blusher, lip gloss, and mascara. I'd seen Dave at lunch and he'd seemed real happy about our date. I gave my hair a good brushing, bringing out the sheen, and then went back on the floor.

As soon as I did, Mrs. Hughes, the manager of sportswear, asked me to unpack and set out a new shipment of sweaters. As I began to do it, I thought about how beautiful they all were. I'm not sure to this day what came over me at that point, but something seemed to whisper to me: They'd never miss one! I felt my pulse throb and my heart pound as my fingers slid over the smooth, fluffy yarn. How soft—how delightfully warm—and all in such lovely pastel colors! The pale yellow one, my favorite color, was especially pretty with little pearl buttons at the neck.

Why not? the voice asked. Then, almost as if my hands had a mind of their own, I slipped the yellow sweater out of the batch, wrapped it in tissue paper, and dropped to my knees so that I was even with the shelves underneath the counter. That's where we kept our handbags, umbrellas, or any other personal things. I zipped open my tote bag and hurriedly stuffed the sweater inside. I heard the stockroom door open behind me, and I jumped to my feet, quickly tagging the rest of the sweaters. I hadn't had time to completely close the zipper on the bag but I'd do it as soon as Dina, the other clerk, went back on the floor. But I didn't have a chance because just then Mrs. Hughes called me to come out and wait on a customer.

We were very busy for the rest of the afternoon and I didn't get back to the stockroom. I kept watching the clock as its hands neared closing time because I was looking forward to the evening with Dave. I figured I could change into the sweater in one of the washroom cubicles, then put on my jacket, button it up to the collar, and leave the store with no one the wiser.

About twenty minutes before closing, Mrs. Hughes came over to me. She seemed irritated and upset.

"Darla, wasn't there a yellow sweater in that new shipment I asked you to unpack?" she asked. "I'm sure I saw it when I opened the box. I have a customer who ordered one when we didn't have it in her size before. It wasn't sold, was it? I told her when one came in I'd hold it for her."

My heart skipped a beat, my hands got clammy, and I wondered if I looked as guilty as I felt. Of course, I knew it hadn't been sold. And, of all the sweaters, it had to be the yellow one that had been ordered, I thought with a sinking sensation.

"Maybe it's in one of the dressing rooms," I managed to stammer. My heart was racing now. Dear God, please don't let me get caught! I prayed frantically. I'll never do it again, I promise. Just give me a chance to slip it back into stock.

By this time, some of the other salesgirls were gathering. When Mrs. Hughes was agitated, everyone reacted.

"Someone must have sold it!" she declared. "I should have had you put it aside, Darla. Mrs. Hansen is a very good customer, and I hate to disappoint her. Let's look through the sales slips. Someone must have written it up by mistake."

152

Although I knew it was futile, I went through the motions of checking my sales book. Mr. Witherspoon was now in the department. He made it a habit at closing time to walk through the store, and I guess seeing the unusual activity in our department made him curious and he walked over.

"Look on the shelves under the counter," someone suggested, and I felt a wave of dizziness sweep over me. I thought I was going to faint. It was Mrs. Hughes herself who stooped down and started searching underneath the counter. She picked up my tote bag from which a bit of pale yellow was showing. She stood up slowly with my tote bag in her hand. Her shocked expression told me she knew what had happened. There was a sharp intake of breath all around me. Everyone recognized my tote bag.

"Darla!" Mrs. Hughes exclaimed. Her glance went from me to Mr. Witherspoon, who was standing there witnessing the whole scene. Mr. Witherspoon was the one who had hired me. He'd always been very kind, asking me about school and my grades, knowing I was working for a scholarship to college.

"Could I see you in my office, Miss Seaver?" he said through stern, tight lips.

My legs were trembling as I followed him. I could feel the eyes of the other clerks and Mrs. Hughes boring into my back, looks of curiosity mixed with pity. I moved like a sleepwalker. This can't really be happening, I told myself.

Mr. Witherspoon closed the door of his office, motioned me to a seat, took a place behind his desk, and riveted his gaze on me.

"I don't know what to say to you, Darla, besides expressing my own shock. You must know shoplifting is a crime and this store has a policy of prosecuting shoplifters." He paused, letting his words sink in. I was too ashamed to raise my eyes to meet his, and my hands twisted and untwisted agonizingly in my lap. "Furthermore," he went on, "your whole future is at stake. I would sincerely like to avoid any unfavorable publicity for you and for the store."

"I'll bring back everything—pay for everything!" I blurted out before I realized that I'd hung myself with my own words. Now I'd revealed this was not the first time or the first thing I'd stolen.

"Then there have been previous times—other things?" Mr. Witherspoon asked.

I burst into tears. Half-hysterical with fright that I'd end up in jail, I heard myself telling Mr. Witherspoon about my life at home— how I never seemed to have any pretty things or clothes . . . how I'd yearned for some of the lovely merchandise I handled in my work at the store . . . how I hadn't meant to do anything really wrong . . . how sorry I was, and how ashamed, too. All the while, Mr. Witherspoon listened intently. When I finally stopped sobbing, he handed me a tissue from the box on his desk.

"Darla, I'd really like to help you," he said. "I know your parents are good, hardworking people and this will be very painful for them. It could also ruin your future." He paused significantly while I held my breath, my hands clenched together. "If you will return everything you have taken and not used, and make restitution for what you have, I will not prosecute—on one condition." He paused. "Our store, along with other retail stores in this area, supports a police program to keep anyone who shoplifts—that is, first-time offenders—from a conviction record. For a fee, you may attend an eight-hour deprogramming class. It provides counseling to help correct what is considered a personality defect rather than a criminal nature. If you are willing to attend this class, I think we will find that the bonus coming to you from your sales commissions while you've been employed here would about cover the fee. Will you do this?"

"Oh, yes, Mr. Witherspoon!" I said instantly. "I'm sorry. I don't know why I did something I knew was wrong. I never will again."

"Well, this program should help you find out why and help you in your determination not to do it again. You realize something this serious could destroy your life, don't you, Darla?"

"Yes, sir, I certainly do," I said, relieved beyond belief that that was all he was going to do. But his next words shattered my hopes and plunged me into deep despair.

"Of course, your parents will have to be notified," he said and picked up the phone. I went rigid with tension. Then he added, "And naturally we can no longer have you working here in the store."

I wish I'd been able to blot out what happened in the next few hours, but it will be etched forever on my mind. It was all as bad or even worse than I could have imagined.

My father, tightlipped, came to get me as I remained sitting like a statue in Mr. Witherspoon's office. Mr. Witherspoon told him briefly what had happened and about the deprogramming class. Then we left. We had to go out through the basement of the store to the parking lot where the pickup truck was parked, for the store was now closed. It was only then I remembered Dave and our date.

I closed my eyes in misery. He was probably waiting and wondering why I'd stood him up. I wondered if the information about me would somehow leak out and I'd be the topic of gossip at school. I huddled in the truck's cab, trying to tune out my father's harsh voice lashing at me as we headed home.

The scene at home was a nightmare, too.

"You wicked girl!" Mama screamed at me. Her face was blotchy and red from weeping, and the veins in her head and neck were pulsing. I was terrified that what I'd done would bring on a heart attack. I was more afraid of that than my father's violent anger. One parent's action triggered the other's reaction. As my father continued to rant and rave, Mama seemed to suddenly remember she was supposed to be a Christian. She fell on her knees, and her voice rose in quavering pleas. "Forgive this lying, thieving girl—save her for my sake. I've tried to raise her to obey Your commandments. But she rebelled against the law that says, 'Thou shalt not steal.' Punish her for her transgressions."

Mama moaned loudly until my father whirled on her and shouted, "Shut up, Mabel." Then he turned toward me. "Now, you listen to me, Darla. You're going to pay back everything yourself. Mr. Witherspoon said they weren't sure just how much you'd taken or how much it was all worth, but it sure isn't coming out of my pocket. I've never taken a dime that didn't belong to me in my life, and I'm not about to take the rap for you."

Yes, I wish I could wipe that horrible scene from my mind. I don't remember just how long they both went at me; I only know when they were finally through I was exhausted and crept off to my room to bed. I wished I could sleep and never wake up.

But of course it wasn't a bad dream—it was real. And when Monday morning came and I had to go to school, I didn't know what I was going to say to Dave, how I'd ever explain. As it turned out, I didn't have to because he cut me cold when I saw him in the cafeteria. He was standing with Sue Ellen Sims, one of the cheerleaders, a pretty girl with shiny blond hair. She was looking up at him and laughing and flirting. They must have made contact at the dance, I thought forlornly. Not that it mattered. I was grounded for the rest of the year as punishment, so I wouldn't have been allowed to date or go out anyway.

At the end of English class, I got a message from the office that Miss Jacoby, my counselor, wanted to see me after school. I immediately wondered if she had been notified about what had happened at Witherspoon's. I worried that I had lost my scholarship eligibility.

I was pretty nervous by the time of my appointment, so nervous that when I found out all she wanted was to show me my grade-point average, and to tell me I had a good chance of obtaining a full scholarship, I was so relieved that I burst into tears.

As Miss Jacoby tried to comfort me, I poured out the whole, terrible story. She was wonderful; she didn't say a word, didn't look shocked or anything. She just waited until I was finished, then talked quietly and calmly.

"I think I understand, Darla," she said, "and I'm sure you're

155

remorseful and unhappy about everything. But this program you're going to be involved in sounds like it will be very helpful. It will probably help you sort things out in your own mind, help you to see how you got to the point where it seemed okay to take something from the store. I really feel you're going to be better off afterward, in every way. Now here's my home address. If you ever feel you need to just come by and talk, you'd be welcome."

I thanked her and left the office feeling as if a weight had been lifted. According to her, I wasn't as bad a person as my parents had hammered into me, but someone who was confused and had her values mixed up.

For the rest of my senior year, my friendship with Miss Jacoby was my lifesaver. She knew I'd lost my job at Witherspoon's and that I now had no way of earning the money I needed for college next fall. So, she suggested I clean her apartment and do some ironing for her each week, and she paid me as much per hour as I was getting at Witherspoon's. It was very kind and generous of her because Dad wasn't about to help me out financially, and even with a full scholarship, there'd be extra expenses.

Actually, I loved the time I spent in her pretty apartment. It was bright, warm—full of flowers, plants, and art. Sometimes after I'd finished and she'd come back from shopping or whatever she'd done while I was cleaning, she'd make tea and serve it in dainty china cups. We'd talk and she helped me so much. In fact, my visits with her made the rest of the year bearable.

In the meantime, I started the program Mr. Witherspoon had offered as an alternative to prosecuting me. At first, I had felt like a drowning person being rescued. But the nearer it got to the date I was to go to the class, the more reluctant I became. But there was no backing out. I knew I had to do it.

Dad dropped me off at City Hall the day of the first meeting. I felt like cringing as I asked directions, but the clerk at the information desk didn't bat an eye. "The Behavioral Modification Workshop is being held on the third floor, Room 302," she told me.

Since the classes were scheduled for Saturday so that those attending didn't have to take off from work or miss school, the building was practically deserted, and I didn't run into anyone I knew.

When I got to Room 302, the room was already half-full of people of all ages, male and female. I was surprised to see a nicely dressed, middle-aged woman, a man in a business suit, two brawny "lumberjack" types, and there was even a little, gray-haired lady who looked like somebody's grandmother! I was soon to learn that there is no shoplifter stereotype, they come in all sizes, shapes, ages, and occupations.

156

The class was informal and conducted by two great counselors: Dr. Collins, a psychologist, who told us to call him Steve, and a woman named Anna.

It would be hard to describe what that class did for me and I think for everyone there. First, there was nothing judgmental or accusing about anything that was said by the counselors. They were there to help us find out why we stole because, like myself, it seems it was against what most of us believed to be right. From their own stories—and we were each encouraged to describe our own experiences—the majority had taken clothing or a small article such as a clock or a pen or a razor.

No one in our particular class had stolen food or medicine. Many of the people actually had credit cards or enough cash with them when they had taken something in a store. What we discovered about ourselves was that each of us had a different reason for stealing, and none had a real need.

The well-dressed woman wept softly as she confessed that her husband neglected her. She thought he was involved with someone else, and had shoplifted just to gain his attention. One of the big, very "macho" guys said he had been fired from a job where he really wasn't very happy anyway, and did it to get even with his ex-employer. Another man had a poor self-image. I guess there were as many reasons for shoplifting as there were people in the program.

By the end of the sessions, we all felt very comfortable in the group and openly shared our feelings. When we finished, all of us had a better understanding of ourselves. It was encouraging to be told by the counselors that the program's success was proven by the fact that over four hundred shoplifters had gone through the course and there had been only one known repeat violation.

It was almost like the parting of old friends after the final session. I was so grateful that this class had been offered. I felt I had a much better handle on my life now and I was sure I would never have the problem again. I would try to remember what Anna had said before we were dismissed: "Remember, being tempted isn't the same as giving in to the urge to take something. You may be tempted, but you have enough tools now to walk away from it."

I worked all summer to get money for college in the fall. Dad said he'd give me bus fare to Cold Valley where Teachers State College was located, but that was all. So in June I started picking fruit, then packed fruit at a cannery for the rest of the summer. It was hard work but good pay and I needed the money. I'd arranged to live with my mother's aunt in Cold Valley. Aunt Angela was a widow and had just had a hip operation, and she told Mama she would be glad for the company and help with the housework.

The thought of college in the fall was all that kept me going during that long, hot summer. I wouldn't be sorry to leave home or Diamond Hill; it held a lot of unhappy memories for me. The last year, since the mess at Witherspoon's, I'd been mostly miserable. When it came time to say good-bye, Mama cried a little. I think she really felt bad about our home life, and how she and Dad had treated me since I was caught stealing. They couldn't seem to accept the fact that I was sorry, or that I'd learned a bitter lesson. As far as Dad was concerned, my going was "good riddance."

Once on the bus, I breathed a sigh of relief. I was starting a new life. Things would be different now. I was leaving the past behind.

Life in Cold Valley was a welcome change. I felt like I was starting over with a clean slate. Aunt Angela was kind and cheerful, and seemed happy to have me. I registered for classes as Crystal Seaver, as if dropping the first part of my name and using my middle name gave me a new identity. A new chapter of my life was opening and I wanted to be rid of the "old me."

That first year was wonderful. Even though I was shy, I made some nice new friends, and life with Aunt Angela was pleasant and comfortable.

I had a chance to work in the summer-school admissions office on campus, so I stayed in Cold Valley with Aunt Angela instead of going home to Diamond Hill. Then in the fall, I enrolled for my second year at college.

In the middle of that year, Mama died.

Dad didn't even let me know she was in the hospital until it was too late for me to go to see her. This made me angry, but he had always been a cold, unloving person so it shouldn't have surprised me. When I got word less than five months later that he had remarried, I felt my last link with Diamond Hill had been broken. Aunt Angela was all the family I had now, and I really felt her home was mine.

Then, during the fall of my third year, two things happened that changed everything for me.

The first was unexpectedly meeting Miss Jacoby, my high-school counselor, one day when I was on an errand. She was attending the nearby university, working toward her master's degree in psychology.

"You look wonderful, Darla!" she exclaimed. "How are things going for you?"

"Really good, Miss Jacoby," I answered.

"Oh, please call me Erica. I'm just a student like you nowadays. Why don't we go have a cup of coffee?" she suggested.

Over coffee, we exchanged some of the things that had happened to both of us since I'd graduated and left Diamond Hill.

Erica's life had changed almost as much as mine. The marriage plans she had then had fallen through, and she had decided to further her career by acquiring an advanced degree. She was now dating a professor at the university and, as a matter of fact, they were having a little get-together that night at her apartment.

"I'd love for you to come, Darla. I want you to meet Aaron, and there'll be others there I'm sure you'd like. Please come," Erica said.

I hesitated, not sure that I wanted to. Even though I'd overcome a lot of my insecurities, I was still shy about meeting new people. "I'll try," I promised before we parted.

Erica gave me her address and I noticed that her apartment was only a few blocks from Aunt Angela's house. But although I got dressed that evening and started out, I turned back twice, undecided about going. I ended up walking by the building a couple of times before forcing myself to ring the doorbell. Lucky for me, the door opened before I could turn and run.

I say lucky because the second life-changing event of that fall for me happened that night. At Erica's party, I met Kyle Simpson, a tall, lanky fellow student with intelligent eyes and a fantastic smile.

Erica greeted me warmly, led me into her small but charming living room, and began introducing me around. She'd been right when she said it was just a casual, informal gathering; everyone was dressed in jeans-and-sweater-type outfits. They were drinking red wine, and there were large platters of cheese, crackers, sour cream dip, and raw vegetables. There were little groups sitting on the floor, others were milling around, and all over was a cozy, pleasant atmosphere. I began to relax after a girl from my English class came up and introduced her date and we all began to talk.

Then I felt a touch on my arm. I turned and looked up into a face I recognized but couldn't quite place.

"Hi," he said, smiling. "Did you ever find a copy of Dr. Zhivago?"

That's when I recognized him. He'd been in my class on Russian novelists last spring. His face seemed especially familiar because I'd noticed him just the other day when I'd been in the secondhand bookstore inquiring about that book.

I shook my head and replied, "No, but I left my name and phone number so they could call me if they got one in."

"You're Crystal Seaver, right?"

"Yes, how did you know?" I asked.

He grinned. "I heard you give your name to the clerk at the bookstore. I remembered you from class but—well, I just never got to meet you." He paused. "Can I get you a refill?" He looked at my wineglass.

"No, I'm fine."

"Well, why don't we find a corner where we can sit down?" he suggested, and he placed his hand under my elbow and led me over to a window seat. Once seated, he said, "By the way, the movie version of Dr. Zhivago is playing this week. It follows the book pretty closely. Have you seen it? If you haven't, how about going with me?"

And that's how our romance began. Later, I discovered Kyle was almost as shy as I was and that it had taken him all the courage he could muster to approach me that night. He told me that he'd wanted to get to know me ever since he first saw me in class.

I remember every detail of our first date—maybe because it was practically my first real date with anyone. Aunt Angela was pleased when I told her, and she liked Kyle right away when he came to pick me up.

The movie was wonderful, and afterward we went to The Old Stand, one of the college hangouts. It was dark, smoky, and teeming with students drinking beer and eating pizza—the kind of place poor Mama would have considered a "den of iniquity." But even over all the noise, we were able to enjoy ourselves.

When Kyle brought me home, he surprised me by leaning down and quickly giving me a light kiss on my lips. "I'll call you," he said. I went inside, humming under my breath.

"I'll call you," Kyle had said, but he didn't. Nearly a week went by and I didn't hear from him. I stopped asking Aunt Angela if there'd been any calls for me while I was in class; I was embarrassed and hurt. Maybe I took a casual remark too seriously, I told myself. Not used to dating, I'd latched on to what might have been just a polite ending to a pleasant evening. For him, it had obviously been no big deal. For me, it had meant a lot. I tried to shrug it off during the next long week, and stopped waiting for the phone to ring.

But then it did ring. It was late Sunday evening ten days after we'd met. I'd given up hoping I'd ever hear from Kyle again.

"May I come by?" he asked.

Aunt Angela had gone out to visit friends and I hesitated. Then I remembered she was always urging me to invite someone over, so impulsively I said yes.

I hardly had time to dash upstairs, do something about my hair, and put on a fresh blouse when the front doorbell rang.

Kyle followed me into the kitchen as I got some cold chicken and potato salad out of the refrigerator. I thought having something to do would make the unexpected visit less awkward. Kyle seemed right at ease.

"I'm sorry about not calling sooner, Crystal," he began.

"Oh?" I tried to sound indifferent, as if it hadn't mattered.

"I intended to, but there was a reason."

"You don't have to explain," I started.

160

"I want to," he persisted. "It was my mother. She had a fall, a pretty bad one, so I had to drive down to Smithtown. You see, I'd called her to tell her I wasn't coming—I usually go visit once a month. She's a widow and can't do all the things that need to be done around the house, so she depends on me. Well, since she knew I wasn't coming, she went ahead and tried to clean out the rain gutters herself. She got on a ladder and she fell."

"That's awful, Kyle. I'm really sorry. Was she badly hurt?"

"Bruised, but not seriously. But I felt guilty," he retorted— somewhat shortly, I thought. "Anyhow, I stayed down there for a few days and got some things done. Then when I got back, I had a lot of studying to do."

There was a long pause while I set two places for us at the kitchen table.

"I'd called her to say I wasn't coming because I'd got two tickets for the musical the drama club is putting on, and I wanted to take you," Kyle went on. "I just hadn't gotten around to asking you yet." He showed me the tickets he'd bought and I knew he was telling the truth.

We talked a lot that evening—actually, Kyle did most of the talking. He seemed to want to tell me all about himself. He was majoring in business and had a job at the local pharmacy three nights a week to help with his college expenses.

"I could've lived at home and gone to school at the local college, but I needed to be on my own," he said. "At least for a while. My problem is Mom. She doesn't need me financially but since I'm her only child, she's inclined to—" He broke off. "She can't understand why I won't come back to Smithtown when I graduate, settle down, and—"

"Live happily ever after?" I finished for him, and we both laughed.

The next few weeks we spent a lot of time together, sharing thoughts, feelings, hopes, and dreams. I couldn't believe it was happening. I'd never had that kind of closeness with anyone. It made me tingle all over. For the first time in my life I actually felt young and lighthearted. Kyle and I either saw each other every day or we talked by phone. Each time we were together my feelings for him grew, and by the end of the month, I knew I was falling in love with him.

Kyle could be serious or carefree. I never knew what kind of mood he'd be in.

Even his unpredictability made me love him more, like the day we went on the picnic. One Saturday morning he called me and said, "Be ready in half an hour. I've got a surprise for you."

161

When I saw his old car pull up, I ran outside. Then I saw the wicker basket on the back seat.

"Jump in!" Kyle said, reaching over and opening the door. Then he kissed me and asked, "How's my girl?"

My heart skipped a beat. That was the first time he'd ever called me "his girl." I smiled back at him and we took off.

We drove up into the hills that circled Cold Valley and found a spot not too far from the road where we parked the car. From there, we could look down and see the campus and the surrounding town.

"It looks like a toy village from here," I said.

"Yes, and it's peaceful and quiet and a great place to escape," Kyle said, spreading out a blanket.

I helped him straighten the edges. "You're trying to escape?"

"Yes. Mom wanted me to come home this weekend. She was planning some kind of dinner party and had people she wanted me to meet. Some such nonsense." He stopped abruptly, giving his attention to a bottle of wine he'd pulled out of the basket. "I know you don't drink as a rule, but since this is a special occasion. . . ." He got out two wineglasses, popped the cork, poured two glasses, and handed me one.

"Special occasion?" I asked, taking a sip. It was light and lovely and cool.

"Very special," he answered. Then he just went on setting out the food he'd brought: cheese, French bread, sliced ham, grapes, pears. He made me a sandwich, gave it to me in a paper napkin, and finally said, "Mom's always trying to fix me up with someone in Smithtown. Trying to trap me into having a reason to come back there. I know when she's got someone she approves of for me to meet and I just refuse to—" Again he stopped and held up his glass in a toasting gesture. "Besides, I like to choose my own women."

I was already feeling slightly lightheaded from the wine when Kyle said suddenly, "How about driving to Smithtown with me next weekend? I'd like Mom to meet you."

I stiffened slightly. "Meet me?"

"Well, she'll have to meet you sometime if you're going to marry me."

My hand started to shake, and I put down the glass so I wouldn't spill the wine. "Did I hear you right or was that a proposal?" I asked.

"What do you think?" he replied holding out his arms. I moved into them and we kissed, tenderly at first, then slowly moving into a deeply passionate kiss. Finally, we parted and I looked into Kyle's eyes.

"Do you mean it?" I asked.

"Never meant anything more. I love you, Crystal, and I have

162

from the start." He kissed me again, long and lingeringly. I could feel his heart pounding against me as he held me tightly. He lifted his head after a while, traced the outline of my mouth with one finger, and said, "So? Will you?"

When I could breathe, I put my arms around his neck and brought his face down to mine again. "Oh, yes, Kyle!"

That afternoon is unforgettable. Kyle folded our sweaters into pillows and we lay on the blanket, holding each other close. The unaccustomed wine, the food, the sunshine had made us both drowsy. I lay cuddled against his lean body, my head cradled on his shoulder, his arms around me. We could hear the sound of rushing water over rocks of the nearby stream like background music playing—a love song. The wind in the trees lulled us, and we slept until the sun lowered and the shadows fell across us and we stirred in the sudden chill.

"Oh, Kyle, I've never been this happy," I said as we left.

It certainly was with many mixed feelings that I went with Kyle to meet his mother. Aside from the natural nervousness any girl would have meeting her prospective mother-in-law, mine was coupled with the guilty knowledge of my past. What would Mrs. Simpson think if she knew the girl her son wanted to marry had barely escaped a jail sentence? Even though it had been over four years ago, every once in a while that whole horrible mess came back to me in nightmarish detail. I relived it all, and although the flashbacks grew less frequent as time went on, they were still haunting me.

As we drove down to Smithtown that bright, sunny spring Saturday, I would glance over at Kyle every so often and experience that same scary sensation. What if he found out I'd gone through a period of stealing—of taking things that didn't belong to me? And if I'd gotten away with it, I might still be doing it. I guess that's what frightened me the most, the chance that the urge to steal might come over me again. Even now it was hard for me to remember how I felt back then. What had been going through my mind when I did steal and how could I have rationalized it?

The course I'd taken had clarified a lot for me. Even though the counselors had warned us we all might have sudden, irrational urges to take something again, we had the "tools" to control it and we didn't have to give in to the temptation.

I'd never placed myself in a position to steal since then. The jobs I'd had in the admissions office were filing, typing, answering the phones—general office work. There hadn't been any temptations. I was almost sure I'd never even be tempted again, but then I wasn't in a place where there was either money or merchandise to take.

Should I tell Kyle about that unhappy period in my life? I

163

thought. Should I explain about my peculiar home life, my parents? Make a clean breast of what happened at the store? Kyle had told me practically everything about his own life: his childhood, his feelings about his father who had died when he was eleven, and his relationship with his mother. But I had said very little about my life before coming to live at Aunt Angela's, only that my mother was dead and my father had remarried.

There'd been a couple of times when I'd almost told Kyle, but then I'd asked myself what purpose it would serve. I guess the bottom line was I was afraid of losing him. I didn't really want him to know about that part of my life.

I'm a different person now, I told myself. Why bring up all the ugliness of the past? So, I hadn't told him. And although it sometimes bothered me, lurking guiltily in the back of my mind, for the most part I was happy. Kyle loved me as I was now. I didn't want to rock the boat.

"Well, here we are," Kyle said, stopping in front of a small white house with window boxes blooming with pink petunias, ruffled curtains at the front windows, and precisely trimmed hedges all around.

I looked at it, then at Kyle, and sat quite still, my hands clasped tensely in my lap.

Even Kyle seemed a bit reluctant to get out of the car, but he put his hand over mine and squeezed it reassuringly.

"Come on, honey, it won't be all that bad. We don't have to stay long. We can leave right after dinner."

All the way up a walkway that was bordered with rows of tulips, I felt my heart banging like a drum against my ribs. I swallowed hard, trying to ease the dryness in my tight throat.

The door was opened by a tall, thin woman who resembled Kyle a little. She immediately held out her arms to Kyle, saying, "I thought you'd be here earlier. I've been waiting all morning! I was afraid you might have had car trouble, or even an accident. Why didn't you at least call and say you'd be late?"

"I didn't say exactly when I'd be here, Mom," Kyle said.

I was just standing there, since Mrs. Simpson had yet to glance my way or acknowledge me in any way. Kyle grabbed my hand and pulled me forward. "Mom, this is Crystal Seaver."

Mrs. Simpson slowly turned toward me, a forced smile on her face as she held out her hand. When I took it, it gave mine no pressure at all.

"How nice of you to keep Kyle company on the drive down, Miss Seaver. Do come in, won't you?"

The old saying "a place for everything and everything in its place" must have been written about Mrs. Simpson's house. I'd never seen such a neat, spotless home. Aunt Angela's was pleasantly shabby, but warm and cozy and looked lived-in. But Mrs. Simpson's house looked like everything was dusted and polished every day. There were lace mats on all the upholstered furniture, plastic covers on lampshades, even the china figurines on the mantelpiece were under glass globes. The house was neither homelike nor inviting: everything had a "don't touch" look about it.

There were framed photographs everywhere of Kyle at different ages. As I looked around, I wondered what it had been like for a little boy growing up in such an atmosphere. How anyone could feel comfortable here? I couldn't imagine. I didn't. I felt on edge all afternoon since I was all but ignored. Mrs. Simpson directed all the conversation to Kyle, and she brought up the story about her fall from the ladder at least three times before Kyle broke in and said he had to get back early to study.

Mrs. Simpson went to see about dinner—she had refused any offer of help from me so Kyle and I were left alone in the living room. He immediately came over to where I was sitting and started kissing me. I was startled, and struggled, slightly afraid his mother would walk back in and see us. But Kyle didn't let me go right away. He kissed me thoroughly, leaving me breathless and dizzy. "I love you," he said almost fiercely as he reluctantly let me pull away.

Dinner depressed me even more as I noticed how possessive Mrs. Simpson was of Kyle. When she finally turned toward me, she fixed me with a penetrating stare and said, "I never dreamed Kyle would choose a college away from home. We have a perfectly fine one right here. I can't wait until he graduates and comes home to stay."

Kyle didn't meet my glance, but I couldn't help thinking that Mrs. Simpson would never willingly give him up. Anxiety knotted in my stomach and I could hardly eat.

Finally, we managed to get away, but not before Mrs. Simpson had told us in detail about the "lovely girl, a minister's daughter" that she wanted Kyle to meet on his next visit.

Once we were in the car and headed back to the freeway, Kyle exploded. He reached over and pulled me close to him, saying between clenched teeth, "Look, Crystal, you've seen my mother for yourself. You know she'll never accept our plans to get married. She'll put up all sorts of objections to it. So why don't we just go ahead and get married, then tell her?"

I stared at him. "You mean elope?"

"No, not exactly. We can have the kind of wedding we talked about—in the college chapel with just a few friends, the way you want it. My mother would put up such a fuss that she'd ruin things. But if

165

we're already married, what can she say?"

Some of my happiness flowed back but there still lingered that nagging anxiety that, no matter what, Mrs. Simpson would never accept me. I agreed with Kyle that she would do whatever she could to prevent our marriage, and I was glad Kyle wanted to marry me in spite of the uproar we'd have to expect afterward. But would his mother ever forgive us for not having her there? I was deeply afraid of her power.

Observing her with him that afternoon, I'd realized what a clever woman she was and how, almost without Kyle's knowing it, she could make him do whatever she wanted. Except one thing: marry the girl of her choice.

So I went along with Kyle's decision with all my doubts about whether it was the right thing to do or not. I wanted to be happy, and Kyle meant my happiness. So I blocked out any guilt about not telling Mrs. Simpson. I was willing to pay any price to secure our future. I wanted Kyle at any cost.

On my wedding day, I was delirious with joy. Erica stood up beside me at the simple ceremony in the college chapel, and Aunt Angela gave us a reception for a few friends at the house afterward. Then Kyle and I went home to the apartment we had found in a rambling old Victorian house that had been renovated into apartments. We had one on the top floor, with slanting ceilings and recessed windows.

Mrs. Parrish, a plump, good-natured woman, was the landlady and had, she admitted, a "soft spot in her heart for newlyweds." A romantic soul, knowing our finances couldn't afford a real honeymoon, she had put flowers and a bottle of champagne in the tiny refrigerator for us and had baked a cake. All that was waiting for us when we climbed the stairs and walked inside.

It didn't take much to make me happy. I had Kyle and it was more than I had ever dreamed of having. I was totally in love with him and still rather stunned that he was in love with me.

The next weekend, Kyle went to see his mother and break the news to her. We both decided it was better that he go alone. I waited nervously for his return, knowing what her reaction would be. Kyle later told me she had been shocked and outraged at first, but before he'd left, she had calmed down. She sent a set of dishes and some embroidered placemats back with him, along with her wishes for our happiness.

"Wow, but I'm glad to be back," Kyle said, gathering me into his arms and holding me close. "Glad to be home!"

I nestled into his embrace, loving him so much, feeling safe now that we belonged to each other.

Kyle graduated in June and decided to go on for a master's degree, which he would need if he were going to apply for a teaching position at the junior college. I had another year of school to go, but decided to skip that year and work so that Kyle could go to school full-time. I could finish the next year.

I had been working part-time at the college while I'd been a student, but now I had to get a full-time job. I started looking and happened to see an ad in the newspaper about a management-trainee program being launched by a big, new department store just opening in the area. I knew my supervisor at the college, as well as Erica and some of my teachers would give me a good reference, so I went to apply.

The morning I went to the personnel office, I had dressed carefully, and Kyle had told me I looked "beautiful," so I felt pretty confident. I took one of the applications and sat down to fill it out, and suddenly I was gripped with terror. One of the first questions to be answered was: "Have you had any previous experience in merchandising?"

I was bathed in cold sweat, and it was as though my blood had turned to ice before I felt it rushing to my head. Beads of perspiration popped out on my forehead and upper lip. I felt dizzy as the ugly nightmare of what had happened at Witherspoon's flooded back. I had that same sick feeling I'd had when my shoplifting had been found out. Somehow, I managed to get up and go over to the water cooler, fill a cup with water, and stand there sipping it very slowly as I tried to recover.

I remembered how the counselors at the course I'd taken had warned us all that there would be moments when the memory would come back, when we might relive all the fear, turmoil, humiliation, and disgrace—something like what soldiers sometimes go through, reliving battle experiences. It was natural, the counselors had said, and gradually those bad moments would occur less and less often. But we would have to learn to control it consciously. They had taught us to take deep breaths until the heart stopped racing. I tried it now, inhaling slowly, exhaling, and little by little the frightening feeling went away. Finally, I stopped shaking.

In a few minutes, I walked back to my seat and after a second's hesitation, wrote "none" in the blank after the question about previous experience.

I knew if I said I'd had experience they would want a reference, and if I listed Witherspoon's my record would come out. If that happened, I'd never have a chance at this well-paying job. I would lose the opportunity to free Kyle from worrying about income while he had to study. So I lied.

167

Within a few days of applying, I was called back for a personal interview at Bloom Department Store for a position as a management trainee. There would be a six-week training program, I was told, so that each trainee could get experience in every department, then each of us would be assigned to a particular one for which we showed the most aptitude. When I left that day, I had a good feeling that I'd be hired.

I was. Kyle and I celebrated that night in our cozy little apartment with a pizza and an inexpensive bottle of red wine.

"Next time it'll be champagne!" Kyle promised, lifting his glass.

"When will that be?" I asked.

"Either when I get my degree or you're made manager!"

We laughed, kissed, and talked happily about the future. The future, that night, looked bright and full of hope and promise.

The training program was very interesting. The heads of each department took turns speaking to the class of about twenty trainees. We learned about buying merchandise months ahead, spotting fashion trends, pricing, marketing, and advertising. We were taken through each department, learning about the stock, familiarizing ourselves with brands carried, keeping inventory, figuring commissions, and the many other details of being on top of everything that went on in each one.

When the course ended, I began working on a regular basis. The first four months I was employed, the trainees were rotated around the store. Eventually I was placed in Fine Jewelry. My supervisor and instructor, Miss Lowell, said she had noticed I had a nice, low-key personality and patience. That surprised me because it was the first time I'd considered shyness and unassertiveness to be assets. She went on to explain that when people were selecting expensive jewelry, decisions did not come easily. It was necessary, she said, to give them plenty of time, not make them feel rushed or pressured because then they might not buy anything.

Kyle and I had begun celebrating our anniversary every month, very simply, of course, with a special dinner, a movie, or maybe small inexpensive gifts—just something to mark the occasion. We had been married seven months by this time and I was more in love with him than ever. I couldn't wait to get home that evening because I had a wonderful surprise. I'd discovered I could get a real bargain in a discontinued model of a computer with my store discount. It would make his schoolwork so much easier.

Of course, as luck would have it, that day had been particularly busy and I was tired and looking forward to closing when a customer approached my counter. She wanted some gold earrings for a gift for her sister, she told me, so I began to show her some of our nicest ones, all very expensive. She was very indecisive and I began to feel the slightest bit edgy as I heard the soft warning gong sounding throughout the store that meant closing time.

Finally, we narrowed down her choice to two pairs. Then, when I was almost biting my tongue in frustration, she decided on the more expensive of the two and asked for a gift box. She gave me her charge card. I wrote up the sale, wrapped the little box, and handed it to her. She thanked me for my patience and went off happily. At least I'll have a good commission on the sale, I thought as I closed out my register. I hurried to get my things from the employees' locker room and was finally on my way home.

The next day, I couldn't have been more surprised when I saw the same woman back at the jewelry counter.

"You'll think I'm crazy," she began, "but after I got home I began to think my sister would really prefer the other pair we looked at. Would you mind if I changed them?"

I smiled and assured her it was perfectly fine. I was feeling pretty good that morning, anyhow. Kyle had been overjoyed about the computer. We had made love, and I had awakened feeling so happy and lucky that I'd practically floated to work. I filled out the necessary forms on the exchange, put the woman's second selection in the tiny box she had brought with her, and she left happily again.

It wasn't until later that a cold feeling of dread crept over me. Had I put the pair she brought in to exchange back into the locked case? I was in the middle of helping another customer when that thought struck me, and I had to wait until I completed the sale to check and make sure.

With hands that trembled, I fumbled with the lock and looked inside the case. There was no sign of those earrings! I felt a sick lurching in my stomach, and I was almost physically ill as I locked the case. I stood for a minute, holding onto the edge of the counter, as waves of nausea swept over me. The whole experience at Witherspoon's shot across my mind in horrifying detail.

Slowly, I got hold of myself. I'd have to report it right away. I must have put the second pair of earrings into the gift box without removing the first pair. And neither of us had noticed. Or was my customer a clever thief? I tried to make sense of the incident as I asked someone to cover my counter. I took the elevator to the third floor to my supervisor's office. I hated the idea of getting involved in something like this. I was terrified that somehow my past at Witherspoon's would be revealed, and that maybe they would think . . . no! I stilled my quivering nerves, and as calmly as I could I told Miss Lowell what had happened.

She suggested I get the woman's name from the sales slip on

which her charge card number was printed, and try to get some explanation of the missing earrings. If the customer denied having them, the store would have to accept that. Losses like that often happen in a big store like Bloom, she told me, but of course, since the earrings were fourteen-carat gold, they would prefer recovering them. But customer relations were the important thing, and it wasn't in the store's best interest to make an issue of it.

In spite of her understanding and kindness, I was terribly upset about the incident. I kept thinking that it might throw suspicion on me in some way, cause the store to check my references, and that somehow my past history of shoplifting would come to light. What if that happened and I was fired, not only for lying about my past experience, but also for losing the valuable earrings through carelessness? By the end of the day, I was a wreck.

If what I dreaded did somehow happen, what could I tell Kyle? He thought I was doing so well on my job, and I really believed I was up for a promotion, maybe to assistant buyer. I'd gained a lot of self-confidence lately. Now all of that was slipping away.

I should have told Kyle about what happened at Witherspoon's—been more honest with him about my upbringing and background. Then maybe he would understand my terror of being discovered now. As it was, he would be so shocked, disillusioned, and angry that I had kept it all from him. And his mother! I shuddered, imagining what Mrs. Simpson would think of a daughter-in-law who had barely escaped jail.

On impulse, I called Erica. She was the only one who knew about my past in Diamond Hill—the only one who would understand and help me. I asked her to meet me after work; I needed to talk to her.

Erica was already waiting in a booth when I pushed open the door of the little coffee shop.

"You're as pale as a ghost," she said as she greeted me. "What happened?"

I poured out the story while Erica listened sympathetically. When I'd finished, she went back over all the things I'd done, and there was still no answer. The customer must have taken the earrings with her, intentionally or maybe by mistake. It was now up to her to report or return them. I nodded in agreement, but that wasn't what was really bothering me.

"It's Kyle I'm thinking about," I said. "This whole incident has brought up the past to me, and I feel so guilty that I never told Kyle about it. I didn't want him to know. He thinks I'm so—so wonderful. I don't want him to think less of me."

"His love is stronger than that. I don't think you're giving him enough credit. Try telling him. I think you'll find out," Erica suggested.

170

Encouraged, I went home, and after a few false starts when Kyle was getting out his books to begin studying, I blurted out, "Honey, I need to tell you something."

I'll never forget how the expression on his face slowly changed from his usual loving interest to disbelief, shock, and then to a sullen, closed look.

I don't know what I expected, but I had hoped for a very different reaction. I guess I wanted Kyle to take me in his arms, to tell me that no matter what, he loved me, believed in me, and that would never change. Instead, Kyle stared at me as if he were looking at a stranger. I slowly turned and walked back into the little kitchen and began washing the dinner dishes. After a few minutes he followed me, leaned against the refrigerator, and said, "Mom called this afternoon while you were at work. She needs me to come down and fix a few things around the house. I'll go early tomorrow morning. I think I need some time to think about what you've told me."

He was still at his desk, head bent over his books when I went to bed. I stifled my sobs into the pillow. When he finally came in, he lay stiffly apart from me. I lay awake a long time after his steady breathing told me he had fallen asleep. I finally drifted off toward dawn into an exhausted slumber, and when I woke up the bed beside me was empty.

How can I describe that weekend? It was the longest, loneliest, most desolate of my life. If I'd lost Kyle, what was the use of anything? I thought he'd be back Sunday night but he didn't come. Discouraged and depressed, I gave up waiting around midnight and went to bed. I dragged myself to work the next day, feeling like my world had come to an end.

I'd only been on the job a few hours when I heard my name being paged over the store's intercom: "Mrs. Simpson, please report to the manager's office."

My heart felt as though it were being squeezed by a cold hand. My mind raced frantically ahead, trying to imagine what I'd been called for, as I took the nearest escalator. At Mr. Chase's door, I knocked and entered. To my amazement, there was my earring customer! And she was smiling. She was the first to speak.

"Mrs. Simpson, I hope I haven't caused you needless worry, but I'm afraid I have. I bought some earrings for a gift for my sister, remember? Well, I left town with them right after I exchanged them, and it wasn't until she opened the box on her birthday that we discovered both pairs of earrings were in the box. I couldn't contact you until I returned to the city late last night."

I almost cried with relief. I can't remember what else was said, but I do remember her praising my patience and graciousness to both

171

Miss Lowell and Mr. Chase. But even that couldn't relieve my worry over probably losing Kyle. I knew he felt betrayed. We'd been so close, shared everything—or at least he'd thought we had. He was probably thinking now that his mother was right. He should have met and married the minister's daughter, not a girl he knew nothing about—someone who had just missed having a criminal record.

I went to the employees' lounge before going back on the floor. I needed a little time to regain my composure. I had spent several highly stressful days, and they had taken their toll. I sat down and tried to sort things out. I felt as if a big burden had been lifted. After all these years, I felt strangely free. I wasn't guilty of anything and I had to forgive myself for what had happened in the past—not let it constantly be a shadow on the present. We have to go on from our mistakes, learn from them, not carry them with us forever. Even if Kyle couldn't forgive me, I forgave myself.

That evening I wearily climbed the three flights of stairs to our apartment. I dreaded facing its emptiness, knowing Kyle had left and might not ever come back. I opened the door and was startled to see him standing in the small kitchen, holding up a bottle of champagne. He was smiling.

"What are we celebrating?" I asked numbly.

He put down the bottle beside the two chilled glasses and took me in his arms. My head was pressed so closely to his chest that I could hardly hear what he was saying.

"Forgive me, Crystal. Forgive me for failing you when you needed me."

I lifted my head and looked up into his eyes misted with tears.

"I'm so ashamed," Kyle went on. "After I left Mom's Sunday, I couldn't come straight home. I still had to work things out.

"I went to a motel and I spent the night pacing, thinking. Then I knew I had to come back—that somehow we had to find our way back to each other. But I didn't know how. I felt you had lied to me by withholding a truth. It was a truth about yourself, and that seemed awfully important to me. Then I found a slip of paper under the glass top of the bedside table in the motel. I don't know how it happened to be there, maybe it was meant to be. I copied it down."

Kyle loosened his hold on me and dug into his pocket. He handed me a folded piece of paper.

I looked at it and read:

"He who cannot forgive breaks the bridge over which he himself must pass."

I searched Kyle's face again and this time found only acceptance, forgiveness, and love. And I knew, as I fell into my husband's arms, that we would never let each other go again.

172

In a way, I'm grateful that the incident with the missing earrings happened, because it forced me to put my past behind me, leaving me free to pursue the future. Things have turned out well. Kyle finished his studies, received his master's degree, and is teaching at the junior college in Cold Valley. And I just found out yesterday that I've been promoted to assistant buyer for the fine-jewelry department—which means my own little cubicle, and a nice raise. The extra money will come in handy, I'm sure, but we don't intend to move out of our little apartment yet. We've been so happy there that it has sentimental value, so we'll stay—at least until we decide to start our family.

Speaking of family, while Kyle's mother and I haven't actually gotten close, we are making progress. I've invited her over for dinner several times and I call her occasionally just to say hello. I figured one of us had to make the first move.

Since then, I've learned that she's not a cold woman, she's just a frightened one. She lost her husband, and was scared of losing her son, too. Hopefully, she'll realize one day that I haven't taken Kyle away from her.

In the meantime, I'm doing all I can to show her how grateful I am to her. After all, she's the woman responsible for bringing Kyle into the world—and to me!

THE END

A TRAMP TRAPPED
MY SON!
Into a life of poverty

After thirteen years and three children, my husband had left me. The shock was almost more than I could bear. Everybody who knew us was shocked, too. They couldn't believe it when the divorce notice appeared in the paper. They came with unbelieving faces and good intentions. I dropped all of our old friends and moved to another part of the city.

We had been through many things together—some very hard times, living sometimes on very low wages. By the 1980s, D.C., as an electrician, was making good money. All the dreams we'd had through the lean years seemed about to come true. How he used to say, "Baby, when I get to making good money, I'm going to buy you fine clothes and diamond rings, fine furs and a car of your own."

I'd laugh and say, "Well, in the meantime, dinner's ready. Come on and eat." He would catch me in his arms and whirl me around until I could hardly breathe.

Maybe it was the debts that first started it. I wanted to pay off everyone who had extended credit to us when we needed it, and then splurge. But he wanted to get up high real quick. It wasn't that he didn't want to pay the debts, but he wanted to pay them a little at a time, while we bought other things, like another car and a house. Since I paid the bills I started to do it my way. It was good to walk into the grocery store and plunk down the money we owed him. Then D.C. would come in and ask how much we had left. We never seemed to have enough to go around.

The kids got sick and doctor bills piled up. D.C. had an accident and we didn't have any insurance to fix the car. It was these things that seemed to take the starch out of his wings. My husband was a handsome man. Women always turned to look again when we walked down the street. I always wondered what he saw in me when he could've had his pick of the girls in our town. But he thought I was beautiful. I knew women ran after him, but he was mine.

Five-foot ten and a half, one hundred sixty-five pounds. His dark brown hair was the same color as the long lashes that fringed the most wonderful pair of indigo blue eyes I'd ever looked into. As he told me how much he loved me, how beautiful I was, his lips smiled a crooked smile, showing sparkling white teeth. His olive skin was smooth and clear, and the dimple turned inside out in his chin. But it was his walk, his way of gesturing with his hands when he talked, all the little things that come to haunt me in the lonely times.

When he was transferred to Smithfield in Georgia, we couldn't get a house to live in, so I had to stay in White Hills with the children. He came home every Friday evening. Then one weekend, we waited for Daddy—and he didn't come. I was nearly beside myself with worry and called his mother. She said D.C. had called her and told her to let me know he wouldn't be home that week. We didn't have a phone and she said she was fixing to come over and let me know. She said he was working overtime. He got time and a half and double time on Sunday.

But when the next week came, he wired me some money with a message, See you next week. Love, Daddy. I knew there was something wrong. I tried to act natural so the children wouldn't be upset, and told myself I was crazy to think such things like him having another woman and so on. If people love truly, it's hard to deceive them. But, they will deceive themselves. I did, and when he came home the next weekend, I tried not to nag at him for staying away. It's so easy for a man to say, "I had to work."

He was cross with the children, yelling at them, "Doesn't your mother teach you anything when I'm gone?" He was building up to something. I knew him too well. I wondered about the new hand-tooled boots he had bought for himself. He pulled them off and set them beside the bed and ordered the kids to be careful and not scar them. I'd had about all I could take and picked them up and set them on a shelf. "No," I said sarcastically, "don't, by all means—we may have to boil and eat them."

I had said the wrong thing. He would've laughed about it a few weeks ago, but now he came back at me, "Yes, because we won't ever have anything decent, as long as we live." The children were looking at him with fearful eyes. I told them to go play and sat down beside him on the bed. He turned his back to me and pretended to go to sleep. I had made my advances as far as I would go, and he knew it. All he had to do was turn over and take me in his arms.

Somehow we got through that miserable weekend, and then, when it was time for him to leave, he held me in his arms and said, "Gosh, honey, if I didn't love you so much. . . ." I asked him what he meant and he said, "Oh, well, it's the same old thing. I work my fool self to death and never seem to get anywhere."

"But, honey, we have to crawl before we can walk."

"Darn, I've crawled now till I doubt if I can ever walk again."

"Maybe," I said with tears in my eyes, "if you didn't have me and the kids, you could do the things you've always wanted to do."

He held me fiercely to him and kissed me over and over.

"Woman," he said, in his growl of a voice, "you're mine and I love you. You just remember that, no matter what happens."

The next week came the petition for a divorce: David Cantrell versus Samantha Cantrell. I went around in a daze getting Sarah off to school, fixing Tommy's breakfast and little Eddie's bottle. For days I was like this. People came and went, offering sympathy. It all went in one ear and out the other.

Then a great urgency to see D.C.'s mother came over me. When I walked into their house, I couldn't believe it. D.C. stood there in the kitchen, as big as life. The kids ran to him and hung onto his hands yelling, "Look, Mama! Here's Daddy." I felt all the blood drain out of my face and saw the floor coming up to hit me.

He pushed the kids away and grabbed me as I went down. But when I come out of the faint I was lying on the bed and he was standing there with clenched fists at his side, looking out the window. I lifted myself up and fell back weakly. My hands were trembling as I put there up to my face and felt the tears streaming down my cheeks. "Why, D.C., why do you want a divorce?" I asked him in a choked voice.

"Divorce?" a small, scared voice said, and I looked into the white stricken face of my little girl. I hadn't seen her standing there in the doorway. "Oh, no, Daddy!" she screamed and threw herself on him, winding her arms and legs around him.

I jumped up and tried to quiet her, but she was D.C.'s problem; he had done this to her. He finally forced her arms and legs loose and got her up in his arms as she convulsively clung to his neck with great sobs shaking her whole body. His mother and grown sister had run into the room. They were crying and frightened, too.

"D.C.," his sister said, "you are a darn fool." Molly was a fat woman, but she was strong. She tried to take Sarah from him, but he told her to leave them alone.

He was saying, "No, honey. Daddy doesn't want a divorce." He gave me a look like he blamed me for the whole thing. He must've sounded convincing, because her sobs began to subside and soon she was blowing her nose on his white handkerchief. All this time, Tommy, who was six, and eighteen-month-old Eddie, had stood against the wall with frightened eyes.

"What's a divorce?" Tommy asked after a while when Sarah was smiling again.

"It's when a mama or a daddy goes off and leaves a mama or daddy and the kids," Sarah said. "Isn't it, Mama?"

I said "yes" barely above a whisper and went into the bathroom. My heart pained me like an abscessed tooth. The tears had just dried up when Sarah went into hysterics. My eyes felt hot and aching. I was

176

sitting on a chair with my face in my hands when D.C. opened the door. I had forgotten to lock it. He stood there for a minute, then he said, "Honey, I'm sorry."

"Why? Why do you want a divorce?"

"Don't look at me like that."

In one stride he had me in his arms and the world began to turn right-side-up-again. He wouldn't answer my questions, just said he was a fool and asked me to forgive him. He swore it wasn't another woman. But there was something that kept me from feeling like everything was all right. I didn't want him to go back to work. He went down and dropped his suit for divorce. We were all almost happy again. But he went back to work, since he was making so much money, and said he would be back Friday.

Friday never came. I got a telegram with enough money to pay the bills and eat on for a week. The message said, Can't make it, see you Friday. Love, Daddy. The eyes of my children were tragic.

"When is Friday?" Tommy asked a hundred times a day.

Sarah would come in from school, calling, "Has Daddy come home?" After my answer each day of, "No, not yet," she grew quiet.

I wrote to my husband telling him how the children asked for him and how we missed him; his answer was another petition for divorce. Sarah saw the letter as I stood with it in my hand, too shocked to cry or try to hide it. She read the lawyer's name and gave a strangled wail as she stumbled off into her room and shut the door.

Tommy followed her and I heard her say through her sobs, "Daddy, and divorce." Tommy came to me with the eyes of a hurt puppy, big velvety brown eyes that hadn't ever known real hurt before. "Mama," he said, in his soft voice as the big tears spilled down his cheeks, "Daddy," he just broke down, unable to go on for a while as he sat in his tiny chair. He buried his head in his little arms and gave way to racking sobs. I stood as though petrified as Eddie bent over and said, "Don't cry, Tom, it be awight, don't cry." He had been talking since he was a year old. Now he was trying to comfort his brother with words I had said to him.

"I don't want Daddy to divorce us," Tommy sobbed out. "I want my daddy. Oh, Mama."

I knelt down beside him and took his shaking little body in my arms. "So do I, son." Sarah came and sat beside me and Eddie scrambled up on one side with his soft little arms around my neck, his baby hand patting my back. And we all cried together.

I knew there wasn't any use for me to fight it, but Sarah made it so hard on me. She said with tears streaming down her face, "Mama, you could beg Daddy not to leave us, you could if you would."

Oh, darling child, only God knows what it cost me to beg. But

177

I did. Letter after letter, "Please don't, you don't realize what you are doing. Please, honey, come home, I can't stand tears, questions anymore, please come back to us." The children all got sick, wearied with sorrow, feverishly calling for Daddy.

I wrote a poem and sent it to the judge. Maybe if he would refuse to grant the divorce, D.C. would come to his senses. If it hadn't been for my children, I'd never have moved a finger to keep him from divorcing me, because I was too independent, too proud. But I felt like I was going to crack up, looking into the staring, wounded eyes of my darling children. I couldn't feel the pain for myself, because of their awful sorrow. Mine would come later, when the weeks turned to months and the months to years.

He had sued me for a divorce, he told the court, because he couldn't stand my nagging anymore. "Oh, God," I prayed in my shamed heart, "have I been guilty?" I thought of everything, not sparing myself. It had only been since he started working away from home that he had accused me of nagging. I remembered the time I had said, "Honey, we have to pay the doctor something this week." He had turned on me with a snarl and said, "Why don't you quit nagging?" I told him I hadn't meant to nag.

But every time I said anything about bills, he had accused me of nagging. Then, when he had gotten in a dice game and lost enough to pay our rent that week, I guess I had really nagged. But I hadn't meant to; he didn't used to call that nagging.

Well, he got his divorce. At two o'clock in the afternoon, and he was married again at five the same day. His new wife was a wealthy widow who couldn't have children. The court ordered him to pay child support, though my rent wasn't covered by that.

The awful truth was borne home to me: I had to get a job to support my family.

I was unskilled, afraid to face the future alone. But those frightened eyes of my children. Oh, how I hated to leave them to go to work! But I took Eddie to a day nursery and Tommy to kindergarten, since he was six.

It seemed that there was nothing I could do. Domestic help received such small wages that I couldn't pay the nursery tuition. Sarah had wanted to stay with D.C.'s folks and go to school. I thought I couldn't stand to be away from her.

They were advertising for women taxi drivers. But as the days went by and I could find nothing, desperately I applied for a job at the Rapid cabstand. I took the examination and received my chauffeur license. I kept thinking: D.C. will have a fit about me doing this. Then the awful truth would slap me in the face: He didn't care what I did. But still, I kept a wary eye out for him; he had always been jealous of me and I was afraid of what he would do.

I don't know why it's so hard to believe that someone doesn't love you anymore. I grieved constantly about being away from my children, even in the daytime. I picked them up every evening, and their haunted eyes came alive when they saw me. They were afraid, always afraid. What if Mama went off like Daddy did? When I came home they would throw their little arms around my legs and sob with relief.

The days went by. I would turn my head when any of the people I knew came by the cabstand. Then one day D.C. motioned for me to pull out of line. In a daze I did and parked. My legs trembled as I got out of the cab and walked toward him.

His eyes were spitting fire and he had a hungry look. He didn't know that I knew he had married. It was all I could do to keep from breaking down. Although I could feel the blood draining out of my face, I held back the tears. He said, "Hello, Samantha.""Hello, D.C."

He just stared at me for at least thirty seconds. "I want you to go home."

I couldn't believe my ears. "Go home? What do you mean?"

"Well, I'm paying you alimony so you don't have to work."

I started laughing and I couldn't stop. "You're paying me?" I asked incredulously. "When did we ever live on that little pittance you pay for child support?"

He said he would quit paying anything if I didn't quit work. I told him when he paid me enough to live on, I would be more than glad to quit—that divorce hadn't been my idea in the first place.

"Listen, woman, I mean for you to quit this job and go home now."

"Well, I can't. I don't have enough to feed the children after the rent gets paid."

He turned pale. The tears began to course unheeded down my face as I said, "Go home, D.C., go home to your new wife. I know all about her, so you go home and enjoy your life, if you can. But if you miss one week with the child support, I'll have you thrown in jail."

He turned and strode away, like he had had to jerk himself loose from me.

I drove, blinded by tears part of the time for the rest of that day. Whatever had made him do it? I felt he still loved me, still loved our children. Then I heard he was out of work. She must've been giving him the money for the court payments.

Six months went by and the money stopped. I was too proud to force him to pay. That's all he had, a woman with a bankroll. I had our precious children. The taxi company sold out to a man who didn't want women drivers, so I was out of work again. This time I got a

179

job with a dry-cleaning shop, driving their old car to pick up clothes. When I got sick they had to get another driver. But I couldn't stay sick, I had to work.

The nursery closed when the owner died. That left me without anyone to keep my children. Sarah was in school and so was Tommy, but he got out early, so I had to get work that enabled me to be there when he was dismissed from school. I took Eddie with me most of the time. Sarah hadn't ever gotten over the separation, but I hadn't, either. I knew I never would. Just the mention of his name made my heart quicken. A glimpse of him on the street and I went home to cry until there were no more tears.

The years rolled by. I had dragged a cotton sack in the broiling sun, sold different things from door to door I learned to make flowers from silk and sold corsages as long as they were the fashion. We even sold fireworks in the heat of July and in a blizzard at Christmastime. But we always had a roof over our heads and something to eat and wear. I loved to see my children dressed nice and in Sunday school every Sunday. I taught them something that had been left out of my upbringing and their father's: faith in God. We seldom ever saw their father. He had money, but he wasn't happy.

I went fishing, hunting, played marbles and even jogged. If I could ease the hurt I felt, it was my duty to do so. Sarah fell in love with a young minister, Jake Kenner, and married when she was eighteen. He was a nice-looking boy with chestnut-colored hair, brown eyes, and a love that made me happy for my daughter.

Tommy was always shy. He never made friends easily and always wanted them so bad it hurt. He was five feet eight, had dark brown hair, soft brown eyes, an olive complexion, and a sweet, sad smile.

Blond Eddie grew tall—five-eleven. He had his daddy's dark, stormy blue eyes. He had a natural talent for making friends. So handsome, so likable that all the girls of his age ran after him—but none after Tommy.

I had told my friends and relatives that the only thing I knew to do was to train my children in the way they should go, and when they were older I would trust in God to do the rest. After Tommy was twenty-two and Eddie almost eighteen, they wanted to go to work in Los Grillos. We lived in White Hills at the time. Sarah lived in Hunter's Run.

The first week Tommy was back, it was the first of September. He had left Eddie in Los Grillos on the job and had come after his old car. I knew he didn't want to leave me, and I have wished with all my heart I had kept him there. Instead I rushed him back to take care of his little brother.

180

I told him I would be up there as soon as I could get things arranged. He went and came back the next week. He just couldn't stay away. He worried about me. But he went back and the last of October I arrived in Los Grillos unexpectedly. Were those boys ever glad to see me, and I was glad to see them, too! They had a room together, and Tommy worked days while Eddie worked nights. They both wanted me to visit my parents, so I decided to go.

Eddie was crazy about his job. He had made lots of friends, but Tommy was lonely. Since they didn't work on the same shift it left Tommy out of Eddie's circle. I lingered a few days before leaving on my trip.

One night Tommy took me proudly around to a cafe behind the station where he worked and bought my supper. We had a lot of fun together. I asked him if he'd like to go with me to see my mother and dad, but he said he guessed he'd rather stay there. I didn't know why. I felt so depressed about leaving him; maybe it was that look in his eyes. "Mom, please don't leave me, too."

Ordinarily, it was Eddie I worried about. But he was so full of plans and his new friends, and he loved his job. Had brought the television up for them and told them to be sure to go to church. But uneasiness followed me all the way to my parents' home.

Tommy hadn't ever really had a girlfriend. He'd been home about three weeks when I got a letter from Eddie that alarmed me. Mama, he wrote, I think Tommy is about to get in a jam, but he won't listen to me.

I got ready to go there, imagining all sorts of things—but my parents laughed me to scorn. "The very idea," Mama said, "if Tommy can't take care of himself now, he never will." Dad all but ordered me to stay there and let Tommy alone.

I began to believe that I was being silly. I couldn't sleep nights for worrying. What had Eddie meant? I'd slip out of bed and sit in the dark, praying and thinking about it. I could see Tommy in a thousand different and beloved postures and think of the gentle way he had of speaking. I always had to tell him to talk louder. If Eddie would just write again. Tommy hated to write letters, just like his daddy had.

This boy of mine had a dry sense of humor that kept us all in stitches. He didn't appreciate being laughed at, either, so he wasn't putting on a show. Like the time he set out to keep us from starving. He reasoned that we should plant things. We lived in a tourist cabin at the time, and the only garden spot we had was the car stall. He dug for hours, planting potato peelings or any kind of seeds he could find. This was before his daddy left us and we got lots of laughs about four-year-old Tommy's garden.

He wanted to live in the country. When he was traveling on a

181

train one time he had seen fields of corn, wheat, maze and other crops and asked what it was. Such thoughts came to haunt me in the night and I finally made up my mind to go back. He might be twenty-two, but lots of kids that age needed help.

When I got ready to leave, Eddie arrived. At his first opportunity, he got me off to myself to tell me about Tommy and the girl he had just met. Eddie said Tommy was walking in the clouds, because she acted like she was crazy about him. Eddie had asked him where he met her, and Tommy acted sheepish about it, but admitted she worked in a bar.

"Tommy in a bar?" I couldn't believe it. Eddie said Tommy had gone in there to get some change. Then the story tumbled out. Eddie had seen the girl in a neighborhood grocery store, drunk and with a man. They had jerked guiltily apart when he cleared his throat. When Tommy introduced Eddie to his girl, it was the same one. I felt faint and sat down. The next news really staggered me: Eddie had come in one morning last week to find this same girl cooking breakfast. Tommy had been drinking the night before. Eddie had run the woman off and he and Tommy had had a fight. So he came for me.

Eddie was pale and there was a deep hurt look in his eyes. I said, "Eddie, you should have helped Tommy get acquainted with some of your friends. Then this might not have happened." He said he had tried to get Tommy interested in his friends, but he got tongue-tied around girls, and this one had gotten Tommy drunk. Now he felt honor-bound to marry her.

"No, no," I said, "he can't do that." I felt like I was going to faint. Eddie jumped up and got me a glass of water.

I felt as if the bottom had dropped out of everything. Dear God, what had I done to deserve this? Well, I would see to it that this tramp didn't drag my son off into a trap like that. Eddie and I set out for Los Grillos. Only a mother who has suffered like this could possibly understand how I felt.

Eddie said he'd heard that this girl, Joanie Becker Lee, had been married several times and had several children. I'd never seen Eddie so upset.

When we got to Los Grillos, we went directly to the trailer court where the boys had been living. The man said he had my television, but Tommy was gone. I got an address from him that Joanie had given him, and left for the small city that was about forty miles north of Los Grillos. The man had said he heard that Tommy had married Joanie.

Oh, God, don't let it be! I prayed as I drove. The sign of the city limits of read 10,000 population—a typical county seat with the business places built in a square around the stone courthouse. As I pulled in and parked at the courthouse, I told Eddie I intended to find out if Tommy had married the woman before I tried to find him. When the girl in the county clerk's office showed me the record and I saw Tommy's scrawled signature, it was all I could do to keep from breaking down right there. She told us he worked in the big supermarket on the corner.

Eddie said, "Mama, I've been thinking. We really don't have any right to say anything to Tommy. After all, he's of age."

"Right. And who has a better right than I? All these years of my life I've given freely to train you boys in the way you ought to go, and now this."

"Yes, I know that, Mama—but you always said that no matter who we married, you wouldn't try to separate us."

Didn't I know it? I clenched the steering wheel so hard my fingers ached. "Who would ever have thought that one of you would marry such trash?"

Eddie said, "Mama, I don't think you ought to see Tommy until you can control yourself." I wiped my eyes and sat there, not daring to think. Then I drove on to the big supermarket where Tommy worked.

He was surprised to see us but seemed on the defensive. My eyes filled with tears as I looked at him and saw his chin quiver.

"Hello, Son," I managed to get out.

He looked off down the street. "How are you, Mama?" he asked in a sort of strangled voice.

I dashed the tears away with my hand. "All right. And how are you?"

I saw him square his shoulders and his mouth became a grim line; the little boy bracing himself for whatever the world had to offer. "I'm fine. Have you been to the house?"

"No."

He told us how to get there. No excuses, no apologies. "I'll be home for lunch in a little while."

Eddie asked, "How do you like your job?"

He grinned. "Just fine. They just don't pay enough."

I drove to the place he told us he'd rented the week before. Nobody was home. Everything was in a mess. The bathtub had a black greasy ring around it; dirty clothes were strung from one end of the apartment to the other. The divan in the living room and the big chair to match it both smelled. I would tell Tommy a thing or two when he got there about the care they were giving their home.

He was pale when he came and I told him his wife was away. I thought he looked a little angry, too, but he took my car and went to look for her. He hadn't been gone but a few minutes when a car drove up.

Eddie said, "There's Joanie, the. . . ." He called her a terrible name.

"Eddie," I said sharply, but I saw the look of unadulterated hatred that he gave the woman who walked in the door.

She didn't even glance at me nor did she speak to Eddie, whom she had met before. Following her were three of the most pitiful specimens of childhood I had seen in a long time. The little girl had mousy-colored hair and big blue eyes and an uncertain smile. But the thing that horrified me was the ringworm on her head where bald spots as big as a half dollar stood out scaly and naked. I smiled at her and she smiled back. But her mother walked on into the kitchen, without a word.

One little boy was also a victim of ringworm. He had it on his white head and all over his arms and neck. His lower lip was thicker than his upper one, which gave him a perpetual pouting expression. He was short and stocky and, like his sister, dressed in dingy, cheap clothing. I asked the girl what her name was, and she smiled and said, "Janie."

She came to lean against my leg. I smiled at her and knew she was hungry for love. Like a happy puppy wagging his tail, she twisted around and kept grinning. The stocky little boy stood there with a sulky expression on his face. I said, "What's your name?"

He jumped up on the divan, on up to the back and squatted down like a monkey in a zoo and began to jerk up and down on his haunches. His brother—a scrawny, slightly older child, jumped up there with him. Joanie was rattling cans and pots around in the kitchen. Up leapt Janie beside her brothers and there they sat, the three of them, like little untrained animals.

I had smelled the awful stench of her, and her clothes looked like they had been wet and then dried on her body countless times. I felt like gagging and had just gotten up to go to the bathroom but stopped when Tommy came back. He went into the kitchen and said something to Joanie. She came in the living room, still not looking at me.

Eddie said, "Joanie, this is my mother," before Tommy had a chance to introduce us.

"Oh," she said indifferently and looked out the glass in the front door.

I squeaked out a little "Hello," and went back into my shell. Tommy told the kids to get down from where they were and not let him catch them up there again. I said, "Son, this furniture smells awful."

He said in a harsh voice unlike himself, "I know it," and looked at Joanie.

She tossed her head. "Humph."

"Fix me something to eat," Tommy told her. "I've got to get back to work."

She whirled and went back into the kitchen. From where I sat I could study this woman who had entered our family with her stinks and her filth, both physical and emotional. Her hair had had a tint on it that made it a sandy blonde. Her eyes were a light hazel, like a tiger's eyes, brown with yellowish specks in them. She had a heavy pregnancy mask on her face. Her legs were long and scarred, as if from some childhood disease. She wore a pair of slippers, and this gave her a sort of boxy look because of her wide hips.

And, I thought, how many nice, young, good-looking girls can't seem to get a husband? It was her attitude of vanity that made a silly giggle want to come out of my mouth. She seemed to think she was a raving beauty. Her long face wasn't so bad-looking—until she grinned at Tommy and I saw the brown-stained short teeth with the gums showing over them.

What had Tommy seen in this girl? It dawned on me that he felt sorry for her. And when he looked at those poor little children, he had softness in his eyes. I remembered how he had wanted to take in every poor little ragged kid. He would give his food and candy away and explain to me that those were "Poor kids."

"Poor kids?" I had asked him one time. "Do you think you're rich?"

"Well, I'm richer than they are." And how he'd always prayed for kids.

Before Eddie was born I had found him, he was four at the time, on his knees in the bedroom. He had looked up at me with shining eyes and said, "Mama, I just prayed for a baby."

A few weeks later I found out I was pregnant with Eddie. He always said Eddie was his kid. When I would have to spank Eddie, invariably I would have to spank Tommy. He would try to take his brother away from me yelling, "Just whose kid do you think this is, anyway?"

Had Tommy married her because of those kids? She finally got his lunch on the table and he asked us to eat, but I had long since lost my appetite and so had Eddie. I went on to the bathroom and came out to hear the boys talking.

Tommy told Eddie he thought he could get a job at the supermarket where he worked. So Eddie went with him back to the store and, sure enough, he was put to work. Joanie came into the living room after they left and sat down with a magazine. She screamed out at her children to, "Get out and go play." They crept away like scared puppies. I hadn't ever hated anyone, not really hated, but I felt a red, searing hatred rising up for this woman in my heart.

I hadn't ever used profanity, but I felt like the only way to describe her would be with profane language. She was rude, ignorant, filthy, and vile. What kind of a woman who would let ringworm eat the scalp from her children's heads and curse them like dogs? I had told Tommy the danger of this awful infection, and he said he had been buying medicine for it but he said nothing seemed to work. I soon found out why: The medicine was supposed to be applied, not left in the bottle. I got worried about her children after a while and went to see about them. They were taking some kitchen utensils and things out of the landlady's storeroom. I told Joanie and she began to curse them and make them put the things back.

I waited for Eddie to bring the car back. If he didn't come back soon, I knew I would have to start walking. I had stood all I could without blowing my top. I had purposed in my heart not to say anything until I could say the right thing in the right way. But this was almost too much for a mother who has tried to bring her child up to honor and respect other people. Joanie had ironed on a pretty little coffee table, with a bath towel to pad it with. When she took it off, the fuzz stuck deeply into the varnish on the table. Everything smelled so terrible, I knew she had allowed Janie to climb around with sopping panties on.

I did what I thought was right. I got up and started cleaning up the dishes. I cleaned the bathtub and straightened up the living room and bedroom. All the time I was thinking: My child is living here; I'm doing this for his protection.

I wanted to scream at that woman to take her kids and get out, but I could say nothing, couldn't even ask her how she had tricked Tommy into marrying her. With an aching heart I was sure I knew. I was the one who had always said, "Boys, don't ever ruin a little girl if anything should ever happen like that, be man enough to marry her." My God, I thought, he ought to have known, ought to have realized, what she was.

There were a few times that afternoon that I wanted to tear the magazine out of that woman's hands and slap her face. But I just kept on cleaning house. And she acted like she had me hired to do her work. I was really at the exploding point when Eddie brought the car. I took him back to the store and went to look for an apartment. Joanie said, "See ya," as we went out the door. Her children were playing under the grease rack at the filling station on the corner. But when I told her, she only squalled out loud enough to be heard a block. "Hey, you kids, get out of there." I backed out in a hurry, so people wouldn't think it was I yelling.

Eddie said, "Mama, I hope you don't say anything to hurt Tommy. I almost hated him when I walked into that rat hole, but now I feel so sorry for him. Don't hurt him any more than he is already hurt Mama, please.'

I thought: Here we go again. When I punished one of them, I had to punish the other! "Did he explain anything to you?" I asked.

"No, Mama. I started chewing him out, and he acted like I was beating him with a wet rope, just hunched down to stand the blows." There were tears in Eddie's voice, and hate, as he went on to say, "That dirty low down . . . I'm sorry, Mama, but if she ever gets smart with me, I'll—"

"Listen, Son, you can't let it ruin your life. Why do you want to stay here, anyway?"

"Because maybe we can help Tommy, and I have a job now. You just go look for an apartment and we'll move this evening."

"Okay, that was my idea, too." He kissed me and got out at the store.

It was late when I found a lovely garage apartment in a nice part of town. It was too late to put up the deposits and have the utilities turned on. I went back to the store for the boys at six and they were just coming out of the door. Tommy's eyes flashed at me in a smile, and then a film of something seemed to come into them. What was it, shame? A sickened soul?

I couldn't tell. Oh, how proud I had always been of my sons—so unlike, and yet so dear to each other. Eddie towered a head taller than Tommy. His blond good looks drew the admiring glances of women. Tommy was handsome, too, but short. Did that have something to do with his self-abasement?

Even relatives, who knew how old he was, treated him like a kid. He needed someone to look up to him. Eddie got in the front seat after he stood back for Tommy to get in the middle. Why did I notice things like this?

He insisted on us spending the night and moving the next day or just when we got ready. He told me, though, that Joanie's first husband's mother had moved in on them with about nine children, and if Joanie acted funny it was because she was afraid I might do the same thing, and he wanted me to know I was welcome to stay with them, regardless of what Joanie said, as long as I wanted to.

"You don't need to worry about me staying in that place," I told him and felt him wince against my shoulder. I told him I'd cleaned up the house and how Joanie cursed her children.

He turned pale at that. "I aim to get some things straightened out, but the landlady has been telling me lies about Joanie. It looks as if I'm going to have to move."

I was afraid to say any more, afraid I couldn't stop and Eddie's tortured eyes pled with me not to hurt his brother.

Those two boys could fight like wildcats, beating each other with their fists until I whaled the daylights out of them, but they didn't want anyone else to hurt the other one. Tommy borrowed a rollaway bed from his landlady and told his wife we were spending the night. Her face looked like a thundercloud, but she didn't say anything. I saw her, though, when she slammed a skillet on the stove to start supper.

I had bought some groceries and had Eddie bring the sack in from the car. "Now, you don't have to buy groceries at my house," Tommy said.

"I know it." I smiled at him. "But I thought you might like some of Ma's cooking for a change."

I knew I had said the wrong thing when he said, "Well, Joanie is a pretty good cook," and put his arm around her.

My heart cried: Why a woman of the streets? The stab of hate went through me like a sword. I said, "Well, I washed your last six baths from the tub, if you want to take another one." Joanie went into the living room with Tommy and Eddie and I was astonished to hear Eddie invite them to play checkers with him.

"Tommy," she said, "let me play him. I know I can beat him."

Tommy laughed, naturally, not a strained laugh like I'd heard before that day. Like he didn't have a right to laugh after what he had done. "Okay, Joanie, go ahead."

Eddie went out to the car and got his checkerboard. I only hoped the boys didn't get into it as they usually did when they played a game. Eddie is a good checker player, but he had to really hump it to beat Joanie. I heard admiration in his voice when he said, "Boy, she can play."

Skyler—I had heard them call the little boy who had answered me so impudently when I asked him what his name was—and Janie came into the kitchen. Toby, the other boy, followed. All were dirty and Janie's panties were wet and black where she had sat in the dirt. Skyler wanted to make the hamburger patties.

"Oh, no," I said. "Look at your dirty hands. You can't put them into the food." He jumped up on chair and leaned over the table, informing me that his mother let him make the meat patties. I shuddered to think what my son had been eating unknowingly.

"Skyler, get out of that kitchen!" yelled his mother.

Tommy then said, "And you'll all wash up now!"

I told him, "If you don't get rid of that ringworm, everyone in the house will have it."

"Well, Mama, I don't know where it came from. Joanie has some medicine the doctor gave her for it, but it didn't work."

"Maybe it's because it hasn't been used."

"What? You've used the medicine—haven't you, honey?"

She didn't answer him. I told Tommy I knew those children hadn't been treated. I could tell by the way it was spreading and I told him about some simple home remedies. Furthermore, I told him they had come from the sick-looking kitten I'd seen the children playing with. Joanie must've had one ear cocked toward the kitchen as she played checkers, because she said, "No, the cat doesn't have ringworm." I shut up then and went on with the meal I was preparing.

When everything was done and on the table, I told them to come on. I was delighted with the way Tommy stuffed himself that night. He didn't have to say the food was good, not the way he put it away. It was at the table that I learned something else about Joanie: She hated her little girl. Skyler and Toby sat next to their mother, stuffing food with both hands. That is, until Tommy told them to eat correctly.

But Janie sat there with one hand in her lap, trying to spear a bite of food with a fork. She sat next to me and I could see her look at her mother out of the corner of her eyes and ease her hand out of her lap to push the bite onto her fork. Then she would jerk her hand down and into her lap again.

Even after Tommy scolded Skyler and Toby, they kept both hands on the table and in their plates half of the time. I nearly jumped out of my chair when Joanie hollered, "Janie, you get your hand out of your plate!" and reached across the table to whack the child on top of the head with a spoon. The little thing screamed and I said, "Joanie, stop that."

Joanie jumped up, cursing terribly and turned her chair over. Slamming it against the wall behind her, she ran into the bedroom. I looked at Eddie, who was as white as a sheet. Tommy was pale and his eyes had a stunned expression. Then he jumped up and ran after Joanie. I heard him tell her in no uncertain terms that he wouldn't stand for any such doings, and if she knew what was good for her she'd better come back in there and apologize to me and Eddie, and she'd better not hit Janie that way again and let him find it out. She came back sniffling and said she was sorry.

I started crying. I couldn't take anymore. "I can't stand to see a little child abused," I told them.

"Now, Mama, don't get upset. I'm going to make some changes here."

"Yes," I wailed, "but Joanie hates that poor little girl! She's partial to the boys, and that ringworm won't get well because she doesn't take care of it."

Joanie stared at me with stony eyes; she didn't even deny hating little Janie. She said, "She's half crazy, her mind has been affected from the time her Daddy hit her on the side of the head when she was four months old."

"I would hate to say that child is crazy," I told her scathingly. "She has more sense than some people I know!"

189

"Now Mama, control yourself!" Eddie scolded me. "These kids are absolutely nothing to you." I saw Tommy glare at Joanie and knew he would have this out with her later. I excused myself from the table and went into the bathroom.

Idiot, I said to my red-nosed reflection. You pray for wisdom and then act like a fool. God forgive me, please, I prayed, the same prayer that would be on my lips almost every day for a long time to come.

I washed my face and saw lines that hadn't been there a month ago. Eyes that were usually merry and blue in spite of the sorrow I had carried for years were bleary from crying and sleepless nights. Forty-nine years old, life had been one long round of heartache for me. I had always thought how wonderful it would be when my boys took wives and I had grandbabies to hold on my lap. Maybe I would have time to baby them, time I hadn't had with mine because I always had to work. Now how could I cuddle stinking, diseased little Janie, or impudent, hardhearted little Skyler, or sly Toby? Or, the unborn baby—who was its father, anyway?

My auburn hair had streaks of white at the temples, lines like miniature crows' feet ran from the corners of my eyes, and there were lines now at the corners of my mouth. It hadn't been long since people would not believe that I was my age, but thought I was much younger. I had put on too much weight, too, and I knew as I surveyed my reflection that most of my life had passed.

The years seemed to have melted away like snow. I wondered if somewhere along the road I had missed the mark. Maybe I should have married again or let D.C. raise the boys. How could Tommy have married a girl who so obviously had lived a wanton life? Then, as I always did in any crisis, I asked myself: What will D.C. say? He had been very angry when Sarah had married and tried to make her leave her husband.

Lost in thought, I jumped when someone knocked on the bathroom door. "Mama," Eddie asked, "are you okay?"

I opened the door and went back into the living room. Tommy and Joanie were sitting on the sofa. I told Tommy he ought to put a stop to the children tearing up the furniture and especially climbing around on it with soiled clothing. He said he had been making them stay away from it when he was home. But I knew the same as he did that Joanie didn't try to make them take care of anything.

Well, it wasn't any of my business, so I decided to go to bed. I had some heavy quilts in the car. Tommy got them for me and I made Eddie a bed with them on the floor.

At six the next morning, I heard the alarm go off and wake the boys. Then I fixed their breakfast. Tommy said he hadn't been eating any breakfast, but he sure put it away just the same. Joanie and the

190

children were still asleep when I got back from taking them to the store. But the children woke up in a few minutes and started dressing.

I asked them if they wanted something to eat and went to fix it. Joanie screamed at Skyler to get into that kitchen and fix their breakfast, like he always did. I sat down completely flabbergasted. Wearing a pair of ragged blue jeans and a dingy T-shirt, he rushed into the kitchen with his white hair tousled and without washing his hands. He climbed up on a chair, then, walking from shelf to shelf, he got two bowls, a box of dry cereal, the sugar bowl and two spoons. These he gently lowered to the drain and then climbed down. My heart went out to the little thing. I knew he was spoiled in a crude way, but his life wasn't very blissful, either.

I hate to admit this, but it's true, I felt like dragging that lazy, good-for-nothing woman out of bed by the hair and whipping her good and proper. She had filled Tommy with the idea that her landlady was lying about her. The poor thing probably didn't tell all she knew.

Skyler carried his things over to the table and gave me a shy grin. "I always fix mine and the kids' breakfast," he said proudly.

Tears came into my eyes, but I brushed them angrily away. That was just like Tommy, I thought, rescuing the perishing, dragging in all the ragged, dirty little kids for me to wait on. He hadn't changed; he'd just been doing what he'd always wanted to do.

Well, I promised myself grimly, if she's going to wear our name and Tommy is going to live with her and raise these children, he's going to do it right. I thought about how sweet my babies always smelled and how careful I was with them. Dear God—what would she do with the new baby?

Janie came in, struggling with the straps on her overalls. "Here, let Grandma button that," I said and nearly bit my tongue. Grandma, indeed! Maybe Tommy wasn't the only nut in the family. Janie looked back over her shoulder toward the bedroom. But I buttoned her clothes for her, even if her mother did yell that she didn't need any help. I decided to doctor that ringworm, too, but I reckoned without the female who had brought these three into the world. I went into the bedroom and told Joanie as kindly as I could under the circumstances that I knew what would cure it and she wouldn't let me even use what Tommy had bought. I knew she hadn't planned on Tommy having a mother.

He was alone in Los Grillos, except for Eddie. She thought she had a real chump with no one to help him. Well, she would learn, I told myself; she would learn.

Well, that day, as soon as the gas, water and electric offices were opened, I put up the deposits and moved our things into the already furnished apartment. I went after Eddie and dropped Tommy off at his place at noon. Eddie was thrilled about the cute place we had to live in and the good lunch I had fixed.

But about halfway through his meal he put down his fork and said, "Mama, can't I take Tommy some of this?"

"No, you can't. The quicker he gets sick of that mess and gets out of it, the better."

Then I told him what had happened that morning. Somehow he lost his appetite; I guess the same way I did, just thinking about Tommy living that way for the rest of his life. We picked him up and took him back to work. None of us had much to say.

But that evening, he got off before Eddie did and I took him home first. I said, "Tommy, I would like to know why you married that woman. You know that baby isn't yours. How come you've made such a fool out of yourself?"

He looked at me with a strange expression in his eyes and said, "Well, lots of reasons, Mama—and I do love her."

"Love her? How in the world could you love a person like that?" Then I told how she talked to her children and that the landlady hadn't lied, it was his wife. "Besides," I said, "what kind of a future can you offer your own children with that kind of a mother?"

He didn't say anything else in answer to all my raving. But when I pulled up at the curb, there, like three dirty pigeons—bare feet, tear-streaked faces, ragged clothes and all—sat Skyler, Toby, and Janie.

When they saw Tommy, their faces lighted up. Tommy grinned at them and I felt the tears start in my eyes. I said, "Don't you wish they were yours?"

A look of something almost holy came into his big brown eyes and he said, "They are—all of them." He meant the one yet to be born, too.

"But, Son, you know that baby isn't yours, and neither are these."

"Yes, Mama, they are mine, all of them." He turned and kissed me and got out. Skyler grabbed one hand and Janie the other, and dancing along by his side, they went into the house. Toby was close behind.

Every day I picked Tommy up, morning, noon, and night. Every day I preached a sermon to him. The kids always waited for him, but I noticed they were cleaner and he managed to buy them some clothes. He got so that he would ask me to drop the subject, and then I would cry. Then he would ask me to forgive him. Always I would be sorry, but that tales were flying thick and fast about Joanie's neglect of her children when she was away at work.

When anyone said anything to Tommy about it, he would scold Joanie. She would convince him that people were lying about her. Everyone except me, that is. I'd found out for myself and told Tommy and he knew I didn't lie.

What if he killed her? I could imagine him behind bars, going to death row, and a thousand different horrible things. Only God knew what I suffered through the next few months.

Tommy didn't kill her, but he told me he really had to move now. Skyler had broken a window in the apartment and he had to pay for it. Joanie was taking more pills and the doctor's bills were piling up. Now the landlady said he had to get out. I went to see Mrs. Terrence, the woman he rented from. She told me that in all her life she had never heard a woman talk to her children like Joanie did. She could hear through the walls. Joanie had convinced Tommy that she was being persecuted.

Mrs. Terrence asked, "Mrs. Cantrell, I love your son very dearly. He's one of the finest boys I've ever met, but please tell me how he got mixed up with that woman." I could only shake my head. How could I tell her?

I went to look for another place for them and found a furnished apartment. Joanie was very contented to let me clean it.

I moved them in my car and told Joanie she ought to be able to keep things clean. I told Tommy, right in front of her, that if she didn't take better care of her children they would both land in jail.

When the baby was born, Tommy proudly escorted me to the nursery to look at the tiny mite they called his new daughter. I saw the look on his face, like he used to have when he found a crippled bird or a skinny, mangy dog.

"She's so little, so helpless," he said.

What kind of a boy had I raised? This man would be ten feet tall to those kids.

"You sure beat all I ever saw in my life, Tommy."

He came out of his dream world then. He told me then that when he met Joanie and he was so lonely, she had been friendly. She told him a story about being stranded with her little children, how each one of her husbands had deserted her and the kids.

She also told him she had been desperately trying to get food for her family when she became pregnant. He knew I'd never done some of the things she had, but to him came the picture of me and my little ones cast out into the world; how he, Eddie, and Sarah had always wanted a daddy. Well, they say that pity is akin to love.

He believed he could change Joanie, and he did, to a certain degree. She now keeps the house clean and the children, too. If she's mean to them, I don't know, because I have to stay away for more reasons than one.

Not that they don't ask and even insist on me visiting, but it's a raw, open wound. Maybe I should be grateful for a son who can be a father to little ones who need him so badly. But I think of the years that I spent preparing him for a better life. It breaks my heart to see that boyish figure toiling wearily homeward in the evening—working, slaving out his young years, bearing the load for others.

I see the evil thing that D.C. did to his family as the predominant factor in this thing that his son did. Is our son trying to erase his father's sin? Well, one day I looked across the table at my youngest child. His eyes seemed to have sunk back into his head and the blue circles around them frightened me. How thin he had become! I asked him if he felt all right, and he said the words that cut me to the heart.

"Mama, I can't stand the way you're eating your heart out over Tommy. After all. . . ." Tears came into his eyes. "You still have me."

What a blind fool I'd been! How lonely he must have felt all of these months, even with his new friends. I realized, too, that he had been staying out too late. When I asked him where he had been, he told me several times, "Oh, just sitting over at Wynona's cafe, talking to people."

I had always palled around with my kids; he missed that fellowship. Wynona stayed open all night, and my son had had to go there to find someone to talk to unless he went out on a date, and I knew he had dropped a lot of his friends lately, too.

That's why I had to start over again. All these years I'd denied myself for my children. I could have married again. Several times during the years, men were interested, but only one had I ever dated. Ted, a commercial fisherman, who Tommy and Eddie thought was great. He had been married, but his wife had divorced him to marry someone else.

My children all but proposed to him, even though he had talked to me of marriage from the first. Two reasons prevented me from marrying him: First, my children. I'd vowed for them to never have a stepfather.

The second reason was a pair of stormy blue eyes that had looked into mine and said, "Woman, I love you, and no one can ever take your place in my life."

That day, I knew I'd failed Eddie. But the grin on his face when I said, "Why don't we go fishing this evening when you get off from work?" was a reward.

"Okay, Mama. I'll get a chance to try out my new rod."

I would find myself missing Tommy, even at the fishing hole. But I would remind myself to live for Eddie now.

It wasn't as easy as it sounded. There were sleepless nights when gallons of tears ran out on my pillow. But in the daytime, it was Eddie and I. People began to tell me how I was aging and I knew it was the worry. But one night, I remembered how I had dedicated my boys to God. There in the church of White Hills, they had stood in their white

194

suits with faces earnest and glowing.

And I had cried through the whole ceremony as I gave my children into the keeping of their Heavenly Father. God had supplied our needs so many times when we were at the end of our rope. Now I would rededicate Tommy in my heart and ask God to help him. All I ever knew was to do the best I could and leave the rest to a higher power. But, if a person contemplating divorce should read this story, especially if he has children, he should think about these things. It isn't just today, it's all the tomorrows, the years to come.

Eddie and I live in another town and so do Tommy and his family, only a few blocks apart but I don't go around them much. So far we haven't heard from D.C., what he thinks about it all, but he forfeited his right long ago. I put forth every effort to make Eddie happy and he seems to be, but he says he learned to pick and choose his friends very carefully when he saw what Tommy got. Maybe something will be accomplished through it all. I hope so.

THE END

THE LAST TIME I HELD
HER IN MY ARMS

There's a funny story about how my wife, Tracy, and I fell in love. I used to like to tell it back in the days when we were first married. Now that Tracy's gone, though, the story doesn't seem funny anymore. When I remember it I think about how maybe I should have been paying more attention then, and all through our marriage, to what was really going on between the two of us.

The story was that I never paid one bit of attention to Tracy, the most beautiful girl in the senior class, and probably in our whole school, until a day she was looking her worst. All through school I'd been interested in girls who were fun to be with, tomboy types who weren't always fussing with their hair and makeup. I'd never thought that Tracy Hansom, Mayville High's homecoming queen and winner of two local beauty pageants, would have anything in common with me.

During my senior year in school I had an after-school job as delivery boy for a local pharmacy. One afternoon in early spring there was a tube of ointment to be delivered to the Hansom house. Tracy was in my English class, and she'd been absent for a couple of days.

No one answered when I rang the Hansoms' bell. I knew Tracy's parents were probably both at the family delicatessen on Main Street, but I was pretty sure Tracy was home. I rang again, then leaned on the bell a third time, and finally heard her voice.

"Okay, okay! I'm coming."

I couldn't believe the girl who answered the door was Tracy. Her usually lustrous hair hung in limp strands, and she wore a terrycloth robe that looked as if she must have gotten it in the seventh or eighth grade. Most surprising of all, she wore a pair of thick glasses I'd never seen before. Behind one of the lenses she'd crammed a compress that she pressed to her eye with one hand while she held the door open with the other.

"Oh, uh, I know you from school, don't I?" she asked, embarrassed. "I didn't expect—" She pulled her hand away from the door and tried to sweep her hair away from her face on one side.

There was something about seeing her looking that way that made me feel differently about her than I had before. She was just a regular person, after all. I thought about my own ratty robe at home that I liked to wear when I was sick. "You've got a sty on your eye, haven't you?" I said. "I get those. They really hurt."

She nodded, looking surprised, and stopped fiddling with her hair. "Come in and I'll get the money for the salve," she said.

In a moment Tracy came back with the money, still holding the compress to her eye. "I've never used this salve before," she said. "I've never even had a sty. My folks think it might be because I was careless with my contact lenses."

"Let me see," I said, moving closer to her.

She took her glasses off and removed the compress. Her eye was red and swollen almost completely shut.

"You should have gotten the salve sooner," I said. "It's really bad."

She nodded miserably and I suddenly felt sorry for her, all alone in the house and hurting.

"If you'll show me somewhere I can wash my hands, I'll help you put this stuff on, okay?" I said.

Meekly, she sat at the kitchen table while I dabbed the salve on her lower lid. I was impressed by the way she didn't cringe, and something about the way she looked right at me as I bent over her made my hand tremble a little.

She must have noticed because she reached out and caught my hand in hers, holding it a moment against the softness of her cheek. "Thanks," she said. "You know, I never realized before how nice you are."

I leaned over her indecisively a moment and then, giving in to my impulse, I kissed her gently on her lips, which were even softer than her cheek. She stood, moving into my arms as naturally as if I were one of the football-hero types I was always seeing her with in the halls at school. She fit into my arms just right. I longed to pull her even closer and savor the curves of her body against me but there was something telling me even then that Tracy was the girl for me, and that I wanted things to be right and good between us.

I moved away, not taking my eyes from her face. "Will you go out with me this weekend?" I asked, still holding her hand.

"If my eye is better," she said, her glance wavering from mine as though she'd suddenly become self-conscious. "I can't go out until it's better."

"Sure you can," I said. "You can see out of it, can't you?"

She shook her head, smiling a little, and wouldn't discuss it any more.

I had to take a lot of razzing from my friends later on about Tracy's eye. "Are you sure she was seeing okay?" they joked the day after our first date. "Otherwise why would she go out with a guy like you?"

Other people's opinions didn't matter to us. We were totally caught up in each other all the rest of that school year and on into the summer. She became the bright center of my world.

At night I'd dream of her lovely face with its high cheekbones, sultry long-lashed eyes and full, perfectly shaped mouth that invited kissing. I was on fire with longing for her almost all the time. By the end of the summer we'd convinced our parents to let us get married. I was positive our love could overcome any obstacles.

And for a while it did. We rented a small apartment near the community college where I took part-time courses in small-business management while Tracy and I took turns helping out in her parents' store. Tracy's father made it clear that eventually he'd like us to take over the store, so we had that knowledge as security when our son, Ben, was born and then, two years later, Joe.

By the time the boys were eight and six, Tracy's father was ready to retire, and we took over the store full time.

After a year of working together we came up with the idea to turn the store into a gourmet food shop. Business picked up right away, and soon we were getting calls to deliver trays for office parties and bridge luncheons. The expense for the new truck, however, didn't leave us any extra cash to hire help. One of us would go out to make deliveries and the other would stay in the store and wait on customers.

Tracy wasn't entirely thrilled by our sudden success. She worried that she wasn't spending enough time with the boys; that our meals at home were too sketchy and that something in our lives was going to be threatened if we kept going at such a pace.

The faster pace was an ego boost for me, though—one I needed as the son-in-law who'd been virtually handed a business—and I pushed aside Tracy's complaints and worries. It was exciting to listen to the phone ringing off the hook and to have people lined up at the cash register.

It was around New Year's, one of our busiest times, that the accident happened. We woke up to snow that morning and the phone ringing. It was a room mother calling to say the boys' school was closed for the day. Tracy asked Stephie, our next-door neighbor, if she could watch the kids, but she was going skiing.

"I'd better stay home with them, Patrick," Tracy said. "They'd go bananas all day at the store."

"We have three deliveries scheduled for today," I pointed out. "There's no way I can be in the store and make the deliveries, too."

Tracy thrust her chin out, her stubborn look. "Maybe if you weren't so obsessed with making money and we had some extra help, this wouldn't keep happening. There's no way the boys can be running around out in that snow all day without supervision."

Finally we reached a compromise. Tracy would ask Mrs. Cheney, an elderly woman who lived across the street from us, to keep an eye on the boys until she could make the noon deliveries and get back home. I wasn't happy about her having to drive the truck on icy roads. I usually made the deliveries while Tracy watched the shop.

"I'll manage fine," she assured me. "I can be home by two or three to look after the boys. Maybe I can even make us a decent dinner for once."

The delivery truck was loaded by eleven and Tracy got behind the wheel. I remember how she looked, like a Russian princess with her white angora hat framing her flushed cheeks and tendrils of hair escaping all around. I kissed her before she slid behind the wheel, and the fur of her hat tickled my nose. Of course, it never occurred to me then that there was anything final about that kiss—that it would seal the closing of a chapter of our lives together.

The truck went into a skid just two blocks from our house. Tracy had made all the deliveries and was hurrying to get home. She was in such a rush to get back to the boys that she hadn't bothered to fasten her seat belt. When the truck finished its skid it smashed into a tree, and Tracy was flung forward against the dashboard. Her nose and right cheekbone were broken, and the metal corner of the visor made a deep slash down her left cheek.

Miraculously those were the only injuries she received. The thing that saved her, the emergency squad said, was the cautious speed at which she had been traveling, as well as the angle at which the truck hit the tree.

I closed the shop and got to the hospital as soon as I heard of the accident. Tracy's face was so swathed in bandages that I couldn't see the full extent of the injuries, and she was too drugged for me to be able to talk to her. I held her hand and sat with her, thanking God that she had been spared.

In the next week, though, after she'd been sent home, it became clear to me just how deeply the accident had affected Tracy. The first morning she was home she turned over in bed, pulling the sheet over her face, and refused to come down for breakfast.

I sat on the bed beside her, gently trying to pull the sheet away, but Tracy wouldn't let me. The night before she'd removed the gauze covering her face because the doctor had told her it would heal better. She hadn't let me see her face then, and she wouldn't let me see it now.

"Hey, it's me, remember?" I said, rubbing her shoulders. "I love you, honey. A few scratches on your face aren't going to make any difference to me, or to the boys, for that matter."

"It's more than a few scratches," she said in a muted voice. "My face will never be like it was before." She drew a shaky breath.

"Please, just let me alone for now, will you?"

I went downstairs and made breakfast for the boys. Before I left for the shop I took some toast and tea upstairs for Tracy. She didn't sit up or acknowledge the food in any way. I set the tray on the bedside table and leaned over to kiss her, but she pulled away. It was going to take time.

Things were so hectic at the shop, with the procession of part-timers coming to help me, that I guess I didn't realize for a while the full extent of Tracy's grief. At first I viewed her refusal to come into the shop or even to go out of the house at all as a quirk that would pass as her face returned to normal.

Soon, though, it became clear that Tracy's face wouldn't ever be exactly the way it had been before, nor would she. As much as she could, she covered her injuries with gauze squares during the day, even though the doctor had told her not to.

"Do you think I want the boys seeing me looking like some kind of Frankenstein's monster?" she said tightly when I encouraged her to leave the gauze off.

By then I'd seen Tracy's face at night when she took the gauze off to sleep, and though her injuries were red and angry looking, she was still the same old Tracy to me, beautiful from an inner radiance.

"You're being silly," I said. "You're making more of it by keeping your face covered like that." It never occurred to me that it was important to Tracy that someone try to understand how she was feeling emotionally about what had happened to her. By telling her she was being silly I made the situation even worse than it was.

As it turned out, Tracy did have something to be upset about. Her first trip back to the doctor revealed that the slash on her left cheek was healing crookedly, pulling her features on that side of her face slightly askew.

"Each person scars differently," the doctor said. "It appears you're forming some rather heavy scar tissue here. Later when the healing process is completed, plastic surgery could alter it."

"How long will the healing process take?" I asked.

"I wouldn't consider scar revision until at least six months have passed," the doctor said.

"Six months looking like this," Tracy said hopelessly. "And, even then, I suppose you can't guarantee me that I'll look the way I did before?"

"There are few guarantees in medicine," he said, "but I'd try not to worry too much about it if I were you. You're a lovely woman with a family who cares about you. Get on with your life. In six months we'll see what can be done."

Tracy kept her face uncovered after that. At first the boys stole

200

secret looks at her, their expressions clearly showing that they were upset about the change in their mother, but soon they grew accustomed to the way she looked, and so did I.

It seemed a natural thing to protect Tracy, to make trips to the store so she wouldn't have to go out, and, finally even to hire a woman to take her place in the shop. Visits to the boys' school, evening P.T.A. meetings, and taking the boys to church became things I did alone.

For weeks after Tracy was injured I didn't approach her sexually. It was clear that she didn't feel well enough. At night I held her tightly to reassure her of my love. When, after the first visit to the doctor, I did try to make love to Tracy, she didn't respond.

"I don't want to, Patrick," she said. "I feel ugly."

I pulled her close, smoothing her hair and kissing her gently. I was so afraid of hurting her, and I guess she sensed my tentativeness, because she stiffened in my arms.

"See?" she accused, "you're even afraid to kiss me like I was a normal woman." She grabbed my hand, rubbing it against the ridge of her scar. "Feel that?" she said in a choked voice. "Sexy, isn't it?"

"Tracy, honey, please don't do this." Gently, I pulled my hand away, gathering her to me.

"I need more time, Patrick—a lot more time," she said, her face against my chest.

"Maybe it would help if you talked to someone—a counselor," I said, stroking her hair.

"I already talked to the doctor," she said tonelessly. "He made it clear he thinks I'm being silly to get so upset over a scar. I don't need someone else to tell me the same thing. Besides, with all the medical bills we don't have the money to pay for any more doctors."

"Sure we do, honey," I said. "You're worth it to me. I want you to be happy. I want things to be the way they used to be." I moved against her, wanting her with a pent-up longing that had been held back too long.

"Soon," she said, moving away from me. "I'll be my old self again soon. I just have to get used to looking a little different, that's all." The pillow muffled her voice but I could tell she was crying. I tangled my fingers in the warm mass of her hair and lay there aching for her until sleep came.

Months went by, and our lives formed a kind of pattern. Maria, the woman I'd hired to help in the shop, gradually picked up the skills Tracy had brought to the business. After a while customers no longer asked for Tracy. Business continued to flourish and I was away from home longer and longer hours.

It was about that time that Tracy began drinking. I'd come home in the evenings to find the boys doing their homework in front of the

201

TV and Tracy deeply asleep upstairs, alcohol on her breath. Meals became haphazard, and Tracy spent a lot of time in bed. Bills came for liquor that had been delivered to the house. When I tried to talk to Tracy about what was happening she became hysterical.

"You'd drink, too, if you looked like this. Don't you think I see the expressions of disgust on people's faces when they look at me?"

I held my tongue. Lately I'd found that no amount of arguing or consoling seemed to convince Tracy that she was wrong about her obsession with the damage to her face.

The six-month visit to the plastic surgeon didn't help, either. The doctor didn't think he'd be able to improve much on the final result of the healing process. "It's natural to have a slight amount of pulling from scar tissue," he reassured Tracy. "It really doesn't affect your appearance that much."

And I guess it didn't. If Tracy had smiled once in a while, if she had let any of the old liveliness return to her face, the scar would hardly have been noticeable. But by then she was caught in a cycle of drinking and self-pity that I didn't know how to get her out of.

At work things were busier than ever. Maria's homemade soups and quiches were a welcome addition to the shop, as was her steady cheerfulness. Fair and even featured, she was very different from Tracy. In a way, she reminded me of the "comfortable" girls I used to go out with before I fell in love with Tracy.

It was our first Christmas after Tracy's accident when my bafflement at her behavior began to turn to anger. She refused to leave the house to shop for the boys' Christmas presents, and I'd had to go out at night after work. Maria volunteered to come along, and together we negotiated the crowded toy store aisles, picking out the latest superheroes and games.

"How do you know about all this stuff?" I asked her.

"Second childhood," she said, grinning. "Really, I'm a TV addict." Then she added a little wistfully, "I wish I could see their faces when they open all this on Christmas morning."

As it turned out, I sort of wished she'd been there, too, because Tracy slept late with a hangover on Christmas morning while the boys and I opened presents without her.

"It's been almost a year since the accident," I told her later in the day. "You've got to get hold of yourself and start living again, for the boys' sake if not your own."

"I'm doing the best I can," Tracy said in a tight voice. "I wish you wouldn't be so critical of me all the time. That might help."

Later I sat in the living room absently watching the boys play with their presents. They were quiet, sensing the tension between Tracy and me. I thought about how I really didn't know her as well as I thought I had. I'd always been surprised and a little awed that I'd been able to attract someone as lovely as Tracy. But though I appreciated her beauty, it certainly hadn't been what made me love her. To her it obviously meant much more. It was up to me to change that, I decided. There was no way we could keep on living the way we had been.

After Christmas was our slow time at the shop. People usually had enough leftovers to tide them over for several days, and they weren't interested in gourmet foods. It would be a good time to get Tracy back to the shop, and back into some kind of life again.I had to practically drag her all the way, but I finally convinced her that I really needed her to come in since Maria had taken off until after New Year's. On the way to the shop we dropped the boys off at Stephie's.

Tracy was really shaky. "I look terrible," she said. "Even if I didn't have the scar, I haven't had anything done with my hair in months. I've put on weight, too."

"You look just fine," I said. "It means a lot to me to have you coming to the shop. It'll be just like old times."

Things got off to a bad start. Tracy had been away from the shop a long time. Maria had her own way of running things. She did the books in a way that Tracy wasn't accustomed to, and she'd stocked the shelves differently. When customers came in Tracy had difficulty finding things and she was painfully shy.

"I feel as though I don't belong here anymore," she said wistfully around noontime. "It's hard to believe I practically grew up in this store."

She'd just finished saying that when Meg Weidmeyer, one of Tracy's old friends from high school, came in. Maybe I shouldn't call Meg an old friend. She'd lost to Tracy as homecoming queen. She stood just inside the doorway, browsing through some herbal teas and stealing a glance at Tracy every few seconds.

"Hello, Meg," she said finally. "Can I help you with something?"

"Oh, then it is you!" Meg said, coming over to the counter. "You look so different I never would have recognized you." She tilted her head and gazed long and hard at Tracy, and I could almost feel her physically recoil. "Where have you been keeping yourself?" Meg went on. She giggled. "Everybody's talking about the sweetheart Patrick has hired to take your place. Believe me, you're smart to come back here and protect your interests!"

There was an awkward silence, and then Meg picked out a box of tea, paid for it, and left.

Tracy slumped on the stool near the chopping block. "I could have faced almost anybody but her," she said dejectedly. "What did she mean about the 'sweetheart' you hired, anyway?"

"You've met Maria," I said defensively. "She's good with the customers, that's all Meg meant. I had to hire someone to help out while you weren't coming in."

"I guess so," Tracy said tiredly. "Well, she can have it as far as I'm concerned. As soon as she comes back from vacation I'm going to stay home with the boys." She rubbed a hand over her cheek.

After that Tracy stayed in the back of the shop making trays and slicing meats and cheeses. The only time she came out was when I had to make a delivery. When Maria came back from vacation, Tracy stayed home and returned to her old pattern.

I had tried and failed. All of a sudden it didn't seem as though my wife was being a wife to me in any way at all. And there was Maria, tanned from a week of skiing, happy to be back, and, most important, cheerful. She was like a breath of fresh air in my life. I began to look at her in a new light.

I can't pinpoint exactly when it was that things began to change between Maria and me. For a very long time I had been aching to hold a woman in my arms. There had been a few times in the past year when Tracy had allowed me to make love to her—but that had been the word for it—allowed. It was clear she wanted no part of sex with me, and that, more than anything else, was what made me turn from her finally.

Ironically it was another snowstorm that started things between Maria and I just as it had been a snowstorm that had caused Tracy's accident.

It was three weeks after Christmas, a leaden-skied January day. The snow began a little after noon, but I didn't pay much attention to it. We'd just gotten in a lot of supplies and I was absorbed in stocking the shelves while Maria waited on customers. People who came in said they'd heard we were in for several inches of snow. From the way everybody was buying food I figured they were right.

Soon the snow was blowing so thickly I could hardly see the few cars that were parked along the curb. "You get home while you still can," I told Maria. "I haven't the heart to close up while people are still coming in."

"That's okay," she said. "You forget, I just got back from a week skiing. I'm not going to let a little snow intimidate me."

We worked side by side until, by six o'clock, the last customer left. As I balanced out the receipts for the day, Maria turned on a small portable TV we had on the counter. Blizzard warnings were in effect, it said. People were not to drive except in cases of dire emergency. I realized then that the people who had been coming into the shop in the last hour all lived within walking distance.

"I wonder if they consider getting home a dire emergency," I quipped.

Maria stood at the front window, squinting out into the snow. "I can't see my car anymore," she said nervously. "I can't even see street lights. It's all just a sheet of white."

I stood besides her, looking out. "Maybe you could leave your car here and I could drive you home," I offered.

"You know how Crooked Lane is when it snows," she said. "It's always the last to be plowed. I don't think there'd even be a way to get down it."

"You could come home with me," I said hesitantly. I never knew how Tracy would be anymore. She might or might not be sober.

"Not a good idea," she said, shaking her head and glancing at me meaningfully.

"You're probably right," I agreed.

"I don't have anywhere I have to be," Maria said. "There's no reason I can't make a couple of calls and then stay right here until the roads are cleared."

She made her calls, and then I called Tracy.

"Why didn't you leave for home about two o'clock when it started to get bad?" she asked irritably. "You'll never make it now."

"People were coming in," I said. "I couldn't just close the place on them."

"That's the way you always think," she told me. "The business comes first—ahead of everything else. Well, it's a good thing you feel that way, Patrick, because it looks as though you'll be staying there tonight. Most of the roads are closed."

"Fine," I said tersely. "I'll see you when I can get through."

Maria looked at me sympathetically as I hung up the phone. "More storms?"

"All the time," I said. "It's cold in here," I added to change the subject.

"We still have hot soup left," Maria said. "At least we can have a gourmet dinner." She gave the soup a stir and began slicing some bread for sandwiches.

Without even needing to ask her I got out the meats and cheeses I knew we both liked and began to put the sandwiches together as she ladled the soup. It was a good, companionable feeling to be with Maria. I realized that I'd been feeling that way about her for a long time.

She leaned over to set the soup on the counter, and her long ponytail swung forward. Standing nearby, I caught her hair in my hand, smoothing the warm silk of it between my fingers. "Let it down," I said softly. "Just let me see it down."

205

She didn't take her eyes from me as she reached around, loosened the band, and began undoing her hair. There was a burning intensity in her gaze, and I felt an immediate yearning for her, but I held myself away from her, just watching as the silky hair fell in ripples around her shoulders.

The soup grew cold as we stood there with only the counter separating us. I watched her lips part and her cheeks begin to flush and I felt my own body respond. It seemed to me that the intensity of actually coming together would be too great for us both, overcome as we were at that point.

But gradually, as though in slow motion, we did come together, her soft body sweetly molded against mine, the mass of perfumed hair around us both, hiding us, making everything beautiful and all right.

Together we walked into the back of the shop to the small daybed there. Maria stood near the daybed and began unbuttoning her blouse and removing her skirt.

In a daze of longing I watched her, knowing I should muster the power to resist, but unable to.

As the storm pounded the window over our heads, passion surged between us that night. I hadn't realized until then how great my need had been for warmth in my life. Holding Maria on the tiny daybed, I felt alive again.

"I've wanted you to make love to me for such a long time," she whispered. "I've dreamed of this happening."

I held her more tightly, saying nothing. I didn't know what I could say. I thought of Tracy, wondering if there was any love left between us. I think that if she'd responded to me just one time, had given me any hope at all, I could have recaptured the old feeling. But she hadn't done that. Yet how could I leave her?

Maria and I slept a little and then made love again. Dawn came, and we got up to dress, a little embarrassed.

"What will we do now?" she asked me.

"You know how it is with Tracy," I told her. "I could never leave as long as things are going so badly for her."

"I wouldn't ask you to," Maria said softly. "Just . . . keep on caring for me the way you did last night. Could you do that?"

"Could I do that?" I said. I was hugging her so hard I was afraid I'd hurt her. "There just seems so little in it for you."

"I'll be the judge of that," she said, breaking away and pulling on her coat and gloves. "Now come on. We have some shoveling to do if we expect to have any customers today. Then there's soup to get on."

"You do the soup and I'll do the shoveling," I said.

"No, I want to be with you." Smiling shyly, she slipped her hand into mine.

That was the most endearing thing about Maria, I realized. Her desire to share things with me was what touched me the most and made me least able to resist her.

In only half an hour we'd cleared the steps and sidewalk in front of the store. We went back inside to warmth, the smell of brewing coffee, and to each other. There were few customers that day, and plenty of time for us to talk together and become more fully acquainted.

"It's hard to believe you'd ever want to look at someone like me, married to such a beautiful woman," she said at one point.

"She doesn't think she's beautiful anymore," I said. "Since the accident, she's felt maimed. I haven't been able to talk her out of it."

"And now I've caused this to happen," she said.

I took her hand. "You haven't caused it, Maria. It was both of us. What I've had with Tracy isn't a life. I realize that now. I couldn't go on that way. I don't think we should blame ourselves for waiting a little happiness."

But those were just words. What I really felt throughout that day was a whole lot different. Not only had I not been able to pull Tracy out of her misery, I had turned away from her in the most unforgivable way of all.

I don't know if my guilt was written on my face, or if Tracy just sensed something, but the first thing she asked me that evening when I got home was if Maria had gotten home all right during the storm.

I wanted to lie to make things easier, but figured someone might have seen Maria's car sitting in front of the shop all night. "I told her to leave early, but she stayed to help me until the storm was too bad," I answered, not meeting Tracy's eyes.

"You mean she spent the night at the shop with you?" Tracy cried.

"Shhh!" I said, glancing into the living room where the boys were. "You were the one who encouraged me to stay at the shop. I wanted to try to come home. I even thought about bringing Maria here with me."

"You sure didn't push very hard for it," she said coldly. "Maybe there is something to what Meg said the other day, after all."

In spite of my guilt I felt defensive, partly because when Meg said what she did I'd had no thoughts of getting involved with Maria. "She's a busybody and you know it," I said shortly. "I really wish we could drop the whole thing."

"I'm supposed to just not think about what went on all night long between the two of you?" Tracy said tightly. "I'm supposed to forget how long it's been since you've made love to me? Of course, you wouldn't want to, the way I look now." Her voice faltered and she rubbed her eyes, then stood and began stacking the dirty dishes.

A wave of deep sadness came over me, watching her hunched over the dishes, her eyes red, her hair uncombed. I wondered what would happen if Tracy found out about Maria and me. The thought of what she'd do really scared me.

I took the plates from her and pulled her close, resting my chin on top of her head. It was such an odd and confusing thing, the deep love I could still feel for Tracy when I had just experienced such a tumult of passion with Maria.

"Stop putting yourself down," I said, running a hand over her tumbled hair, feeling her relax against me.

"I just feel so bad all the time, Patrick," she said in a low voice against my chest. "How do I stop feeling so bad?"

Holding her, I moved my hands against her back, kneading gently, easing away the tension. Tracy turned her face up to me, and I kissed her, tasting the saltiness of her tears.

"Make love to me, Patrick," she whispered. "That will help, I know it. The boys are watching TV. We can slip upstairs."

Up in our room, Tracy turned her back beside the bed and shed her clothes. I undressed slowly, trying desperately not to think of how it had been with Maria the night before. When I made love to her I hadn't thought that it would affect my ability to react to Tracy. But as I undressed and slipped under the covers I wasn't able to give myself over to what was happening between my wife and me as I used to be able to.

Tracy and I caressed each other silently, our hands cold. What we'd been experiencing down in the kitchen had dissipated, and we both knew it. Still her body was warm and smooth against me, and I willed myself to respond to her. Finally I did, but what went on between us was perfunctory and bittersweet.

Afterward Tracy turned over on her stomach and lay very still.

"Honey," I said finally, touching her shoulder. "Are you okay?"

"I was wrong," she said dully. "It didn't help."

"I'm sorry," I said. "I'm a little tired."

"You know that's not it," she said.

I didn't know what else to say, so I got up and started to put my clothes on.

Before I left, she said in a low voice, "I hate living, Patrick."

"Don't say that," I told her, suddenly alarmed. "There has to be someone who can help you with this, Tracy, a therapist maybe."

"It would be a waste of money," she said dully. "Do you really think a stranger can make me like myself again? Do you think he can give me a new face?"

"You don't need a new face," I said desperately. "I love your face, Tracy. I love you. Please, honey."

"I don't think you know what I need at all," she said, her back to me. "I'm not sure you ever knew."

I couldn't sit there and listen anymore so I went downstairs to wash the dishes, Tracy's unhappiness pressing down on me like a weight. As I worked I thought of Maria. How different I felt when I was with her. It was like the contrast between darkness and light. A sharp stab of desire for her left me feeling weak and ashamed. It was as if I had no control over choosing to do what was decent.

Wanting the reassurance of the way things used to be, I went into the living room and lay on the floor between the two boys, who were glued to a space war movie. I watched along with them, glad for the distraction and their company. Maybe if Tracy and I could just recreate some of our old happiness, get rid of the misery that her lingering depression had spread around us, we'd all be okay.

"Who's for popcorn?" I asked when a commercial came.

"Me, me!" both boys shouted, and I went into the kitchen to make it.

"Here, Dad, I'll shake it," Ben said, appearing at my elbow in a few moments. "Joe, why don't you go ask Mom if she wants some?"

Ben and I took turns shaking the popcorn over the burner until Joe came back. "She says she just wants to sleep," Joe said, pouting. "Why does she need to sleep so much, anyway? Other people's moms don't sleep that much."

"Other people's moms don't have to put up with you," Ben said. "Just lay off her, will you?"

"Try and make me!" Joe taunted.

Ben took a swipe at him, and I was left to dish up the popcorn. When I took the popcorn into the living room, the boys were sitting at opposite sides of the room, glaring at the TV screen. They barely touched the popcorn. Things were going to be harder to change than I'd thought.

Driving to the shop the next morning, I found myself hurrying, wanting to see Maria, wanting to feel the way I did when I was with her. I didn't know how to begin to fight the feeling, powerful as it was, and I wasn't even sure I wanted to.

"Hi," Maria said shyly as I came in. She'd gotten to the store early. Already, the rich aroma of simmering chicken broth filled the place. "I was up early, so I decided to come in," she said. "Actually, I couldn't wait to see you."

"That's the way I felt, too," I admitted, steeling myself not to touch her. I knew if I did, I wouldn't be able to let her go. "Things didn't go so well with Tracy last night. I think she suspects what's going on with us."

"How could she know?" Maria asked, wide-eyed.

209

"She knows you were here all night," I said. "And she knows that something's going on with me. It's enough."

"Let's not think about it," Maria whispered, touching my hand. "Please, Patrick, let's just take it a moment at a time."

The bell over the door rang as a customer came in, and she jerked her hand away.

It seemed to me all that day that people could see, just looking at Maria and me, the desire that simmered between us. I could barely think, I wanted her so. Yet it was more than physical longing. I felt contentment just to be near her. I could hardly remember when I'd felt that way about Tracy. Even back at the beginning, before the accident, I'd always had to be the one to reach out to Tracy, to do the courting.

With Maria there was the newness of someone courting me, seeking to please, wanting me. I'd never fully experienced that kind of thing with any woman before and it totally carried me away.

Maria and I managed to stay away from each other that whole week. I couldn't reconcile making love to her and then going home to Tracy. At home, though, things were worse than ever. The doctor had given Tracy some pills that were supposed to alleviate her depression, and she was sleeping more than ever. It worried me that she was mixing the pills with alcohol, but I couldn't get her to listen to me. As many afternoons as I could, I'd leave Maria watching the shop and pick up the boys from school and bring them back with me. It didn't seem that Tracy was capable of taking care of them the way she was.

"There's nothing to do here, Dad," Ben complained. "Besides, we should be at home, making sure Mom's all right."

I hated hearing that my sons felt they had to take care of their mother. I also hated needing to have my sons around so that I could trust myself with Maria.

One evening I came home late with the boys, and Tracy met us at the door. Torment was clear in her swollen face. I couldn't tell if she was groggy from pills or if she had been drinking.

"Good for nothing, that's me!" she slurred. "Can't even take care of the kids anymore, according to you." Leaning down, she addressed Joe, who backed away. "Do you like that lady who works for Daddy? Do you like her better than me?"

Joe began to whimper, and I laid my hand on top of his head. "That's enough, Tracy," I said as calmly as I could. "I've brought home some soup and sandwiches. Why don't you get a robe and—"

"Don't you patronize me!" she shouted, anger flaring in her eyes. "Think you're so great, don't you, taking care of it all? Think you're doing such a good job. You can just have it all then. I don't want it!" She swept out of the kitchen and up the stairs.

"What does she mean, Dad?" Ben asked, his face white.

My hands were shaking. I was angry and disgusted with Tracy. How long could things go on that way? "That's not your mother talking, Ben," I said. "She's—"

"She's drunk, is what she is," Joe burst out.

"Shut up, you brat!" Ben said. He swung around to face me. "I told you we should stay here to make sure she's all right. It's your fault, Dad, for dragging us to the shop. She just needs somebody to be with her, that's all." He headed for the stairs.

I started to call him back, but changed my mind. Maybe Ben could do what I couldn't seem to.

Later that night, after I'd gotten the boys to bed, I went out for a drive. I had to think, figure out what to do about my marriage.

I was sick at heart. None of my attempts to help Tracy had worked. She seemed bent on destroying herself, our marriage, and even her relationship with the kids. Without really planning to, I drove down Crooked Lane to Maria's house. Lights were on, spreading a bright welcoming pool over the banked-up snow outside. I pulled into her driveway, sat in the car a moment trying to reason with myself, and then gave in.

"Patrick, you don't even have a coat on," was the first thing Maria said when she opened her door. "Something has happened, hasn't it?" She guided me inside.

Her concern and her steady, reassuring manner made me feel worse, playing up the horrible scene with Tracy as they did. Things at home seemed even more hopeless in the light of Maria's rationality.

I sat down in front of the fireplace. "I can't stay," I said. "Tracy's in really bad shape. The boys shouldn't be alone with her. Oh, Maria!" I went on, feeling as though I might start to weep at any minute. "I feel so much to blame for everything. Maybe if I could have loved her the way she needed to be loved. . . ."

Maria sat on the floor, her head resting against my knees. She was so alive, so much of everything I seemed destined to be denied. "A woman should be glad to have a man like you," she said, gazing in to the fire. "A person loves the way he loves. Nobody's responsible for another person's happiness."

"Maybe not," I said, and because I wanted so much to believe her, I slid down to the floor to join her. The fire crackled and blazed higher as a log settled. We were in each other's arms, Maria's touch bringing me alive.

"I'd be so happy if you loved me," she whispered. "Even if it was only the tiniest bit."

"Why do you think I'm here?" I breathed, hungry for her kiss. Then there was no more talk, only the quickening of our breathing as we were joined in the sweet oblivion of lovemaking. There

211

was no misery waiting at home for me then—only that interval of forgetfulness, and the dawning of the realization that this was the woman I really loved.

Later, tenderness swept over me as I pulled a knitted afghan over Maria where she had fallen asleep on the rug. I knew I could never turn my back on her sweetness, her willingness to love me no matter how little was in it for her. She was a part of me, far beyond the physical need we felt for each other.

I felt calmed as I drove home. The words Maria had said about a person "loving the way he loved" stayed with me. It was true that I had loved Tracy in the only way I knew how—that is, until I fell in love with Maria. But that had happened long after things had gotten bad between Tracy and me. It was hard to know, though, how much of my thinking was rationalization and how much was an unbiased assessment of the situation.

Tracy was awake when I came in. She was sitting up in bed, her knees pulled up and her chin resting on them. She looked like a little girl that way—very different from the sloppy drunk person of a few hours before.

"I know where you've been," she said, turning her face to look at me. Her expression was passive, uncaring.

I didn't want to lie anymore. I wasn't sure how telling the truth could make things any worse than they were. Maybe it would help. "Can you blame me, after the way you acted in front of the boys tonight?" I said.

"So you're punishing me then?" she said.

I shook my head. "I'm not punishing you, Tracy. It's just that I want to be someplace cheerful for a change. This unhappiness between us is hard on all of us, especially the boys."

"I see," she said, straightening out her legs and nodding. "Well, I think I know what I can do about it."

I hesitated in the middle of unbuttoning my shirt. "I thought a lot about that tonight, Tracy," I said. "I'm not sure there's anything left to do."

"Oh, but there is," she said, smiling oddly. "You'll see. Everything will work out just fine." Then she slid down in the bed and turned on her side, refusing to say anything else.

I didn't sleep much that night, and I was pretty sure Tracy was also lying awake, rigid and still beside me. It was awful, as if we were strangers, and I felt a twinge of fear that things could change so drastically between two people who had loved each other so much.

In the morning, though, things were much better. For the first time in months, Tracy got up, showered, put on makeup, and dressed before breakfast. I had mixed feelings about that, realizing as I had the night before how much I cared for Maria. If Tracy really did change, how could I justifiably leave her?

It was a wonderful thing to see the boys' response to Tracy's efforts. "You look nice, Mom," Ben said happily.

"Thanks, Ben," Tracy said, glancing at him abstractedly. There was something about her—something I couldn't put my finger on. It was as though her mind was elsewhere. No matter how much her appearance told us she was with us, she was still somewhere else. "I've been thinking, though," she said. "I don't have anything really stylish to wear. It's been so long since I've been shopping. And my hair needs cutting and shaping. Don't you think so, Patrick?"

"You look fine the way you are, but I wouldn't mind if you spent some money on yourself," I said, not sure what she was getting at.

"Good," she said, smiling. "Then you won't mind if I go into the city tomorrow. The boys can go to Stephie's after school. I'll probably be late getting home, so she can take them out for a fast-food dinner. I'll leave something in the refrigerator for you, Patrick."

I stared at her. It didn't seem possible that she could be planning to drive into the city by herself when she'd been practically a recluse for so many months. "Why don't you hold off, honey? Wait until I can come with you."

"You work six days a week, Patrick. Most of the shops aren't open on Sunday, and certainly not the beauty salon."

"I could take a day off," I said. "A slow time is coming up."

"Sure, you could," she said sarcastically. "I'll be old and gray by then. I'll manage fine, don't worry." Then she said something strange, something I wish I'd paid more attention to at the time. "Just make sure you come home for dinner before you pick up the boys, okay?"

I figured maybe it was her way of emphasizing how important it was to her that I come home to eat instead of maybe using the opportunity to spend time with Maria, so I didn't pursue it.

That night Tracy had a nice dinner made, and afterward she sat down with the boys and me to watch TV. The boys were hungry for her presence, vying for chances to sit close to her and to compliment her. I think they were as uneasy as I was, about the sudden change in Tracy. It seemed almost too good to be true.

When we went up to bed Tracy snuggled close as she hadn't in a long time. As I held her I became aware of dampness on my shoulder where her head lay. Reaching out, I could feel tears on her face. She'd been crying with no sound or movement—just tears streaming steadily down her cheeks. I wiped them away with my hand, saying nothing at all.

The next morning Tracy looked lovelier than I'd seen her since the early days of our marriage. There was cheerfulness about her that

213

belied her tears of the night before. Had I imagined them?

She spent a lot of time getting the boys off to school, hugging them, and making sure they had their instructions for that afternoon. "Remember, you're to go to Stephie's," she told Ben. "Don't forget and come home. Okay?"

"Sure, Mom," Ben said. "We won't forget."

As I was leaving, Tracy came to the door with me, wrapping her arms around my neck and hugging me hard. "Things will be better, Patrick. I promise," she said. Then she kissed me. It was a kiss like the kisses of our early marriage, full of promise.

I was confused. Seeing Maria when I got to the shop, I still felt an inexorable pull toward her, a definite sense of the rightness of us being together. But Tracy's kiss lingered with me all through the morning, nagging at me. There was something wrong. I knew it.

"You're a million miles away," Maria said. "What's on your mind?"

"It's Tracy," I told her. "She said she was going to the city to get some new clothes, but I don't know. There was something strange about the way she was acting."

"Why don't you go home to see if she left the house all right?" Maria suggested. "I'll take care of things here."

I called the house first, and, of course there was no answer. Still, I thought I'd feel better just checking things out. A few minutes later when I saw Tracy's car still sitting in the driveway, I knew that I'd been right about something being wrong.

The house was silent when I went in. Tracy didn't answer my call. In the kitchen I opened the refrigerator. There was no dinner waiting to be warmed, as Tracy had said there would be. A strong pulse began to throb in my throat. She hadn't planned to go to the city at all!

Slamming the refrigerator shut, I raced for the stairs. "Tracy! Tracy, for God's sake, no!" I shouted, tripping in my hurry to get up the stairs.

But I was too late. Early as I'd come home, it hadn't been early enough. Tracy lay on our bed, dressed as she'd been when she'd kissed me good-bye that morning. Her skin was bluish and very cold. Beside her on the bed was her empty pill vial. I touched her neck with a trembling finger. I could feel no pulse. Even as I dialed for an ambulance I knew it was no use. She was dead.

An eerie fog of unreality carried me through the arrival of the ambulance squad, my trip with Tracy to the hospital, and, finally, the doctor telling me what I already knew. For so long there'd been Tracy's misery, haunting me, requiring something of me. Suddenly it wasn't there anymore. In its place was a reproach. I wouldn't have another chance to help her ever again. Realizing that, I was filled with shame.

I called Stephie from the hospital. She said the boys had just arrived there from school. "Keep them inside," I told her. "Don't let them talk to anyone. There's been an—accident."

"I know," she whispered. "I saw all the activity next door. I'll keep them occupied until you get here."

The drive to Stephie's house seemed like the longest of my life. How could I tell the boys that their mother was gone? It didn't seem possible to me yet. Clutching the wheel, I wept for Tracy, for the boys, and for all our lost chances.

Stephie had Ben and Joe in the kitchen. They were glumly helping her make cookies.

"Oh, good, here's Dad," Joe said. "Maybe he'll let us watch TV!"

Stephie met my eyes over the boys' heads. She looked as though she felt almost as scared as I did about what I had to tell them.

"She didn't let you watch TV because something has happened," I said. "It's something I wanted to tell you myself. We didn't want you finding out on TV."

Both boys were suddenly very still, staring at me. She slipped out of the room to leave us alone.

"It's your mother," I said, going around the counter and putting an arm around each of them. "She didn't go to the city today. Instead, she—she took some pills. A lot of them. I took her to the hospital but it was too late." I held on to the boys tightly, feeling the shock vibrate through them.

Ben began to sob.

"Did she do it on purpose, Daddy?" Joe asked, his eyes filling.

"No one can ever answer that, honey," I said. "I do know Mom was awfully sad for a long time."

"We should have done something!" Ben wailed. "I told you a long time ago we should have done something!"

I could only nod, though Ben had his hands over his face and didn't see me. After a while the boys and I went back to our house. I thought about what Tracy had said about my coming home to dinner before I picked up the boys. Of course, she hadn't wanted them to be the ones to find her. Still, the horror of what she had done lingered in the house.

Maria called that night. She had heard about Tracy on the news. I could tell from her voice that she was hurt that I hadn't called her. "Patrick, you must be devastated," she said. "I'm so sorry, so very sorry. Tell me what I can do to help."

"There's nothing," I said wearily. "Just close up the shop for a few days. Take care of anything perishable. I'll be in touch about

215

when we'll open again. Right now I just can't think straight."

"You sound so cold," she said. "Would it help if we talked? You know you did everything you could for Tracy. We've discussed it before."

"I wish I could believe that," I said. "But I can't."

I knew as I hung up the phone that it was over for Maria and me. We would never be alone, just the two of us. Tracy would always be there between us. As far as I was concerned, I had as good as killed her.

More important, there was Ben. Young as he was, he sensed that there had been something between Maria and me. Late that night, when Joe was asleep, he came down to the kitchen where I was sitting over a cup of coffee. There was no way I could make myself go up to the bedroom.

"Are you going to marry Maria now, Dad?" Ben asked out of the blue. His face was twisted with contempt. "I remember Mommy asked us if we liked Maria better than her. You did, I'll bet."

"No, Ben, I'm not going to marry Maria," I said, looking into my coffee. We were both silent for a long moment. "But you're right, I did like her. I liked her cheerfulness. I liked her liking me. Grownups aren't perfect, Ben. I'm sure not. I made a mistake not giving your mom more attention. I admit that. If there was anything I could do now to turn that around, I would. Really." I looked at Ben, and he nodded, his face softening.

"I know you would, Dad," he said.

Tracy would have been pleased at how beautiful she looked at her funeral. Her makeup was perfect. There was almost no sign of the scar that had twisted her face and our lives. She looked peaceful, and I tried very hard to imprint her expression on my memory to help during the days ahead.

I wanted to get back to a semi-normal life as soon as possible. A couple of days after the funeral I got the boys back in school, arranged for someone to be with them in the afternoons, and reopened the shop.

Seeing Maria that first day back was painful. I knew I wouldn't be able to work with her any longer, and told her that I was giving her notice.

"How can you do this?" she said. "It's as though you're blaming me for what happened. At least let me work with you, see you every day. I told you before I'd settle for that."

"It isn't just what you'd settle for, Maria," I told her. "I can't be around you every day and not want you."

"Then want me," she said. "It's not so wrong to love somebody, to want to have a little happiness."

I shook my head, thinking that those were the things that Tracy

216

had wanted. Things I hadn't given her.

Several months have passed since Tracy died, and it's spring now. Through the help of counseling, the boys and I have tried to come to terms with what happened to her. More and more, as we've learned to get in touch with our feelings, I wish I'd forced Tracy to get counseling before it was too late.

But there's no going back. Finally, I've accepted the fact that a person can take only so much responsibility for another person's happiness. I couldn't create happiness for Tracy. It had to come from somewhere inside her—from her sense of herself.

I want my boys to have a good sense of themselves, to know that they're loved for who they are, and because we're a family and belong to one another. For that reason I've tried to spend a lot of time with them after school and on the weekends. My family comes first with me now, as it should have long ago.

I've cut down on business and have been running the store single-handedly except for after school hours when a high-school boy comes in to make deliveries for me. The work is good. It helps me to heal and forget.

One thing, though, I don't want to forget. It's important not to minimize another person's pain. From the beginning I couldn't understand how a scar could upset Tracy so much. I never really said to her, "I know how you feel." If I'd said that, just that, I might have penetrated her aloneness.

Ironically, it was that very quality, that sense of someone else knowing how I felt, that appealed to me most about Maria. I still see her now and then around town, and knowing that she's somewhere nearby comforts me. Someday she'll probably leave here, but I won't forget her and the warmth she spread in my life. There will always be a part of me that loves Maria, even though we couldn't make things work. Maybe in letting her go, I'll finally be demonstrating some unselfishness.

THE END

MY LITTLE GIRL
WAS TRAPPED!
I had to save her from drowning

I tried to control my shaking knees as I walked up the steps of the familiar, old house. I was thinking only of my baby, and yet I noticed the bed of chrysanthemums just beginning to bloom by the side of the porch. There were two new red rose bushes, too. Rebecca, I thought. Of course! She would plant flowers! I took a deep breath and knocked. Please, God, let me say and do the right thing! I prayed.

What if Brittany cried and refused to go with me? I hadn't seen her in almost two years, and she was only three and a half now. Oh, I had waited so long for this moment, and I was scared to death.

Rebecca opened the door so suddenly, I jumped back, startled. She stood there for a moment, just looking at me. Not even a "hello." I had dressed carefully, but I cringed inside as Rebecca's acool stare took in my hair, my clothes, my shoes. She could have been inspecting a bug that she had found in her kitchen.

I tried to push back the anger. It's all right, I told myself fiercely. Just don't say anything. She'll have to bring Brittany out.

"Brittany will be ready in a minute," she said stiffly. "Wait here."

Well, she hasn't changed any, I thought bitterly, watching her disappear through the hallway. She still thinks she's the Queen of England. Oh, I didn't expect her to invite me in, but she could have at least been civil. After all, she had everything that had once belonged to me—my husband, my baby, the house I used to live in. And my mother-in-law. That last part of it served her right!

Another thing I didn't begrudge Rebecca was the old house. It dated back to the Civil War, and I hated it. I craned my neck until I could see into the living room. The cracked plaster had been repaired, and some of the shabby old pieces of furniture had been replaced with modern things. There were new drapes, too, bright floral ones.

I tried to swallow the ache in my throat. But the ache quickly vanished at the sight of Rebecca reappearing in the hallway, leading a little girl by the hand.

Rebecca opened the door, and she and Brittany came out on the porch. I could feel my heart pounding hard.

I stared at the little girl. She was so tall, taller than I had imagined! Oh, I knew she'd be a lot bigger than the last time I had seen her, but somehow in my mind I had still imagined her a baby. Her hair was still as dark, but it had grown into a thick ponytail and was tied back with a red ribbon to match her dress. But her wide brown eyes looking curiously up into mine were the same, exactly the same as I had remembered them. They had haunted all of my waking moments, and most of my sleeping ones, too, for the last two years.

"Hello, Brittany," I said hesitantly, stooping down to her. "You've grown so tall! The last time I saw you, you were still just a baby."

Brittany looked shyly down at her bright patent-leather shoes.

"She's shy with strangers," Rebecca said, emphasizing the last word. Her words cut me like a knife, but only for a second.

"Would you like to go to the beach with me, Brittany?" I asked, forcing my voice to be light and gay. "We'll go to the playground if you want to, and ride the merry-go-round."

"The merry-go-round makes her sick," Rebecca said. But I guess the pleading in my eyes softened her a little, because she added that Brittany could go on the other rides.

"But don't let her eat peanuts," she ordered, "and please have her home promptly at six."

I stood up and extended my hand to Brittany, holding my breath. Wonder of wonders! She instantly put her warm little hand trustingly in mine.

"Does she know?" I whispered to Rebecca over Brittany's head. I still didn't know what they had told Brittany about me.

"Yes," Rebecca whispered back. "Justin told her." She paused a moment, and her eyes hardened. "If you really loved Brittany, you wouldn't have come back."

"Rebecca, please," I pleaded. "I came back because I do love her—I'm her mother. Please try to understand."

"Oh, I understand. Brittany isn't the only reason you're here. You're tired of playing around now, and you think you can get Justin back. Well, you're wasting your time. He despises you!"

I gasped. I couldn't have been more surprised if she had struck me!

"That isn't true—I mean about wanting to get Justin back," I stammered. "I don't want to cause any trouble. All I want is to see Brittany once in a while."

I think Rebecca and I both realized at the same time that we weren't whispering anymore, and that Brittany's eyes were round and questioning.

"You'd better go now," Rebecca said, looking a little shamefaced. She leaned down and gave Brittany a brief kiss. "Be a good girl," she said, and went inside.

I was alone with my daughter! I managed to brush the conversation with Rebecca out of my mind. I wasn't going to let anything spoil this precious afternoon.

Brittany climbed eagerly into the car, and then sat very primly, arranging her underskirt and dress just so. A little feeling of panic rushed over me. What should I say? What does one say to a three-year-old?

"That's a very pretty dress," I said in sheer desperation.

"Thank you," she answered politely, but she didn't look up. She was busy inspecting her gleaming shoes. It had rained that morning and a few blades of wet grass had stuck to them while we were walking to the car. It seemed to upset her, so I carefully wiped the wet grass off with my handkerchief.

"Are you really my mother?" she asked suddenly.

"Yes," I said, scarcely breathing.

She looked thoughtful for a minute, and then a little frown wrinkled her forehead. My heart sank. "Well," she said slowly, and then a look of pure delight lit up her face. "I have this many mothers!" She looked gleeful as she held up three fingers. "You, and my really mother, and my grandma!"

I breathed a sigh of relief and grinned back at her. "Lucky you," I said, "to have so many mothers."

We hit it off fine from there on. Brittany was soon chattering happily, and she kept it up all the way to the beach. She told me about her cat, her Sunday-school class, the little boy she played with, and the hole she was digging in the backyard. I hung on her every word completely fascinated. When she was talking about the hole, though, something kept nagging at the back of my mind.

Suddenly I remembered—the old well! It was a well that Justin's father had started digging before he discovered it was on a rock deposit. There wasn't any water in it, but I had almost stepped in it one day and it had frightened me.

"Do you have any more little girls?" Brittany asked, interrupting my thoughts.

"No," I said softly, aching to hold her in my arms. "Just you."

She still looks like me, I thought. Even more now than when she was a baby. I wondered if Justin ever noticed the resemblance.

It was a beautiful afternoon, and when we got to the beach, it was already crowded. The water looked so inviting I was sorry I hadn't asked Rebecca about taking Brittany in. Next time I will, I thought, and the idea filled me with a deep contentment.

Remembering Rebecca's warnings, Brittany rode the miniature train instead of the merry-go-round. She looked so cute sitting in the boxcar, my heart felt as if it would burst with love. After that, we ate cotton candy, and Brittany laughed with delight at the way it disappeared on her tongue. I pushed her on the swings, caught her as she came zooming down the slide, and held a little paper cup while she filled it with sand. I wanted to absorb every single moment of the afternoon—it would have to last me a whole week.

All too soon it was time to go.

"Can't we stay a little while longer?" Brittany begged.

"No, dear," I said firmly. "If I don't get you back when your mommy said to, she'll be mad at us."

"Well, all right," Brittany said. Then her face brightened. "I'm going to tell Grandma I rode the train. Grandma can't walk. She has to stay in bed all the time."

"I'm sorry," I mumbled, and the conversation I had with Justin on the phone the week before came rushing back. He had called me at the restaurant where I was working, and as soon as I heard his voice I knew my lawyer had contacted him. Justin sounded harsh and angry, just as he had the last time I'd seen him two years before.

"There's no need to sue for visitation rights, Sarah," he said. "Mother isn't well, and I don't think she could stand the strain of going to court now. How often do you feel you should see Brittany?"

"Once a week would be fine," I stammered. I was so surprised at his cooperation that I reached for the stool by the phone to support myself. I had been prepared for a bitter fight.

"We can try it and see how it works out," he said coldly. "Of course, we don't want Brittany upset. If it becomes a strain on her. . . ." His voice was threatening.

Hastily I assured him that I didn't intend to divide her affections—that all I wanted was to be with her once a week on my day off. We agreed on an afternoon, and he hung up.

I had been using the phone in the restaurant's kitchen, and it wasn't until I noticed Jim, the cook, staring at me that I realized tears were streaming down my cheeks. I fled to the rest room then and let the sobs come, wonderful sobs of relief after a two-year nightmare!

Brittany was tugging on my arm, trying to get my attention.

"Honey," I said, bending down to her and putting my arms around her, "would you like to go somewhere again next week? Would you like me to come for you again?"

"Yes," she said, smiling. "Will you?"

"Well, I might," I answered. "If you gave me a great big hug, I just might."

Shyly, she put her arms around my neck, and I pulled her sturdy little body close. I buried my face in the sweet little-girl smell of her hair. "My real mother," she had called Rebecca. The pain stabbed at me again and I pulled her closer.

Brittany pulled away and looked up into my face. "Why are you crying?" she asked, her own lips beginning to tremble.

"I'm not crying, honey," I said. "I just have something in my eye."

"Both of them?" she asked.

"Yes, but it's all right now," I said, gathering up her shoes and socks.

I got Brittany home just as Justin was pulling into the driveway. He had got out of his car and had started up the walk when he heard my car. He turned around and just stood there, waiting. Oh, no, I thought. I can't drive in with him standing there! Somehow I just couldn't face him, not yet. With shaking hands I carefully parked on the side of the road and helped Brittany out of the car. I walked her across the street, and then let go of her hand.

"That's my daddy," she said proudly, pointing to Justin.

"I know, honey," I whispered. "I'll see you next week. Okay?"

"Okay," she said, but her mind was on Justin and she ran to him. Justin caught her in his arms, but our eyes met for a long moment across the length of the lawn. I felt paralyzed. I wanted to turn and run, but I couldn't move. I just stood there, looking. Justin turned away first, carrying Brittany in his arms. I stumbled back into the car and drove away as fast as I could. Although I'd known I was bound to run into Justin sooner or later, I hadn't been prepared for it.

I felt too keyed up to go right to my apartment then, so I drove by the restaurant where I worked. Mr. Garner, my boss, smiled when he saw me come in, and he walked over and sat down on the stool next to me.

"Might as well give me a cup, too," he said when I ordered coffee from Carrie.

As soon as Carrie had served our coffee and moved away to wait on a customer, he asked, "Well, how did it go?"

"Oh, wonderful," I said. I launched into all the details of the afternoon, describing just how Brittany looked and everything we did.

Mr. Garner listened attentively, as if it was really important to him. I had only been working for him three weeks, just since I got back to town, but I felt I had known him forever. He was a swell boss, and somehow I had found myself telling him all my troubles. He was new in town, and had only had the restaurant a couple of months. He didn't even know the Minors and that made me feel at ease with him. I didn't have to worry about what he was thinking about me, the way I did with the rest of the people in town that I had known all my life.

"Well, I'd better go," I said, realizing how long I had been talking and knowing he had other things to do. It was just a small restaurant, but it kept him and a waitress jumping mostly the time.

"I'm happy you got to see your little girl," he said warmly. The sincerity of his words touched me. I looked at his rugged, homely face. He didn't look a bit like Papa, yet somehow he reminded me of him. It's his kindness, I thought. He has the same kindness.

Briefly, I wondered about his wife. Carrie told me she was dead,

222

but she didn't know anything other than that. Mr. Garner had never talked about her.

When I got back to my apartment, it seemed smaller and lonelier than ever. I should be getting used to tiny, lonely rooms by now, I thought. But somehow, I never did.

I took a shower and set my hair. I put on a pot of coffee and fixed a sandwich that I couldn't eat. I drank the coffee, though, and pressed my uniform for the next day. I couldn't think of anything else to do, so I went to bed.

It was a mistake—sleep was impossible. I kept hearing Rebecca's voice saying, "Justin despises you."

Maybe if Mrs. Minor hadn't set her heart on Justin's marrying Rebecca, things might have been different. I don't think she even considered the possibility that Justin might marry somebody else—especially somebody like me. Me and Papa and Dave were just—well, in her eyes, we were just nothing.

Papa raised Dave and me alone after Mama ran off with another man. I was eight, but Dave was only six, and I knew even then that the neighbors felt sorry for us. Well, it didn't bother me much—the nearest neighbor was a mile away, and, to tell the truth, Mama's running off seemed to bother other people more than it did us. We didn't like Mama much anyway. She was pretty, but she didn't care about Dave and me the way Papa did, and was always yelling at Papa about living in a shack where everything smelled like fish. Mama didn't care a thing about the water. In fact, she hated it.

But Papa! Well, Papa came from seagoing people, and he loved the water more than anything else in the world, I guess, except Dave and me. He respected the water, too, the kind of respect that comes from making your living from it and being dependent on it.

One time when we were treading water for clams, he got mad at Dave for needlessly killing a small crab.

"But, Papa, he pinched me!" Dave said, trying to find a mark on his arm to show Papa.

"You are in his house," Papa said, his voice rough and his eyes all dark with anger. "How would you like it if somebody came stomping around your house? You'd feel like pinching, too! If you ever deliberately kill anything again, except if it's to be used for food, I'll pinch you in a spot you won't forget in a hurry!"

That's the way Papa was. He yelled as much as Mama did, but he was always fair, and somehow, we never minded his yelling at us.

At first, I hated Mama when she left, because I thought Papa would feel bad. But I guess the love between them had been destroyed long ago, because Papa didn't seem sad over losing her. And Mama was wrong about our house. It was small, but it wasn't a shack. Papa had built it with his own hands, and it was beautiful. Best of all, our front porch looked out over the vast, exciting waters of Chesapeake Bay.

It's true we didn't live the way a lot of people live, but it was good enough for us. Dave and I grew up in a sort of rough-and-tumble way, but we went to school and did all right. I wasn't crazy about housework then, and the house got kind of messy sometimes, but nobody really minded.

Papa was a boatbuilder by trade, and he fished a lot, too. But by the time Dave and I were in high school, Papa's business started falling off and he went to work part time in the shipyards. Dave went into the Army as soon as he turned seventeen, the month after I graduated. I tried to get him to wait until he finished school, but he was crazy to see the world.

After Dave left, Papa wanted me to get a job in Rapids Park and stay with his sister. We had been carrying on a running argument about it most of the summer. It wasn't the money Papa was worried about. He was afraid I was going to be an old maid! Bronson's Point was a small town, hardly more than a fishing village, and Papa thought I ought to move to greener pastures. He was seriously worried about it, and while I was amused, I was puzzled, too.

"Papa, I don't like Rapids Park, I like it here," I said over and over again. "Besides, Dave won't be home to stay for two years. You'll get lonesome out here by yourself."

"I get along fine," he said. "You want to be an old maid?"

I laughed. "At nineteen? Really, Papa! Besides, I have dates. I'll get married sometime. Don't rush me!"

Papa and I were sitting on the back steps, and I was trying to decide whether or not to go in and wash the supper dishes. Just then a car turned into our road.

"Probably one of your boys now," Papa said hopefully. But I didn't recognize the car or the fellow until he got out, and then a little thrill shot through me. Justin Minor! What was he doing here?

"Mr. Waldon?" Justin asked pleasantly, walking up to where we were sitting. . . .

Stop it! Stop it! I told myself fiercely, getting out of bed. Why did my mind keep going over and over every little detail? I poured a glass of water and got some aspirins out of the cupboard. I took them and went back to bed. Think of Brittany, I told myself, only of Brittany.

But sleep still wouldn't come. If only I could figure out how Justin and I had reached the point where we couldn't talk anymore. Maybe we had never been able to talk. Oh, but we had, we had!

I pulled the pillow down tight over my head to blot out the images of Justin and me strolling hand in hand on the beach, talking

224

a mile a minute, discovering all the wonderful little things about each other. I remembered how Justin's gray eyes lit up when he was telling me about the appliance shop he wanted to open, the thrill of his strong arm around me in the darkness of a movie theater, the way there was just enough curl in his reddish-blond hair to wrap around one of my fingers, and, later, all the nights I slept in his arms. Maybe that's all we ever had, I thought, just a wild, crazy sort of hunger for each other.

That first time, Justin had come to talk to Papa about a boat he wanted to build, but after that he came because of me. It was common knowledge that he and Rebecca Hardy had an understanding, but they weren't married yet, and Rebecca wasn't even wearing his ring.

He and Rebecca were three years ahead of me in school, so I didn't know them very well, but they were going steady even then. Her father owned the cannery in Bronson's Point, the only industry in town. Rebecca's father and Justin's mother were third cousins, so Rebecca and Justin were fourth cousins. But after they grew up, they looked more like brother and sister.

Oh, they made a handsome couple! They slummed around the local places once in a while, and I would see them occasionally. They were both tall, but while Justin's hair had a reddish tint, Rebecca's was like ripe wheat. She wore it piled high, and that made her look even taller. But standing next to Justin, she looked delicate and fragile. It was their faces that were so similar—they both had an aristocratic look that set them apart from other people.

But Justin was friendly with everybody—the younger kids in school adored him—while Rebecca was snooty. I didn't like her even then, and after Justin started taking me out, I hated her. I knew it was because of her that Justin always took me to places where we wouldn't see anybody we knew. Justin came to my house often, to see me and to talk to Papa, but he never asked me to his. Poor Papa! He thought everything was fine, and he was delighted that I had a steady boyfriend.

I knew everything was all wrong, but I didn't have the courage to have a showdown with Justin. By that time, I was madly in love with him, and I just couldn't risk losing him! Besides, I felt sure he was falling in love with me, too. Oh, he never came right out and said so, but he was spending more and more time with me instead of Rebecca.

Yet we were still going the way of the back roads and the deserted strips of beach. And because it wasn't a normal relationship, our dates had a desperation about them. The time came when just being together wasn't enough. I knew it was wrong. I told myself that a thousand times a day. But when I was with Justin, nothing mattered except our love.

When I discovered I was pregnant, I was terrified. I dreaded telling Justin. I didn't know what he would do about it, but I was sure he wouldn't be pleased.

I was right. He was furious at first—not just with me, but with himself, too.

We were down on the beach when I told him.

"Well, I can't think of anything to do about it except get married," he said finally.

Relief flooded my feverish mind, but it hurt, too, the way he said it. Justin must have sensed what I was feeling, because he reached out and pulled me to him.

"Don't look like that," he said softly. "You know I'm crazy about you. It's just that this is a shock. I haven't had time to think. I don't know how I'll break it to Mother and Rebecca. Maybe this is the only way I would ever have got up enough courage to tell them about you."

He kissed me then, gently, as if he loved me, and my heart overflowed with gratitude.

We went home and told Papa that we were going to be married. I thought I saw tears in Papa's eyes, but he hurried out to the little shed to get a bottle of wine to celebrate the occasion. We were so happy, just the three of us, and we drank the wine and laughed and joked.

I should have known then that Papa wasn't well, but I was too wrapped up in my own happiness to notice. Papa died in his sleep a week later, and it wasn't until then that Dr. Jacobs told me about the two other heart attacks Papa had had.

"Why didn't he tell me he was sick?" I sobbed to Dr. Jacobs.

"He didn't want to worry you. Besides, there was no sure way of telling just how serious it was." Dr. Jacobs patted my shoulder. "There was nothing you could do, Sarah. He lived a good, happy life. That's the important thing."

I remembered how anxious Papa was for me to get married, and how happy he had been the night when Justin told him about us. He must have known he didn't have long, and he didn't want to leave me alone.

Justin and I were married quietly, just three days after Papa's funeral, while Dave was still home to be best man. Dave was leaving right after the ceremony, so we told him good-bye on the steps of the parsonage and then went straight to Justin's mother's house.

"Have you told your mother about—about the baby?" I asked.

"No, let's wait a while, until she gets used to the idea of having you for a daughter-in-law." His eyes were troubled, and I longed to comfort him. He had explained that we couldn't afford a place of our own yet, and I'd understood. He had just opened the appliance shop two months before, and it would take at least a year before it got on its feet.

"You can stand it just for a while, can't you?" he asked. "You and Mother will get along all right once you get to know each other."

I smiled and nodded, feeling I could get along with the devil himself to please Justin.

Only it didn't take me long to discover that was just what Mrs. Minor was—the devil! She hated me because I wasn't Rebecca. She and I would have been natural enemies, anyway, even if we had met under different circumstances. She was a hateful, domineering woman, and she made my life miserable from the day I moved in.

She was a tall woman, with a cloud of beautiful white hair. She had a grand-lady manner that awed me at first, and later just plain got on my nerves. It wouldn't have been so bad if she had just come out with the things that were on her mind—we could have fought then, and cleared the air. But not her! She would gently nag and criticize, always harping on little things. My clothes, my makeup, even the way I talked offended her. She was constantly correcting me, and in front of Justin, too. I thought at first that Justin would stand up for me, but he didn't, and after a while I stopped expecting him to.

"Oh, honey, Mother doesn't mean to offend you," he'd say. "That's just her way. You'll get used to her after a while." He'd take me in his arms then, and I'd forget about everything—for the moment.

Of course it didn't take Mrs. Minor long to discover I was pregnant. The morning sickness that had first aroused my suspicions didn't show any signs of letting up, and it got to the point where I couldn't even face the breakfast table.

Mrs. Minor came into my room one morning, after Justin had left for work. I was lying across the bed, too sick to even feel angry that she hadn't knocked.

"Have you seen a doctor, Sarah?" she asked.

"No," I answered weakly, trying to sit up. It was no use—the room whirled.

"That's why Justin married you, isn't it? You're pregnant, aren't you?"

"Yes," I said, and suddenly, I burst into tears. I couldn't stop crying. Everything had been building up until I felt I could stand it no longer. I cried for Papa and the little house I'd loved so, for Justin who seemed to love me only at night when we were alone in our room, for my happy, wonderful childhood that would never return. I didn't even think about the baby then. It was too unreal.

Mrs. Minor just stood there until my sobs had quieted down. Then she said, "I'm going downstairs to make an appointment with Dr. Jacobs. You had better stay in bed today. I'll send Christine up to see if you need anything."

Her voice was cold and detached, but because the words sounded kind, I reached out and touched her hand.

"Please don't blame Justin—it just happened," I began.

She drew back her hand as if she had touched a hot poker.

"I don't blame Justin," she said. "Getting pregnant is one way to get a man—if the man is a gentleman like Justin."

She turned and went downstairs then, and my despair turned to sheer rage. She thought I had deliberately trapped Justin! I knew then that there wasn't even the remotest possibility that we would ever be friends.

Things went from bad to worse after that. Justin was putting in long hours at the shop, but he wouldn't let me go down and help. And it was useless to pitch in around the house, because Mrs. Minor turned up her nose at everything I did. Besides, there was Christine who came in during the day. I tried to tell Justin there was no reason for Christine to come in—Mrs. Minor and I together could have kept up the house, even if it was old and rambling. But I might as well have been talking to thin air. If I even so much as mentioned his mother, he'd get angry. So as the months went by and I got heavier, I just settled back miserably to wait for the baby.

Just three weeks before the baby was born, I discovered, quite by accident, that Rebecca was helping Justin in the shop. That night, alone in our room, I faced Justin with it. I was trembling, I was so furious.

"Why didn't you tell me?" I demanded. "Why is she there? You told me you didn't need any help."

He was sitting on the side of the bed, taking off his shoes, and he paused, a shoe in one hand. He brushed the other hand tiredly across his eyes, and, in spite of myself, I felt a little pang of sympathy. He was working so hard!

"I couldn't very well keep her out," he said slowly. "I didn't want to tell you this before because you get so upset over everything, but Rebecca's father put up all the money that's in the shop. Mother sold all the land that Father left, trying to keep things together while I was in school. So when they offered to lend the money. . . ."

"But they thought you and Rebecca were going to get married when they lent it, didn't they?"

"Yes, I suppose they did."

"That's fine," I said bitterly. "Just dandy! We have absolutely nothing that belongs to us. I wonder what it would be like to breathe free air again."

Justin's eyes narrowed dangerously, and suddenly, I was afraid. We just couldn't go on like this!

"Justin, please let's get a place of our own," I begged. "We could even live in Papa's house. We won't be able to sell it until Dave's twenty-one."

"Mother can't stay in this house by herself," Justin answered. "And the money that's coming in now has to go for repairs, or it's going to fall apart."

"Then let her sell it," I said, "and rent an apartment."

"Sarah, Mother came to this house as a bride. It would kill her to leave it now."

"Let it!" I said angrily, the words just slipping out. Instantly I put my hand to my mouth, my eyes mutely begging Justin's forgiveness. He turned and went downstairs, and when he finally came to bed he slept far over on his own side, as if he couldn't bear to touch me.

I lay awake, listening to the sounds of the house and the night, wondering what was going to become of us.

It was the first of many such nights, and if I had any hopes of the baby making a difference, they quickly vanished. After Brittany was born, the tension was still there between Justin and me.

Oh, Justin tried to act happy about the baby, but I knew he was deeply disappointed that Brittany wasn't a boy. And the way his mother acted first surprised and then alarmed me. She so obviously despised me, I couldn't understand how she could be so crazy about my little girl. Brittany had my dark hair and coloring. She looked nothing like the Minors. But to hear Mrs. Minor tell it, Brittany was a chip off the old block.

This didn't bring Mrs. Minor and me any closer together. In fact, our conflicts now often erupted into open warfare. I think I could have held my own against her if Justin had just stayed out of it altogether. But he always sided with his mother, and between the three of them—Justin, Mrs. Minor, and Christine—sometimes I felt I was going to lose my sanity. Often I would get the feeling that the baby didn't even belong to me.

Or Justin, either, for that matter. I was sure that his love for me had faded or he wouldn't have deserted me for his mother. Oh, he still reached for me at night sometimes. But I couldn't feel the same anymore, and Justin knew it.

It was during the following summer that I started taking walks along the beach. I took the baby with me sometimes. Of course, Mrs. Minor thought of a million reasons why I shouldn't take her, but I took her, anyway.

I'd spread a blanket on the sand and let Brittany play there for a while, and then we'd go into Papa's house while she had her bottle. Those were the only times that I really felt she was mine.

Then one day when the weather had turned chilly, Brittany got sick after a trip to the beach. It frightened me, and, for once, I was happy to let Mrs. Minor take over. As it worked out, it was just a cold, but I had to agree it would be foolish to take Brittany on any more of my outings, at least not until the next spring.

But I kept on going even after winter had set in for good. There was just so much I could stand, and then I had to get out of the house.

It came as a surprise the day I noticed smoke coming out of the chimney of Papa's house. I hesitated, wondering if it was a trap. Then I felt a little flick of anger and marched up to the door. Whoever was there had no right. I knocked, and then stepped back when the door opened.

It was a young man dressed in a turtleneck sweater and slacks. He was lean-looking and tall, and he smiled very pleasantly.

"This is indeed an unexpected pleasure," he said. "Won't you come in?"

"What are you doing here?" I asked. "This is my house."

His smile faded, and he looked a little startled. "Oh, well, I'm sorry—I was under the impression that it belonged to a Mrs. Minor. At any rate, she took my money as though it belonged to her."

"You mean you rented this house from Mrs. Minor?"

"Yes," he said, looking slightly amused. "Do you know her?"

I could feel the anger starting in the pit of my stomach. The least she could have done was to tell me about it. "She's my mother-in-law," I said, beginning to feel foolish.

"Oh!"

"I'm sorry I bothered you—"

"Oh, that's all right," he said. "I hope there isn't any trouble. I mean, I like it here. It's ideal for my work, such a beautiful view."

I was interested in spite of myself. People didn't usually rent any of the waterfront places except in the summer.

"What kind of work do you do?" I asked.

"I'm an artist," he said. "Would you like to see some of my work?"

I almost said "yes," but I remembered just in time how it would look if I went in. "Maybe some other time," I said. "I walk down by the beach pretty often. I lived here as a child."

"Of course," he said. "Then I'll probably run into you again. I intend to paint down there quite often."

In the weeks that followed, I did run into him down on the beach. His name was Craig Tavis, and I had never known anyone like him before. He was wonderful company, witty and charming. We would talk while he painted beautiful pictures of the bay. I poured out all my troubles, and Craig listened and seemed to understand. Oh, I knew the situation was dangerous—I looked forward to seeing Craig too much for it to be just a casual thing, but I was so lonely for companionship. And he had never once stepped out of line in any way.

"I'll be leaving in a couple of days now," he said one afternoon, wiping his brushes off.

230

I felt a little pang of regret. Somehow, he had made my life more bearable. "I'll miss you," I said, turning my face away.

"Why don't we go to the house and have a hot cup of coffee?" he said. "You're shivering. Anyway, I really would like to show you the rest of my work before I leave."

His smile was so nice, and he had been such a good friend, I felt it wouldn't hurt to have a cup of coffee with him.

"All right," I said.

He took my hand and we started walking to the house, talking a mile a minute about his future plans. When we got inside, he took my coat and put the coffeepot on.

I was looking around the room, wondering what kind of a housekeeper Craig was, when it occurred to me that he was acting terribly nervous, not at all like his usual smooth self. He went to the window a couple of times—as if he were afraid that someone was watching. A strange, uneasy feeling came over me. I decided my coming in hadn't been a good idea, and I stood up to leave, a flimsy excuse on my lips.

Suddenly, there was a knock on the door. As if it were some kind of signal, Craig started acting like a crazy man!

He grabbed me with one hand and rumpled my hair up with the other. I started fighting, terror rising in me, but I couldn't stop the clawing hands, tearing at me, ripping at my clothes. I tried to bite his arm, but he yanked my head back with such force I felt the floor slipping from beneath my feet. Then he forced me to him again and kissed me brutally.

Nausea welled up in me and I felt a scream of terror begin somewhere in my throat, but suddenly Craig released me! I staggered back, grasping at the side of the table for support.

"Do you believe me now? Do you believe me now that she's been cheating on you all this time?"

I was stunned as the words lashed out at me. It was Mrs. Minor! And Justin! Justin was standing right behind her with an unbelieving look on his face. I rushed toward Justin, unable to understand what he and his mother were doing there, but weak with relief at seeing him.

Justin pushed me away from him so violently that I landed against the wall. I'll never forget the look in his eyes.

"Don't ever touch me again," he said slowly and deliberately. "I never want to see you again." He turned and walked out then, and Mrs. Minor followed, a smile of triumph on her face.

I cowered back against the wall, not able to understand what was going on.

"Here, better put this on," Craig said, throwing me one of his sweaters. I looked down at my blouse. The neckline was torn so I couldn't keep it up around me. I flung the sweater back at him and grabbed my coat. As I put it on, a glimmer of truth began to dawn on me. I faced Craig, trying not to look at the lipstick smeared across his face.

"Mrs. Minor paid you, didn't she, for what you just did!" I said. He shrugged his shoulders.

"Why—why—" My voice rose hysterically.

"Look at it this way—I really did you a favor," Craig said. "You were unhappy, they were unhappy. Now you can all go your separate ways and everything's peachy keen. Besides, I needed the money. Now why don't you just sit down and calm yourself, and we'll have that cup of coffee."

I stared at him unbelievingly. I couldn't believe anyone could be so wicked. Then I turned and ran out of the house.

I ran for almost two whole years. I signed the papers giving Justin complete custody of Brittany. I didn't know what else to do. Sick with shame and desperately hurt that Justin didn't believe me, I was too crushed to fight Mrs. Minor any more. She told me they would take Brittany away in court, and it would be easier on everybody if I just agreed.

"You can't possibly take care of Brittany," she said. "I don't think we'll have any trouble proving that you're an unfit mother. Brittany is much better off with us, and you'll be free."

Her face was cold as ice, and I realized for the first time how much I hated her. Free—she said I would be free!

Immediately after the divorce, I took the money that Justin had given me and left town. I worked in Rapids Park a while, waiting on tables, and then decided to push on. I went to Yorktown, and, after that, Jacobsburg. From Jacobsburg I moved on to Baltimore, and from Baltimore to Washington.

After a year and a half of wandering, I knew what I should have known from the beginning: I would never be free. I was chained, chained to the memory of a fat little baby's arms, and there wasn't anywhere in the world I could go that would free me of it. There was no escape. I had to see Brittany or I would lose my sanity.

Once I realized that, I came to a decision. I would talk to a lawyer. I picked one out of the phone book and made an appointment for my next afternoon off. Somehow, before I even talked to the lawyer, hope came alive in me. After talking to him, it grew tall and strong. He told me that I could go back and sue for visitation privileges, that there were very few instances where either parent was absolutely cut off from the child.

I started saving every penny I could lay my hands on. My boss gave me permission to work overtime, and I spread the word among the other girls that I was available if anyone wanted an extra day off. Four months later, I had what I thought was enough money and I took the bus back to Bronson's Point.

The first thing I learned when I got back was that Justin and Rebecca were married. I was expecting it, I guess, and yet for just a second my heart opened and bled. I heard the news from the woman who rented me my apartment. She watched me closely to see my reaction, but I managed to look disinterested.

The next day I walked into the little restaurant that had been built during my absence and asked Mr. Garner for a job. I was in luck—one of the girls had just quit and he needed a girl for the evening shift.

Oh, it was wonderful, just to be back! Everybody acted glad to see me, although they also seemed to be wondering why I'd come back.

I waited two weeks before I went to see a lawyer. I went to one in Rapids Park, and he told me the same thing the other one had. He said he would draw up the papers, contact Justin, and then we would wait to hear from him. Well, I heard, and sooner than I had expected. And so I had had my first visit with my little girl.

Tomorrow, I thought, drifting into an exhausted sleep, tomorrow, I'll go see about Papa's house.

The next evening after work, I got into the little jalopy that I'd bought to take Brittany out in and drove to the house. I had expected it to bring back only the memory of that last ghastly scene, but, instead, all of the warm, wonderful memories of Papa and Dave came floating back. I decided to move there. It would be a long drive back and forth to work, but at least I would have memories for company. When Dave came home, we could decide what to do with the house.

I had it all fixed up by Wednesday, my next day with Brittany. She loved it. I fixed her a little pole and line so she could "fish." She didn't catch a fish, but she smashed a little crab with a rock.

"Is he hurt?" she asked innocently.

"Not really," I said, silently asking Papa's pardon.

After Brittany got tired of fishing, we had a tea party and she sang for me, all the little songs that she had learned in Sunday school. "God is love—God is love," she sang, her voice cracking sweetly on the high notes. Something tugged at my heart. I hadn't thought much about God in a long time.

Christine was waiting for Brittany at the door when I brought her home, but I didn't think anything of it other than that Rebecca probably couldn't stand the sight of me. I'd brought Brittany home a little earlier this time, because I didn't want to run the risk of meeting Justin. I didn't know it then, but Justin and Rebecca both were at the hospital with Mrs. Minor.

233

Mr. Garner had told me to drop by the restaurant after I took Brittany home, and if he wasn't busy he would take me to a movie. Wednesday was the slowest night of the week, and Carrie assured him she could handle everything.

"You know what they say about girls who go out with the boss," I teased, smiling up at him as we walked to the theater.

"Well, it isn't true," he said. "You're the nicest girl I know, besides being the prettiest."

I felt good. It was awfully pleasant to be going to a movie with a nice man.

Just as Mr. Garner and I were coming out, I saw Justin driving by. He stopped for a red light, and Mr. Garner took my arm to cross the street. We had to pass right in front of Justin's car. He was looking, taking it all in—me and Mr. Garner. I don't care, I thought angrily. Let him look!

The car drove off, but Mr. Garner knew something was wrong.

"That was him, wasn't it?" he asked.

"Yes," I said, "but it doesn't matter." And for the first time since I'd met Justin, I knew it didn't matter. Justin had deserted me for his mother long before he'd divorced me.

I smiled up at Mr. Garner, and he took my hand in his. "My name is Seth," he said.

He walked me to my car and kissed me lightly on the cheek. "I'll see you tomorrow," he said, and I drove home in a happy little glow.

I went to sleep as soon as my head hit the pillow.

Seth was sitting at the counter reading a newspaper when I came in the next day. Wordlessly he shoved the paper at me. Mrs. Minor's picture stared back at me. With shaking fingers I picked up the paper and read the account of Mrs. Minor's illness and death the night before at ten o'clock. Justin must have been going for Rebecca when I saw him.

I put the paper down and walked to the back to hang up my coat. Funny, I didn't feel anything. Mrs. Minor had destroyed my marriage and taken my baby away. It was impossible for me to feel sorry that she was dead, but I couldn't feel glad, either.

I tried to put her out of my mind as I went about my work, but I couldn't shake off a vague, steadily mounting feeling of apprehension.

Two days later, I went to the funeral. I felt I had to. After all, Mrs. Minor was my daughter's grandmother. Rebecca looked poised and lovely in her black mourning dress. At the cemetery, she stood with her eyes downcast—it was impossible to tell what she was feeling. Justin's grief was terrible. I had never seen him cry before, and the tears were streaming down his cheeks. My own heart reached out, longing to comfort him. Horrified at what I was feeling, I quietly stole away before the services were over.

Justin knew I hated his mother, so I didn't see any point in making a hypocrite of myself by making a personal visit to extend my condolences. Rebecca probably wouldn't let me in the house, anyway.

Still, it bothered me. In spite of what Mrs. Minor had done to me, she had loved my baby.

The following Monday, I worked the breakfast shift. Carrie had asked me to change shifts with her because she had to go to the dentist. I got off at two-thirty, and, on impulse, I drove by Justin's store. I didn't usually pass that way, but I thought that if there weren't any customers, I would just walk in and tell Justin I was sorry about his mother.

I was in luck—no one was there except Justin. He was sitting behind the desk, going over some papers, and he looked up as I walked in. He didn't say anything, he didn't even get up, and I couldn't tell if he was mad or even surprised to see me.

Suddenly, I was sorry that I had come, and I couldn't remember what I had planned to say. My head started to throb. "Justin," I finally began, "I—I just wanted to tell you that I'm sorry about your mother." My words hung in the air. He just sat there, toying with a pencil.

"Yes, I think I know how sorry you are about my mother." His words were cold and contemptuous.

"Justin, please!" I begged. "Can't we even talk like decent people?" My voice broke and ended in a sob, and I whirled and ran out, shaking with fury. I cursed myself all the way home for being so stupid as to think that Justin would understand anything.

Once I got home, I defrosted the refrigerator, cleaned the stove, and mopped the floors, trying to work off my anger. I decided to take a swim after that. The tide was high, and a swim might tire me out so I could sleep. But even the water was against me, full of jellyfish and seaweed, so I gave up in disgust and went back to the house.

Later, as I was sitting on the back steps in the dusk, I saw a car turn in our road. As it came nearer, I recognized it as Justin's. He got out and started walking up the path to the house I sat rooted to the spot. It was like a dream. How many times in the past had I sat on those steps, waiting in the dusk for Justin's car!

For a moment, time turned backward. But as Justin came closer, reality struck me. Justin had never walked clumsily and hesitantly before. All at once his face was looming over me, and he pulled me to my feet, his hands rough and hurting. I caught a whiff of his breath, and then I knew. Justin was drunk.

"You wanted to talk, didn't you?" he snarled. "Well, we're going to talk."

He pushed me back into the house and closed the door. My

surprise turned to fear. I was afraid, unbelievably afraid of him. Never, in all the time I had known Justin, had it ever occurred to me to be physically afraid of him. But this man was a terrifying stranger, and I shrank back from him.

"Go ahead, tell me how sorry you are!" he demanded. "I want to hear you say it!"

He was holding my wrists, and when I didn't answer he pressed harder till I cried out, "Justin, please—you're hurting me!"

I was crying then, sobs of pure terror. The nearest house was a mile away—nobody would ever hear my screams. He'll kill me, I thought frantically.

"You're afraid of me now, aren't you?" he asked. "You weren't afraid, though, when you were sleeping with Craig Tavis, were you? Were you?"

With an enormous effort at self-control, I forced myself to stop struggling. I had to try to reason with him. "Justin, that isn't true," I said quietly. "Your mother set it up so it would look that way."

"Oh, sure," he said. "The way she set it up with that new boyfriend of yours, I suppose."

"Seth Garner is my boss—and just a friend," I said. "There's nothing between us."

"You're lying!" Justin shouted, and slapped me hard across the face.

I tasted blood, and suddenly, I didn't care what he did to me. The whole thing was too horrible. I felt dead inside, and I couldn't even fight when Justin picked me up and carried me to the bedroom. My mind refused to grasp what was happening. I seemed to be floating in a sea of nothingness, and I was only dimly aware, later, when Justin got up and left.

I went through the next couple of days in the same gray fog, working and waiting on people, talking to Seth and Carrie as usual, but my heart was dead. I thought I had been hurt before, hurt badly enough so that Justin couldn't touch my mind and heart again, but I was wrong. He had, and it hurt as much as it had the first time.

When Tuesday night finally came, the night before the day I could see Brittany, my spirits lifted in spite of what had happened. But just before I got off, Rebecca called and said Brittany had come down with the measles. I hung up, feeling desperately alone and lonely. My baby was sick and I couldn't be with her.

Seth noticed my downcast expression and asked me what was the matter. I told him about Brittany and that I wouldn't be able to see her for at least two weeks. "That's a shame," he said, looking honestly concerned. "Well, maybe I can figure out some way to help you spend part of the day tomorrow—that is, if you want to."

I dropped my eyes, looking at the bluish bruises on my wrists where Justin had held me. I couldn't go on encouraging Seth. I would only be using him to help kill my loneliness, and he was much too nice a person for that. I should hate Justin, but I didn't. I knew then without the shadow of a doubt, that as long as I lived Justin would be the only man in the world for me.

"That's all right," I said. "I have some things I have to do anyway." I turned away from the hurt in his eyes, hating myself for being a fool.

The next day, to keep busy, I dragged out one of Papa's rowboats, looked it over, and decided to paint it. I was busy painting when I saw the mailman come. He stopped and put something in the mailbox, so I put the brush aside and walked down to get it.

A letter from Dave, I thought. When Dave's first enlistment was up, he had enlisted again, but his time was almost completed now. Eagerly I reached for the letter. Maybe he was coming home! But it was a plain white envelope with no return address, and the handwriting looked familiar. It was Justin's! I opened the envelope with trembling fingers. It read:

Sarah, please forgive me. I must have been crazy. The only excuse I have is that I was drunk. It's a poor excuse, I know, but if you can find it in your heart to forgive me, I promise I will never come near you again. Justin.

I folded the letter carefully and put it in my shirt pocket. I promise I'll never come near you again—the words echoed over and over in my mind.

In the weeks that followed, Justin kept his promise. My life fell into a routine of managing to get through the days for my one day with Brittany. I planned all of our afternoons down to the last detail. I liked to think that Brittany was really fond of me now—at least she seemed to enjoy and look forward to our times together. While I knew she didn't think of me as her mother still I had become a part of her life. Seth never asked me out again, but I could feel him watching me sometimes. I guess he knew how things were, and it made me feel bad.

The little world that I was carefully building came tumbling down one afternoon back in the kitchen of the restaurant. I was looking for the big box of napkins to fill up the dispensers. Thinking they must be on top shelf, I got the stepladder stool and climbed up. Just as I reached for the box, everything began to whirl around me, and I almost fainted. I leaned against the ladder for a minute until the feeling passed, but a horrible suspicion nagged at the back of my mind. I couldn't be pregnant, I told myself. Not from just that one time! I pushed back the feeling of panic and went on about my work.

But I couldn't kid myself any longer when the terrible morning sickness started a couple of days later. Justin, Justin, my heart cried out—how could you do this to me? Is there no end to the hurt that comes from you?

That night, I decided there was only one thing to do to. I would go away, leave Brittany. But leaving Brittany would be different this time, because I knew it had to be, I told myself. She would be hurt a little at first. But she was young. She would forget quickly. It was Rebecca who took care of her, who nursed her when she was sick, who cooked and cleaned and ironed her little clothes. I was just a part-time playmate. But with this baby I am carrying, it will be different, I thought, hugging the warm feeling to me. This baby will be all mine.

I wrote Dave and told him I wanted to sell the house. He wrote back his permission and I sold the house to a real-estate agent in Rapids Park. I sent Dave his half of the money, and I gave Seth notice that I was leaving.

"I hope you find what you're looking for, Sarah," he said. "I wish I could persuade you that it's right here in Bronson's Point."

I smiled and thanked him, but I knew my life was finished in Bronson's Point. I worked my last day and drove home that evening, feeling only relief. I was already packed—the only unfinished business I had was telling Brittany good-bye.

Deciding how to do it proved to be harder than I thought. Maybe if I just called Rebecca and asked her to do it for me, it might be easier. She would be so happy that I was leaving, she would gladly do it. I just couldn't bear to face Brittany's big brown eyes and tell her I was going away from her.

Well, that was that! I'd leave quickly—before I changed my mind. I could call Rebecca from the next town.

Hurriedly, I changed from my white uniform to slacks and a blouse. I got my suitcases together and checked through the house to see if I had taken everything. I carried the suitcases out to the car, but paused before I put them in. The sky looked awfully dark. The wind had become strong, just in the short time since I'd come home. Might be a hurricane, I thought. We got them fairly often that time of the year.

I took the suitcases back inside, drove the car to a high spot out in the main road, and walked back to the house. The water came up in the yard if the wind was strong enough, and I didn't want to be stranded.

I turned on the radio, but I couldn't get anything because of the static. I made a fire in the fireplace to take the dampness out of the room, and then I settled back to wait. After a while the lights went off, and I knew the lines were down. I got a blanket out of a suitcase and stretched out on it in front of the warmth from the fire. The wind grew steadily worse, and the rain was lashing as if it were something alive. The little house shook and rattled, but I wasn't really afraid. I had confidence in Papa's handiwork. It was just the loneliness that got to me. I felt as if I were the only person in the world, and the only sounds were the wind and the rain beating against the house.

I wondered if Brittany was frightened. And Rebecca—was she afraid of storms? No, they wouldn't be frightened. They had Justin. I could almost picture them—Justin holding Brittany on his lap, with one arm around Rebecca. He would be comforting them, soothing the fears away. . . .

I must have fallen asleep, because the next thing I knew, somebody was pounding on the door. I got up, still groggy from sleep. For a minute I didn't know where I was. The fire had died down to a faint, glowing ember, and I felt my way to the door. I opened it. Whoever was there had a flashlight, but I still couldn't see who it was in the darkness.

"Who is it?" I asked, raising my voice so it could be heard over the wind.

"It's me! Justin!" the voice answered. "Are you all right?"

My heart lurched like a crazy thing. "Yes, but you shouldn't be out in this."

He came through the doorway and I shut the door against the howling wind.

"Here, hold this," he said, handing me the flashlight. I held it, throwing the beam ahead of him as he went to the woodpile and started throwing wood on the fire. Soon, the flames of the fire were leaping again, making magic shadows on the walls and on Justin's raincoat.

"Was Brittany afraid?" I asked.

"She's sleeping now. It's almost over. But I couldn't rest wondering if you were out here all by yourself." He stopped abruptly, noticing the suitcases by the door. He looked at me, questioningly.

"I've decided to leave," I said.

"Why?" he asked, his face registering surprise. "Are you afraid of me? I told you—"

"No, it isn't that," I said quickly. "I just think now that I was wrong to have come back. Brittany will be better off if I'm not around."

I turned away from Justin—I was afraid he would read the truth in my face.

"Sarah, please look at me," he begged.

"Don't—please, just don't," I whispered. But he put his hand gently on my arm and turned me around. For one wild moment I wanted to tell him that I was carrying his baby, but I shoved the impulse aside. He wouldn't believe it was his anyway. Besides, even if he did, there wasn't anything he could do about it.

"Listen to me for just one minute, please," he went on. "I know now that you were telling the truth about Craig Tavis. This morning, I decided to go through Mother's things and throw away a lot of stuff that was just cluttering up the place. I went through her little steel box where she kept all of her papers, and I found. . . ." He paused as if the memory was too painful. "It was in her returned checks from the bank—a canceled check made out to Craig Tavis for the sum of five thousand dollars. There isn't anything else it could be, except a payoff. I didn't even know Mother had any money—you know how hard up we were then. Sarah, please forgive me. I know you're a fit mother, and I want you to be able to see Brittany whenever you please."

"That's fine," I said, anger rising in me. I wanted to hurt him. I wanted to hurt him the way he had hurt me.

"But you didn't believe me until you had proof," I said. "You wouldn't believe me now in spite of the check—if your mother was here to tell you it wasn't so. You had to have your mother's permission to take a good deep breath. When she called me an unfit mother, you just stood there and let her. And now when you find out the truth, your conscience hurts you and you come begging forgiveness. Well, it's too late! It's two years too late!" I was shouting and I couldn't stop. "I'll tell you why I'm leaving. I'm leaving because I can't stand the sight of you! Even seeing Brittany isn't enough to compensate for having to look at you for five seconds. I hate you! Get out! Get out!"

He looked stunned for a second, but then he turned and went back out into the darkness, slamming the door behind him.

I was breathing heavily, as if I had run a long way. I looked at my watch; it was only five o'clock. I would have to wait a while, at least until the rain stopped. I walked nervously back and forth. Finally, I sat down at the table. My fingertips kept running over the design on the edge of the table. Papa had made the table—he had made most of the furniture in the house. I felt a sinking feeling in the pit of my stomach. I would never see this house again!

Suddenly, I heard the shed door slamming back and forth in the wind. I would have to close it before it broke off. I picked up the flashlight that Justin had left and walked out to close the shed. Holding the light on the inside of the shed as I pulled the door to, I saw Papa's rod and reel leaning against the wall. Then I remembered. I had promised Brittany we would drive into Rapids Park on our next day together and buy one for her. She wanted one more than anything and I had seen a little plastic one in one of the store windows.

She would be looking forward to it—she never forgot a promise. I couldn't go all the way into Rapids Park, but maybe, just maybe, Mr. Schmit would have one in his store. I would go by and see. And if he did, I would take it to Brittany.

The rain didn't let up until almost ten o'clock, and then I had trouble getting the car started. When I finally got going, it was noon.

At Mr. Schmit's store, I talked with him about the hurricane. Afterward, he went to the back of the store to see if he had what I wanted. My nerves were raw. It seemed an eternity before he came back with the rod and reel. I thanked him and made my way back through the mud and water to the car.

As I turned down the road where the Minors lived, I was amazed at all the flooded areas. Then I remembered—the canal must have overflowed. All of the residents on this particular road had pitched in and dug a canal from the back of their houses to the water. Well, there was nothing for me to do but get out and walk, even if it was more than a mile. I pulled on my boots and started off. The sun came out just as I was going past the big, old gate. I leaned against the gate a minute to catch my breath. There the Minor house stood, proud and ugly. For just a minute, I saw it with different eyes. It was ugly, all right, and yet, there was something else about it—the word "classy" came into my mind. That's right, I thought, ugly and classy, just like Mrs. Minor herself. Maybe that's why she hated me so—because she felt I wasn't good enough.

Well, let's get this over with, I told myself, and I walked up to the door.

I knocked and waited. Nobody answered. I knocked again, louder, pushing back a little feeling of dismay. Maybe Rebecca had taken Brittany somewhere. Just then I thought I heard Brittany's laughter out in the back. I walked around the house and there was Brittany, wading around in the water in her red rubber boots, having the time of her life. She was chasing a paper boat in the water, and I stood and watched a minute, drinking in the sight of her. This will have to last a lifetime, I thought, and it wasn't until then that the full realization of what it meant to leave her hit me. I can't stand it, I thought, knowing all the time I had to.

Just then, Rebecca stood up from the top step, where she had been sitting, watching Brittany.

"I came to tell Brittany good-bye," I said. "I'm leaving town."

A look of surprise came over Rebecca's face, but she didn't say anything because Brittany spotted me then and came running toward me. She gave me a hug and eagerly showed me the boat that Rebecca had made for her.

"I won't be able to come see you any more, Brittany," I said after

I had exclaimed over the boat. "I'm going away."

"No! I don't want you to go away," she said, shaking her head.

"Well, I tell you what," I said, forcing back the tears, and trying to keep my voice even, "I'll write you a letter, and when you get to be a big girl and learn how to write, you can write back to me. Won't that be fun?"

"Okay," she said, her bottom lip trembling, "I guess so."

"And if you're a great big girl, I'll show you what I brought you today," I said. I took the wrapped rod and reel out from under my raincoat and handed it to her.

She took it and started tearing at the wrapping. When she saw what was inside, she squealed with delight. "Oh, boy!" she cried, and promptly took the rod over to one of the larger puddles and started to fish.

Once I was alone with Rebecca, she said, "So you've given up at last." And there was an amused smile playing around her lips.

"I—I don't know what you mean," I said.

"Oh, don't you?" she sneered. "You were so sure Justin would fall right into your arms, and I would just fade out of the picture."

"That isn't true," I began, and then stopped. My nerves had been on edge for so long that I could feel violent anger threatening to overwhelm me. I was trembling. My hands, clutching my handbag, were shaking. I had already turned to go, but then she laughed, a scornful, contemptuous laugh.

"Isn't it?" she asked. "Then why are you leaving? Did you really think Justin would fall for your cheap little tricks? He knows what kind of a woman you are."

I looked at her, and her face was all twisted up with hate. Her words fell on my ears like physical blows, and something in me snapped. The hate rose up in me strong, as strong as hers a searing, blinding hate that could lash out at her just as cruelly as she had lashed out at me.

"I'm leaving because I'm pregnant," I said softly, deliberately. "I'm pregnant, and it's Justin's baby."

Her face blanched. In her eyes I saw disbelief, then uncertainty, then rage.

"You lie!" she hissed. "Justin loves me! He wouldn't have anything to do with a woman like you! He knows what you are!" She started to come at me, and as I backed away, I caught a glimpse of Brittany way out past the barns, heading for the canal. Instantly, sanity came rushing back into my blinded brain. I forgot all about Rebecca. I started to run toward the barns faster than I ever dreamed I could go.

"Brittany!" I shouted above my pounding heart. "Wait, Brittany!" After not having caught any fish in any of the puddles, she must have decided to try the canal!

"Brittany, Brittany—" Oh, thank God, she heard me! She stopped

242

and turned around. She was waving the rod and saying something, but I couldn't hear. As I came closer, she started walking backward, still saying something. I slowed down a little. She was, after all, quite a distance from the canal. But suddenly she seemed to stumble and fall.

My heart froze with terror! The well—the old well! It would be full of water now, with the seepage from the canal and the storm! Half-fainting with fear, I raced toward it. I could see the top of Brittany's head—she was still holding on to the well side! Sobbing with relief, I knelt down and grabbed her hands. She was screaming at the top of her lungs.

"Hush, my darling. Mother's here." I leaned forward to get a better grip when the earth began to slide out from under my feet! I screamed in terror, but my grip on Brittany was like iron. The dirt had half-covered her little body, but we had stopped sliding. I was partly lying down, throwing all my weight against the caved-out section of the well, frantically trying to keep from slipping down. Brittany wasn't screaming any more. I could hear soft, helpless little sobs. I wouldn't be able to hold her very long. My arms felt as though they were breaking. I had to pull her up. But every time I tried, the muck beneath my feet started giving way.

God, help me! I prayed. Just this once. I'll never ask for anything else, if You will help me get Brittany out.

My feet slid down a couple of more inches. We were going to fall into the well! I braced myself for the fall but suddenly my foot scraped something solid as a rock. Slowly I eased my whole weight on it. It held me. I braced myself and, using all my strength, I managed to pull Brittany up. I couldn't see clearly now—we were too far down.

"Brittany, hold tight to Mother," I said, and she didn't answer; she just clutched at me with frantic arms. I could feel her terrified little heart going like a trip hammer.

"Be still, honey," I whispered. "Be perfectly still. Don't move."

Suddenly I heard Rebecca calling Brittany's name and mine. We weren't more than five feet from the top, but I yelled at her to stay back. "The sides are soft," I said. "Don't come any nearer. Get a rope and throw it down, but stay back. And hurry! I don't know how long this rock will hold!"

"I'll be right back," she shouted, panic in her voice.

"It's all right, honey," I whispered as Brittany whimpered. "Mother's going to get a rope, and we'll have you out of here in no time."

"Daddy," she sobbed softly. "I want Daddy!"

It seemed like an eternity before Rebecca came back with a rope. But finally, her voice called, "Sarah, I'm throwing the rope! Sarah, can you hear me?"

"Yes, yes," I shouted. "Hurry!"

Looking up, I could see the rope, but by the time it slid down within my reach, I couldn't see it. I flung my arm out into the darkness, reaching. Brittany moved and I almost lost my balance. I pushed back, trying to steady myself.

"Bring it up and throw it again," I shouted. "Try a little more to the left." We couldn't fail now! Please, God!

The rope came down again, and this time I caught it. With desperate fingers I eased the rope under Brittany's shoulders, feeling the knot, tying it tighter.

"It hurts," Brittany whimpered.

"It's just for a little while," I said. "Be a brave girl now."

"Okay, pull!" I shouted to Rebecca. I clutched to the side of the well as Brittany's little body slowly slid over mine. I held my breath until I saw the little red rainboots disappear overhead.

A moment later, I heard Brittany talking to Rebecca.

"Thank You, God," I said, my heart overflowing. "Oh, thank You."

Suddenly a searing pain caught me in the lower part of my stomach, and a moan escaped my chattering lips. My stomach—it felt so hot! Slowly, I moved my feet around so I was facing the side. I pressed my body into the soft, cool mud.

"Can you hold on a little longer?" It was Rebecca again. "I'm going to get the horse," she yelled. "For God's sake, hold on."

What in the world is she going to do with the horse? I wondered. It doesn't matter, I thought. I'm going to die. The pain hit me again, and I strained into the mud, crying out. Nobody could feel like this and live anyway. The pain left and I looked up at the patch of sky. It started whirling around, and I closed my eyes. Everything seemed so far away, but I knew I must stay still as long as I possibly could. I was only dimly aware of Rebecca's voice shouting at me. I couldn't make out what she was saying, but I felt the rope as it slid over my face. Weakly I grabbed it, and managed to get it around my waist. My fingers were stiff and slow, and it took me a long time to tie the knot.

"Can you get it tied around you?" Rebecca shouted.

"Yes, yes, it's tied." I couldn't tell if I was thinking the words or saying them, but Rebecca must have heard me. I felt myself being slowly pulled—but right into the side of the wall! My shoulder was buried in the soft, gooey mud. It was covering my neck. I spit some out of my mouth.

"Rebecca, stop!" I shouted, coming out of my daze to the awful reality. I gasped for breath. "I'm suffocating!"

"The rope around you—is it tight?"

"Yes, it's all right," I answered weakly.

I waited a while, listening for Rebecca's voice, but she must have gone away. I couldn't hear anything. I stared upwards. The only thing I could see was the sky and the couple of remaining pieces of board that had covered the well before the storm. I was so tired, and it was so terribly hot! I felt as though I was floating, and I must have drifted into unconsciousness.

Once, I thought Justin was there. He was holding me and looking at me as he used to a long time ago. But he went away and the nightmares came. There was Papa—he was slipping down into the sea and I was trying to hold him up. I was calling for Dave, but a huge giant crab came scooting sideways across the water and lifted me and Papa both up in his gigantic claws. I heard voices then, but I couldn't make them out. Arms were lifting me, but I thought it was the crab, and I was fighting and screaming.

I came to in a hospital bed. For a minute, I couldn't remember anything, but then it all came back to me. I struggled to get up, but the sudden pain left me gasping, and I sank back.

"Lie still!" a voice said.

"Brittany," I whispered, and opened my eyes to see a nurse.

"Your little girl is all right," the nurse said. "She's suffering from shock, but she'll be fine."

Oh, thank God! Brittany was all that mattered. Then suddenly, again, I felt the pain. With a sinking heart, I looked at the nurse. "The baby?" I whispered.

"You lost your baby. I'm sorry. There was nothing the doctor could do. The strain of the ordeal you went through was just too much."

I turned my face to the wall, but I couldn't even cry. So I was to be left with nothing. My baby, I had wanted my baby! God was punishing me! He must be! He was punishing me for hating Mrs. Minor and Rebecca. But I had reason to hate Mrs. Minor! And Rebecca—she hated me more than I hated her!

"You have a visitor waiting outside, if you feel well enough," the nurse said. I nodded my head, feeling numb. What difference does it make? I thought.

"How do you feel?" a voice asked. I looked up. It was Rebecca.

"All right, I guess," I stammered as she took a chair and sat down by my bed.

"Well, you look almost normal again," she said briskly. "When they pulled you out of there, you were the nearest thing to a human mud pie I've ever seen."

"You saved my life, I know, but I can't remember what happened," I said. "The last thing I remember, you were trying to pull me out—" I paused, wondering.

"Well, I went for the horse. I tried to get the horse to try to pull

245

you up. But instead I only succeeded in nearly drowning you in the mud." She was pulling off her gloves.

"How did you get me out?" I asked.

"I had to tie the horse to get him to be still and not wander off while I went for help. You were out by then—at least I couldn't get an answer out of you, and I was pretty sure the rope was all that was holding you." She paused.

"You saved my life," I whispered.

"Don't think about it," she said quickly. "I did what I had to do—nothing more." Then she took a long, shuddering breath. "I'm giving you back your husband and your child," she said.

I couldn't believe I'd heard her right. "You're—you're what?"

"It's true. I am," she said. "And I'm sorry you lost your baby. I feel it's my fault! Oh, I could have cheerfully murdered you and your baby there for a little while. But when I got Brittany out of the mud, that's when I knew I had to leave Justin. My terrible jealousy has been driving me out of my mind." She got up and started walking around the room, not looking at me.

"You see, I didn't know how to cope with the situation," she continued. "Justin just didn't love me. Even before you came back, I guess I knew he never would—not in the way I wanted him to. Oh, I tried hard. I took good care of Mrs. Minor until she died. I worked very hard at being a good mother to Brittany, and I think I succeeded in that.

"Justin and I have always been close friends—" She turned around to face me again. "But the one thing I couldn't be to him was a wife. You see, Justin didn't really want a wife. He already had one—you. I think I must have known he still loved you all along, otherwise I wouldn't have hated you so."

"You mean, you've left Justin?" I asked, trying to make sense out of what she was saying.

"Yes," she said, pulling on her gloves again and picking up her purse. "I moved out after I brought you and Brittany here. I think I'm capable of getting a man of my own—and a child of my own." She smiled then and walked to the door. "Besides," she said, turning for just a second, "lightning striking twice in the same place is just too much for me."

She was gone then, and I lay there, completely stunned! I couldn't understand it! My brain was reeling with her words. She had said that Justin still loved me! And I could have Brittany back!

The nurse came in and gave me a sedative, but I must have been too excited, because it didn't work. Anyway, I kept waiting, waiting. Just when I thought I couldn't stand it any longer, and then there was a soft knock, and Justin stuck his head in.

"Come in," I said breathlessly.

246

He walked over to the side of my bed, a peculiar expression on his face. It was an uneasy expression, as if he didn't know what to say. "Why didn't you tell me about the baby?" he blurted out roughly.

I looked away, fighting back the tears. I didn't want to start blubbering then. "I guess I thought you wouldn't believe it was yours. That night you came, you accused me of so many things. Besides, there wasn't anything you could do about it, so I decided to go away. But there isn't any baby now to worry about—" My voice trailed off and ended in a sob.

Justin threw himself down by the side of my bed, and hid his face in the crook of my arm. "Oh, God, I hate myself," he groaned. "If you only knew how I hate myself! Not only for messing up your life, but Rebecca's, too. I've always loved you, Sarah. Please believe that. Even when I thought you had actually been unfaithful to me, I couldn't stop loving you. When I saw you that day in Craig's arms, I wanted to hurt you back for hurting me so. I shouldn't have listened to my mother, but I did—"

I realized I was soothing back the stray strands of hair over his forehead. How I had been longing to do that!

"And when you came back," Justin went on, "I tried to tell myself it wouldn't make any difference, but I couldn't even sleep at night. Rebecca knew, but she never said anything. That day you came into the store, I don't know what happened—I just cracked. I was still shook up over Mother, and after you left I closed the store and started drinking. And then, I knew I had to see you—but I was angry at myself for having to see you."

"Don't, please, darling! Don't!" I whispered.

"Rebecca was waiting up for me that night. But when she saw I was drunk, she just put me to bed. The next morning she offered me a divorce. But I couldn't tell her I wanted a divorce. I grew up with Rebecca. I always protected her, even when I was a little boy. I couldn't tell her that I no longer cared about her—"

"I know, I know," I said softly.

"And after what I'd done to you, I knew you hated me."

"I've never hated you, my darling."

"Give me another chance! I'll spend the rest of my life trying to make it up to you. When I think I almost lost you and Brittany—"

"What about Rebecca?" I whispered.

"She left me this afternoon. She's really a good woman. She deserves better than what she got from me. But she'll find it. She'll meet somebody who can really love her—the way I love you." He held me then, and we clung to each other for a long time, until the nurse came back and made Justin leave.

Rebecca divorced Justin, and Justin and I were remarried. Our little town was quite busy with gossip for a while, but it all died down the way gossip eventually does. We still live in the big, old house, but I feel different about it now. Now I feel as though I belong. Brittany has two little sisters who are as rough and rowdy as most children. But I try to make them speak softly and mind their manners—just in case Mrs. Minor is watching. I wouldn't want her to think her grandchildren aren't good enough.

Rebecca moved to New York, and got a job as a buyer in one of the big department stores. She hasn't married, but I'm sure she will someday. She sends things for the children quite frequently, especially Brittany. I know she still misses her. In her last letter, she said she would come to see us on her vacation. I cried when I read it, full of joy and thankfulness that God in His mercy had erased all trace of hate and bitterness.

THE END

www.ingramcontent.com/pod-product-compliance
Lightning Source LLC
Chambersburg PA
CBHW072218170626
46813CB00003B/996